TEEN BOAT!

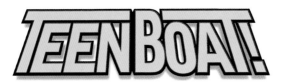

TEEN BOAT!

The *RACE* for *BOATLANTIS*

BY **DAVE ROMAN** AND **JOHN GREEN**

Clarion Books | Houghton Mifflin Harcourt | Boston   New York   2015

Lead colorist:
WES DZIOBA

Additional colors by
JOHN GREEN
MOLLY OSTERTAG
AMANDA SCURTI
ALISA HARRIS

Color flats by
RACHEL POLK

Letters by
JOHN GREEN

Clarion Books

215 Park Avenue South

New York, New York 10003

Text and illustrations copyright © 2015
by Dave Roman and John Green

For information about permission to reproduce selections from this book,
write to Permissions, Houghton Mifflin Harcourt Publishing Company,
215 Park Avenue South, New York, New York 10003.

Clarion Books is an imprint of Houghton Mifflin Harcourt Publishing Company.

www.hmhco.com
www.teenboatcomics.com

Library of Congress Cataloging-in-Publication Data is available.
LCCN 2015932323

Manufactured in China
SCP 10 9 8 7 6 5 4 3 2 1
4500529176

To my mom, who is still waiting for me to buy her a boat.

—DAVE

To my parents, who taught me to fear and respect boats.
Mostly fear.

—JOHN

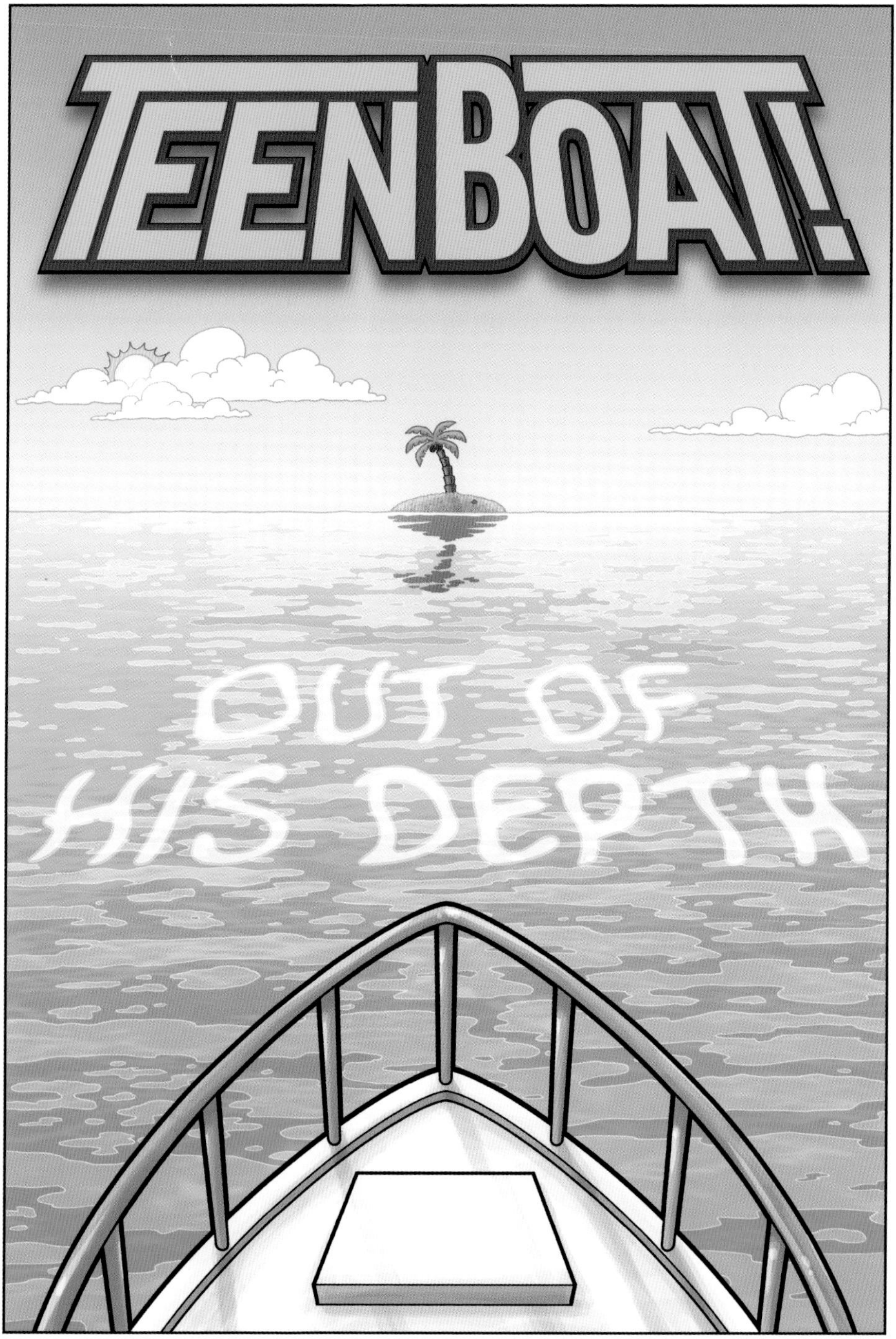
TEEN BOAT!
OUT OF
HIS DEPTH

The ***ANGST*** of being a Teen—the ***THRILL*** of being a Boat!

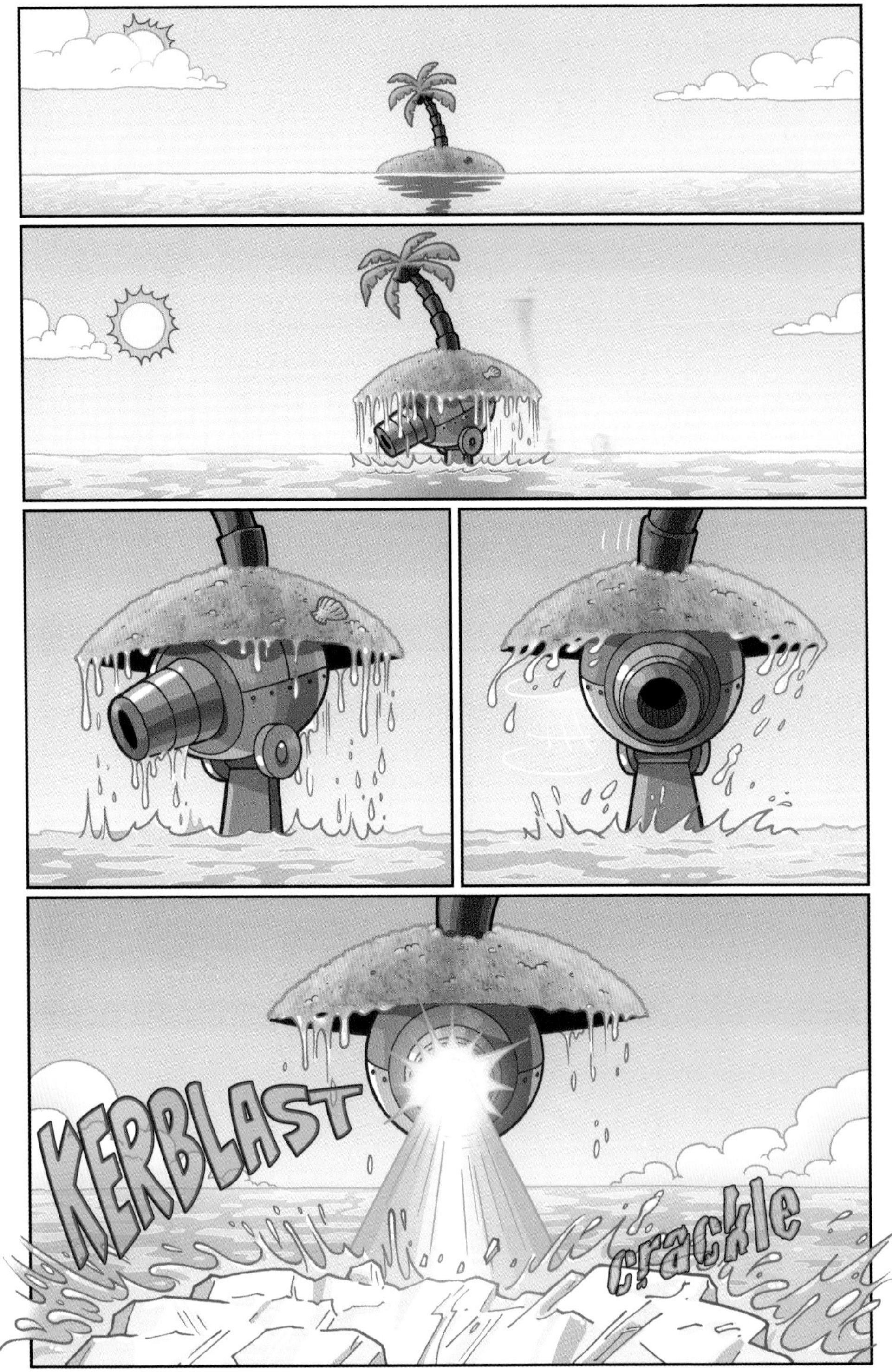
KERBLAST
crackle

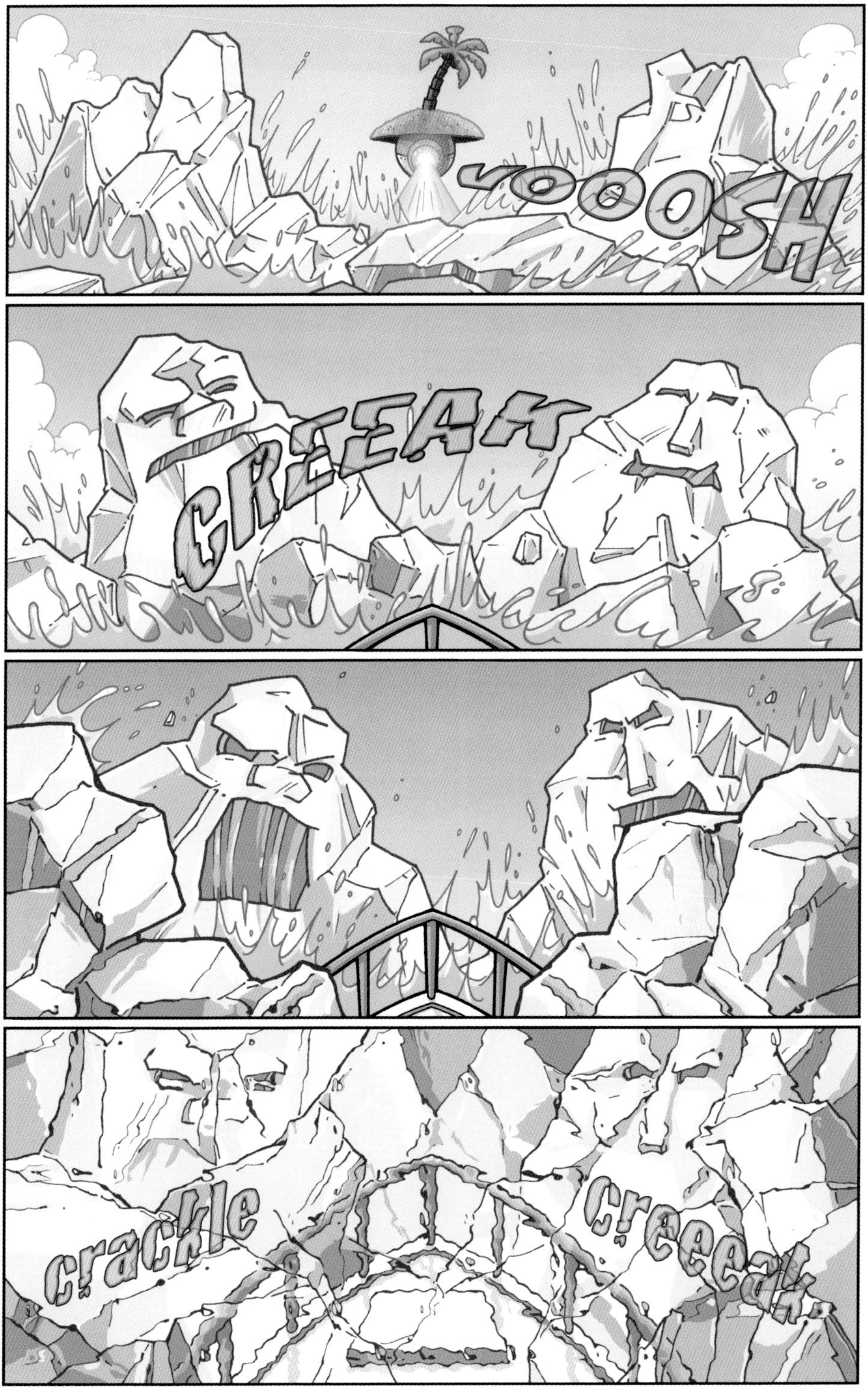
VOOOSH
CREEAK
crackle
creeeak

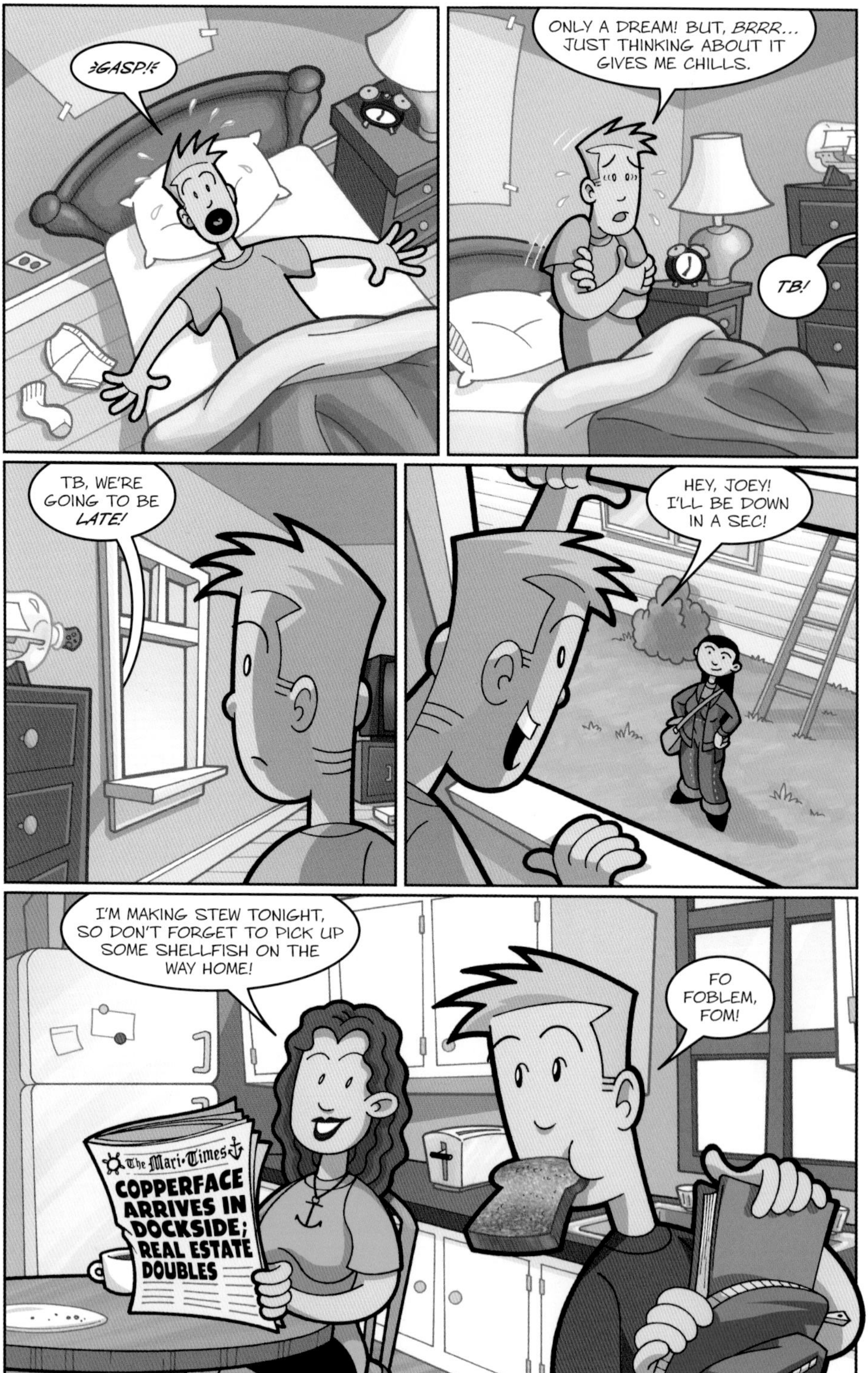
GASP!
ONLY A DREAM! BUT, BRRR... JUST THINKING ABOUT IT GIVES ME CHILLS.
TB!
TB, WE'RE GOING TO BE LATE!
HEY, JOEY! I'LL BE DOWN IN A SEC!
I'M MAKING STEW TONIGHT, SO DON'T FORGET TO PICK UP SOME SHELLFISH ON THE WAY HOME!
The Mari-Times
COPPERFACE ARRIVES IN DOCKSIDE; REAL ESTATE DOUBLES
FO FOBLEM, FOM!

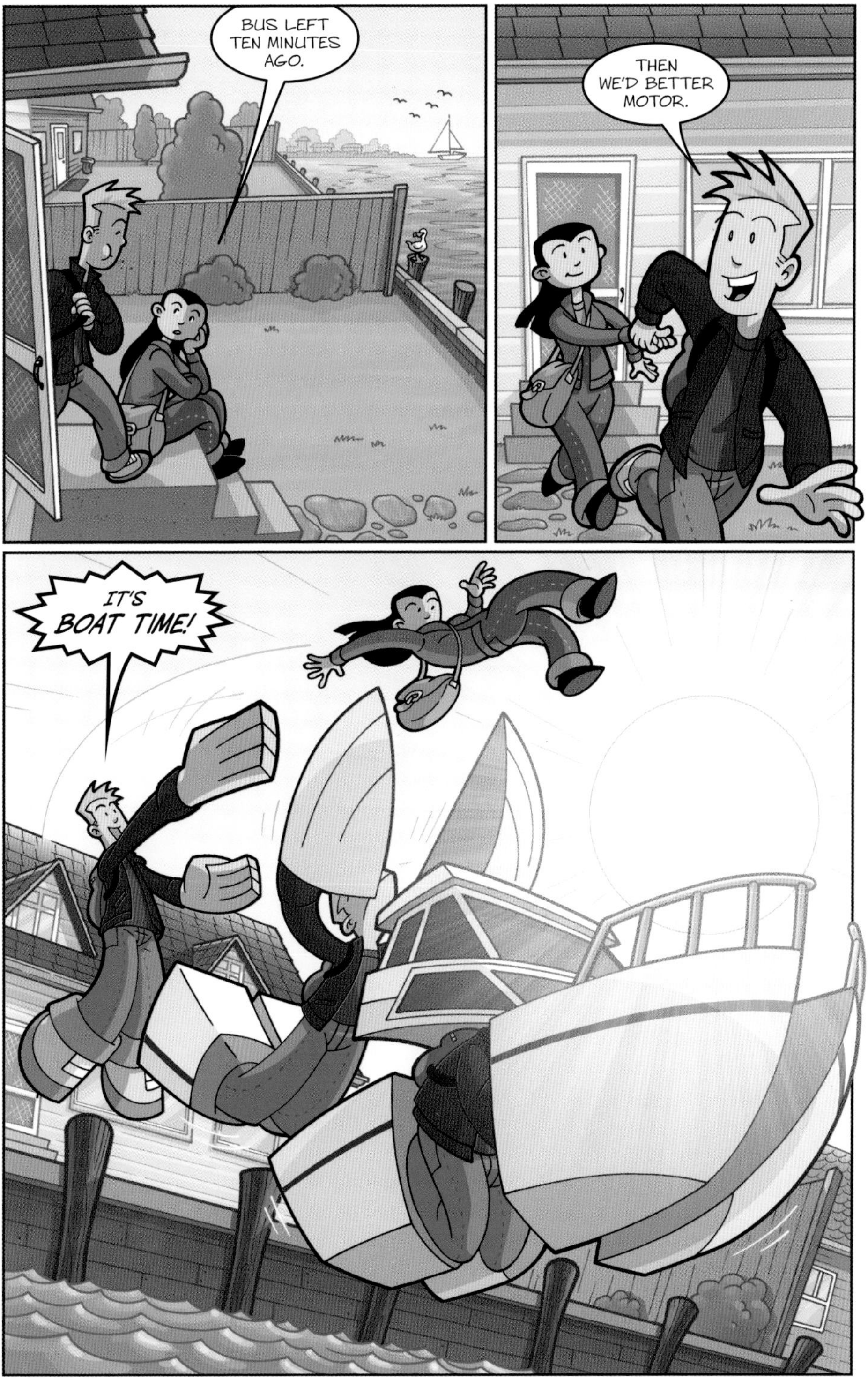
BUS LEFT TEN MINUTES AGO.
THEN WE'D BETTER MOTOR.
IT'S BOAT TIME!

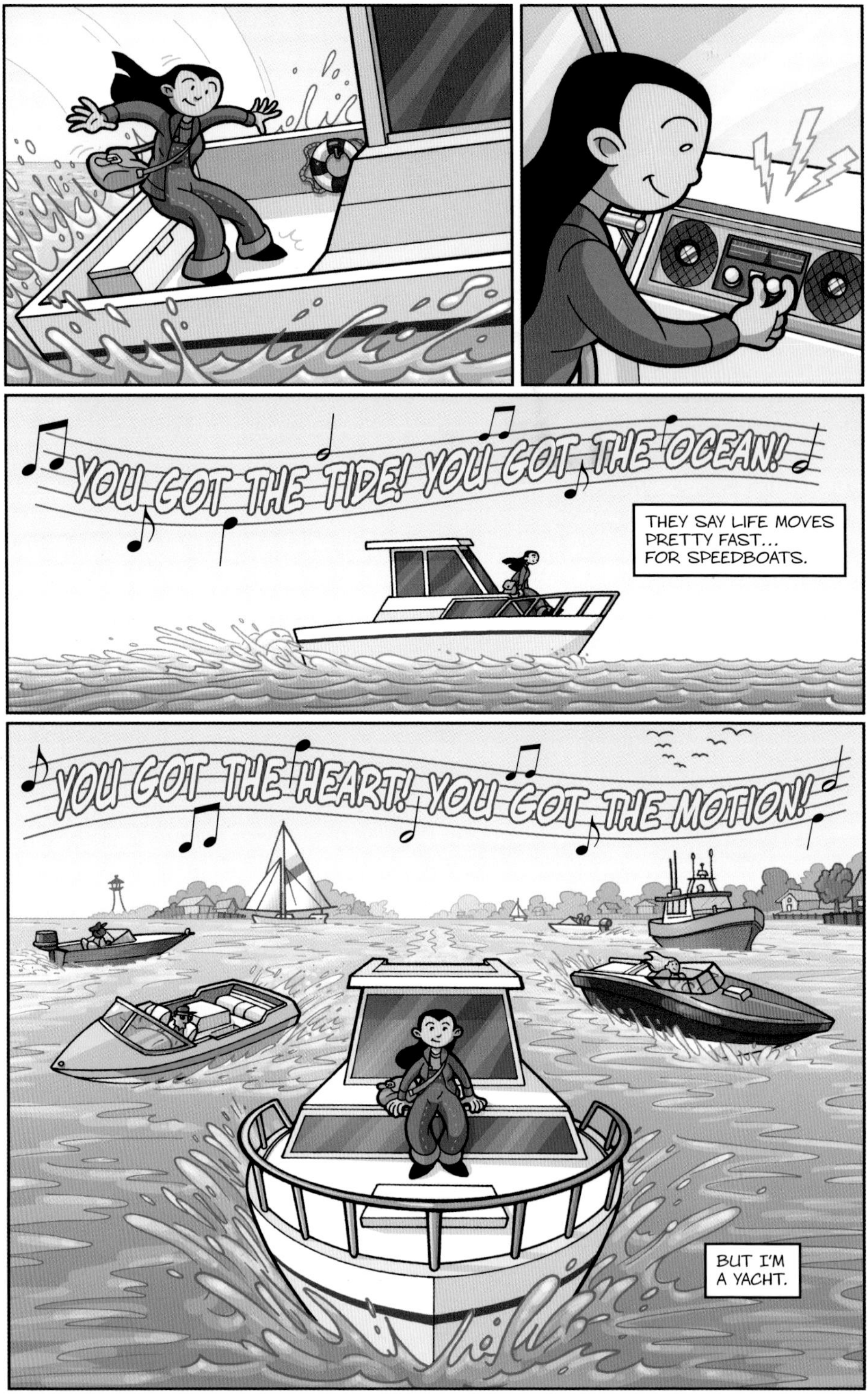
YOU GOT THE TIDE! YOU GOT THE OCEAN!
THEY SAY LIFE MOVES PRETTY FAST... FOR SPEEDBOATS.
YOU GOT THE HEART! YOU GOT THE MOTION!
BUT I'M A YACHT.

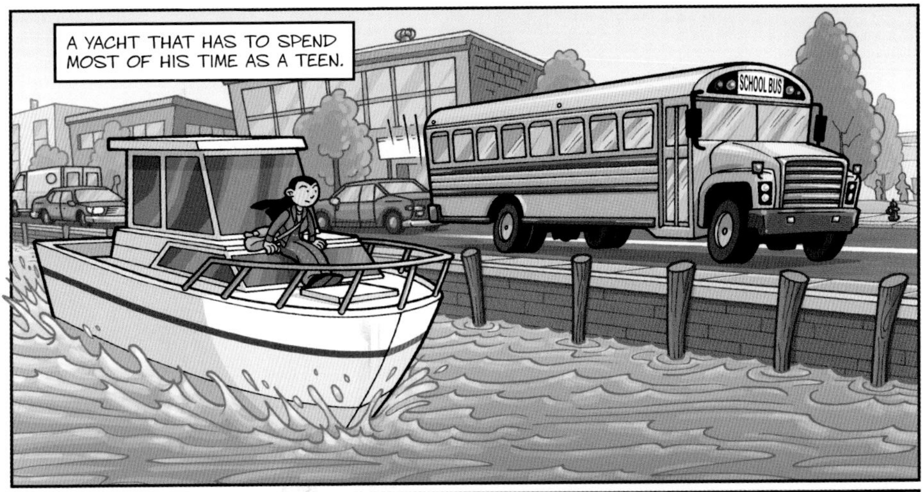
A YACHT THAT HAS TO SPEND MOST OF HIS TIME AS A TEEN.
SCHOOL BUS

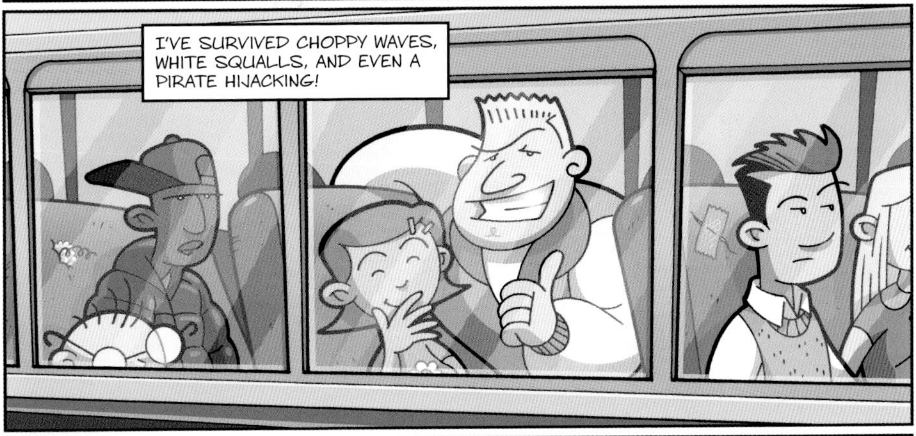
I'VE SURVIVED CHOPPY WAVES, WHITE SQUALLS, AND EVEN A PIRATE HIJACKING!

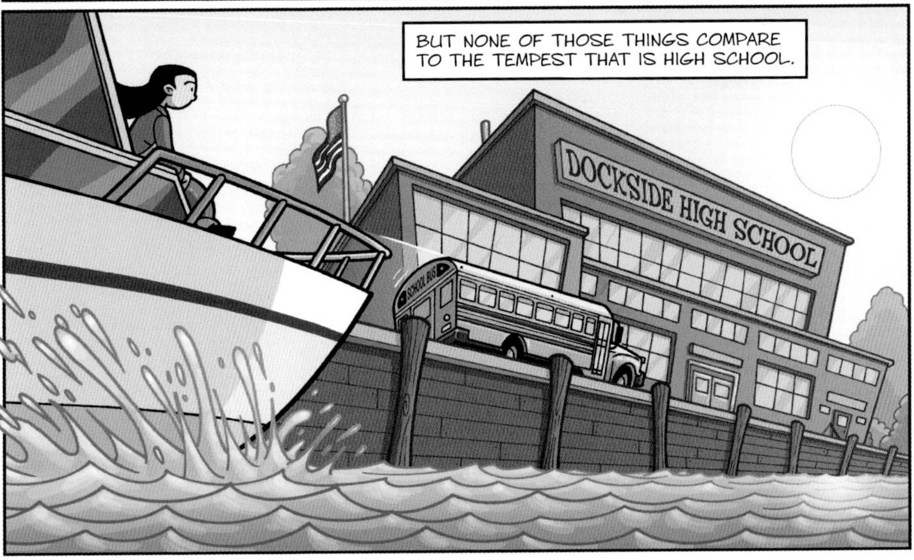
BUT NONE OF THOSE THINGS COMPARE TO THE TEMPEST THAT IS HIGH SCHOOL.
DOCKSIDE HIGH SCHOOL
SCHOOL BUS

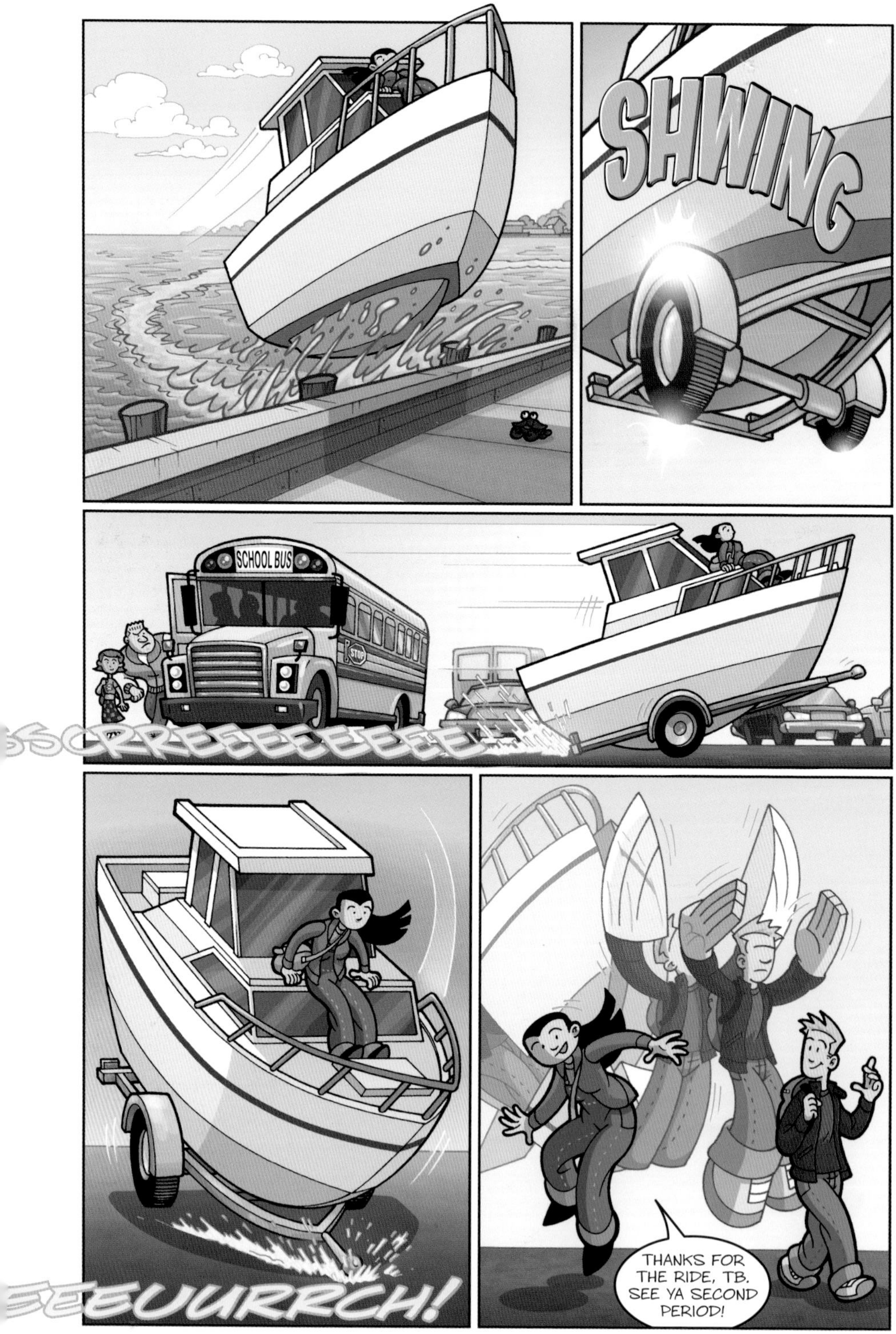

SHWING
SCHOOL BUS
STOP
SSCRREEEEEEEEEEE
EEEUURRCH!
THANKS FOR THE RIDE, TB. SEE YA SECOND PERIOD!

NO MATTER HOW HARD I TRY TO FIT IN, IT SEEMS LIKE I'VE ALWAYS BEEN THE BOAT OF EVERYONE'S JOKES.

HEY, TB! EVER HEARD OF *OLD SPICE?* MIGHT HELP YOU GET RID OF THAT SALTWATER REEK!

HEY, **TEEN BOAT!** GOOD LUCK AT THE BIG GAME TODAY!

I'M SURE YOU'LL *DOMINATE* THE FIELD! HA HA HA!

YOU'D THINK THAT AS A SENIOR, I'D FINALLY WISE UP AND STOP GETTING SUCKERED INTO FOOLISH ATTEMPTS AT BEING POPULAR.

AND YET, JUST TWO DAYS AGO, I DOCKED RIGHT BACK INTO IT...

HEY! BOAT DUDE! TODAY IS YOUR LUCKY DAY!

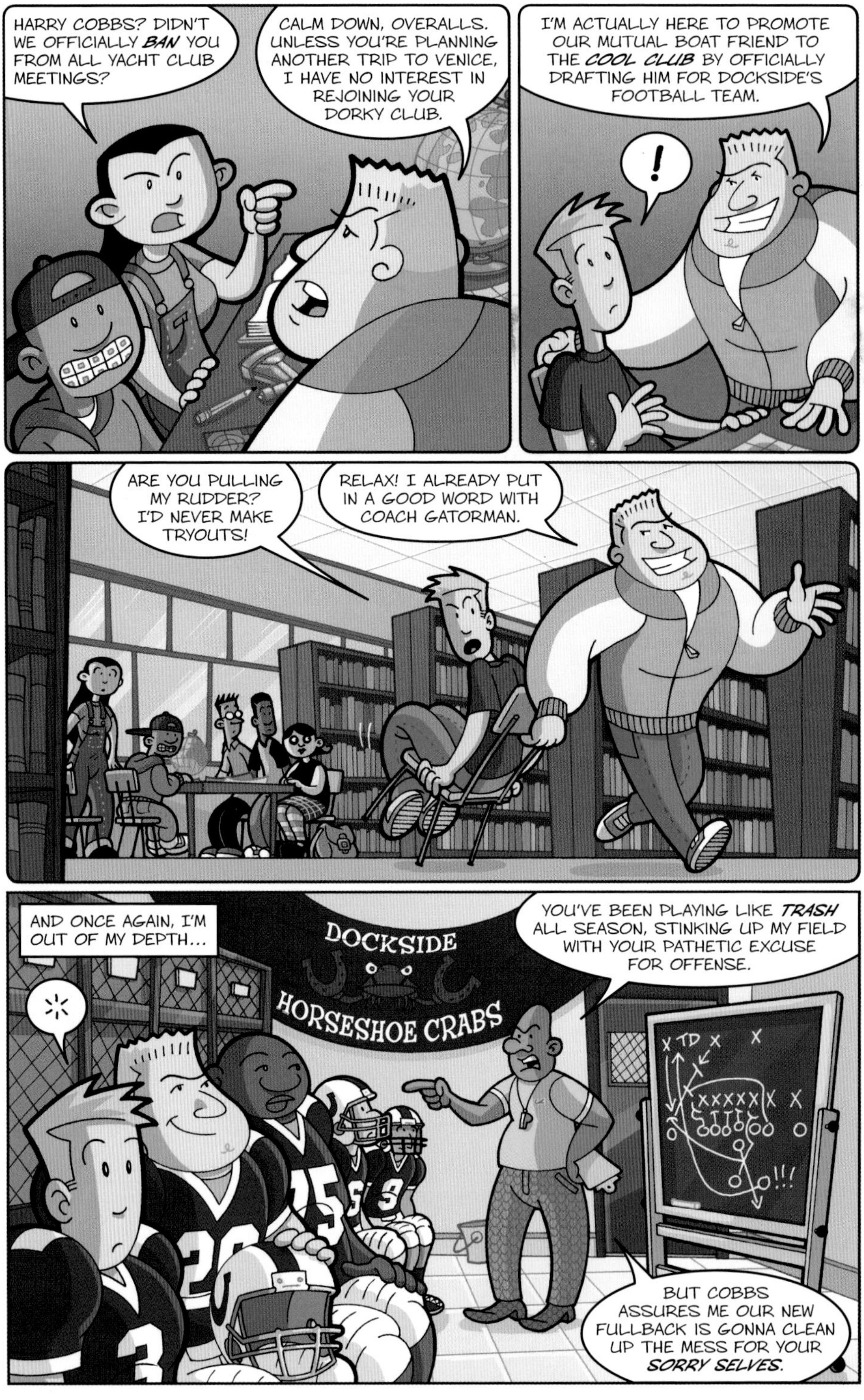
HARRY COBBS? DIDN'T WE OFFICIALLY BAN YOU FROM ALL YACHT CLUB MEETINGS?
CALM DOWN, OVERALLS. UNLESS YOU'RE PLANNING ANOTHER TRIP TO VENICE, I HAVE NO INTEREST IN REJOINING YOUR DORKY CLUB.
I'M ACTUALLY HERE TO PROMOTE OUR MUTUAL BOAT FRIEND TO THE COOL CLUB BY OFFICIALLY DRAFTING HIM FOR DOCKSIDE'S FOOTBALL TEAM.
!
ARE YOU PULLING MY RUDDER? I'D NEVER MAKE TRYOUTS!
RELAX! I ALREADY PUT IN A GOOD WORD WITH COACH GATORMAN.
AND ONCE AGAIN, I'M OUT OF MY DEPTH...
DOCKSIDE
HORSESHOE CRABS
YOU'VE BEEN PLAYING LIKE TRASH ALL SEASON, STINKING UP MY FIELD WITH YOUR PATHETIC EXCUSE FOR OFFENSE.
BUT COBBS ASSURES ME OUR NEW FULLBACK IS GONNA CLEAN UP THE MESS FOR YOUR SORRY SELVES.

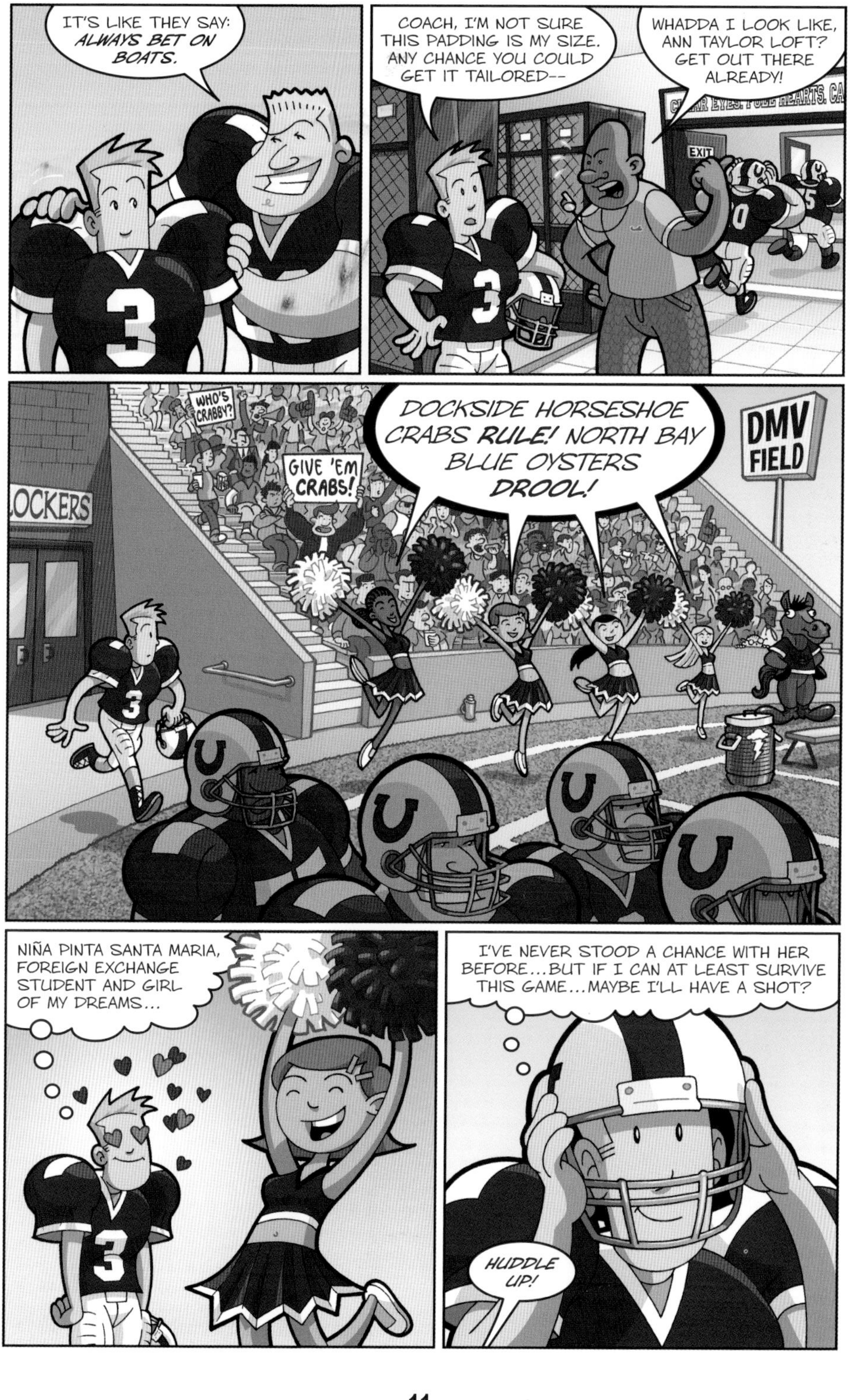
IT'S LIKE THEY SAY: *ALWAYS BET ON BOATS.*
COACH, I'M NOT SURE THIS PADDING IS MY SIZE. ANY CHANCE YOU COULD GET IT TAILORED--
WHADDA I LOOK LIKE, ANN TAYLOR LOFT? GET OUT THERE ALREADY!
EXIT
WHO'S CRABBY?
GIVE 'EM CRABS!
DOCKSIDE HORSESHOE CRABS **RULE!** NORTH BAY BLUE OYSTERS **DROOL!**
DMV FIELD
NIÑA PINTA SANTA MARIA, FOREIGN EXCHANGE STUDENT AND GIRL OF MY DREAMS...
I'VE NEVER STOOD A CHANCE WITH HER BEFORE...BUT IF I CAN AT LEAST SURVIVE THIS GAME...MAYBE I'LL HAVE A SHOT?
HUDDLE UP!

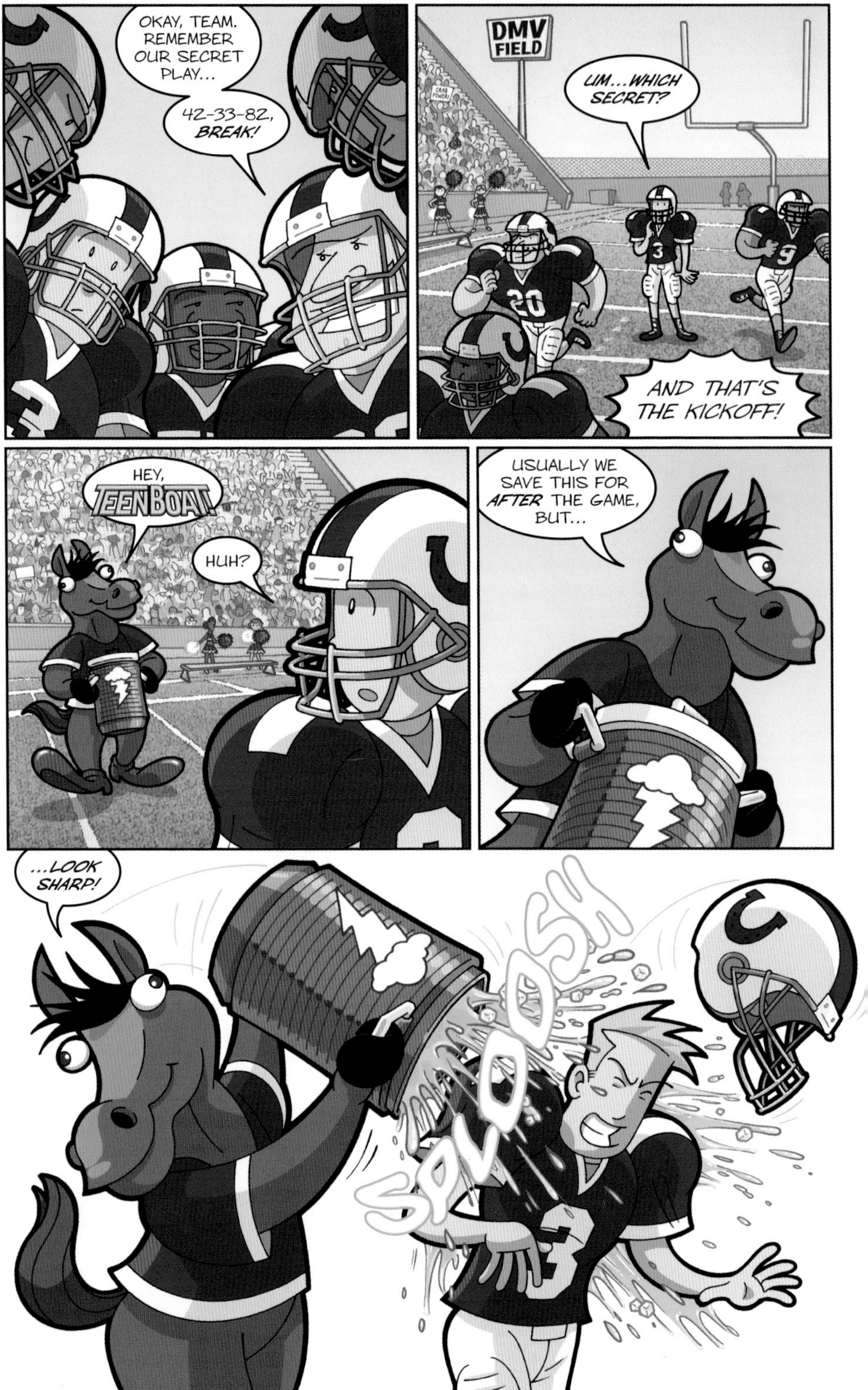
OKAY, TEAM. REMEMBER OUR SECRET PLAY...
42-33-82, *BREAK!*
DMV FIELD
CRAB POWER!
UM...WHICH SECRET?
AND THAT'S THE KICKOFF!
HEY, TEENBOAT!
HUH?
USUALLY WE SAVE THIS FOR *AFTER* THE GAME, BUT...
...LOOK SHARP!
SPLOOSH

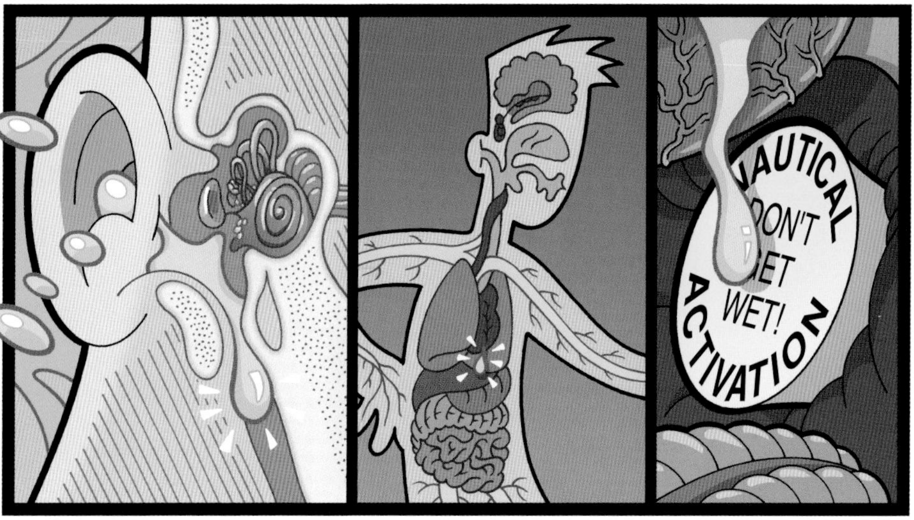
NAUTICAL ACTIVATION
DON'T GET WET!

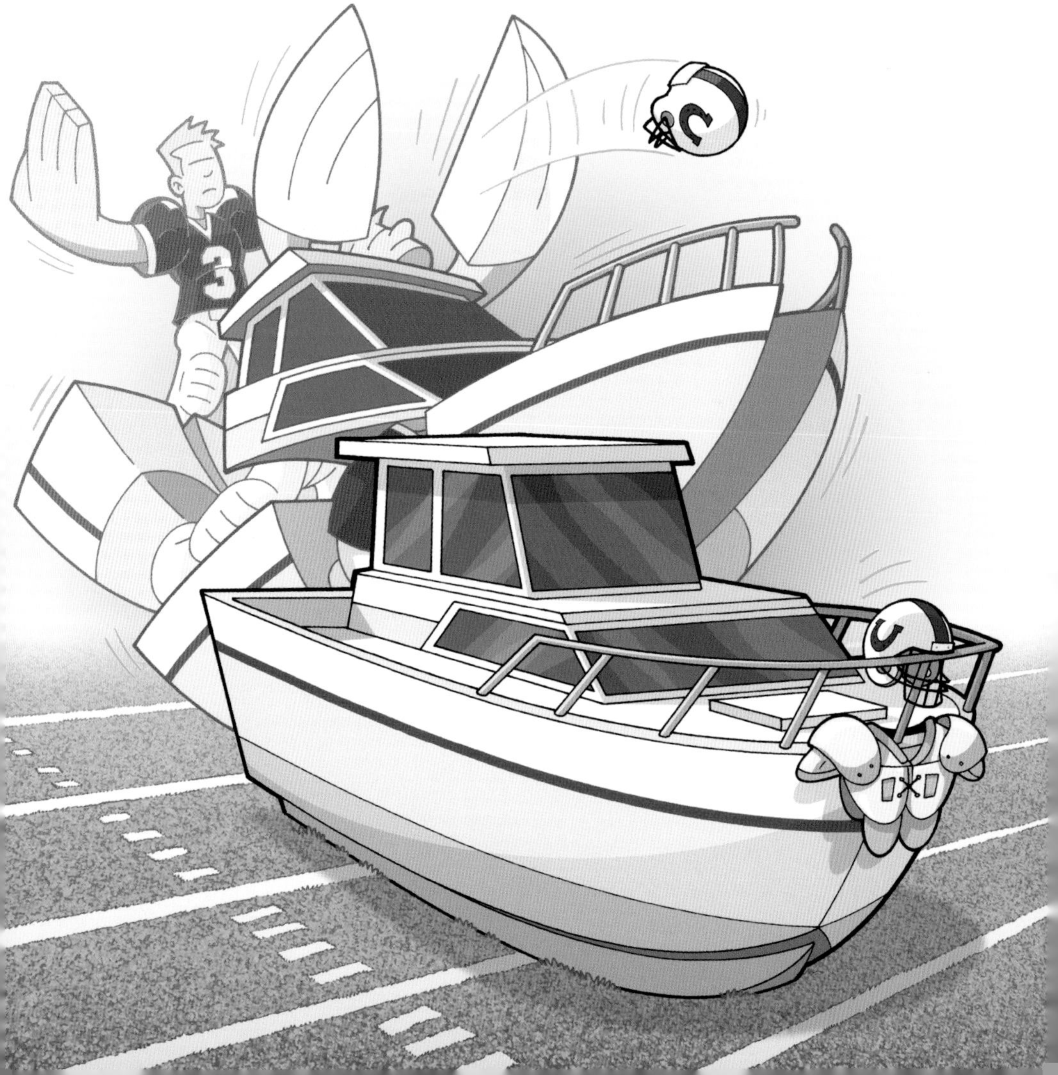

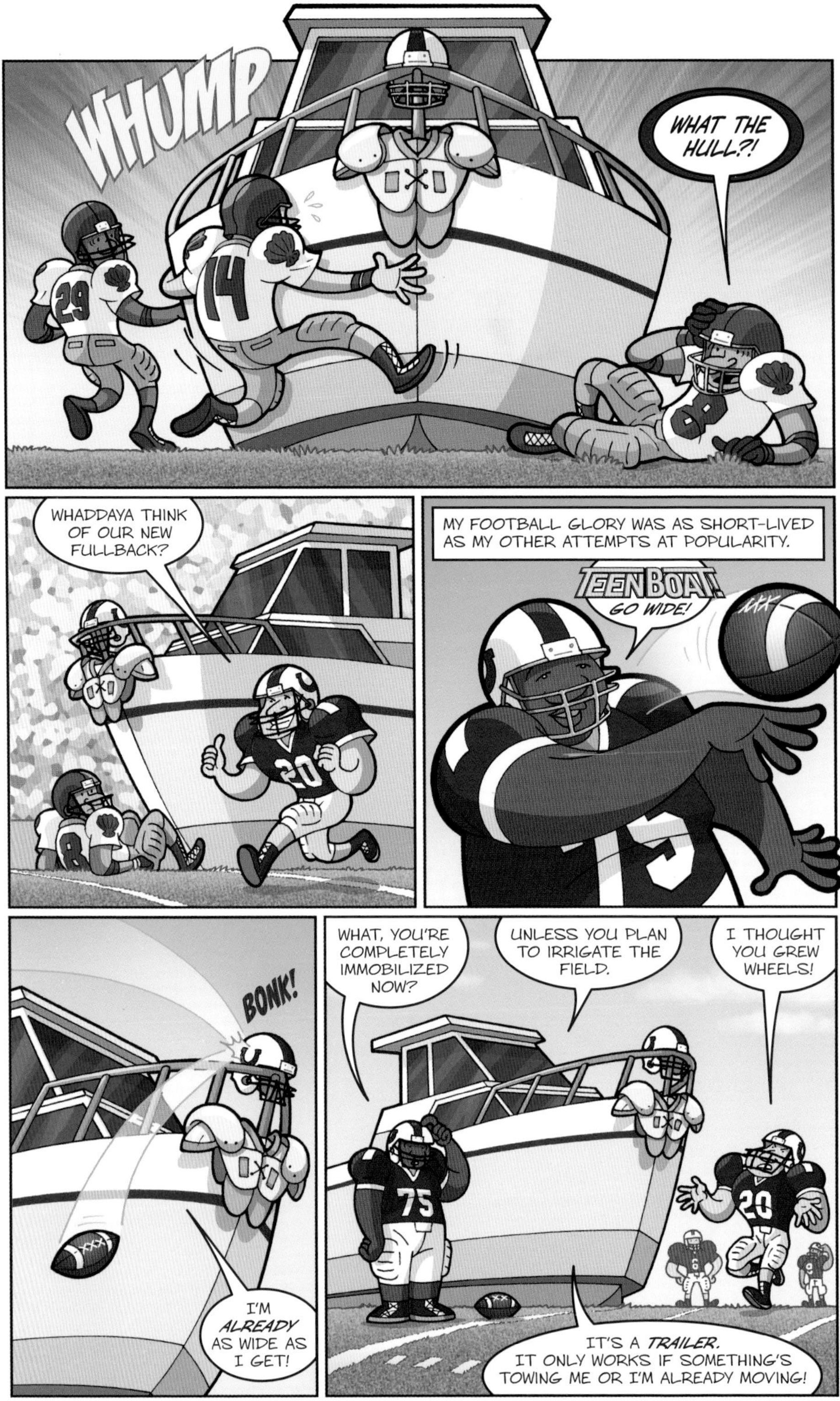
WHUMP
WHAT THE HULL?!
WHADDAYA THINK OF OUR NEW FULLBACK?
MY FOOTBALL GLORY WAS AS SHORT-LIVED AS MY OTHER ATTEMPTS AT POPULARITY.
TEEN BOAT! GO WIDE!
BONK!
I'M *ALREADY* AS WIDE AS I GET!
WHAT, YOU'RE COMPLETELY IMMOBILIZED NOW?
UNLESS YOU PLAN TO IRRIGATE THE FIELD.
I THOUGHT YOU GREW WHEELS!
IT'S A *TRAILER.* IT ONLY WORKS IF SOMETHING'S TOWING ME OR I'M ALREADY MOVING!

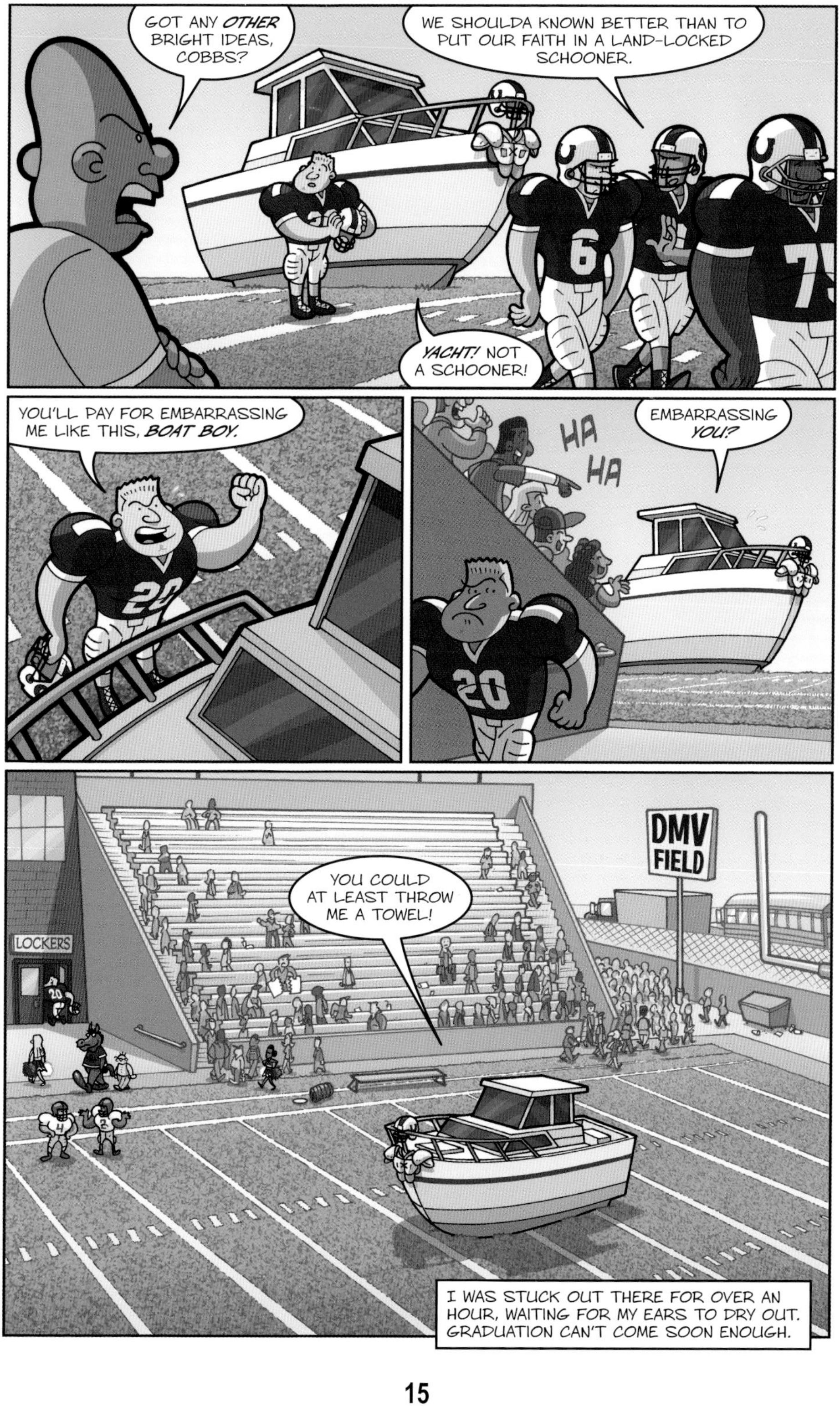
GOT ANY OTHER BRIGHT IDEAS, COBBS?
WE SHOULDA KNOWN BETTER THAN TO PUT OUR FAITH IN A LAND-LOCKED SCHOONER.
YACHT! NOT A SCHOONER!
YOU'LL PAY FOR EMBARRASSING ME LIKE THIS, BOAT BOY.
HA
HA
EMBARRASSING YOU?
DMV FIELD
LOCKERS
YOU COULD AT LEAST THROW ME A TOWEL!
I WAS STUCK OUT THERE FOR OVER AN HOUR, WAITING FOR MY EARS TO DRY OUT. GRADUATION CAN'T COME SOON ENOUGH.

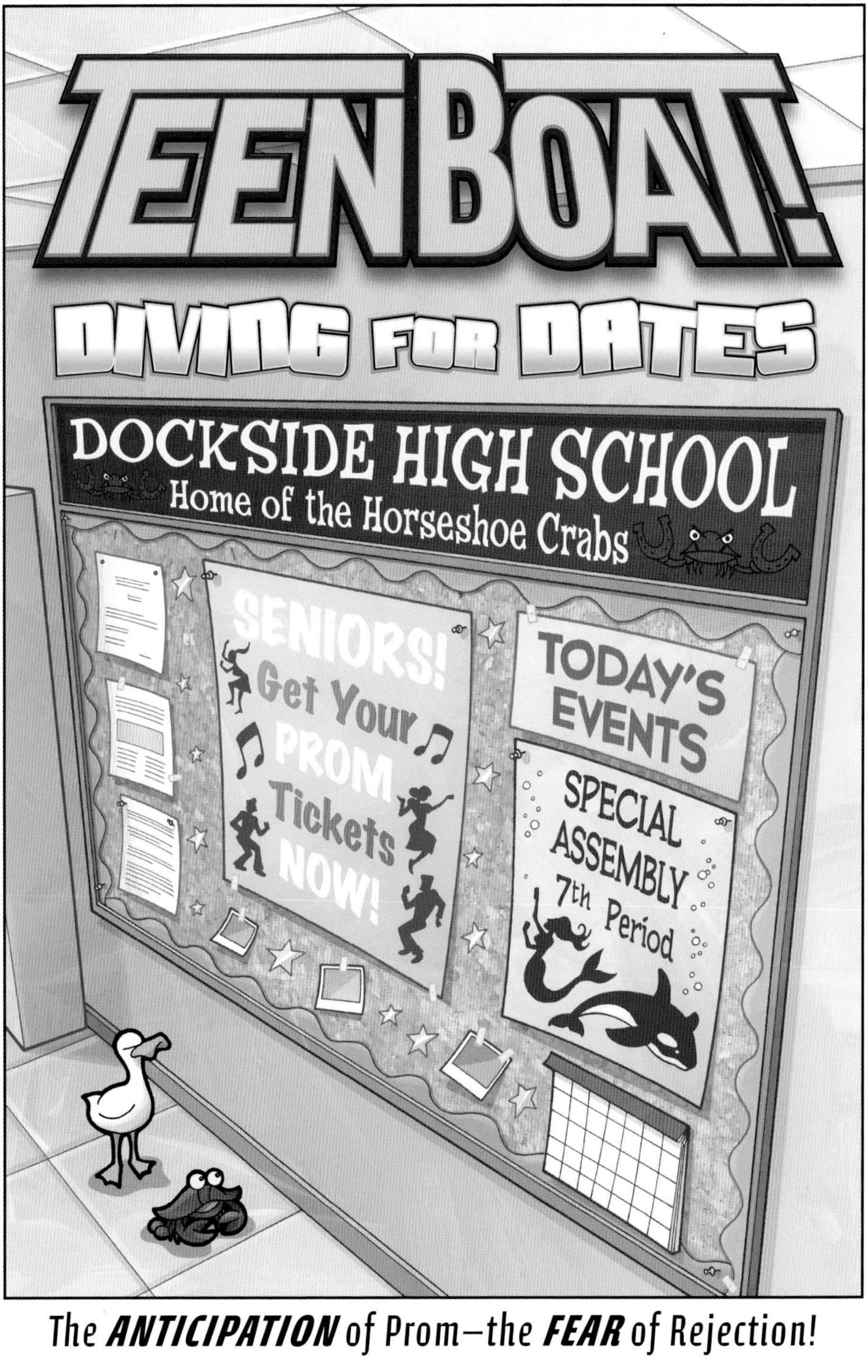
TEEN BOAT!
DIVING FOR DATES
DOCKSIDE HIGH SCHOOL
Home of the Horseshoe Crabs
SENIORS!
Get Your
PROM
Tickets
NOW!
TODAY'S
EVENTS
SPECIAL
ASSEMBLY
7th Period

The ***ANTICIPATION*** of Prom—the ***FEAR*** of Rejection!

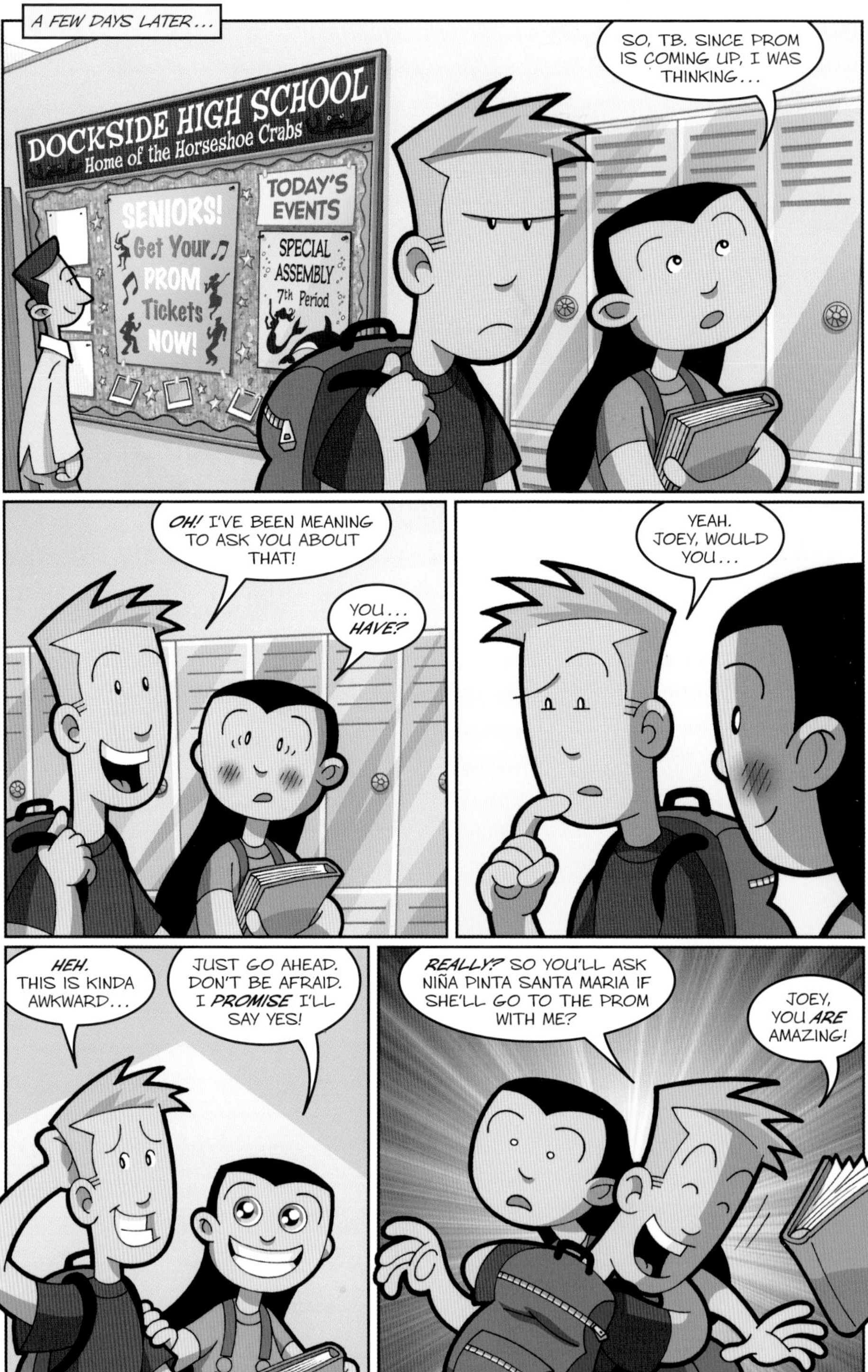
A FEW DAYS LATER...
DOCKSIDE HIGH SCHOOL
Home of the Horseshoe Crabs
SENIORS! Get Your PROM Tickets NOW!
TODAY'S EVENTS
SPECIAL ASSEMBLY 7th Period
SO, TB. SINCE PROM IS COMING UP, I WAS THINKING...
OH! I'VE BEEN MEANING TO ASK YOU ABOUT THAT!
YOU... HAVE?
YEAH. JOEY, WOULD YOU...
HEH. THIS IS KINDA AWKWARD...
JUST GO AHEAD. DON'T BE AFRAID. I PROMISE I'LL SAY YES!
REALLY? SO YOU'LL ASK NIÑA PINTA SANTA MARIA IF SHE'LL GO TO THE PROM WITH ME?
JOEY, YOU ARE AMAZING!

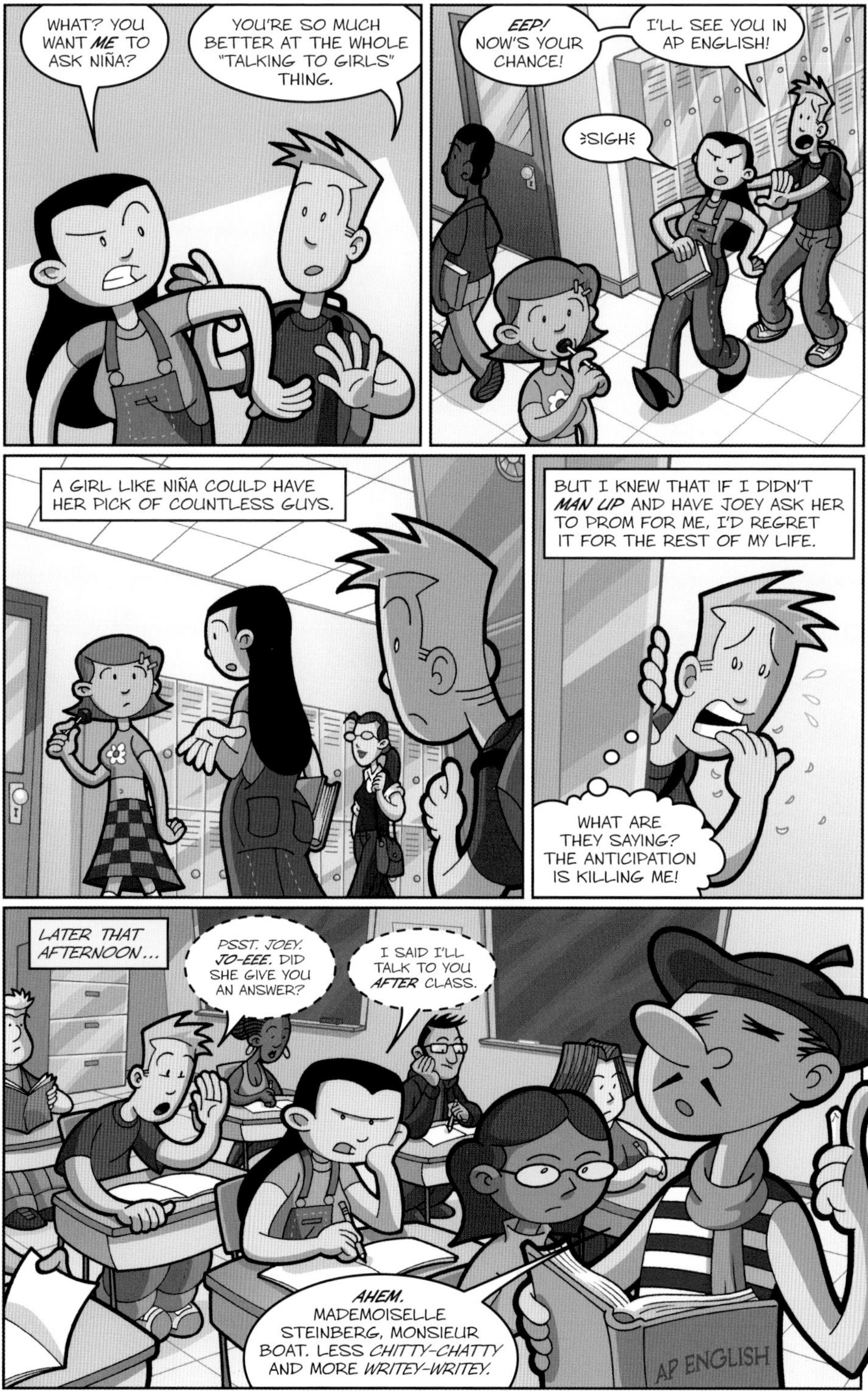
WHAT? YOU WANT *ME* TO ASK NIÑA?
YOU'RE SO MUCH BETTER AT THE WHOLE "TALKING TO GIRLS" THING.
EEP! NOW'S YOUR CHANCE!
I'LL SEE YOU IN AP ENGLISH!
SIGH
A GIRL LIKE NIÑA COULD HAVE HER PICK OF COUNTLESS GUYS.
BUT I KNEW THAT IF I DIDN'T *MAN UP* AND HAVE JOEY ASK HER TO PROM FOR ME, I'D REGRET IT FOR THE REST OF MY LIFE.
WHAT ARE THEY SAYING? THE ANTICIPATION IS KILLING ME!
LATER THAT AFTERNOON...
*PSST. JOEY. **JO-EEE.** DID SHE GIVE YOU AN ANSWER?*
I SAID I'LL TALK TO YOU *AFTER* CLASS.
AHEM. MADEMOISELLE STEINBERG, MONSIEUR BOAT. LESS *CHITTY-CHATTY* AND MORE *WRITEY-WRITEY.*
AP ENGLISH

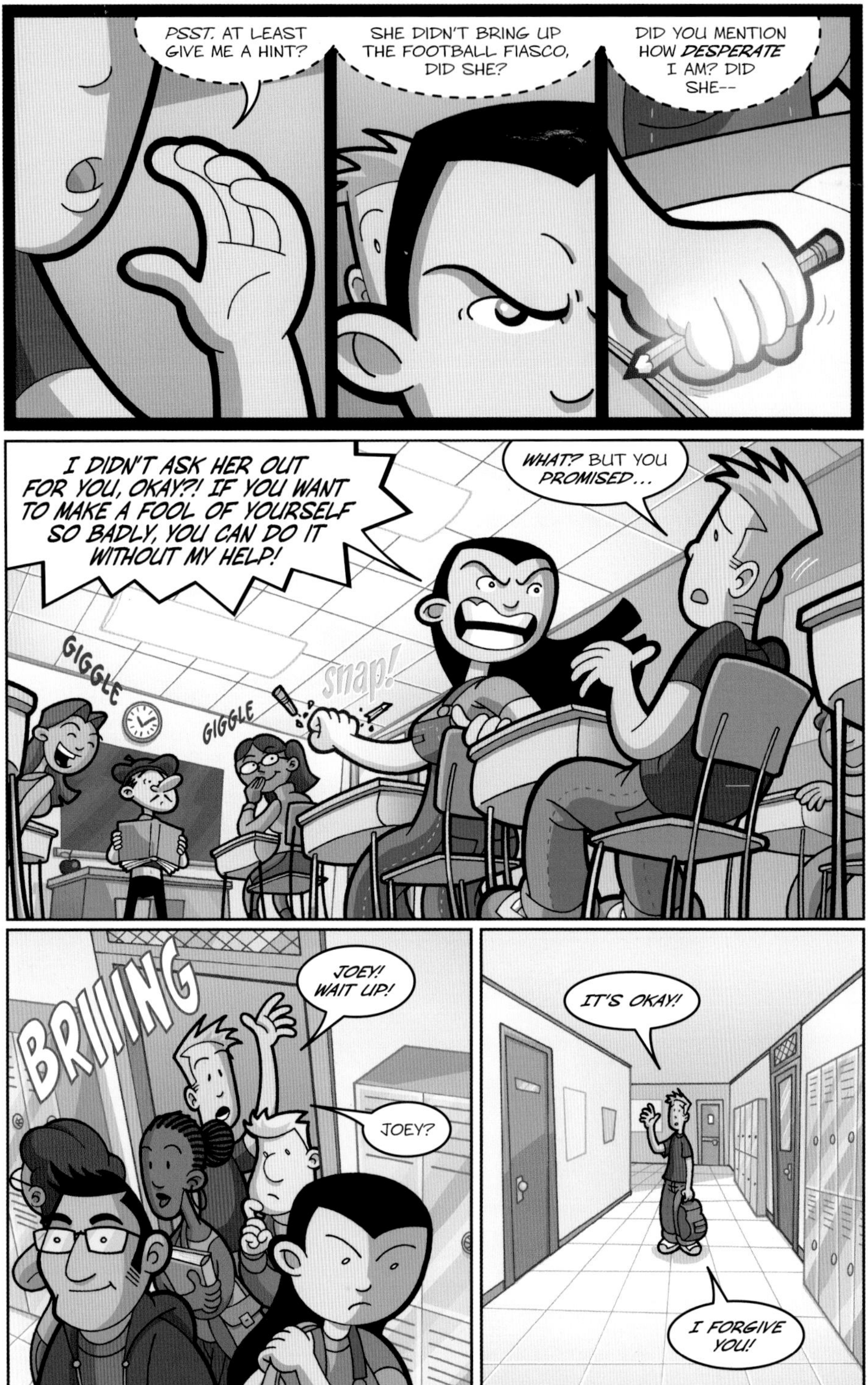
PSST. AT LEAST GIVE ME A HINT?
SHE DIDN'T BRING UP THE FOOTBALL FIASCO, DID SHE?
DID YOU MENTION HOW DESPERATE I AM? DID SHE--
I DIDN'T ASK HER OUT FOR YOU, OKAY?! IF YOU WANT TO MAKE A FOOL OF YOURSELF SO BADLY, YOU CAN DO IT WITHOUT MY HELP!
WHAT? BUT YOU PROMISED...
GIGGLE
GIGGLE
snap!
BRIIIING
JOEY! WAIT UP!
JOEY?
IT'S OKAY!
I FORGIVE YOU!

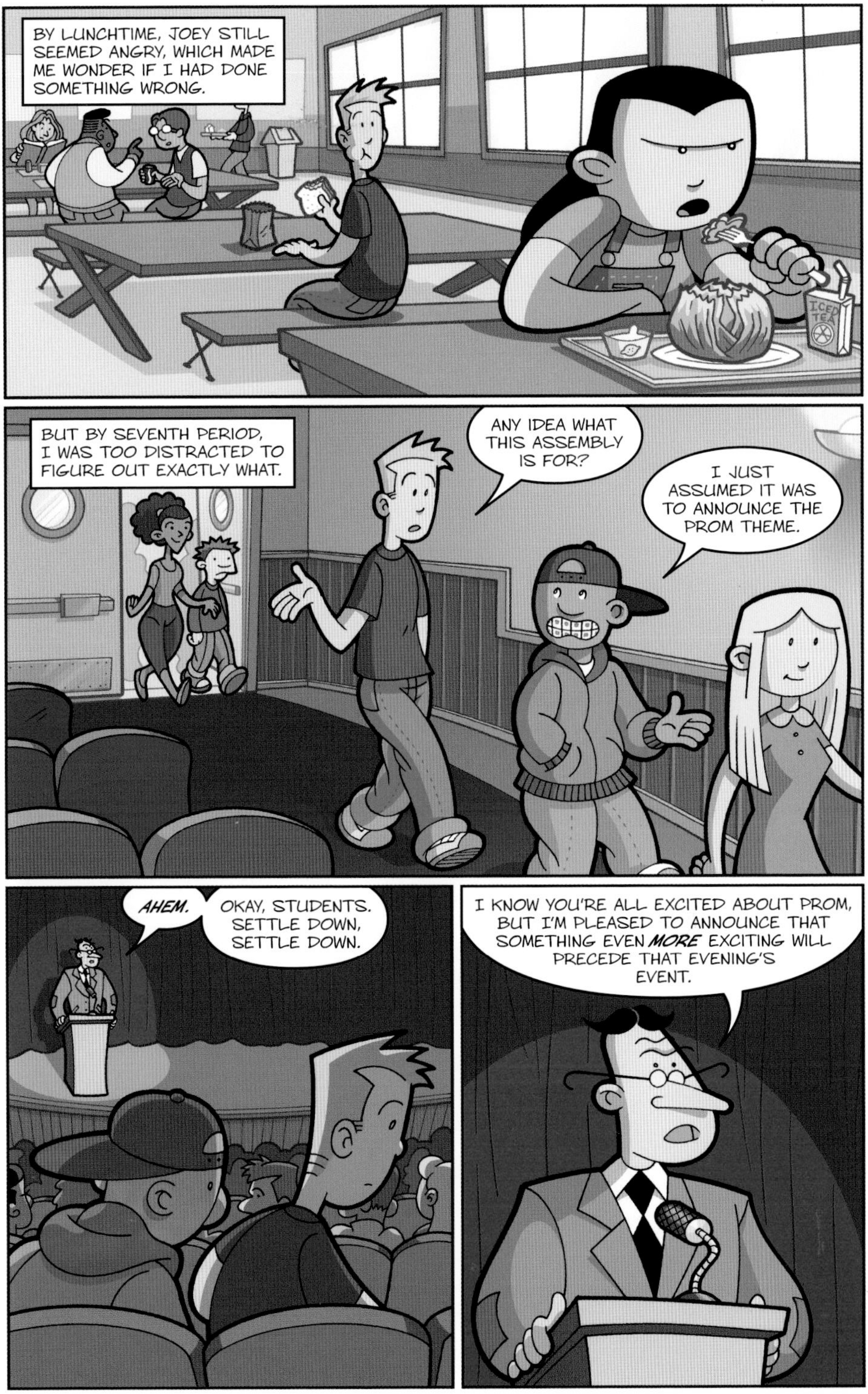
BY LUNCHTIME, JOEY STILL SEEMED ANGRY, WHICH MADE ME WONDER IF I HAD DONE SOMETHING WRONG.
ICED TEA
BUT BY SEVENTH PERIOD, I WAS TOO DISTRACTED TO FIGURE OUT EXACTLY WHAT.
ANY IDEA WHAT THIS ASSEMBLY IS FOR?
I JUST ASSUMED IT WAS TO ANNOUNCE THE PROM THEME.
AHEM.
OKAY, STUDENTS. SETTLE DOWN, SETTLE DOWN.
I KNOW YOU'RE ALL EXCITED ABOUT PROM, BUT I'M PLEASED TO ANNOUNCE THAT SOMETHING EVEN MORE EXCITING WILL PRECEDE THAT EVENING'S EVENT.

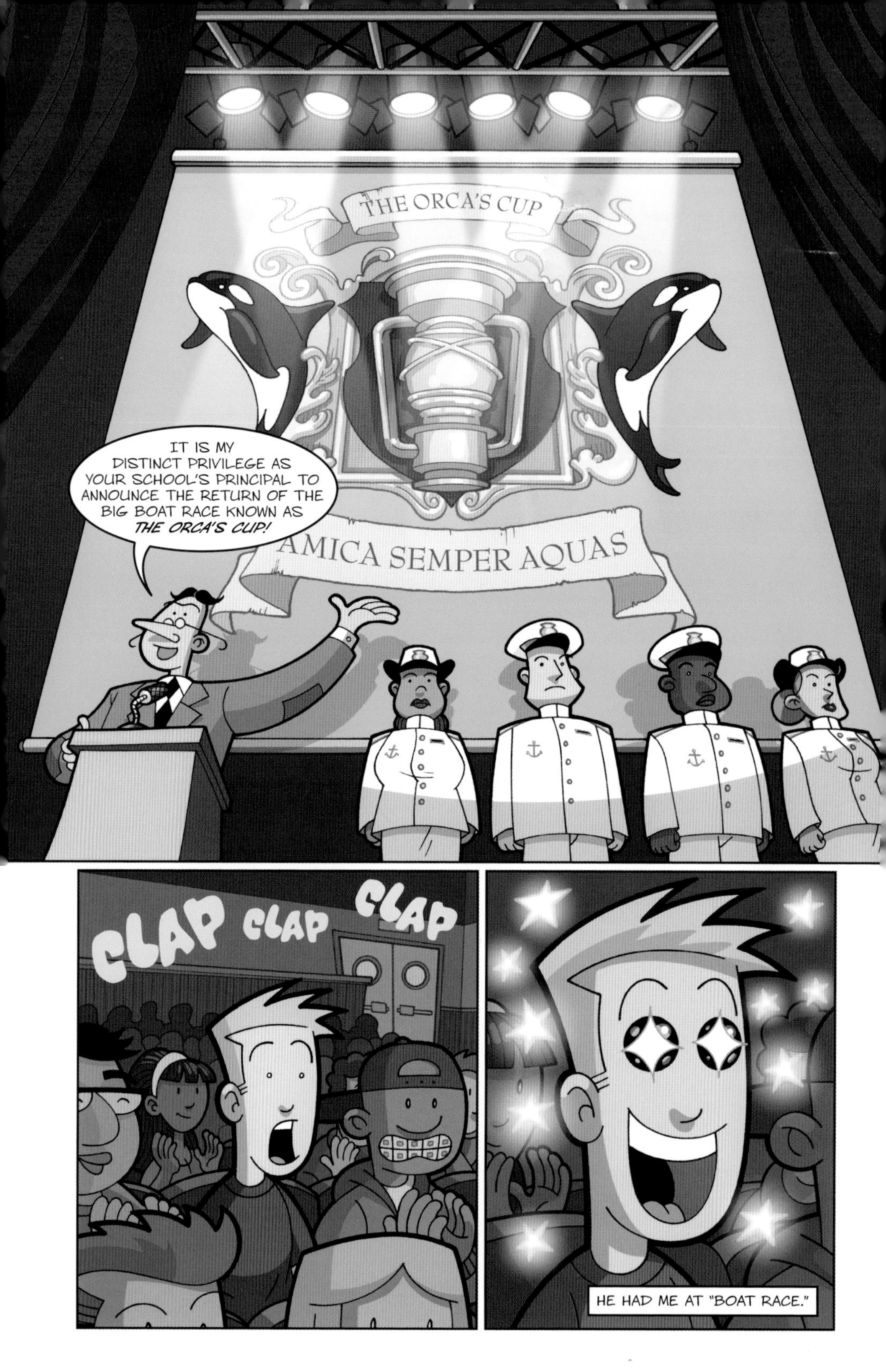
THE ORCA'S CUP
AMICA SEMPER AQUAS
IT IS MY DISTINCT PRIVILEGE AS YOUR SCHOOL'S PRINCIPAL TO ANNOUNCE THE RETURN OF THE BIG BOAT RACE KNOWN AS *THE ORCA'S CUP!*
CLAP CLAP CLAP
HE HAD ME AT "BOAT RACE."

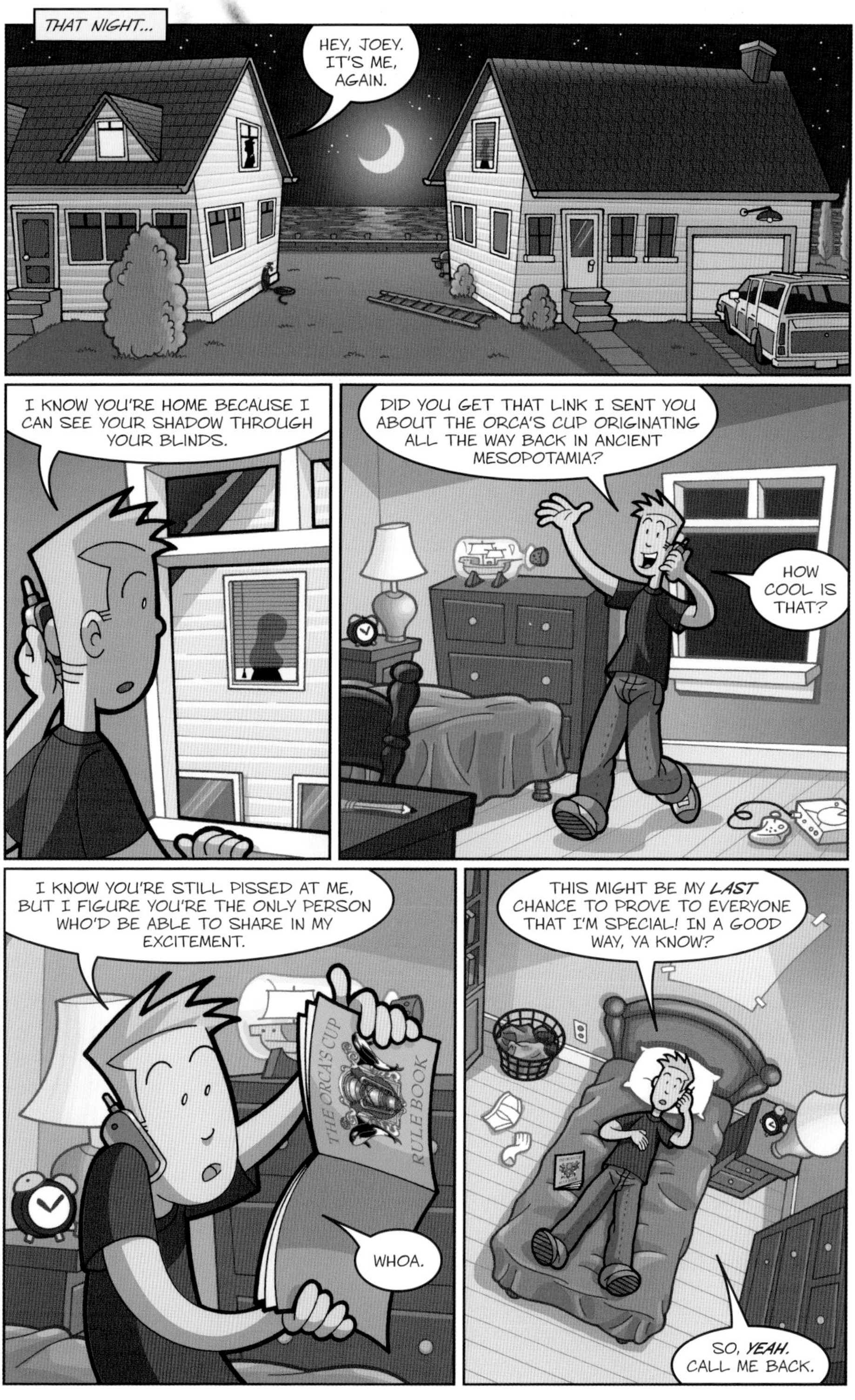
THAT NIGHT...
HEY, JOEY. IT'S ME, AGAIN.
I KNOW YOU'RE HOME BECAUSE I CAN SEE YOUR SHADOW THROUGH YOUR BLINDS.
DID YOU GET THAT LINK I SENT YOU ABOUT THE ORCA'S CUP ORIGINATING ALL THE WAY BACK IN ANCIENT MESOPOTAMIA?
HOW COOL IS THAT?
I KNOW YOU'RE STILL PISSED AT ME, BUT I FIGURE YOU'RE THE ONLY PERSON WHO'D BE ABLE TO SHARE IN MY EXCITEMENT.
THE ORCA'S CUP RULE BOOK
WHOA.
THIS MIGHT BE MY *LAST* CHANCE TO PROVE TO EVERYONE THAT I'M SPECIAL! IN A GOOD WAY, YA KNOW?
SO, ***YEAH.*** CALL ME BACK.

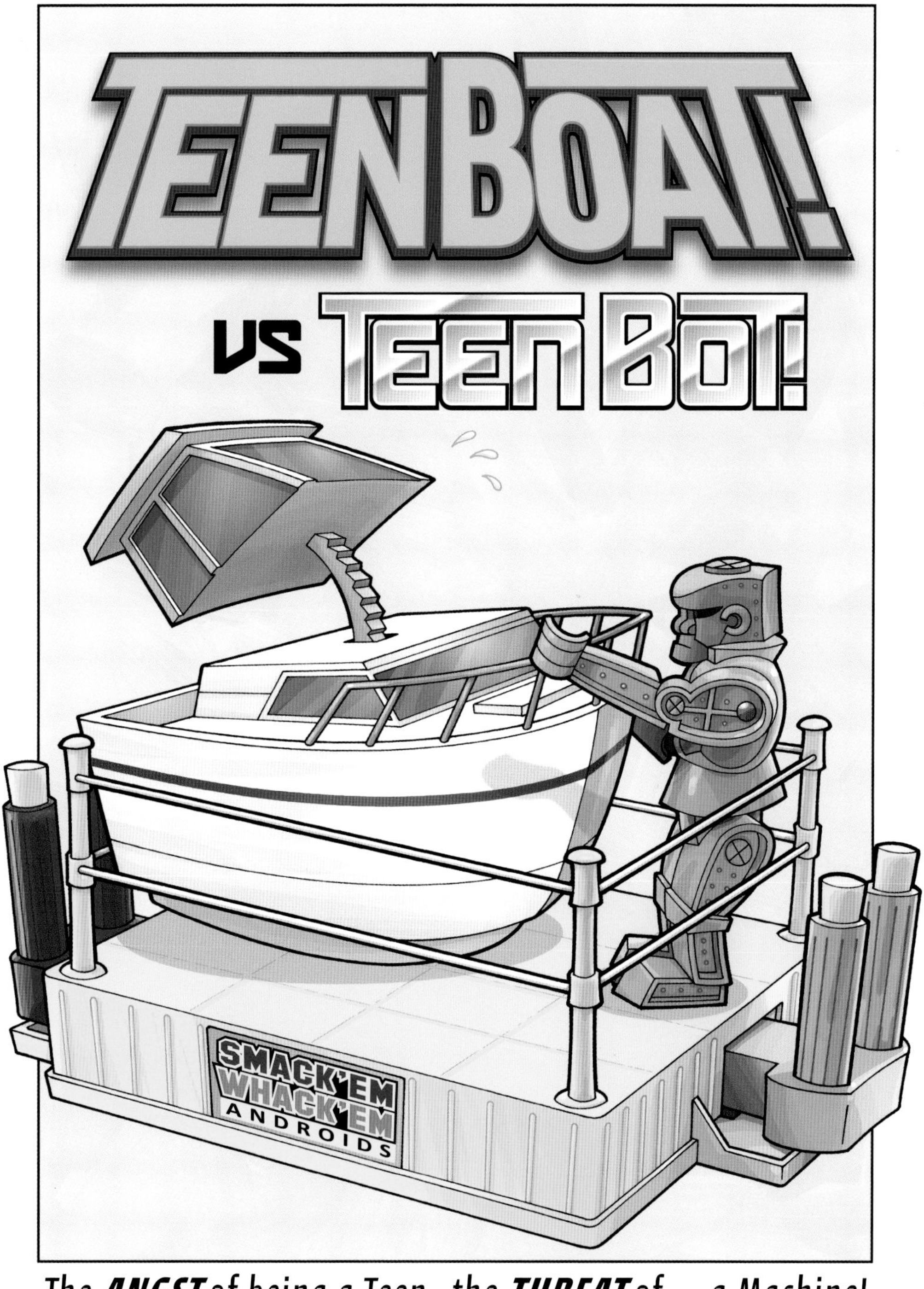
TEEN BOAT!
VS TEEN BOT!
SMACK'EM
WHACK'EM
ANDROIDS

The ***ANGST*** of being a Teen—the ***THREAT*** of. . . a Machine!

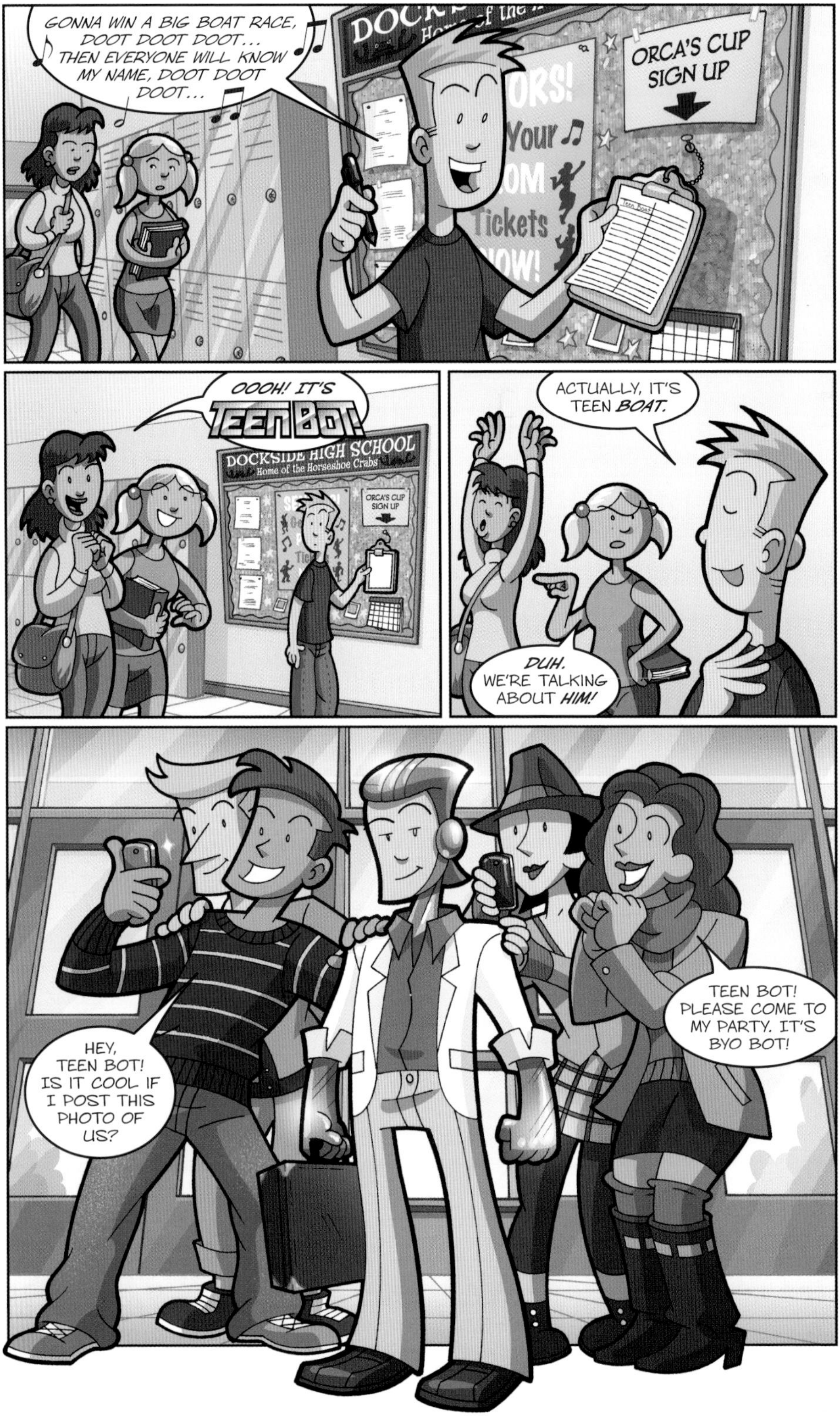
GONNA WIN A BIG BOAT RACE, DOOT DOOT DOOT... THEN EVERYONE WILL KNOW MY NAME, DOOT DOOT DOOT...
ORCA'S CUP SIGN UP
Teen Boat
DOCKSIDE HIGH SCHOOL
Home of the Horseshoe Crabs
ORCA'S CUP SIGN UP
OOOH! IT'S TEEN BOT!
ACTUALLY, IT'S TEEN BOAT.
DUH. WE'RE TALKING ABOUT HIM!
HEY, TEEN BOT! IS IT COOL IF I POST THIS PHOTO OF US?
TEEN BOT! PLEASE COME TO MY PARTY. IT'S BYO BOT!

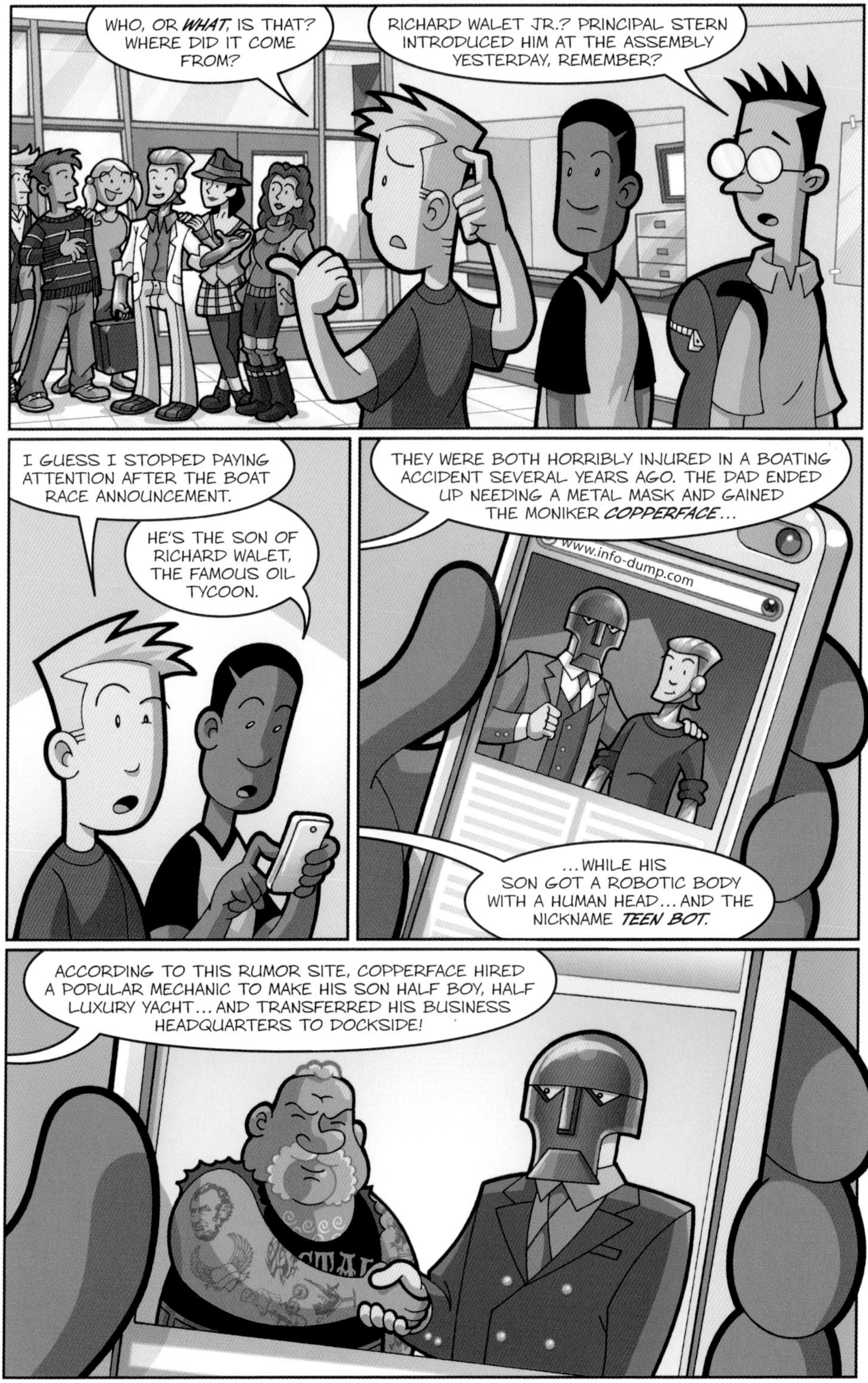
WHO, OR WHAT, IS THAT? WHERE DID IT COME FROM?
RICHARD WALET JR.? PRINCIPAL STERN INTRODUCED HIM AT THE ASSEMBLY YESTERDAY, REMEMBER?
I GUESS I STOPPED PAYING ATTENTION AFTER THE BOAT RACE ANNOUNCEMENT.
HE'S THE SON OF RICHARD WALET, THE FAMOUS OIL TYCOON.
THEY WERE BOTH HORRIBLY INJURED IN A BOATING ACCIDENT SEVERAL YEARS AGO. THE DAD ENDED UP NEEDING A METAL MASK AND GAINED THE MONIKER COPPERFACE...
www.info-dump.com
...WHILE HIS SON GOT A ROBOTIC BODY WITH A HUMAN HEAD... AND THE NICKNAME TEEN BOT.
ACCORDING TO THIS RUMOR SITE, COPPERFACE HIRED A POPULAR MECHANIC TO MAKE HIS SON HALF BOY, HALF LUXURY YACHT... AND TRANSFERRED HIS BUSINESS HEADQUARTERS TO DOCKSIDE!

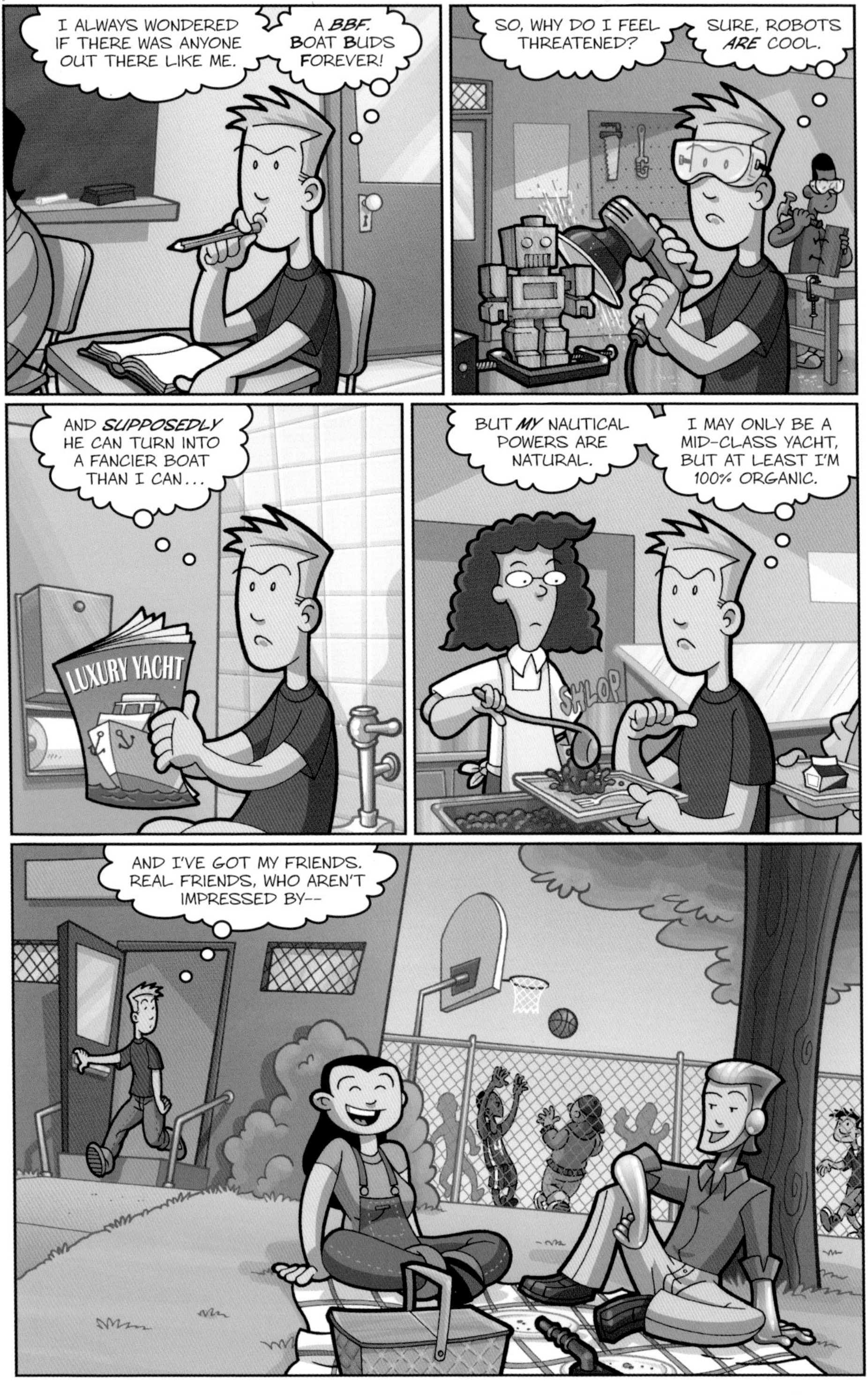
I ALWAYS WONDERED IF THERE WAS ANYONE OUT THERE LIKE ME.
A BBF. BOAT BUDS FOREVER!
SO, WHY DO I FEEL THREATENED?
SURE, ROBOTS ARE COOL.
AND SUPPOSEDLY HE CAN TURN INTO A FANCIER BOAT THAN I CAN...
LUXURY YACHT
BUT MY NAUTICAL POWERS ARE NATURAL.
I MAY ONLY BE A MID-CLASS YACHT, BUT AT LEAST I'M 100% ORGANIC.
SHLOP
AND I'VE GOT MY FRIENDS. REAL FRIENDS, WHO AREN'T IMPRESSED BY--

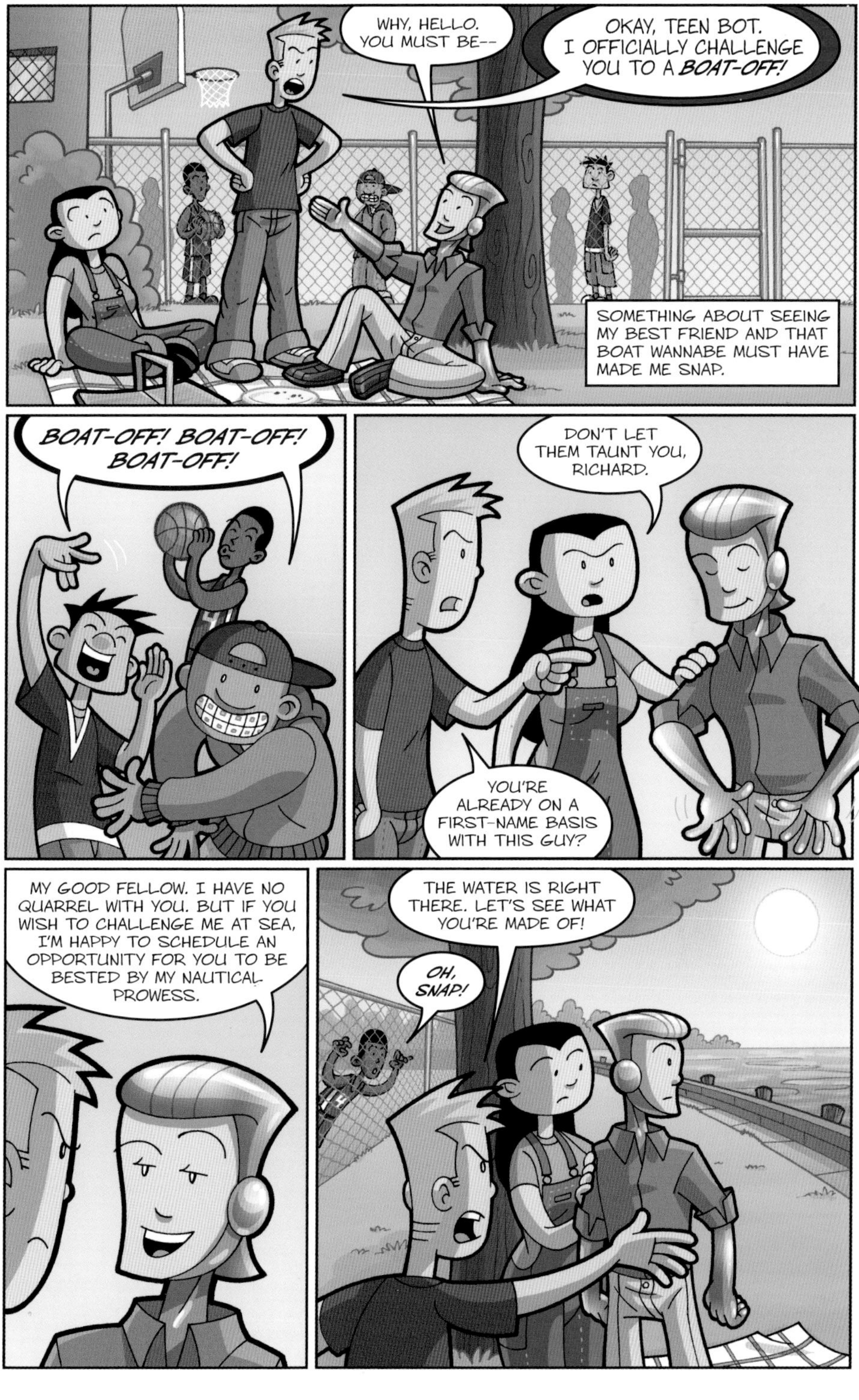

WHY, HELLO. YOU MUST BE--
OKAY, TEEN BOT. I OFFICIALLY CHALLENGE YOU TO A *BOAT-OFF!*
SOMETHING ABOUT SEEING MY BEST FRIEND AND THAT BOAT WANNABE MUST HAVE MADE ME SNAP.
BOAT-OFF! BOAT-OFF! BOAT-OFF!
DON'T LET THEM TAUNT YOU, RICHARD.
YOU'RE ALREADY ON A FIRST-NAME BASIS WITH THIS GUY?
MY GOOD FELLOW. I HAVE NO QUARREL WITH YOU. BUT IF YOU WISH TO CHALLENGE ME AT SEA, I'M HAPPY TO SCHEDULE AN OPPORTUNITY FOR YOU TO BE BESTED BY MY NAUTICAL PROWESS.
THE WATER IS RIGHT THERE. LET'S SEE WHAT YOU'RE MADE OF!
OH, SNAP!

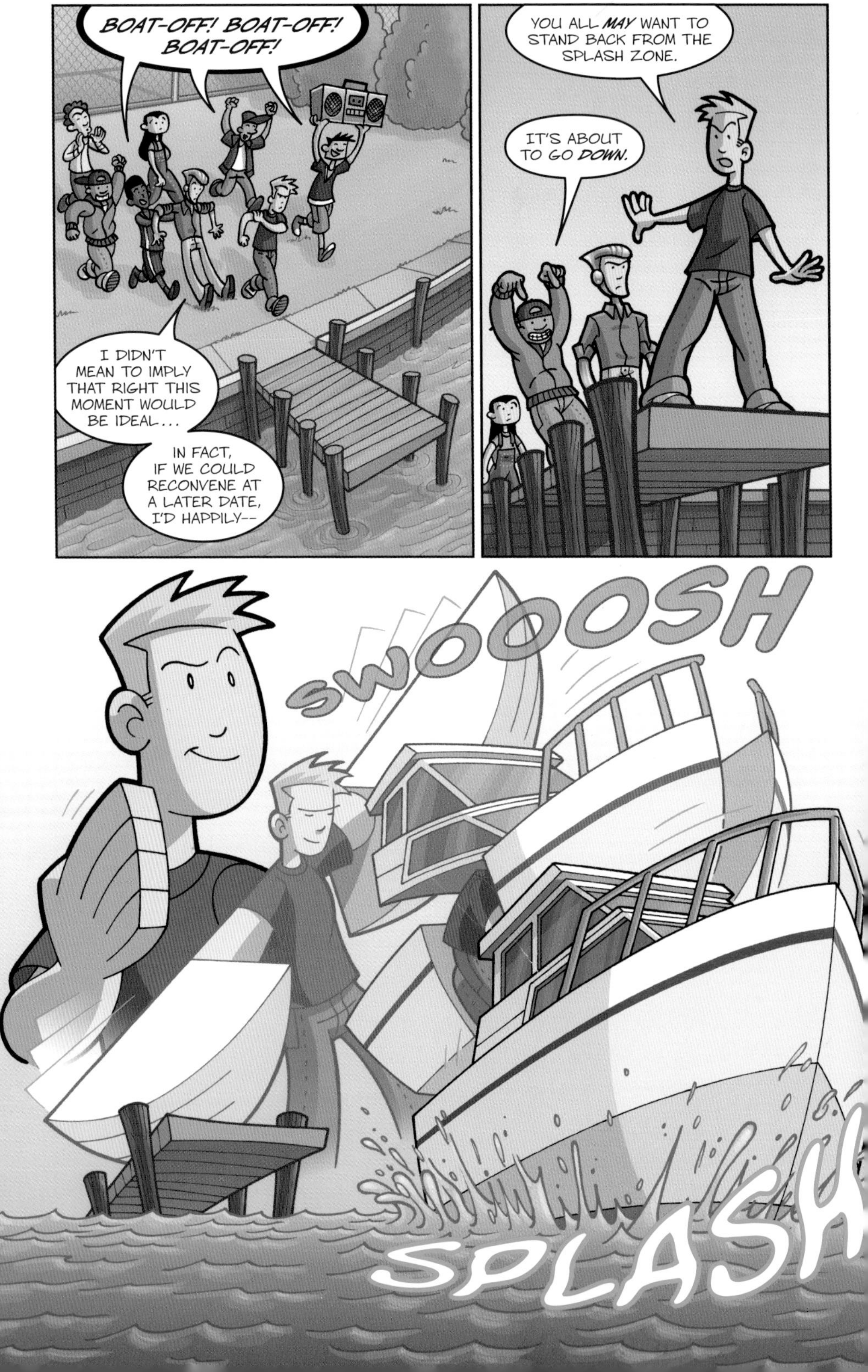
BOAT-OFF! BOAT-OFF! BOAT-OFF!
I DIDN'T MEAN TO IMPLY THAT RIGHT THIS MOMENT WOULD BE IDEAL...
IN FACT, IF WE COULD RECONVENE AT A LATER DATE, I'D HAPPILY--
YOU ALL MAY WANT TO STAND BACK FROM THE SPLASH ZONE.
IT'S ABOUT TO GO DOWN.
SWOOOSH
SPLASH

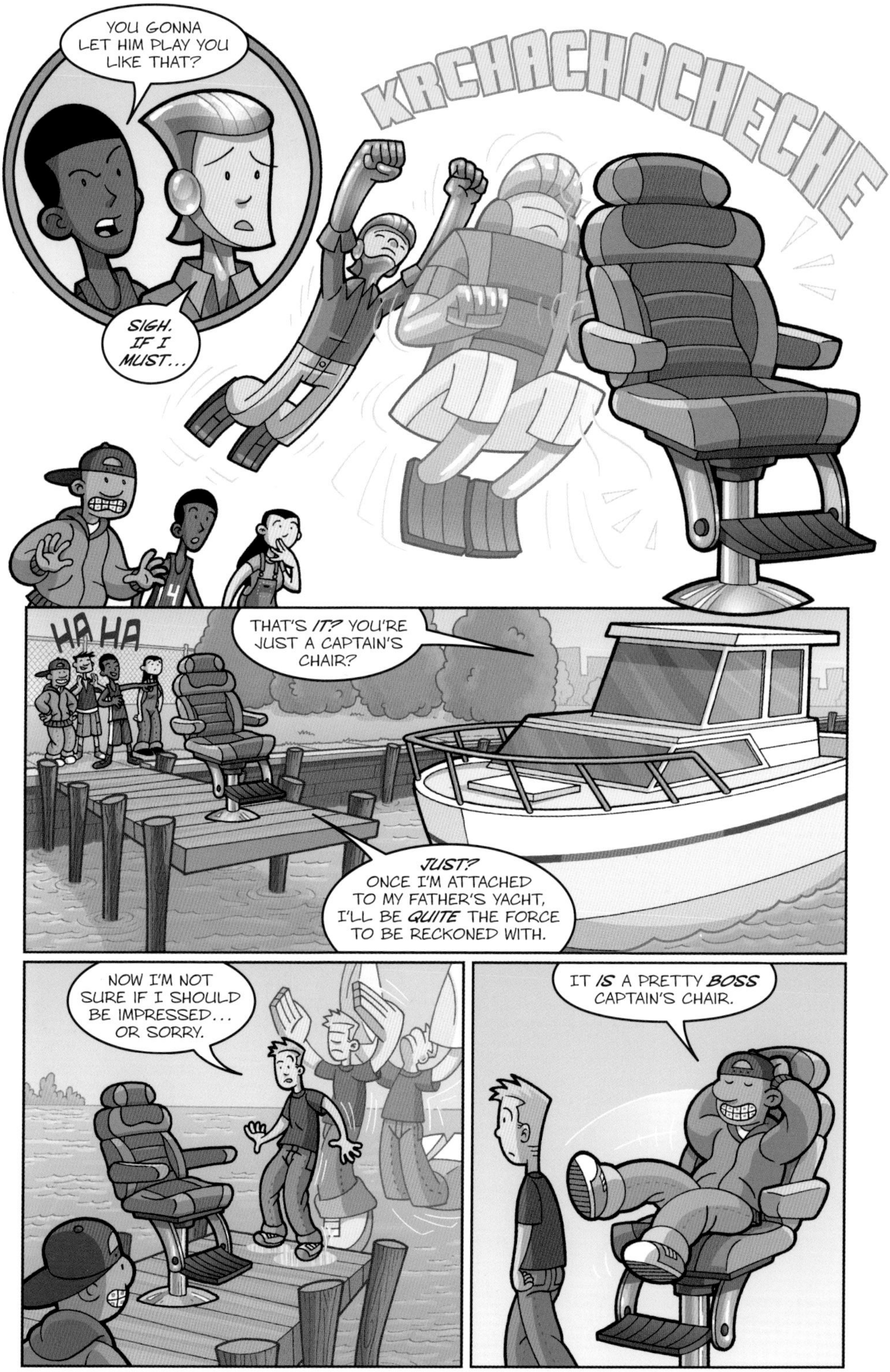
YOU GONNA LET HIM PLAY YOU LIKE THAT?
SIGH. IF I MUST...
KRCHACHACHECHE
HA HA
THAT'S IT? YOU'RE JUST A CAPTAIN'S CHAIR?
JUST? ONCE I'M ATTACHED TO MY FATHER'S YACHT, I'LL BE QUITE THE FORCE TO BE RECKONED WITH.
NOW I'M NOT SURE IF I SHOULD BE IMPRESSED... OR SORRY.
IT IS A PRETTY BOSS CAPTAIN'S CHAIR.

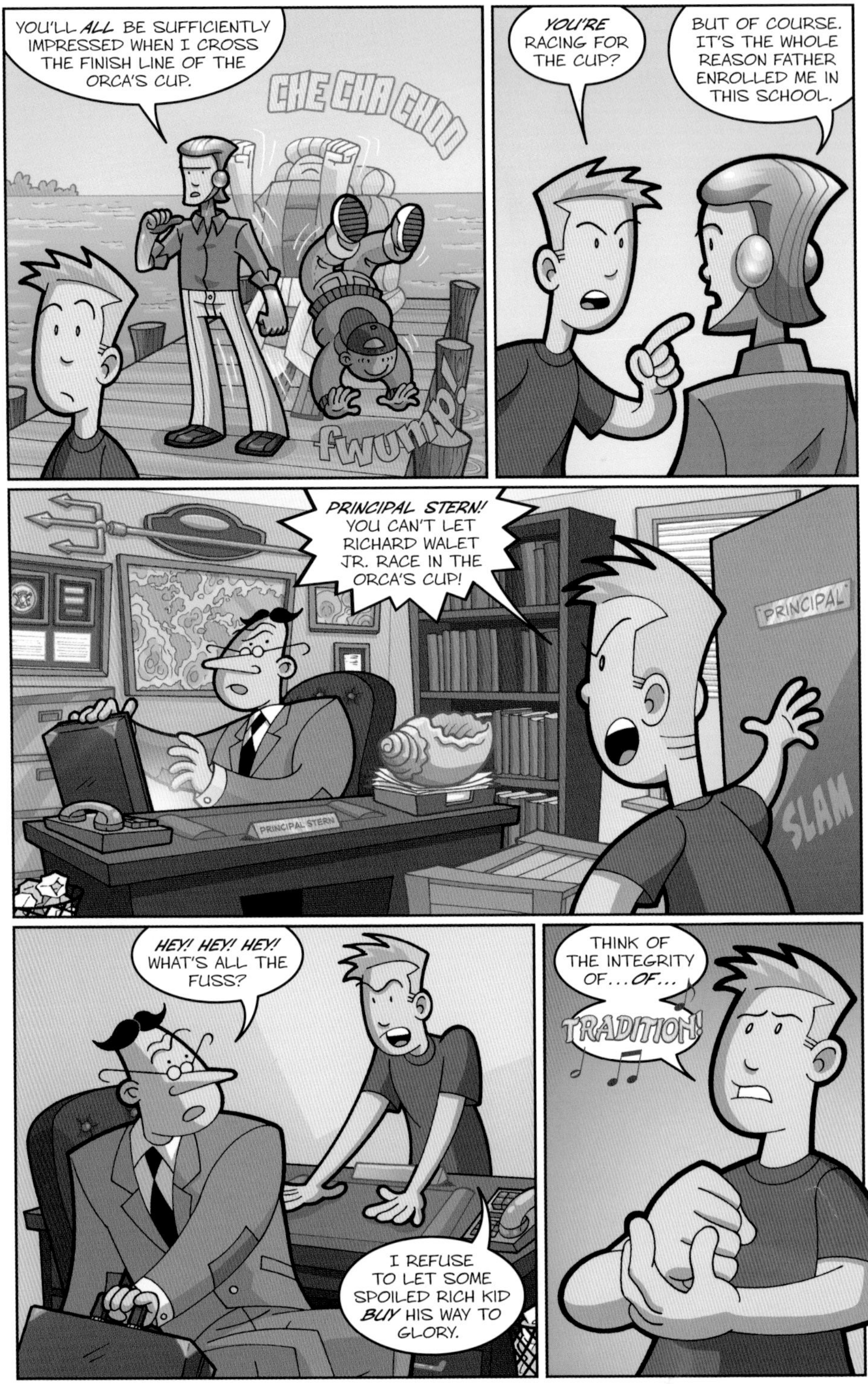
YOU'LL ALL BE SUFFICIENTLY IMPRESSED WHEN I CROSS THE FINISH LINE OF THE ORCA'S CUP.
CHE CHA CHOO
fwump!
YOU'RE RACING FOR THE CUP?
BUT OF COURSE. IT'S THE WHOLE REASON FATHER ENROLLED ME IN THIS SCHOOL.
PRINCIPAL STERN! YOU CAN'T LET RICHARD WALET JR. RACE IN THE ORCA'S CUP!
PRINCIPAL
PRINCIPAL STERN
SLAM
HEY! HEY! HEY! WHAT'S ALL THE FUSS?
I REFUSE TO LET SOME SPOILED RICH KID BUY HIS WAY TO GLORY.
THINK OF THE INTEGRITY OF... OF...
TRADITION!

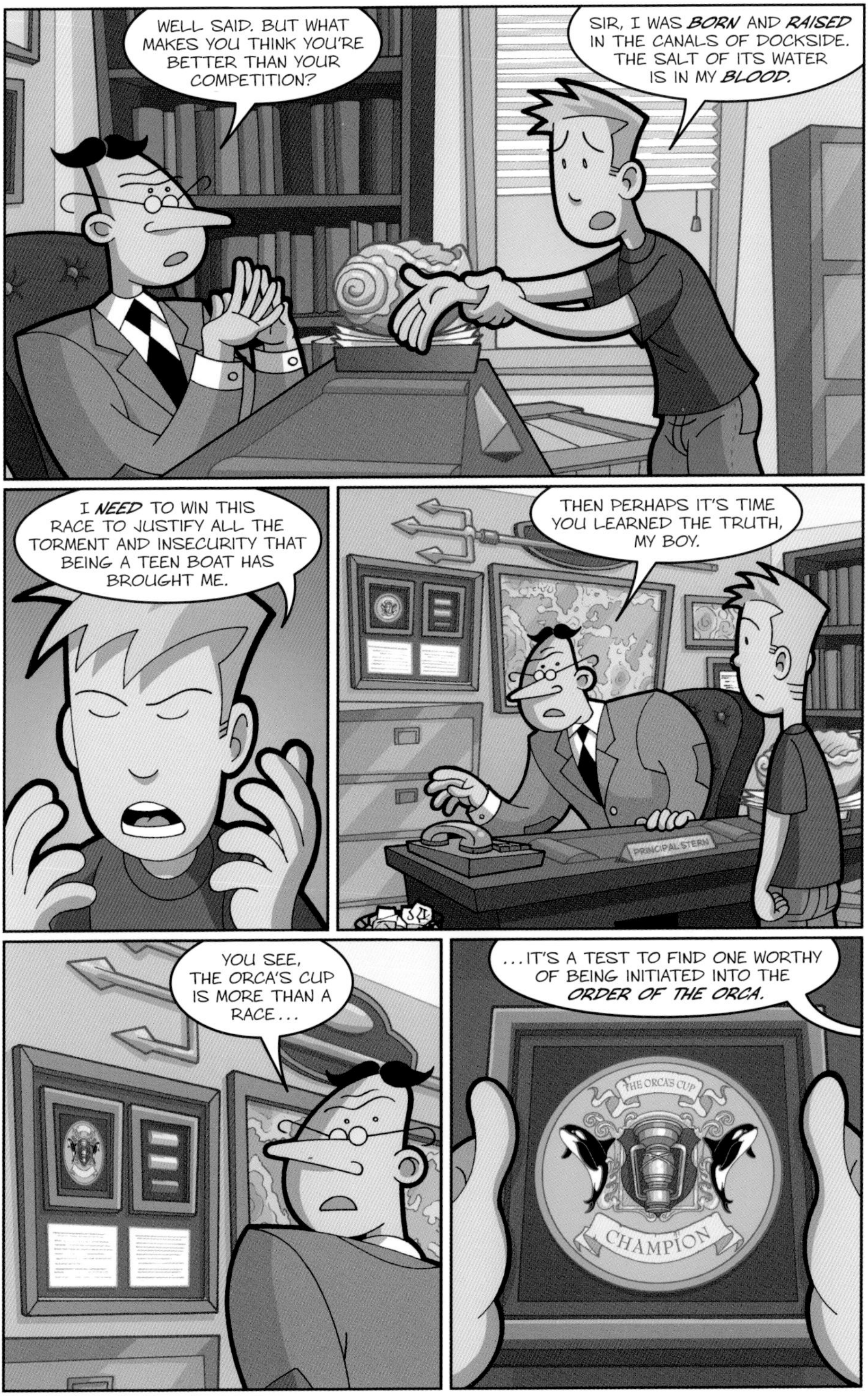
WELL SAID. BUT WHAT MAKES YOU THINK YOU'RE BETTER THAN YOUR COMPETITION?
SIR, I WAS *BORN* AND *RAISED* IN THE CANALS OF DOCKSIDE. THE SALT OF ITS WATER IS IN MY *BLOOD.*
I *NEED* TO WIN THIS RACE TO JUSTIFY ALL THE TORMENT AND INSECURITY THAT BEING A TEEN BOAT HAS BROUGHT ME.
THEN PERHAPS IT'S TIME YOU LEARNED THE TRUTH, MY BOY.
PRINCIPAL STERN
YOU SEE, THE ORCA'S CUP IS MORE THAN A RACE...
...IT'S A TEST TO FIND ONE WORTHY OF BEING INITIATED INTO THE *ORDER OF THE ORCA.*
THE ORCA'S CUP
CHAMPION

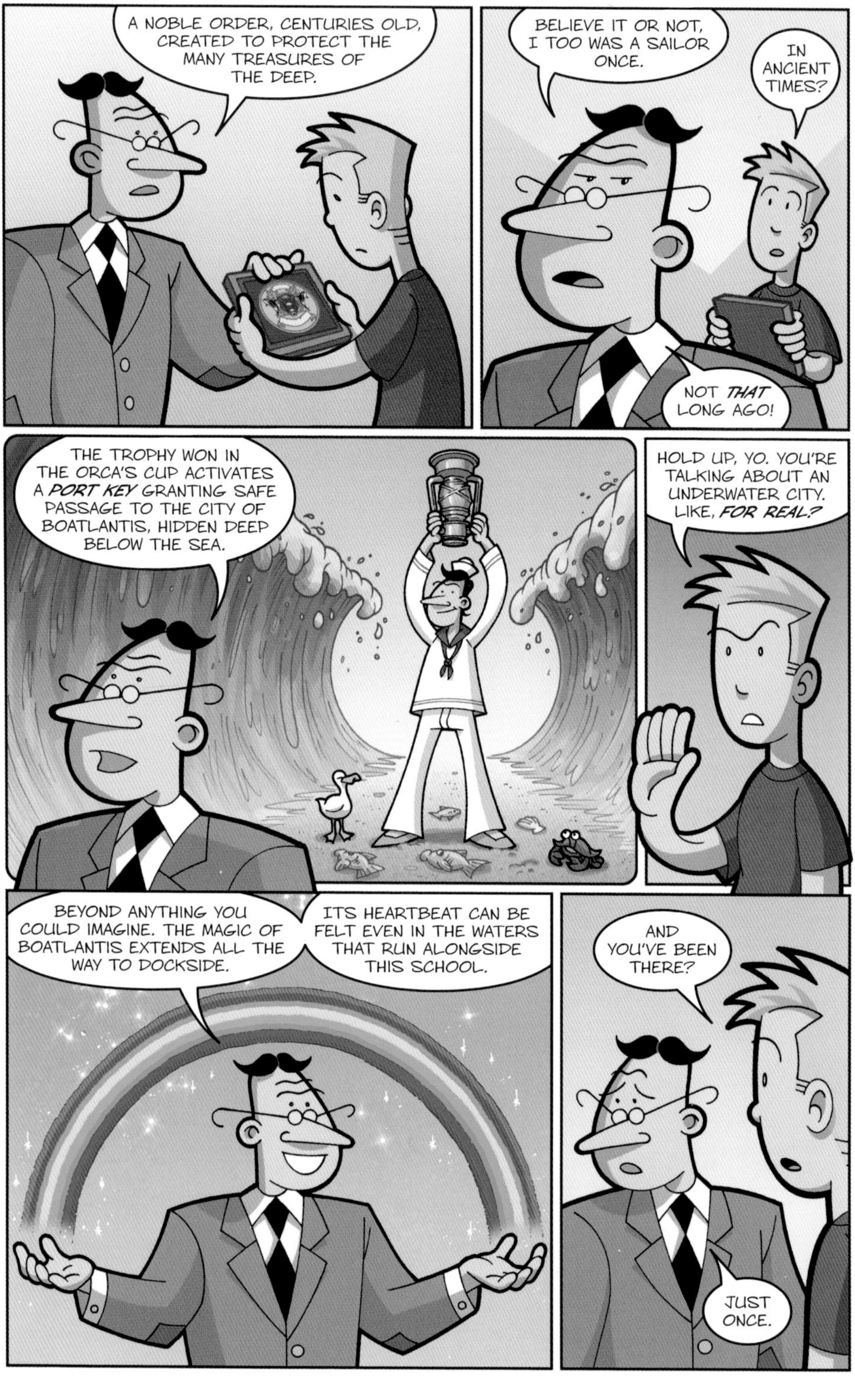

A NOBLE ORDER, CENTURIES OLD, CREATED TO PROTECT THE MANY TREASURES OF THE DEEP.
BELIEVE IT OR NOT, I TOO WAS A SAILOR ONCE.
IN ANCIENT TIMES?
NOT *THAT* LONG AGO!
THE TROPHY WON IN THE ORCA'S CUP ACTIVATES A *PORT KEY* GRANTING SAFE PASSAGE TO THE CITY OF BOATLANTIS, HIDDEN DEEP BELOW THE SEA.
HOLD UP, YO. YOU'RE TALKING ABOUT AN UNDERWATER CITY. LIKE, *FOR REAL?*
BEYOND ANYTHING YOU COULD IMAGINE. THE MAGIC OF BOATLANTIS EXTENDS ALL THE WAY TO DOCKSIDE.
ITS HEARTBEAT CAN BE FELT EVEN IN THE WATERS THAT RUN ALONGSIDE THIS SCHOOL.
AND YOU'VE BEEN THERE?
JUST ONCE.

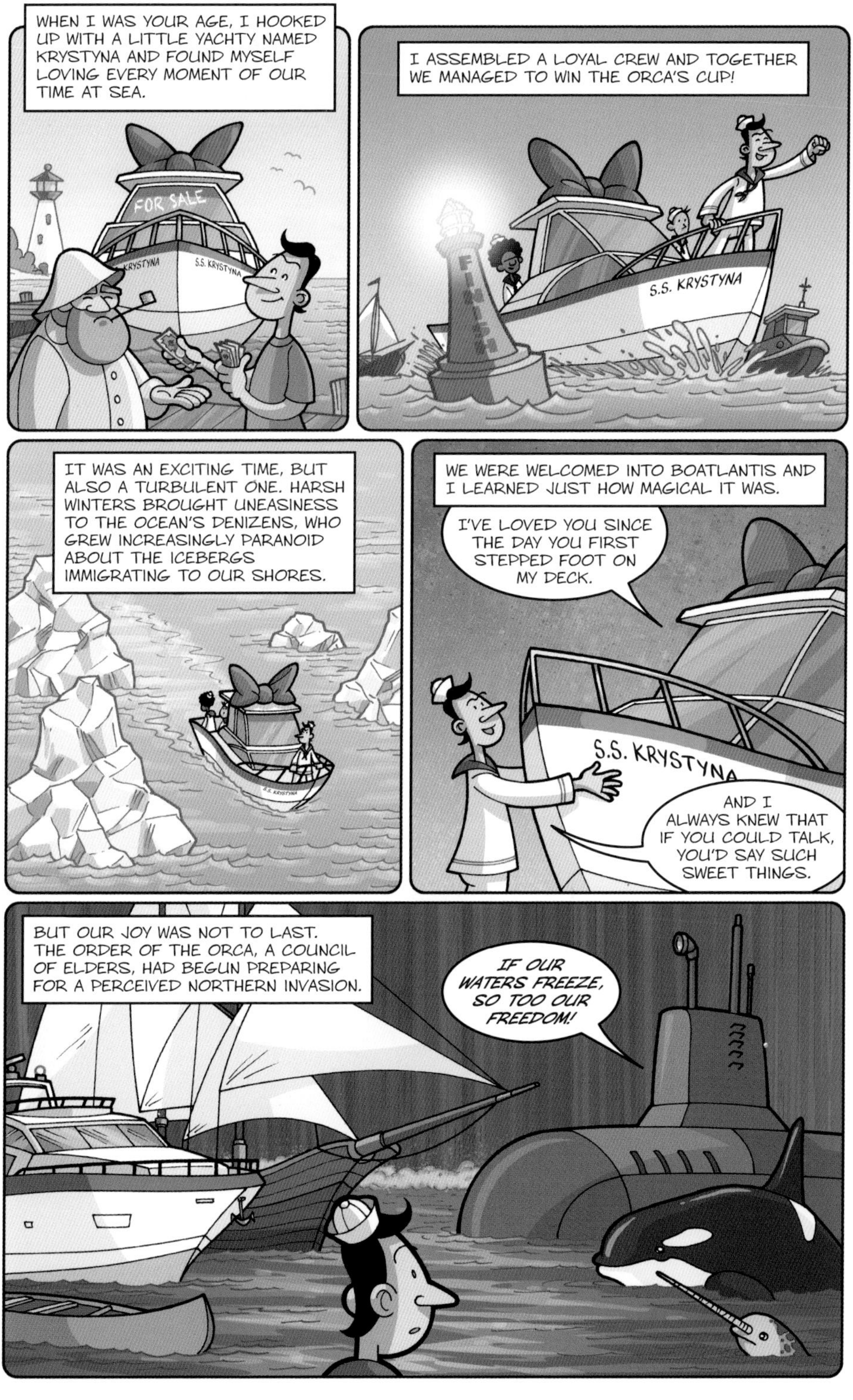
WHEN I WAS YOUR AGE, I HOOKED UP WITH A LITTLE YACHTY NAMED KRYSTYNA AND FOUND MYSELF LOVING EVERY MOMENT OF OUR TIME AT SEA.
FOR SALE
KRYSTYNA
S.S. KRYSTYNA
I ASSEMBLED A LOYAL CREW AND TOGETHER WE MANAGED TO WIN THE ORCA'S CUP!
FINISH
S.S. KRYSTYNA
IT WAS AN EXCITING TIME, BUT ALSO A TURBULENT ONE. HARSH WINTERS BROUGHT UNEASINESS TO THE OCEAN'S DENIZENS, WHO GREW INCREASINGLY PARANOID ABOUT THE ICEBERGS IMMIGRATING TO OUR SHORES.
WE WERE WELCOMED INTO BOATLANTIS AND I LEARNED JUST HOW MAGICAL IT WAS.
I'VE LOVED YOU SINCE THE DAY YOU FIRST STEPPED FOOT ON MY DECK.
S.S. KRYSTYNA
AND I ALWAYS KNEW THAT IF YOU COULD TALK, YOU'D SAY SUCH SWEET THINGS.
BUT OUR JOY WAS NOT TO LAST. THE ORDER OF THE ORCA, A COUNCIL OF ELDERS, HAD BEGUN PREPARING FOR A PERCEIVED NORTHERN INVASION.
IF OUR WATERS FREEZE, SO TOO OUR FREEDOM!

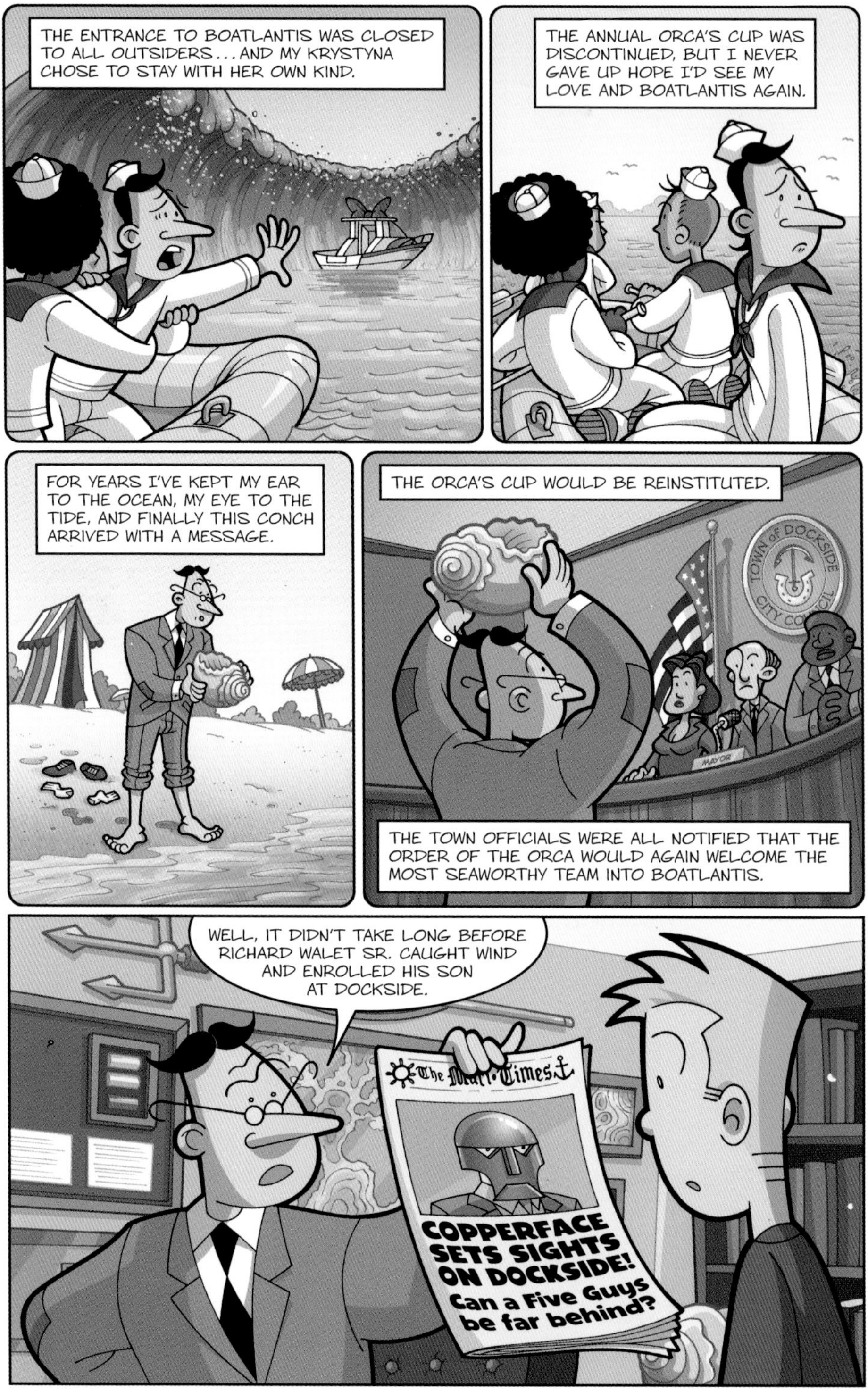
THE ENTRANCE TO BOATLANTIS WAS CLOSED TO ALL OUTSIDERS . . . AND MY KRYSTYNA CHOSE TO STAY WITH HER OWN KIND.
THE ANNUAL ORCA'S CUP WAS DISCONTINUED, BUT I NEVER GAVE UP HOPE I'D SEE MY LOVE AND BOATLANTIS AGAIN.
FOR YEARS I'VE KEPT MY EAR TO THE OCEAN, MY EYE TO THE TIDE, AND FINALLY THIS CONCH ARRIVED WITH A MESSAGE.
THE ORCA'S CUP WOULD BE REINSTITUTED.
TOWN of DOCKSIDE
CITY COUNCIL
MAYOR
THE TOWN OFFICIALS WERE ALL NOTIFIED THAT THE ORDER OF THE ORCA WOULD AGAIN WELCOME THE MOST SEAWORTHY TEAM INTO BOATLANTIS.
WELL, IT DIDN'T TAKE LONG BEFORE RICHARD WALET SR. CAUGHT WIND AND ENROLLED HIS SON AT DOCKSIDE.
COPPERFACE SETS SIGHTS ON DOCKSIDE!
Can a Five Guys be far behind?

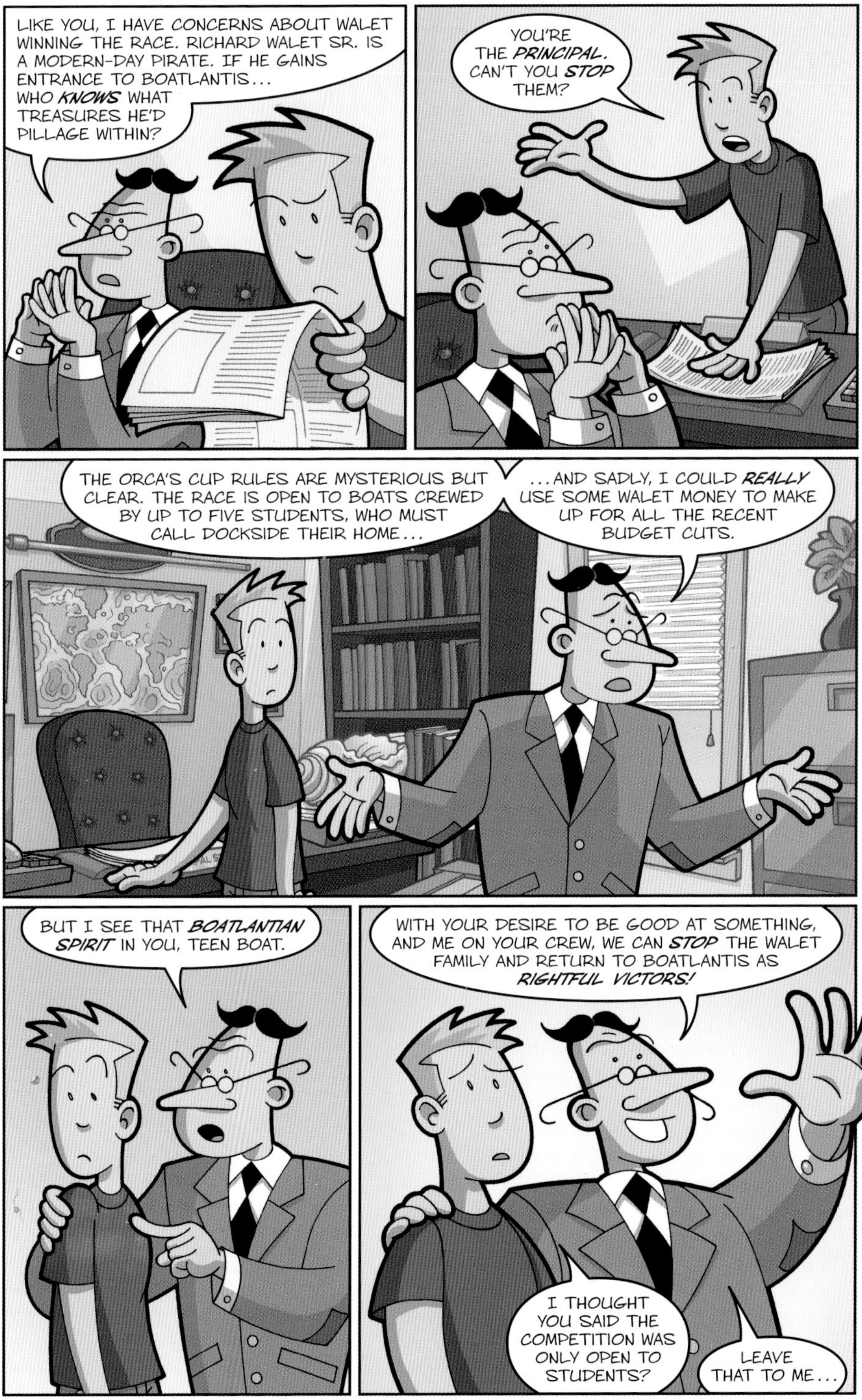
LIKE YOU, I HAVE CONCERNS ABOUT WALET WINNING THE RACE. RICHARD WALET SR. IS A MODERN-DAY PIRATE. IF HE GAINS ENTRANCE TO BOATLANTIS... WHO KNOWS WHAT TREASURES HE'D PILLAGE WITHIN?
YOU'RE THE PRINCIPAL. CAN'T YOU STOP THEM?
THE ORCA'S CUP RULES ARE MYSTERIOUS BUT CLEAR. THE RACE IS OPEN TO BOATS CREWED BY UP TO FIVE STUDENTS, WHO MUST CALL DOCKSIDE THEIR HOME...
...AND SADLY, I COULD REALLY USE SOME WALET MONEY TO MAKE UP FOR ALL THE RECENT BUDGET CUTS.
BUT I SEE THAT BOATLANTIAN SPIRIT IN YOU, TEEN BOAT.
WITH YOUR DESIRE TO BE GOOD AT SOMETHING, AND ME ON YOUR CREW, WE CAN STOP THE WALET FAMILY AND RETURN TO BOATLANTIS AS RIGHTFUL VICTORS!
I THOUGHT YOU SAID THE COMPETITION WAS ONLY OPEN TO STUDENTS?
LEAVE THAT TO ME...

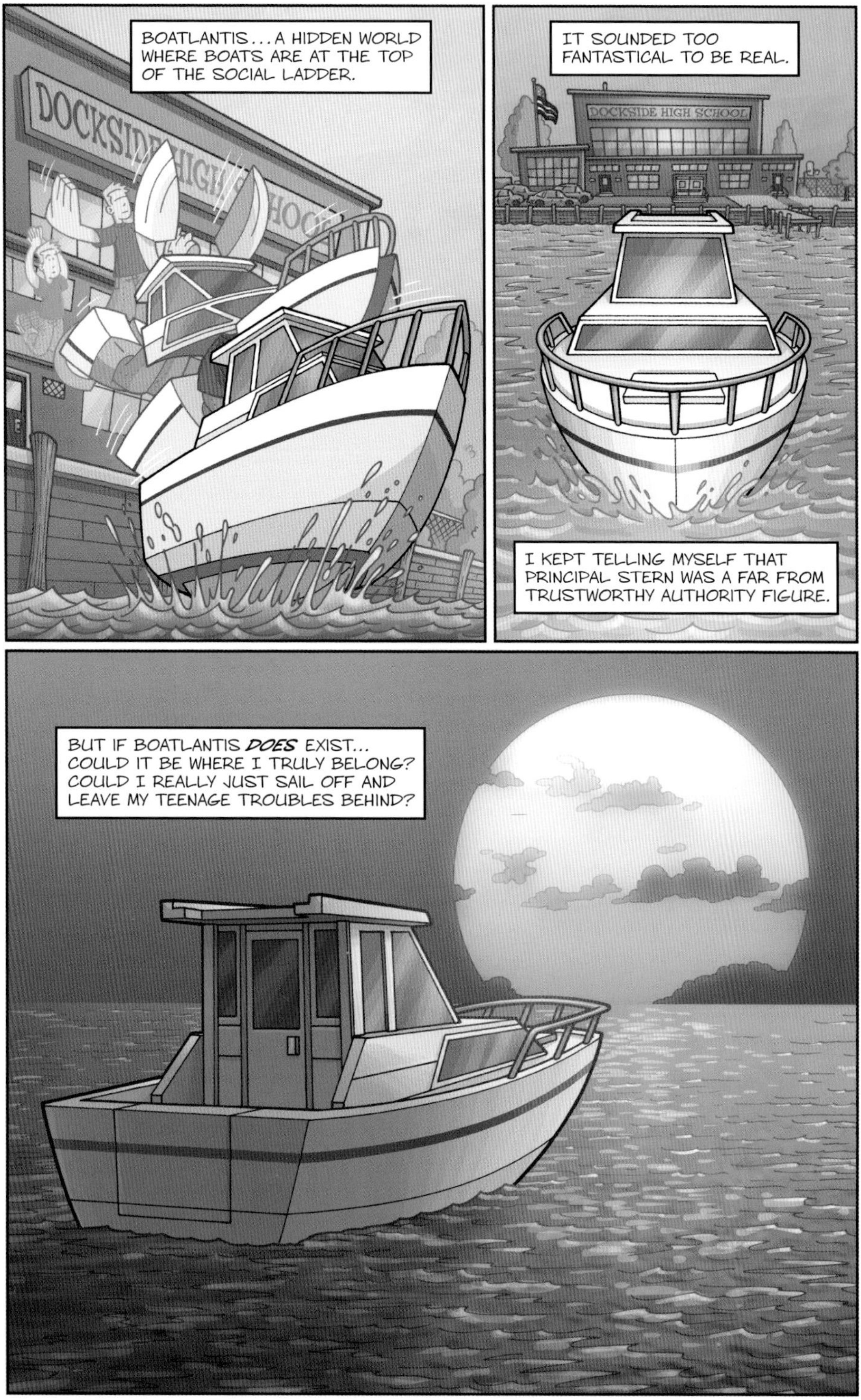
BOATLANTIS...A HIDDEN WORLD WHERE BOATS ARE AT THE TOP OF THE SOCIAL LADDER.
DOCKSIDE HIGH SCHOOL
IT SOUNDED TOO FANTASTICAL TO BE REAL.
DOCKSIDE HIGH SCHOOL
I KEPT TELLING MYSELF THAT PRINCIPAL STERN WAS A FAR FROM TRUSTWORTHY AUTHORITY FIGURE.
BUT IF BOATLANTIS *DOES* EXIST... COULD IT BE WHERE I TRULY BELONG? COULD I REALLY JUST SAIL OFF AND LEAVE MY TEENAGE TROUBLES BEHIND?

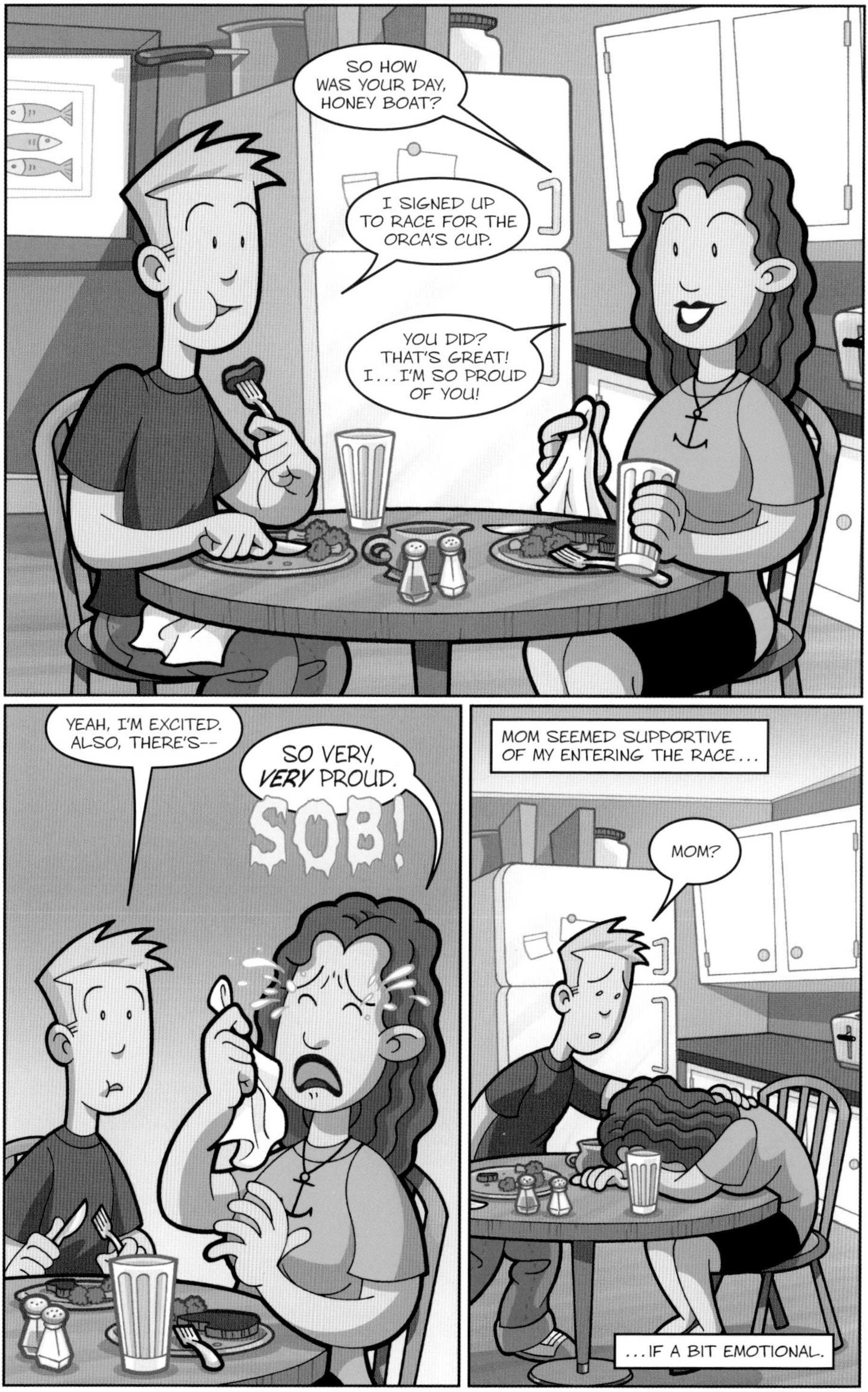
SO HOW WAS YOUR DAY, HONEY BOAT?
I SIGNED UP TO RACE FOR THE ORCA'S CUP.
YOU DID? THAT'S GREAT! I... I'M SO PROUD OF YOU!
YEAH, I'M EXCITED. ALSO, THERE'S--
SO VERY, *VERY* PROUD.
SOB!
MOM SEEMED SUPPORTIVE OF MY ENTERING THE RACE...
MOM?
...IF A BIT EMOTIONAL.

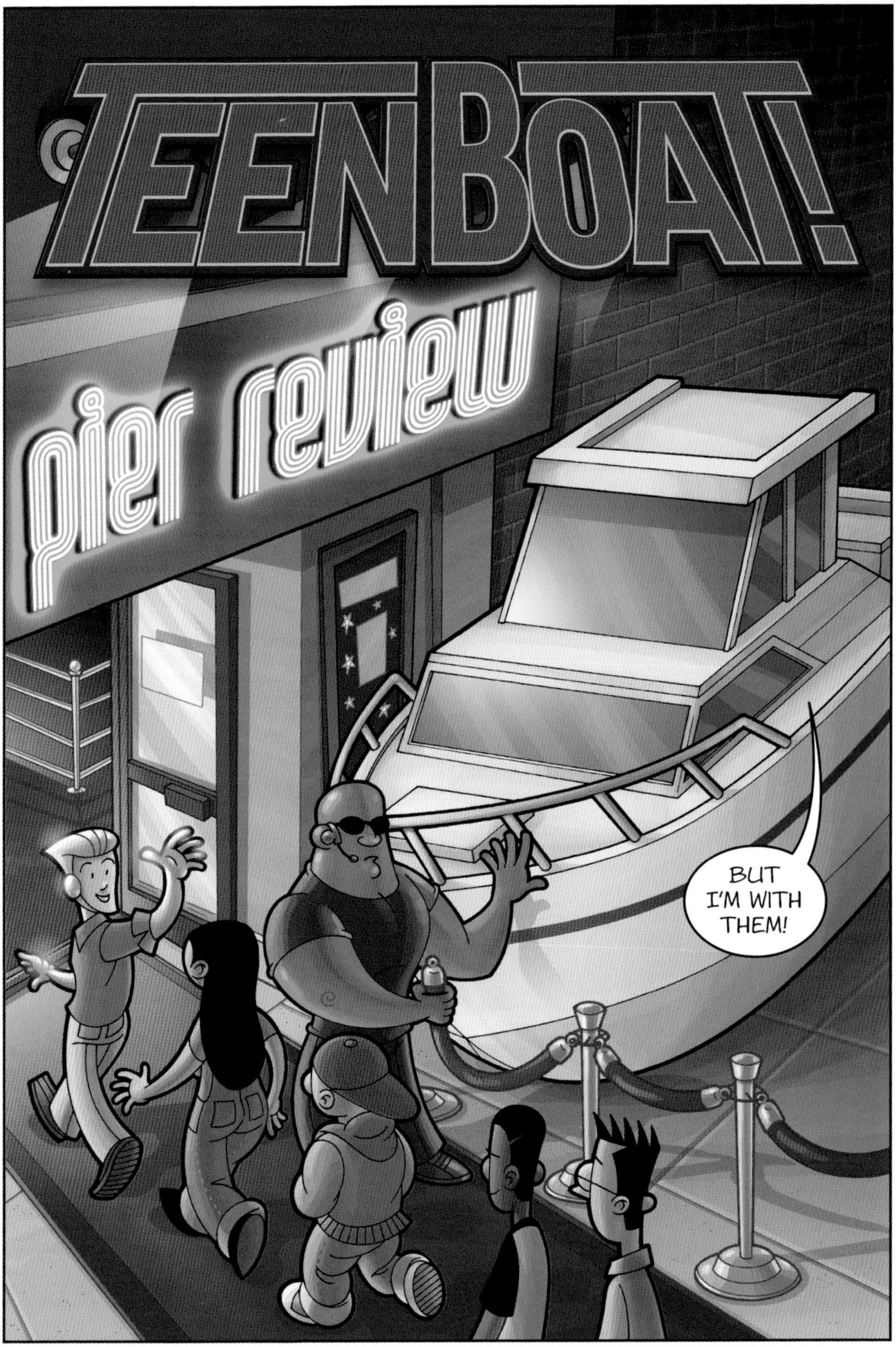
TEENBOAT!
pier review
BUT I'M WITH THEM!

The ***ANGST*** of being a Teen—the ***ANGST*** of being a Boat!

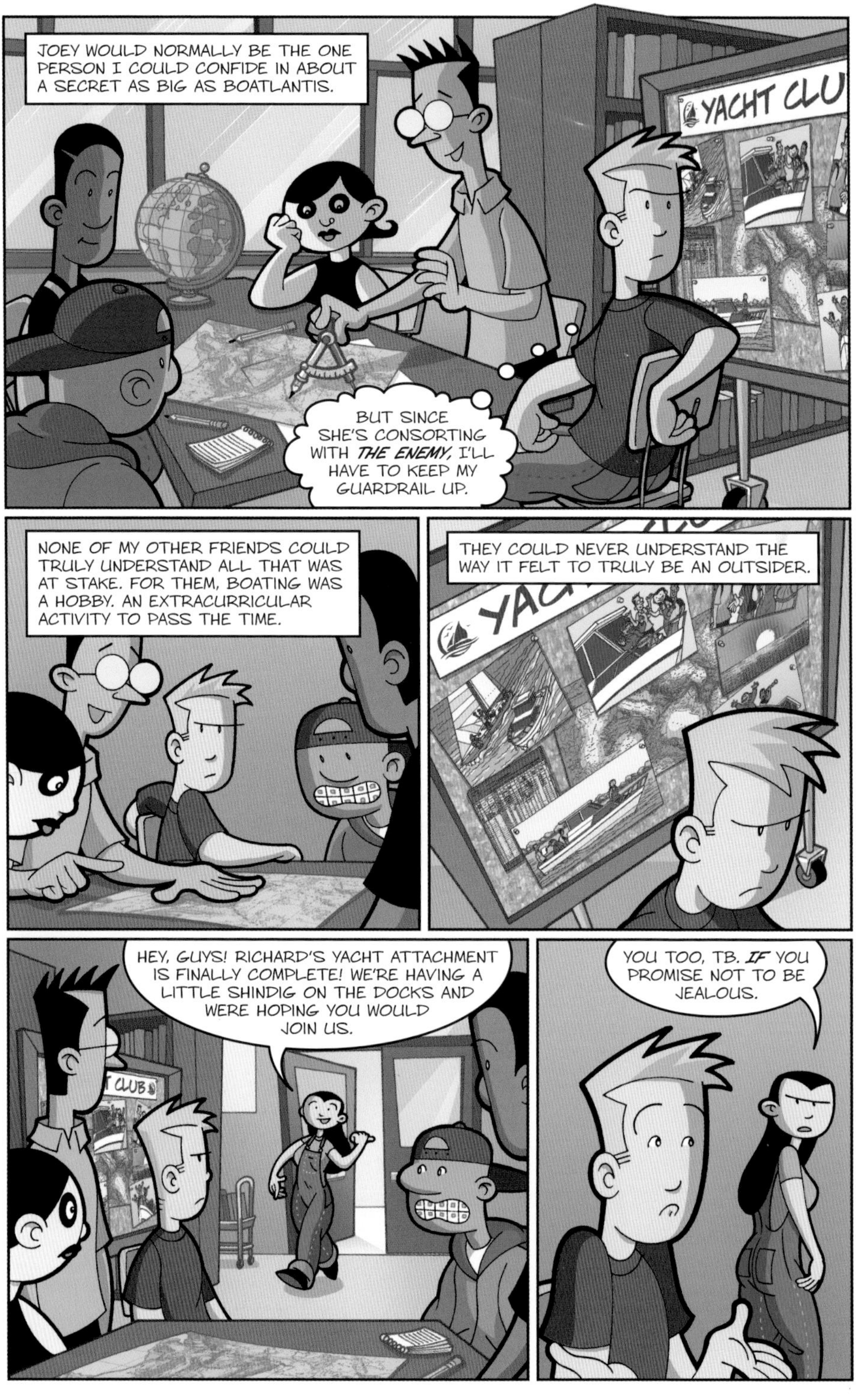

JOEY WOULD NORMALLY BE THE ONE PERSON I COULD CONFIDE IN ABOUT A SECRET AS BIG AS BOATLANTIS.
YACHT CLU
BUT SINCE SHE'S CONSORTING WITH *THE ENEMY*, I'LL HAVE TO KEEP MY GUARDRAIL UP.
NONE OF MY OTHER FRIENDS COULD TRULY UNDERSTAND ALL THAT WAS AT STAKE. FOR THEM, BOATING WAS A HOBBY. AN EXTRACURRICULAR ACTIVITY TO PASS THE TIME.
THEY COULD NEVER UNDERSTAND THE WAY IT FELT TO TRULY BE AN OUTSIDER.
HEY, GUYS! RICHARD'S YACHT ATTACHMENT IS FINALLY COMPLETE! WE'RE HAVING A LITTLE SHINDIG ON THE DOCKS AND WERE HOPING YOU WOULD JOIN US.
YOU TOO, TB. *IF* YOU PROMISE NOT TO BE JEALOUS.

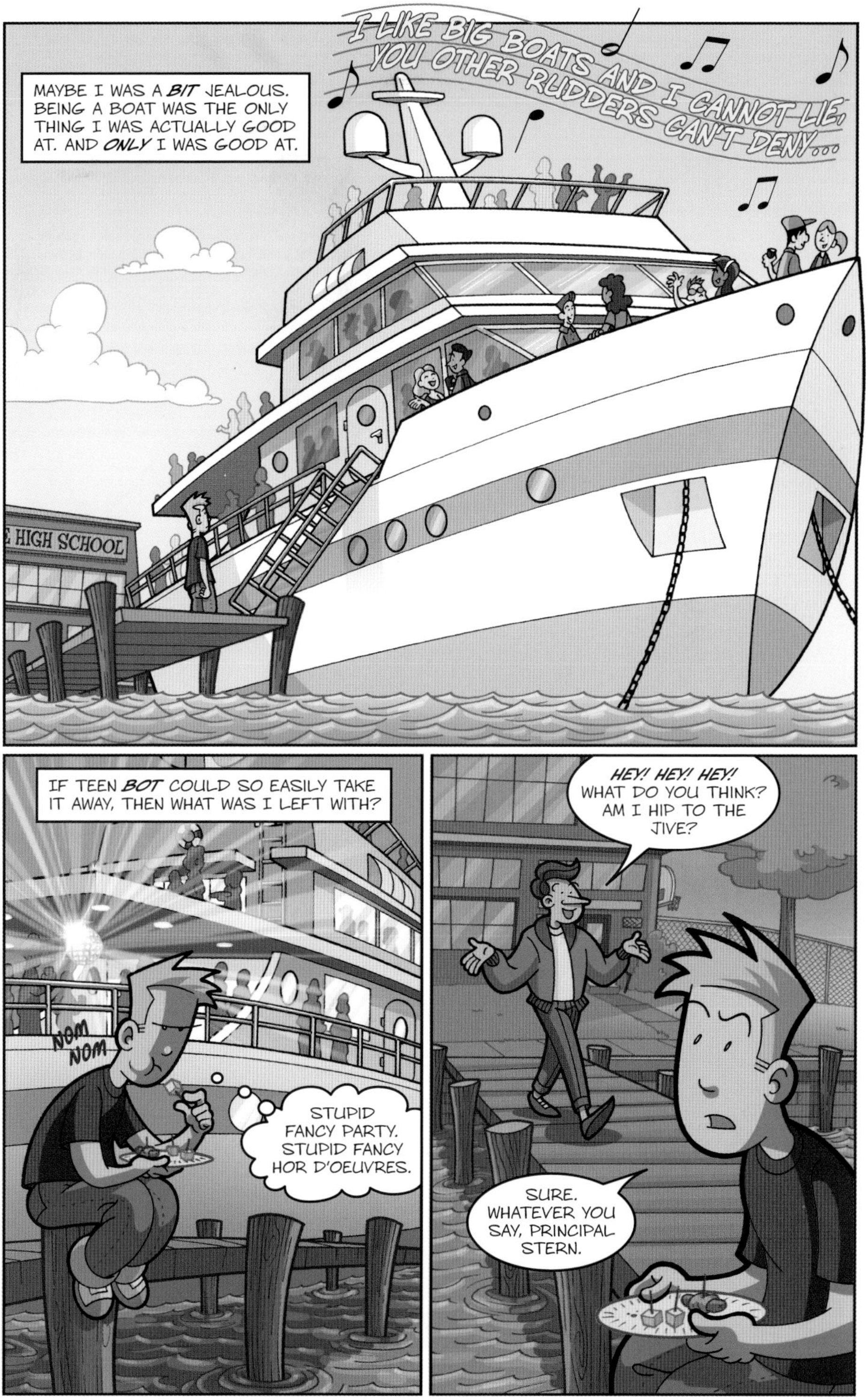
MAYBE I WAS A BIT JEALOUS. BEING A BOAT WAS THE ONLY THING I WAS ACTUALLY GOOD AT. AND ONLY I WAS GOOD AT.
I LIKE BIG BOATS AND I CANNOT LIE, YOU OTHER RUDDERS CAN'T DENY...
HIGH SCHOOL
IF TEEN BOT COULD SO EASILY TAKE IT AWAY, THEN WHAT WAS I LEFT WITH?
NOM NOM
STUPID FANCY PARTY. STUPID FANCY HOR D'OEUVRES.
HEY! HEY! HEY! WHAT DO YOU THINK? AM I HIP TO THE JIVE?
SURE. WHATEVER YOU SAY, PRINCIPAL STERN.

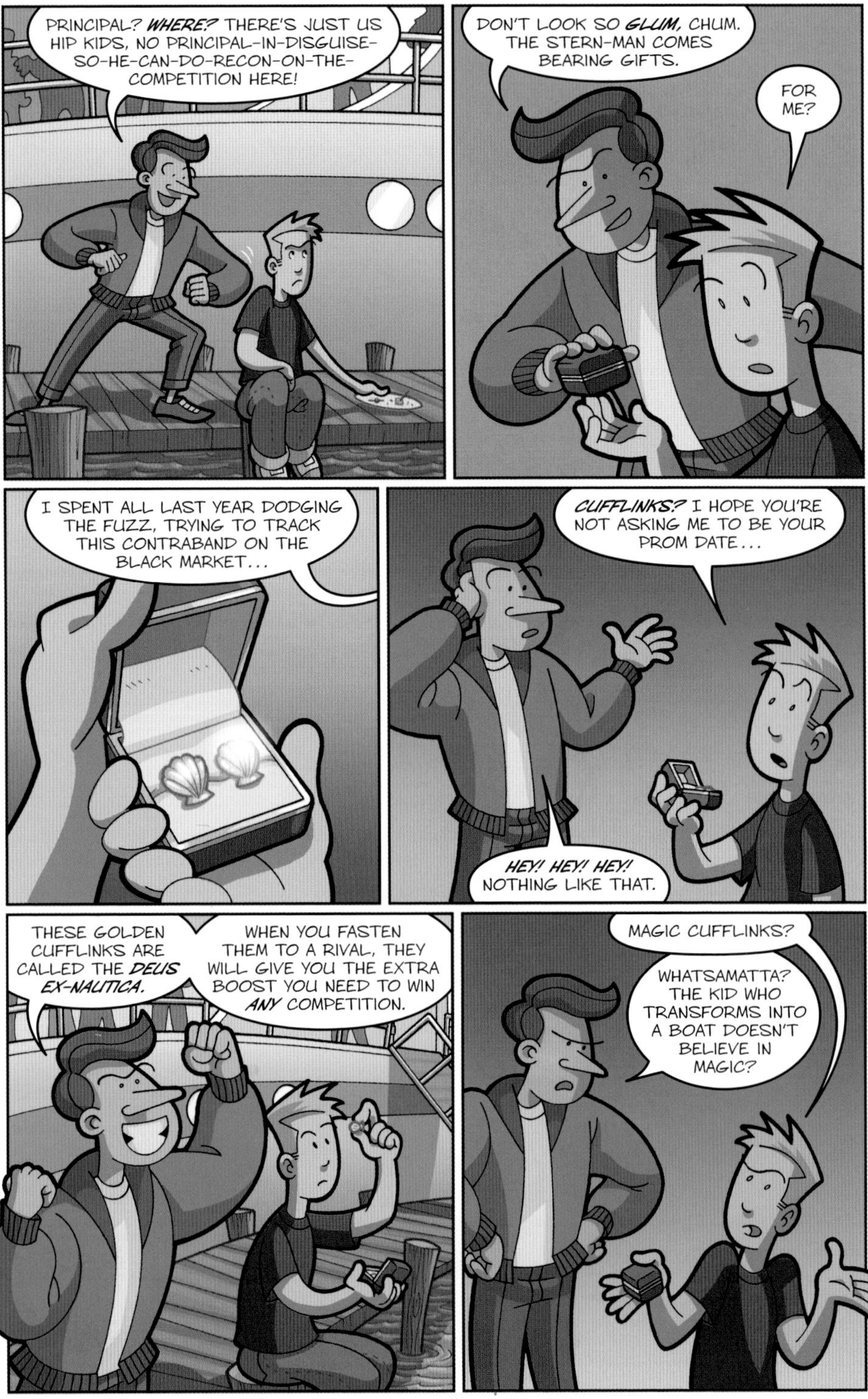
PRINCIPAL? WHERE? THERE'S JUST US HIP KIDS, NO PRINCIPAL-IN-DISGUISE-SO-HE-CAN-DO-RECON-ON-THE-COMPETITION HERE!
DON'T LOOK SO GLUM, CHUM. THE STERN-MAN COMES BEARING GIFTS.
FOR ME?
I SPENT ALL LAST YEAR DODGING THE FUZZ, TRYING TO TRACK THIS CONTRABAND ON THE BLACK MARKET...
CUFFLINKS? I HOPE YOU'RE NOT ASKING ME TO BE YOUR PROM DATE...
HEY! HEY! HEY! NOTHING LIKE THAT.
THESE GOLDEN CUFFLINKS ARE CALLED THE DEUS EX-NAUTICA.
WHEN YOU FASTEN THEM TO A RIVAL, THEY WILL GIVE YOU THE EXTRA BOOST YOU NEED TO WIN ANY COMPETITION.
MAGIC CUFFLINKS?
WHATSAMATTA? THE KID WHO TRANSFORMS INTO A BOAT DOESN'T BELIEVE IN MAGIC?

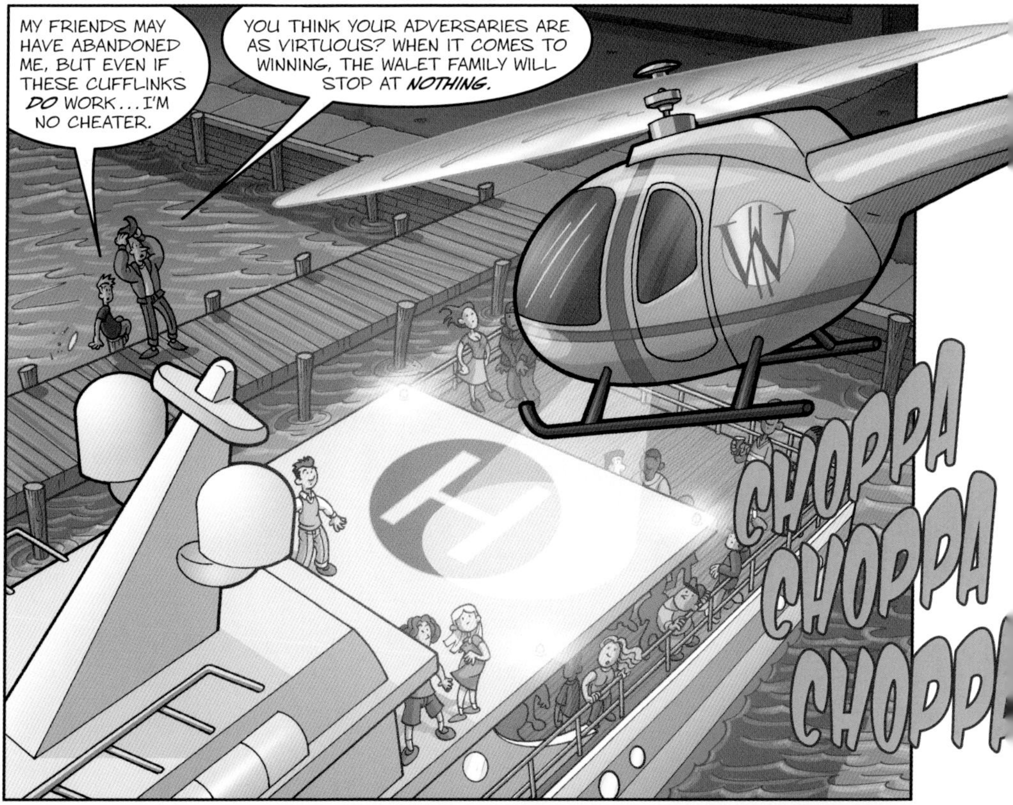
MY FRIENDS MAY HAVE ABANDONED ME, BUT EVEN IF THESE CUFFLINKS *DO* WORK...I'M NO CHEATER.
YOU THINK YOUR ADVERSARIES ARE AS VIRTUOUS? WHEN IT COMES TO WINNING, THE WALET FAMILY WILL STOP AT *NOTHING*.
CHOPPA
CHOPPA
CHOPP

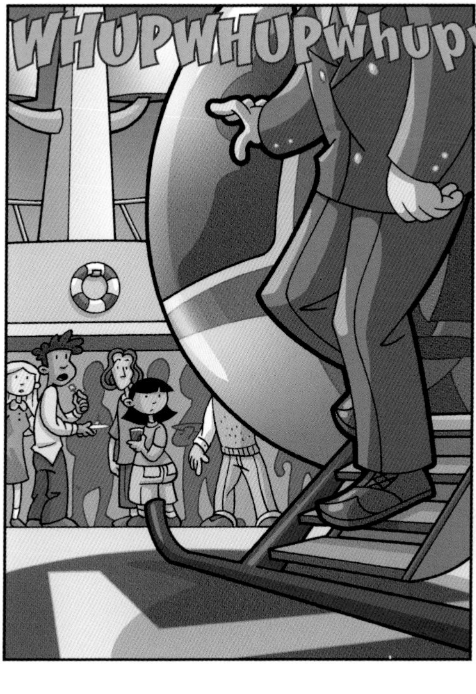
WHUPWHUPwhupwhupwhup

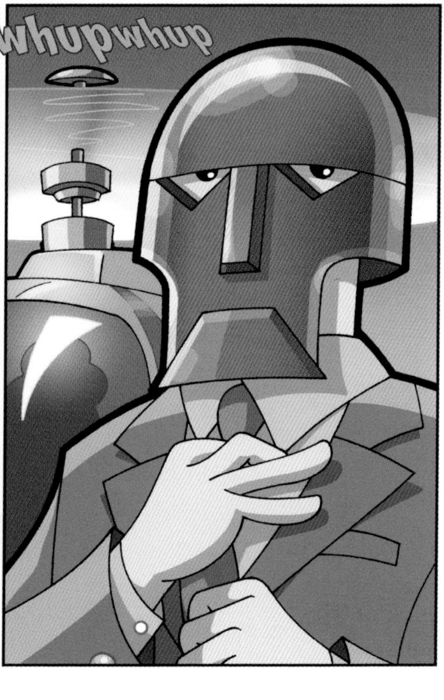

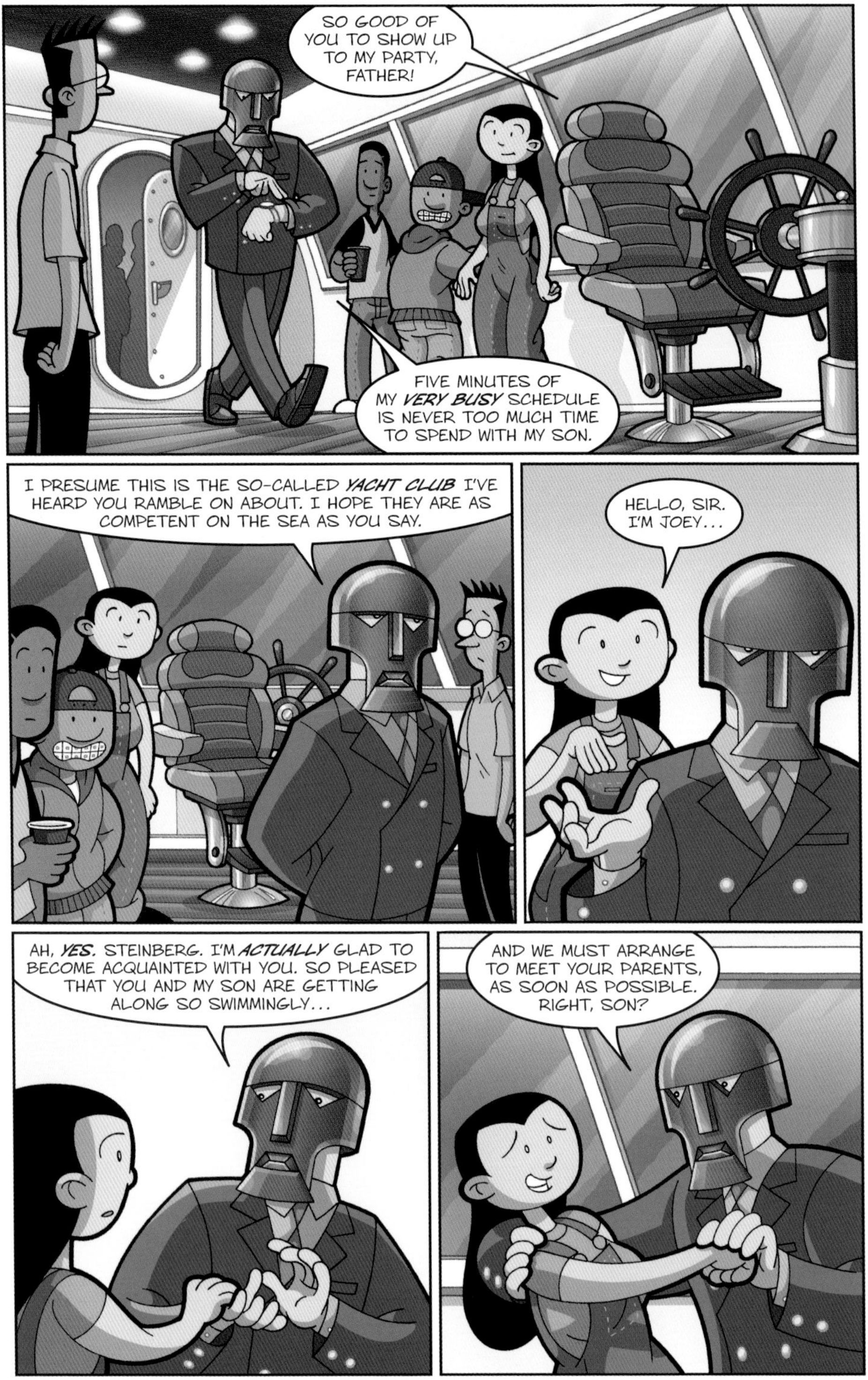
SO GOOD OF YOU TO SHOW UP TO MY PARTY, FATHER!
FIVE MINUTES OF MY VERY BUSY SCHEDULE IS NEVER TOO MUCH TIME TO SPEND WITH MY SON.
I PRESUME THIS IS THE SO-CALLED YACHT CLUB I'VE HEARD YOU RAMBLE ON ABOUT. I HOPE THEY ARE AS COMPETENT ON THE SEA AS YOU SAY.
HELLO, SIR. I'M JOEY...
AH, YES. STEINBERG. I'M ACTUALLY GLAD TO BECOME ACQUAINTED WITH YOU. SO PLEASED THAT YOU AND MY SON ARE GETTING ALONG SO SWIMMINGLY...
AND WE MUST ARRANGE TO MEET YOUR PARENTS, AS SOON AS POSSIBLE. RIGHT, SON?

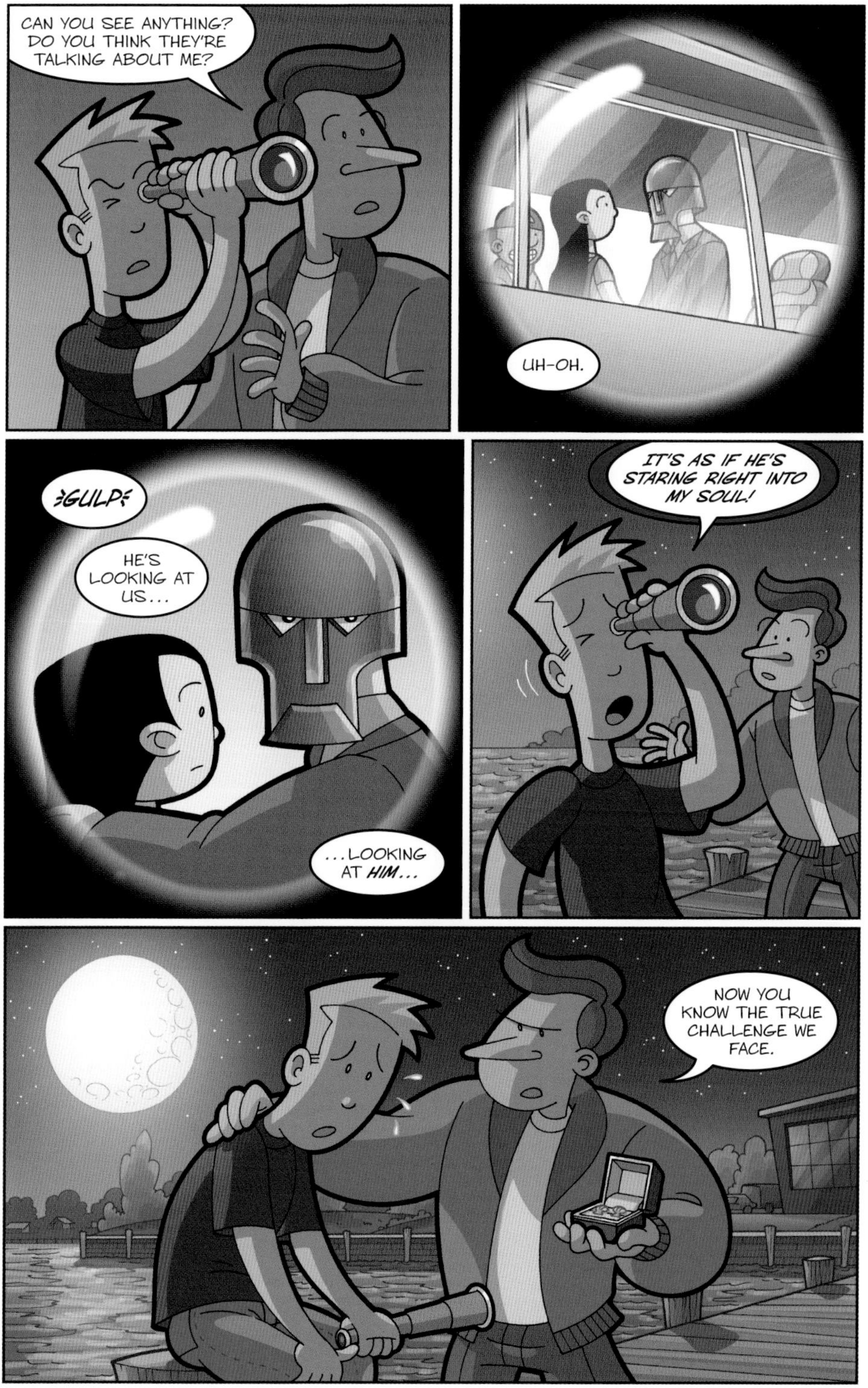
CAN YOU SEE ANYTHING? DO YOU THINK THEY'RE TALKING ABOUT ME?
UH-OH.
GULP
HE'S LOOKING AT US...
...LOOKING AT *HIM*...
IT'S AS IF HE'S STARING RIGHT INTO MY SOUL!
NOW YOU KNOW THE TRUE CHALLENGE WE FACE.

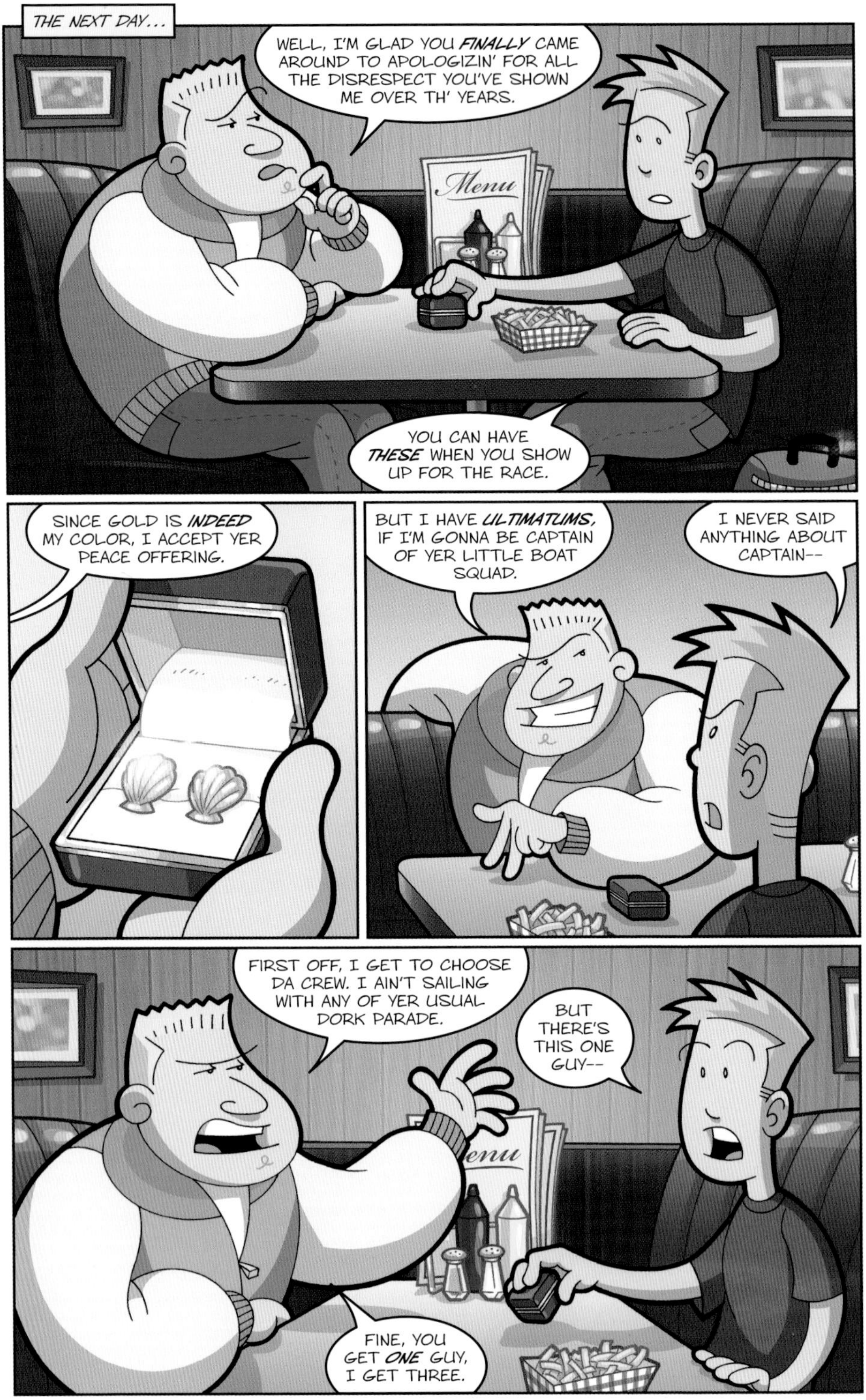
THE NEXT DAY...
WELL, I'M GLAD YOU FINALLY CAME AROUND TO APOLOGIZIN' FOR ALL THE DISRESPECT YOU'VE SHOWN ME OVER TH' YEARS.
Menu
YOU CAN HAVE THESE WHEN YOU SHOW UP FOR THE RACE.
SINCE GOLD IS INDEED MY COLOR, I ACCEPT YER PEACE OFFERING.
BUT I HAVE ULTIMATUMS, IF I'M GONNA BE CAPTAIN OF YER LITTLE BOAT SQUAD.
I NEVER SAID ANYTHING ABOUT CAPTAIN--
FIRST OFF, I GET TO CHOOSE DA CREW. I AIN'T SAILING WITH ANY OF YER USUAL DORK PARADE.
BUT THERE'S THIS ONE GUY--
FINE, YOU GET ONE GUY, I GET THREE.

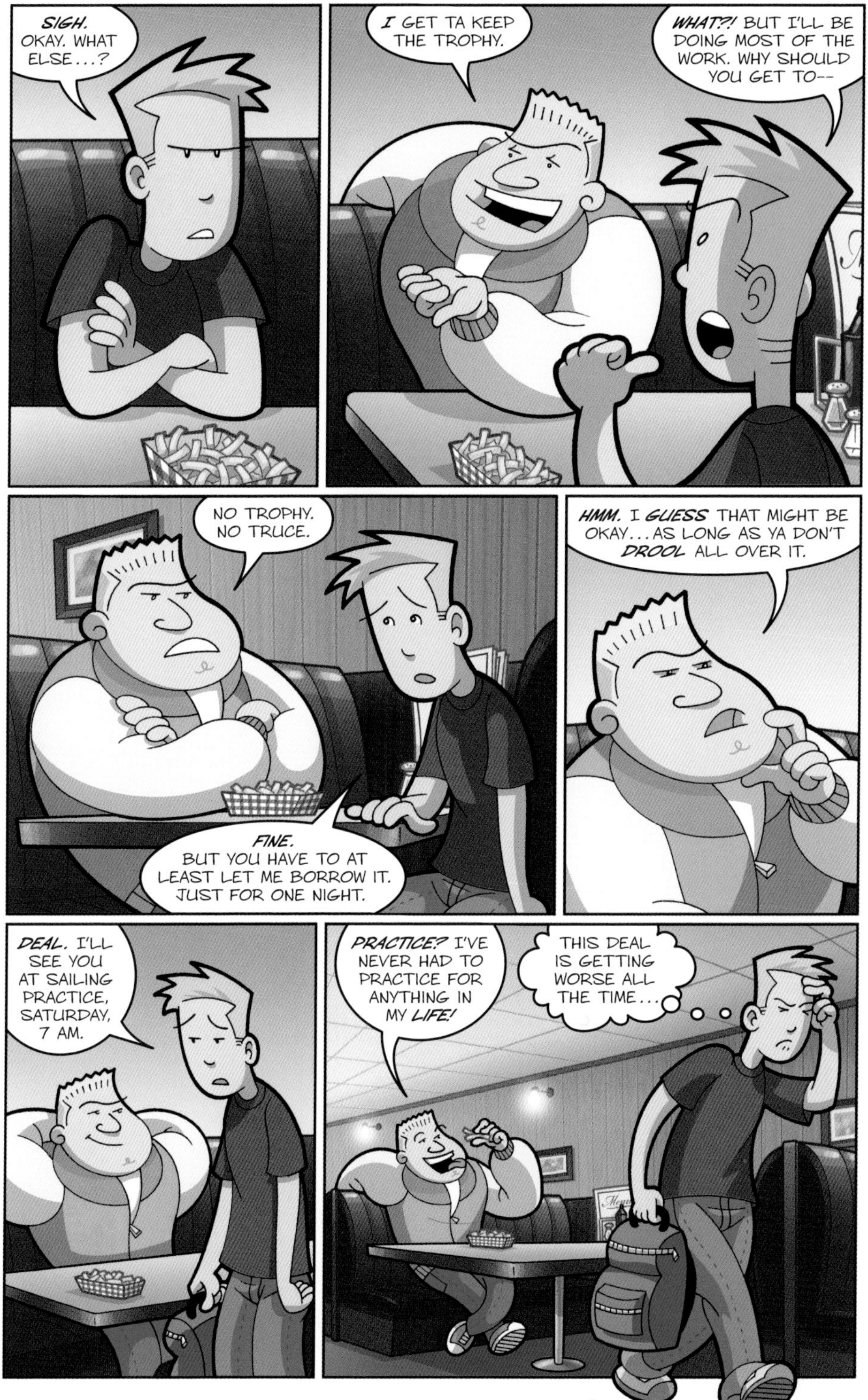
SIGH. OKAY. WHAT ELSE...?
I GET TA KEEP THE TROPHY.
WHAT?! BUT I'LL BE DOING MOST OF THE WORK. WHY SHOULD YOU GET TO--
NO TROPHY. NO TRUCE.
FINE. BUT YOU HAVE TO AT LEAST LET ME BORROW IT. JUST FOR ONE NIGHT.
HMM. I GUESS THAT MIGHT BE OKAY...AS LONG AS YA DON'T DROOL ALL OVER IT.
DEAL. I'LL SEE YOU AT SAILING PRACTICE, SATURDAY, 7 AM.
PRACTICE? I'VE NEVER HAD TO PRACTICE FOR ANYTHING IN MY LIFE!
THIS DEAL IS GETTING WORSE ALL THE TIME...

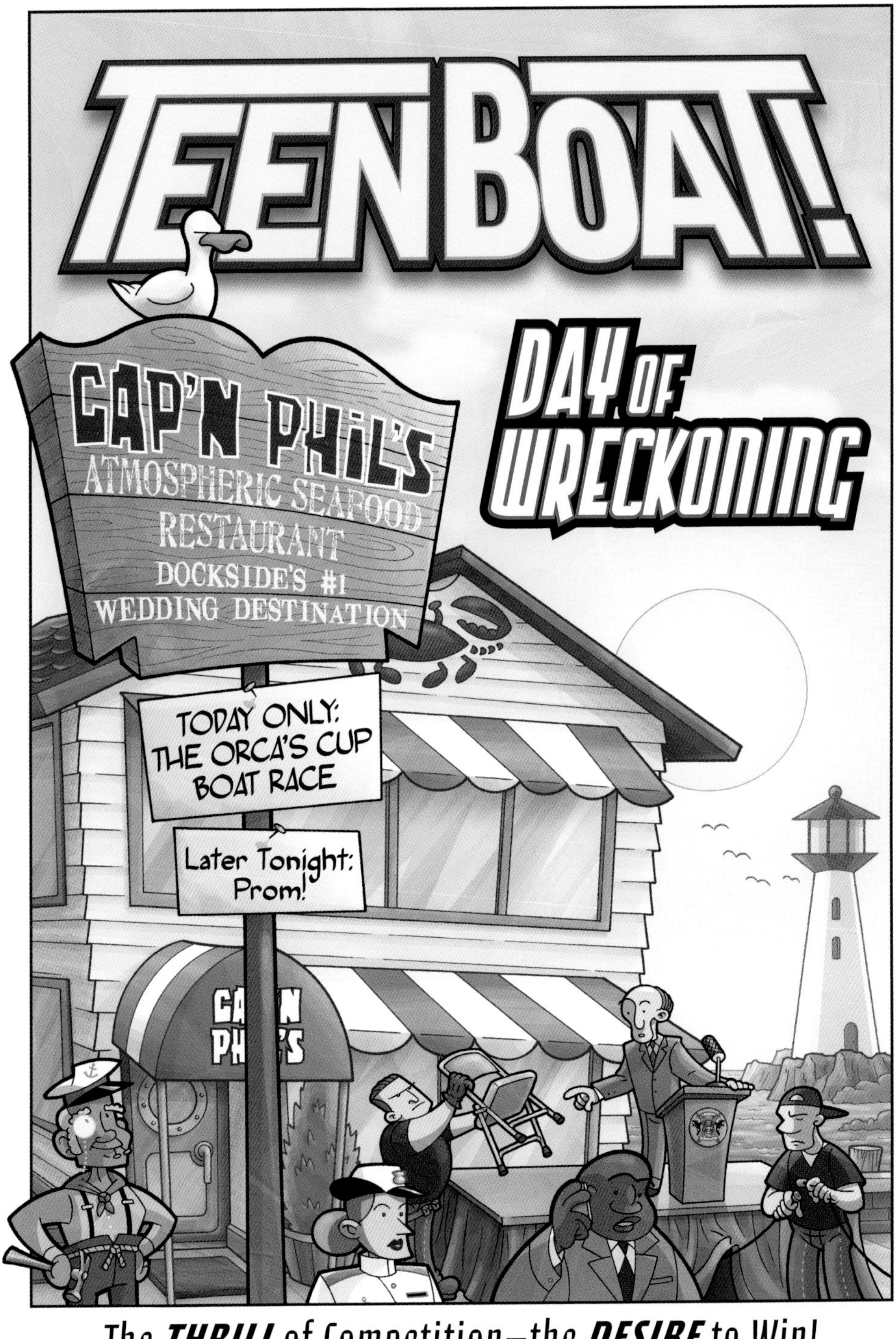
TEENBOAT!
DAY OF WRECKONING
CAP'N PHIL'S
ATMOSPHERIC SEAFOOD
RESTAURANT
DOCKSIDE'S #1
WEDDING DESTINATION
TODAY ONLY:
THE ORCA'S CUP
BOAT RACE
Later Tonight:
Prom!

The ***THRILL*** of Competition—the ***DESIRE*** to Win!

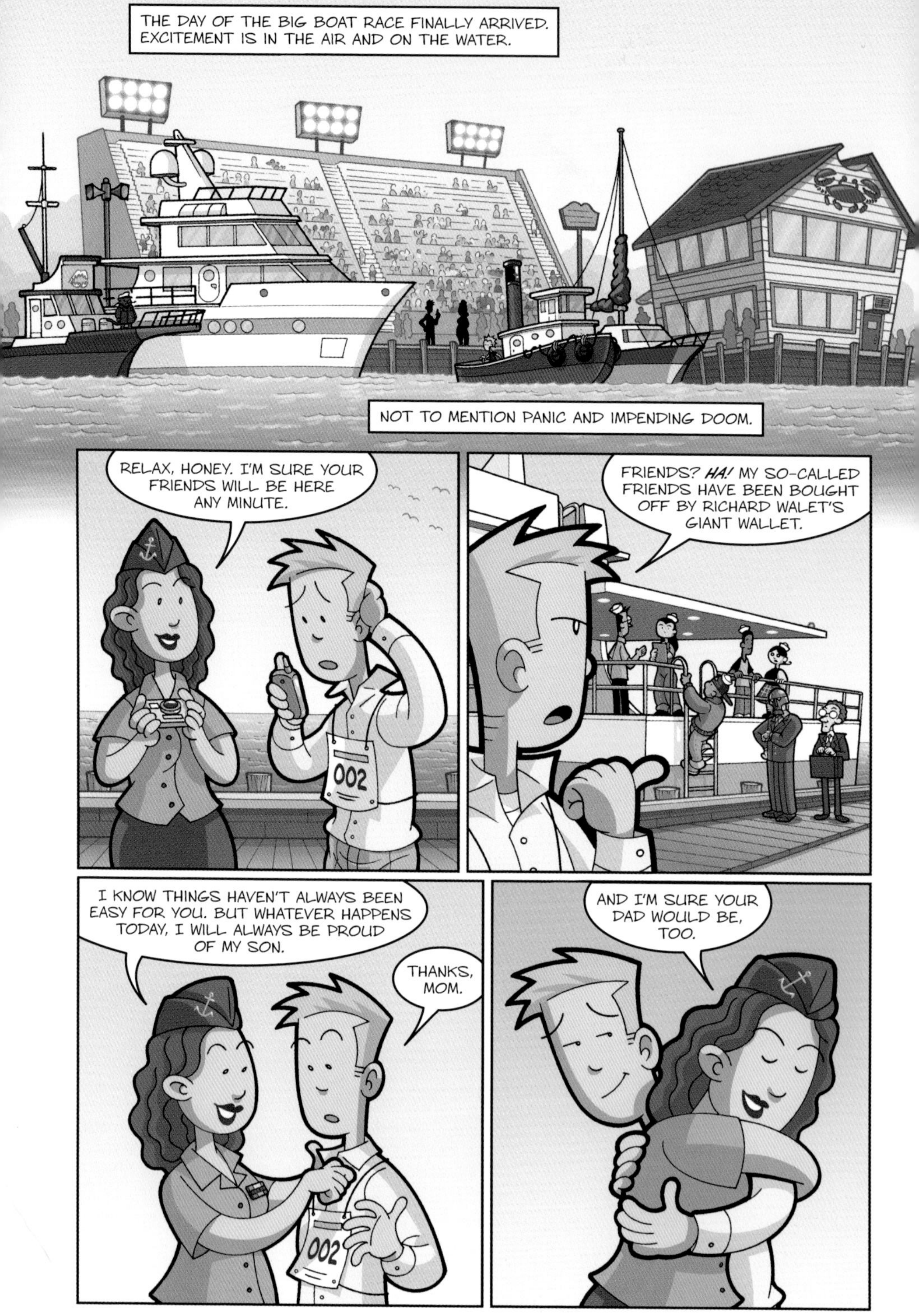
THE DAY OF THE BIG BOAT RACE FINALLY ARRIVED. EXCITEMENT IS IN THE AIR AND ON THE WATER.
NOT TO MENTION PANIC AND IMPENDING DOOM.
RELAX, HONEY. I'M SURE YOUR FRIENDS WILL BE HERE ANY MINUTE.
002
FRIENDS? HA! MY SO-CALLED FRIENDS HAVE BEEN BOUGHT OFF BY RICHARD WALET'S GIANT WALLET.
I KNOW THINGS HAVEN'T ALWAYS BEEN EASY FOR YOU. BUT WHATEVER HAPPENS TODAY, I WILL ALWAYS BE PROUD OF MY SON.
THANKS, MOM.
002
AND I'M SURE YOUR DAD WOULD BE, TOO.

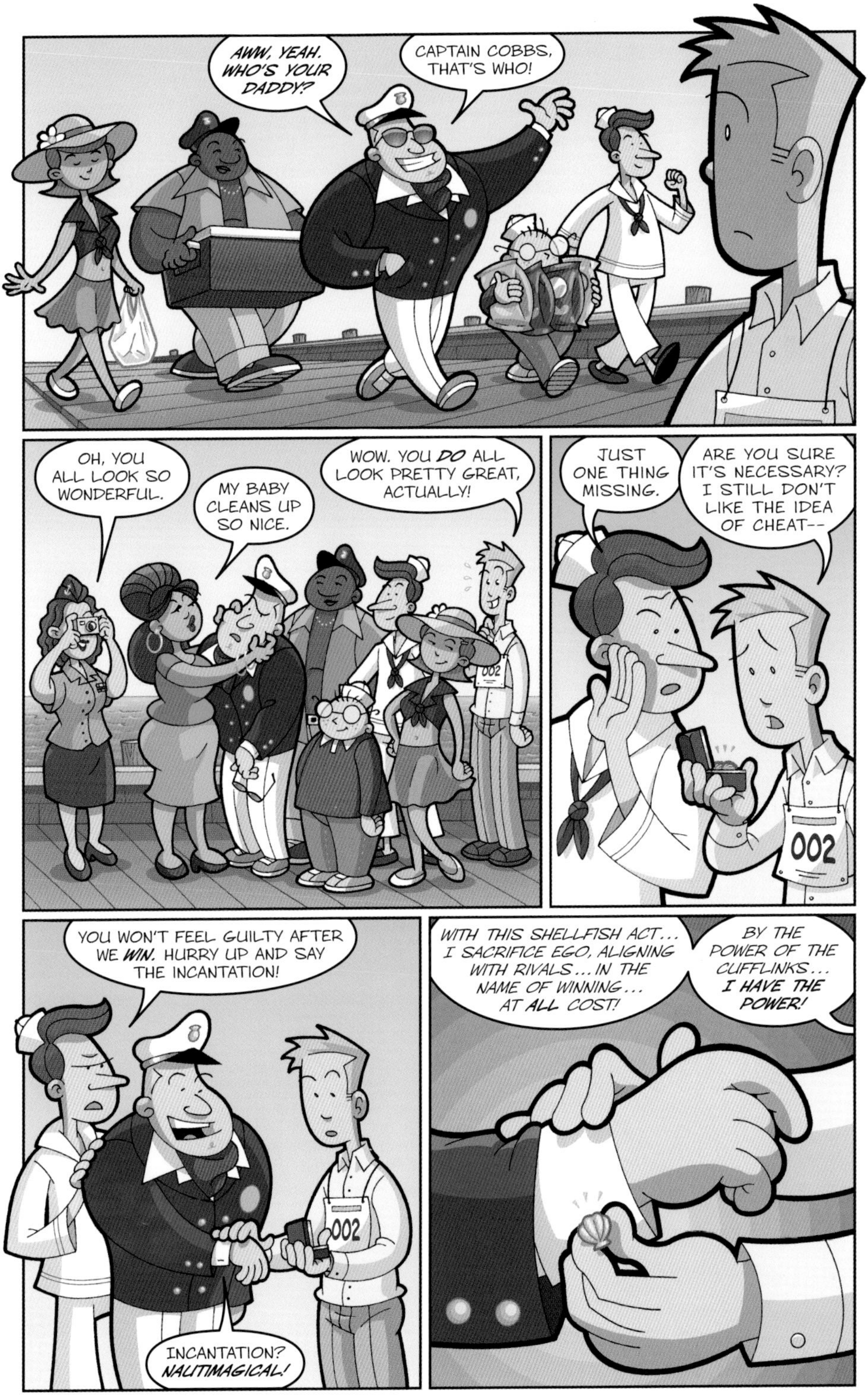
AWW, YEAH. WHO'S YOUR DADDY?
CAPTAIN COBBS, THAT'S WHO!
OH, YOU ALL LOOK SO WONDERFUL.
MY BABY CLEANS UP SO NICE.
WOW. YOU DO ALL LOOK PRETTY GREAT, ACTUALLY!
002
JUST ONE THING MISSING.
ARE YOU SURE IT'S NECESSARY? I STILL DON'T LIKE THE IDEA OF CHEAT--
002
YOU WON'T FEEL GUILTY AFTER WE WIN. HURRY UP AND SAY THE INCANTATION!
002
INCANTATION? NAUTIMAGICAL!
WITH THIS SHELLFISH ACT... I SACRIFICE EGO, ALIGNING WITH RIVALS... IN THE NAME OF WINNING... AT ALL COST!
BY THE POWER OF THE CUFFLINKS... I HAVE THE POWER!

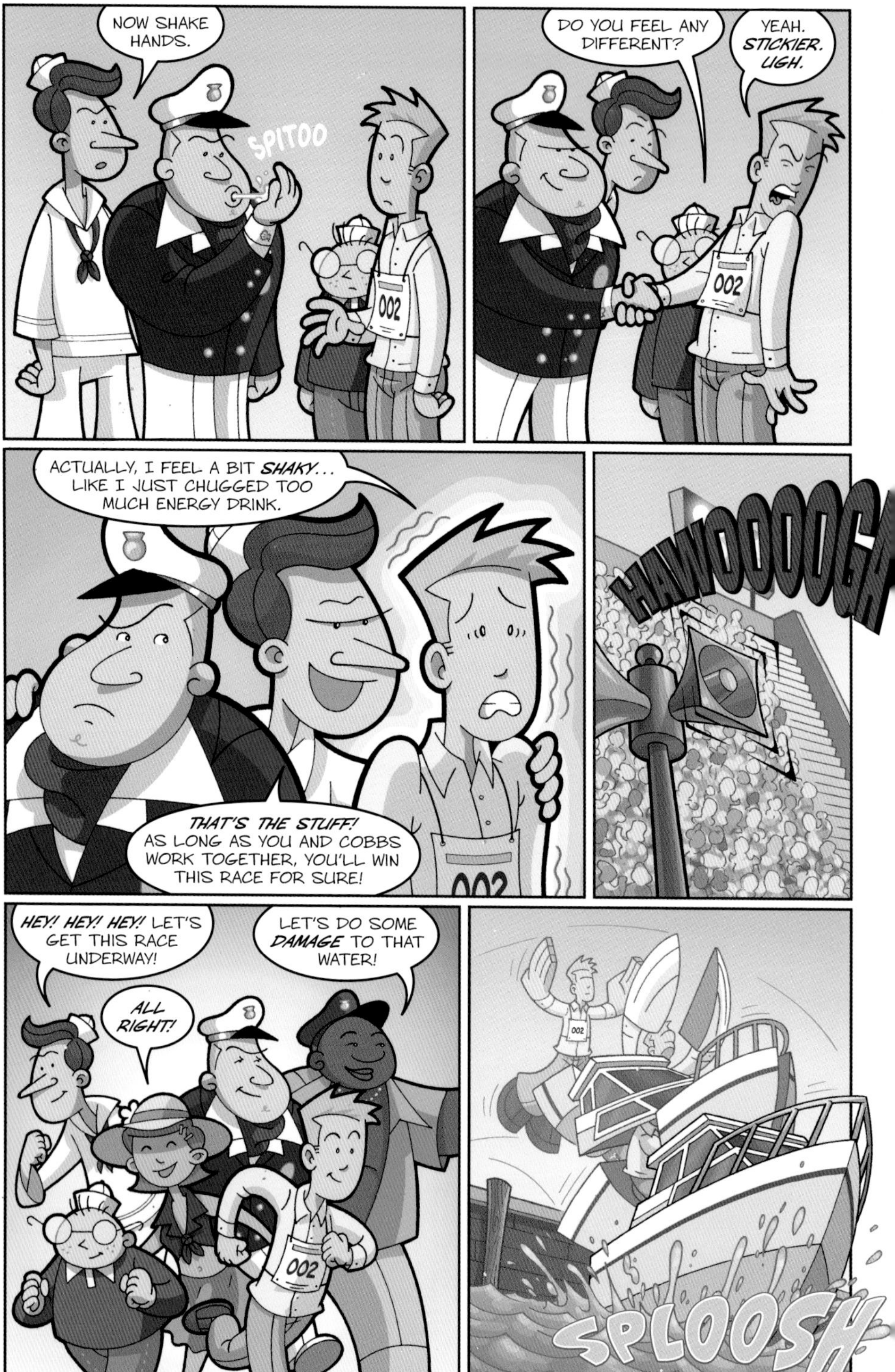
NOW SHAKE HANDS.
SPITOO
DO YOU FEEL ANY DIFFERENT?
YEAH. *STICKIER.* *UGH.*
002
ACTUALLY, I FEEL A BIT *SHAKY*... LIKE I JUST CHUGGED TOO MUCH ENERGY DRINK.
THAT'S THE STUFF! AS LONG AS YOU AND COBBS WORK TOGETHER, YOU'LL WIN THIS RACE FOR SURE!
HAWOOOGA
HEY! HEY! HEY! LET'S GET THIS RACE UNDERWAY!
ALL RIGHT!
LET'S DO SOME *DAMAGE* TO THAT WATER!
SPLOOSH

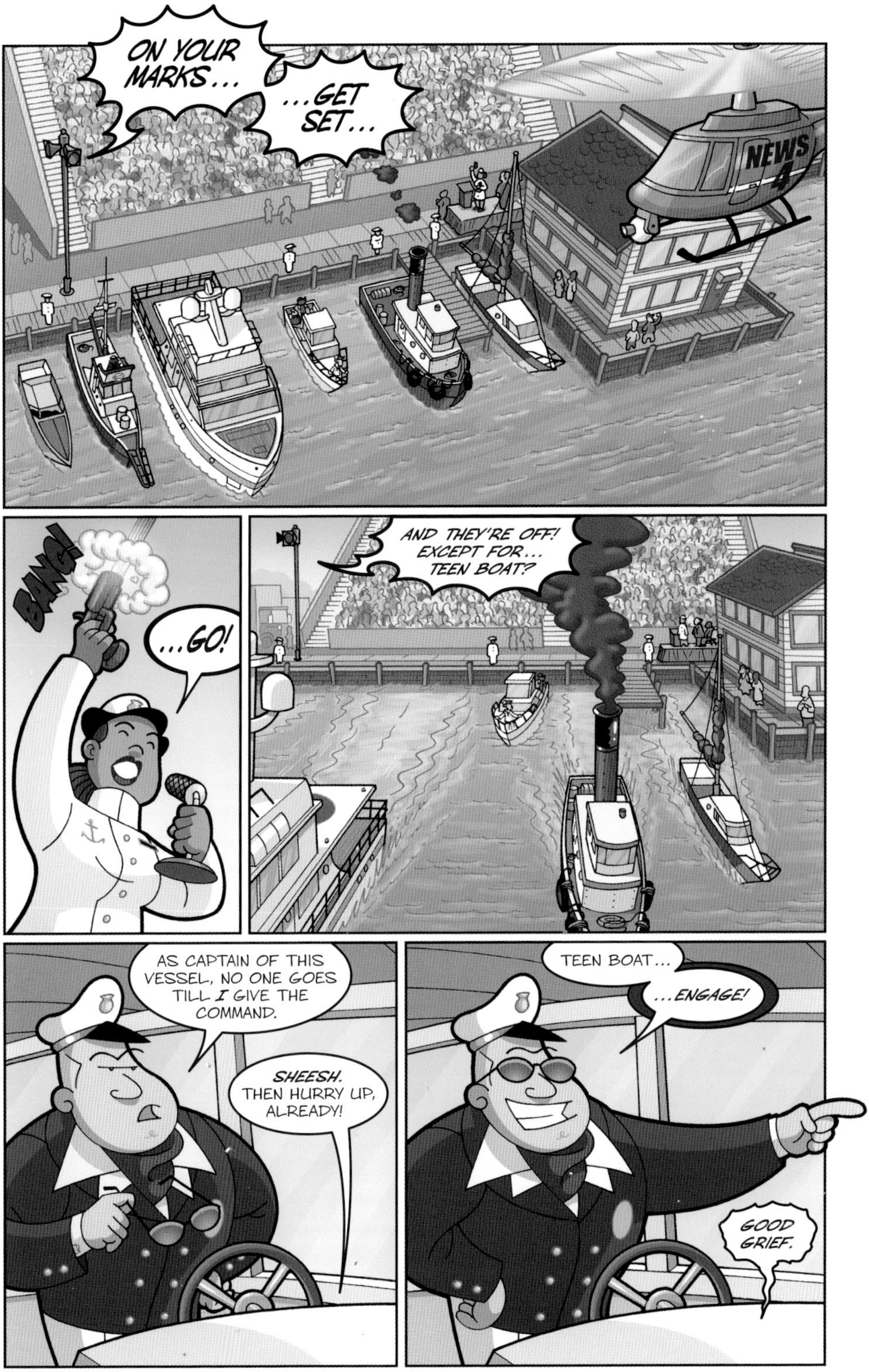
ON YOUR MARKS...
...GET SET...
NEWS 4
BANG!
...GO!
AND THEY'RE OFF! EXCEPT FOR... TEEN BOAT?
AS CAPTAIN OF THIS VESSEL, NO ONE GOES TILL *I* GIVE THE COMMAND.
SHEESH. THEN HURRY UP, ALREADY!
TEEN BOAT...
...ENGAGE!
GOOD GRIEF.

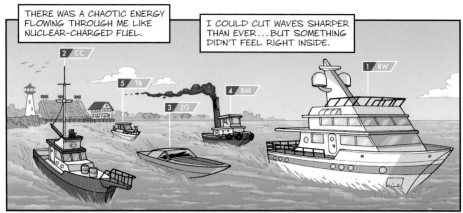

THERE WAS A CHAOTIC ENERGY FLOWING THROUGH ME LIKE NUCLEAR-CHARGED FUEL.

I COULD CUT WAVES SHARPER THAN EVER... BUT SOMETHING DIDN'T FEEL RIGHT INSIDE.

THAT'S *IT*, TEEN BOAT! WE'RE CATCHING UP!

NO THANKS TO ANY OF MY "CREW."

HEY, THESE HOT DOGS AIN'T GONNA COOK *THEMSELVES.*

≋MUNCH, MUNCH≋

I'M LIVE-TWEETING THE RACE. THAT'S PRODUCTIVE.

AND I'M... *THE CAPTAIN!*

CLICK

WAIT--WHY ARE YOU TURNING? YOU'RE HEADING AWAY FROM THE OTHER BOATS!

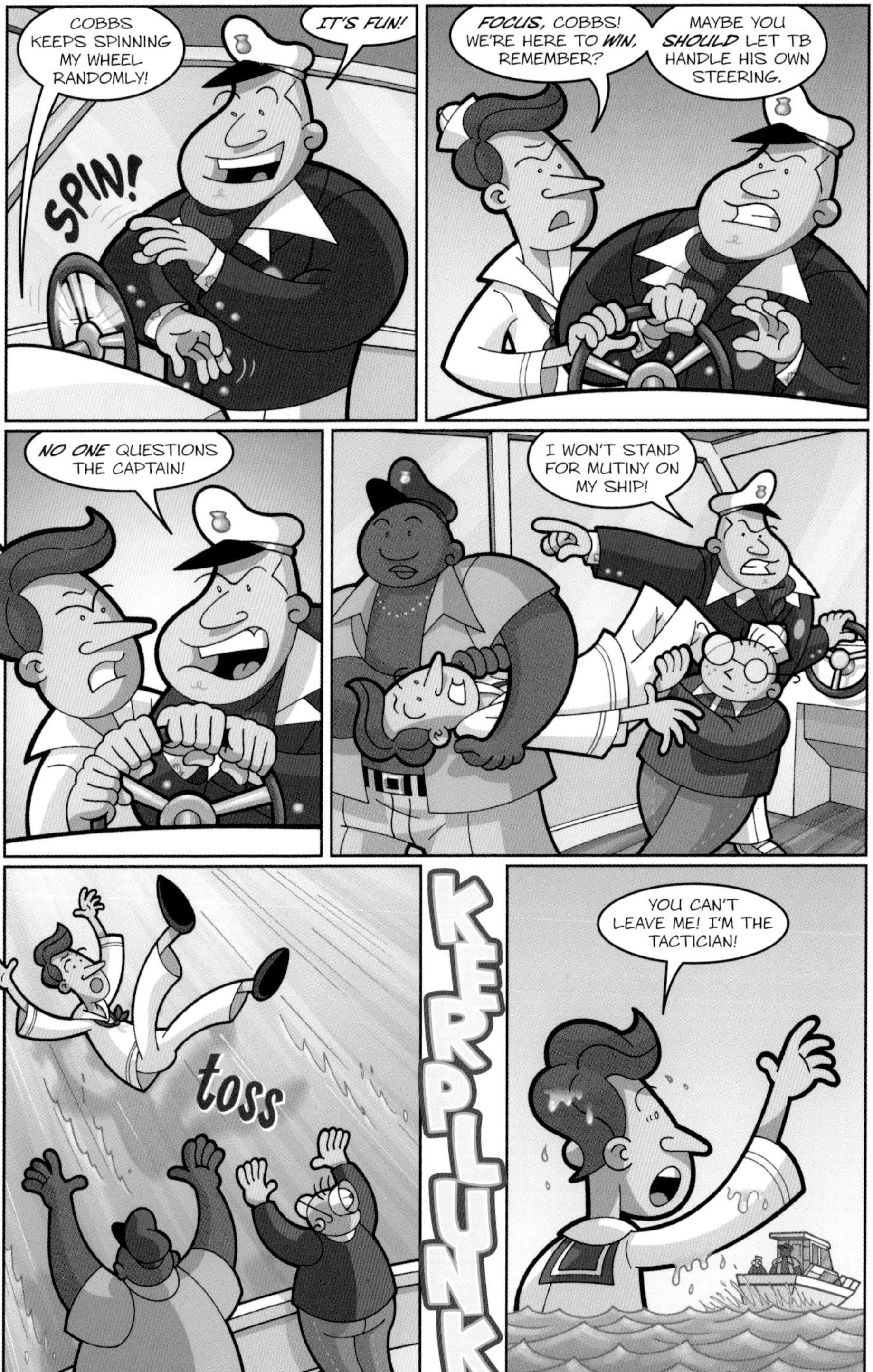
COBBS KEEPS SPINNING MY WHEEL RANDOMLY!
IT'S FUN!
SPIN!
FOCUS, COBBS! WE'RE HERE TO WIN, REMEMBER?
MAYBE YOU SHOULD LET TB HANDLE HIS OWN STEERING.
NO ONE QUESTIONS THE CAPTAIN!
I WON'T STAND FOR MUTINY ON MY SHIP!
toss
KERPLUNK
YOU CAN'T LEAVE ME! I'M THE TACTICIAN!

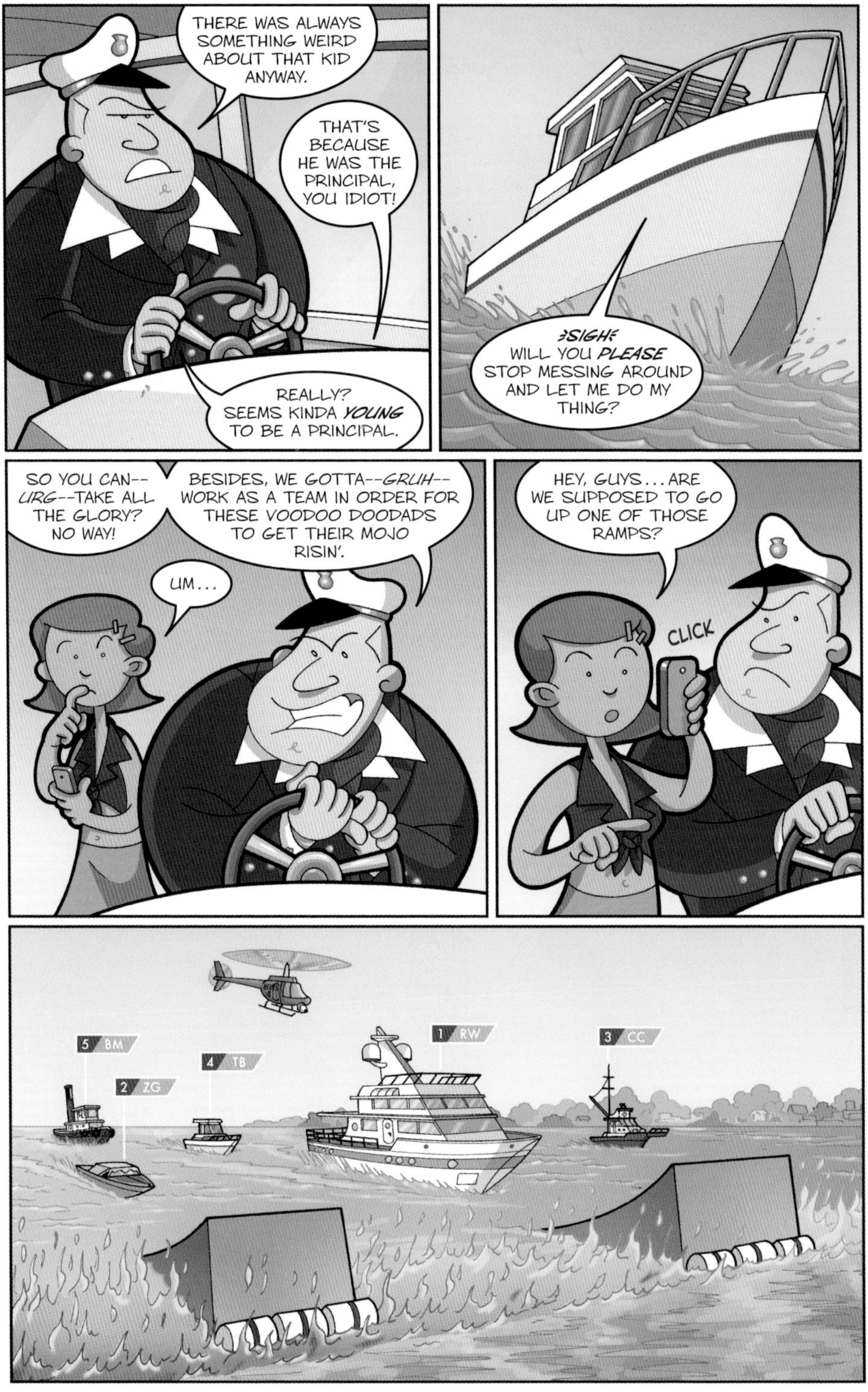
THERE WAS ALWAYS SOMETHING WEIRD ABOUT THAT KID ANYWAY.
THAT'S BECAUSE HE WAS THE PRINCIPAL, YOU IDIOT!
REALLY? SEEMS KINDA YOUNG TO BE A PRINCIPAL.
SIGH
WILL YOU PLEASE STOP MESSING AROUND AND LET ME DO MY THING?
SO YOU CAN-- URG--TAKE ALL THE GLORY? NO WAY!
BESIDES, WE GOTTA--GRUH-- WORK AS A TEAM IN ORDER FOR THESE VOODOO DOODADS TO GET THEIR MOJO RISIN'.
UM...
HEY, GUYS... ARE WE SUPPOSED TO GO UP ONE OF THOSE RAMPS?
CLICK
5 BM
2 ZG
4 TB
1 RW
3 CC

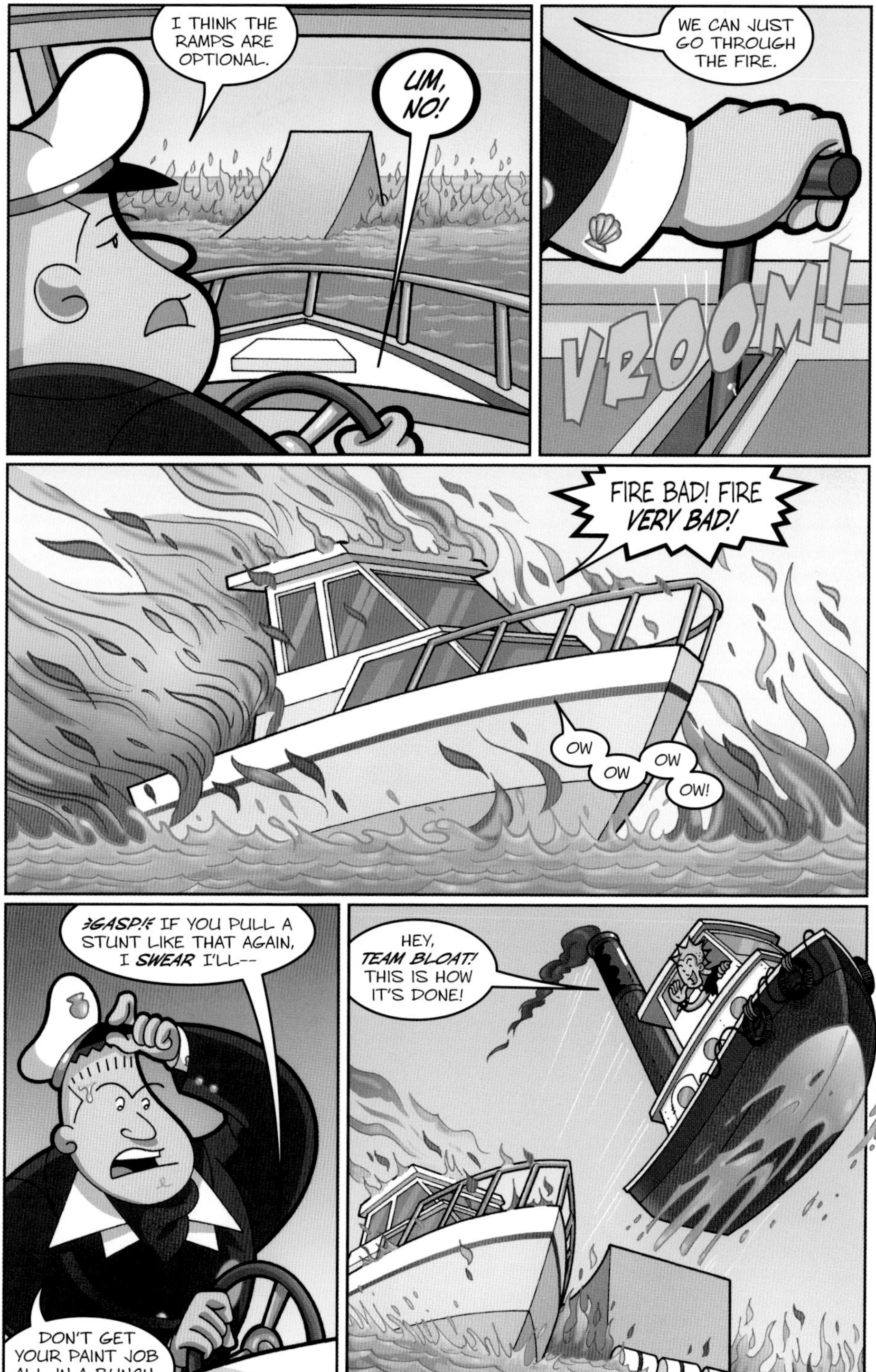
I THINK THE RAMPS ARE OPTIONAL.
UM, NO!
WE CAN JUST GO THROUGH THE FIRE.
VROOM!
FIRE BAD! FIRE VERY BAD!
OW
OW
OW
OW!
GASP! IF YOU PULL A STUNT LIKE THAT AGAIN, I SWEAR I'LL--
DON'T GET YOUR PAINT JOB ALL IN A BUNCH.
HEY, TEAM BLOAT! THIS IS HOW IT'S DONE!

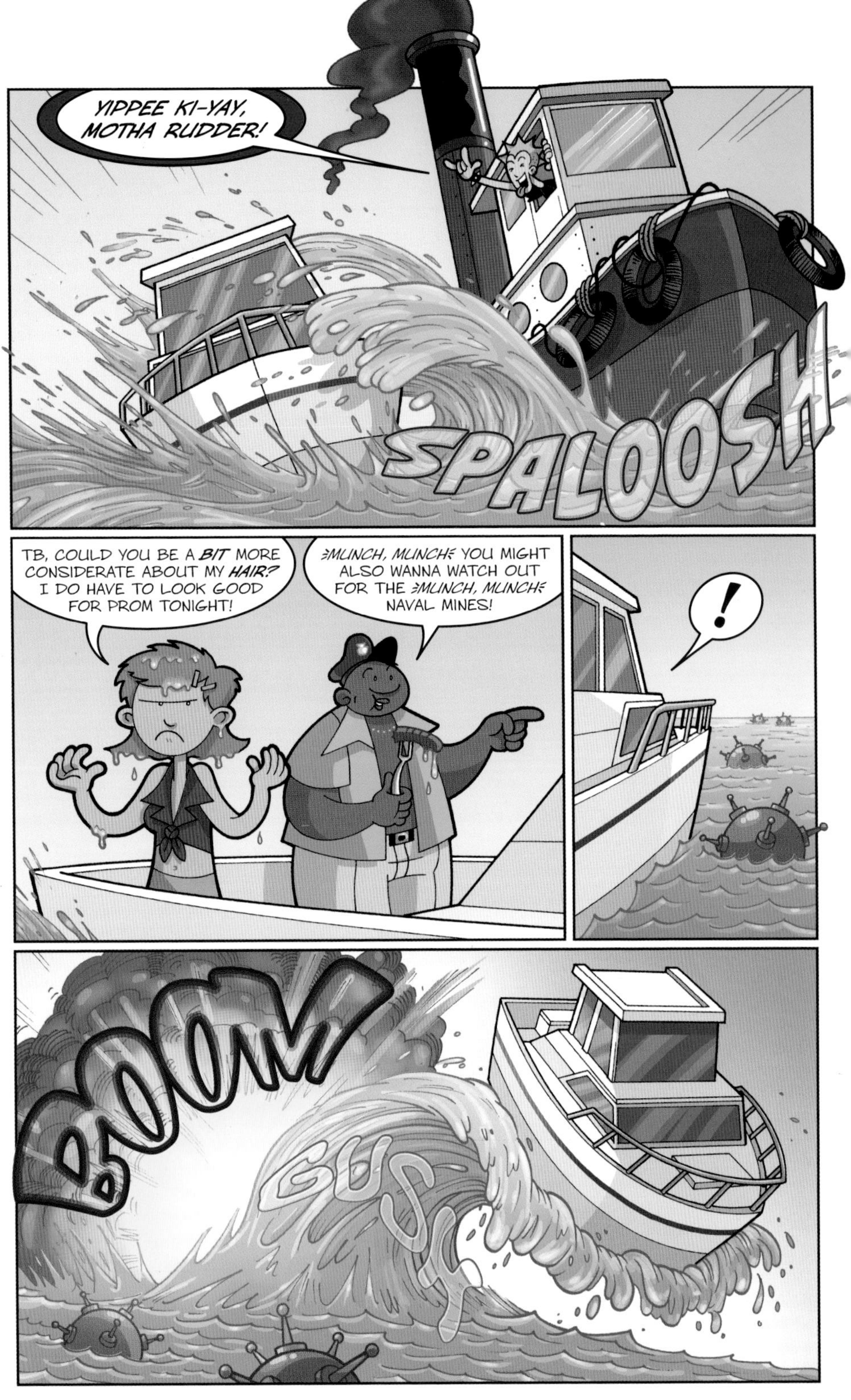
YIPPEE KI-YAY, MOTHA RUDDER!
SPALOOSH
TB, COULD YOU BE A *BIT* MORE CONSIDERATE ABOUT MY *HAIR?* I DO HAVE TO LOOK GOOD FOR PROM TONIGHT!
MUNCH, MUNCH YOU MIGHT ALSO WANNA WATCH OUT FOR THE *MUNCH, MUNCH* NAVAL MINES!
!
BOOM
GUSH

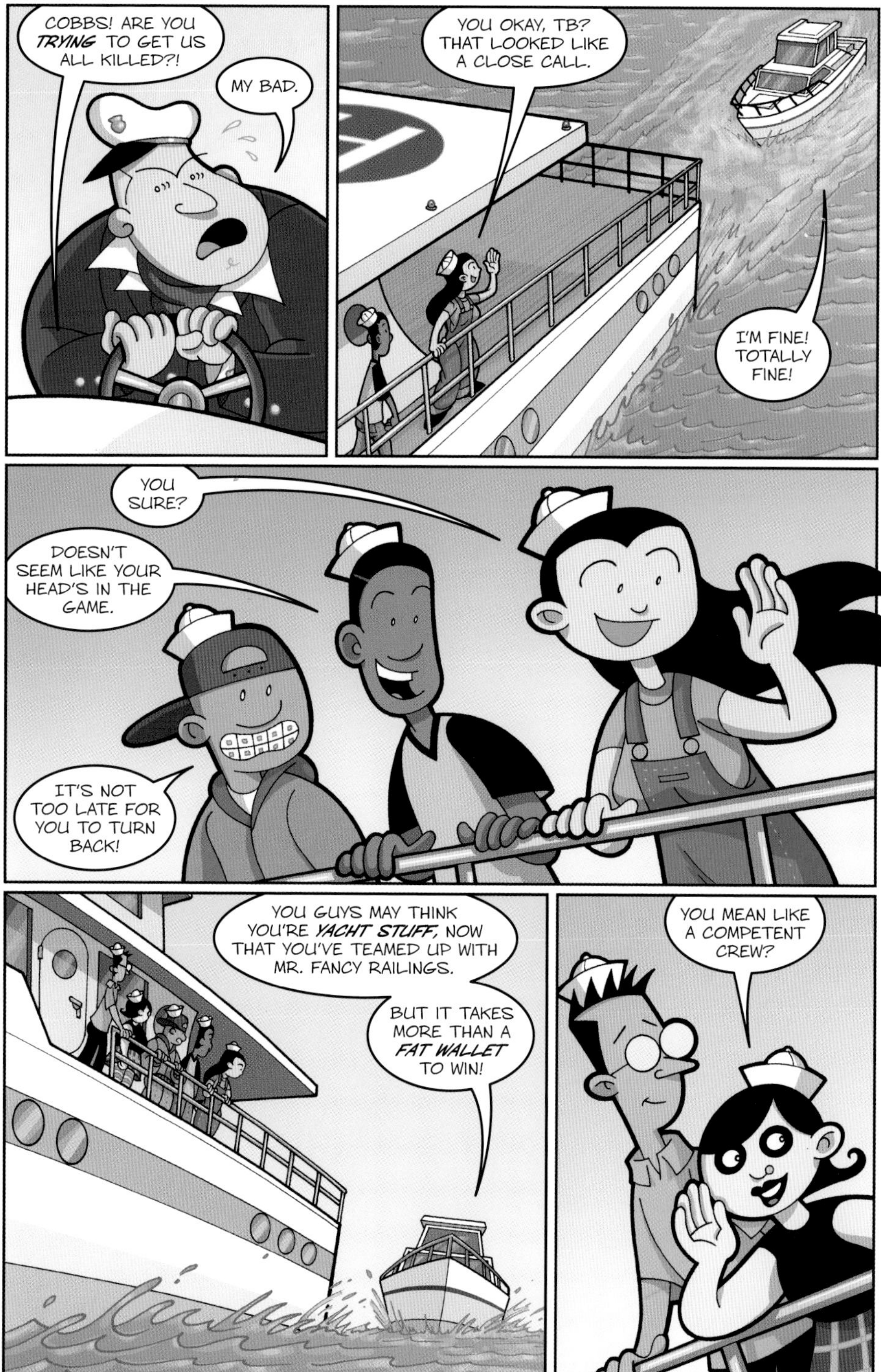
COBBS! ARE YOU *TRYING* TO GET US ALL KILLED?!
MY BAD.
YOU OKAY, TB? THAT LOOKED LIKE A CLOSE CALL.
I'M FINE! TOTALLY FINE!
YOU SURE?
DOESN'T SEEM LIKE YOUR HEAD'S IN THE GAME.
IT'S NOT TOO LATE FOR YOU TO TURN BACK!
YOU GUYS MAY THINK YOU'RE *YACHT STUFF*, NOW THAT YOU'VE TEAMED UP WITH MR. FANCY RAILINGS.
BUT IT TAKES MORE THAN A *FAT WALLET* TO WIN!
YOU MEAN LIKE A COMPETENT CREW?

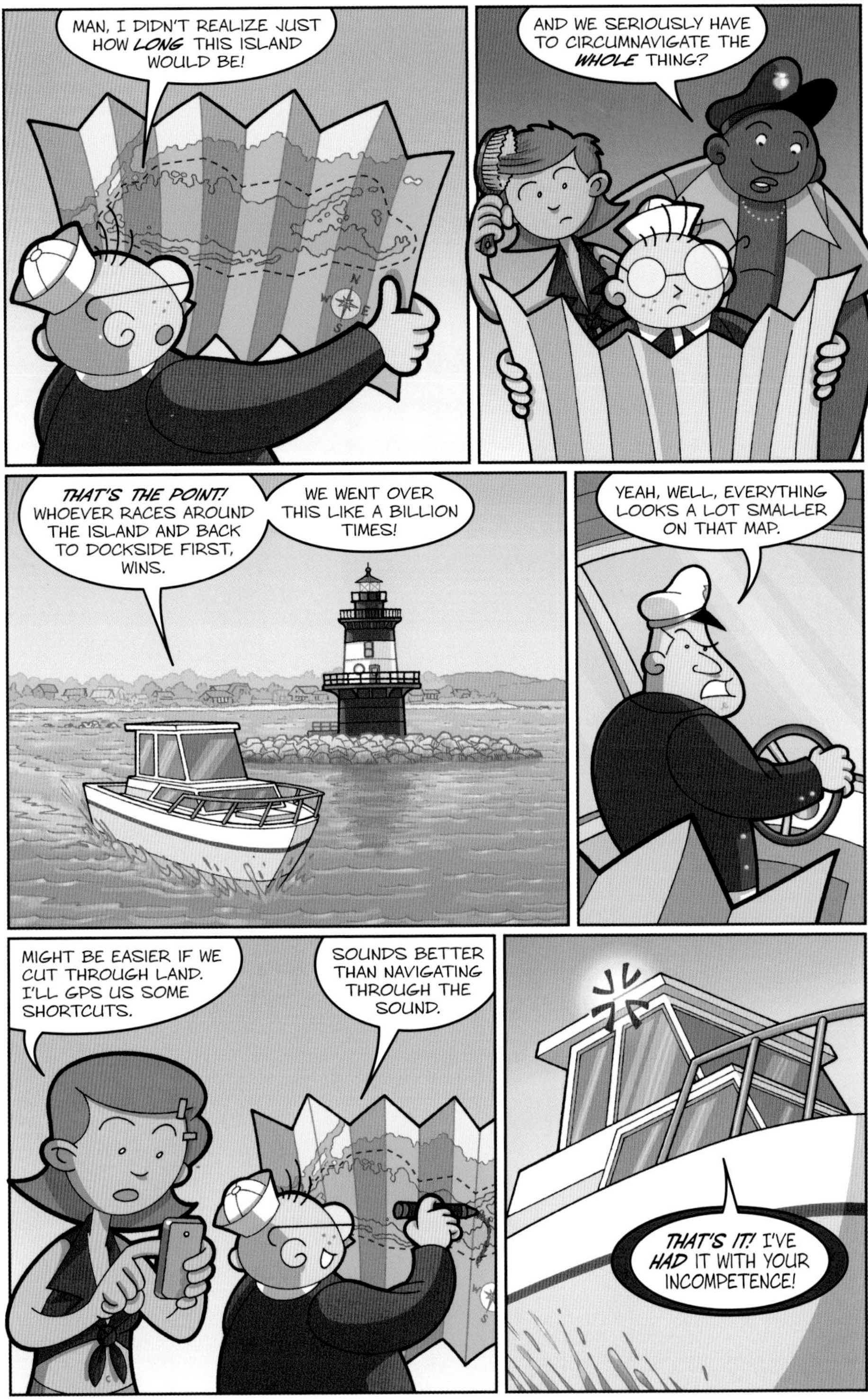
MAN, I DIDN'T REALIZE JUST HOW LONG THIS ISLAND WOULD BE!
AND WE SERIOUSLY HAVE TO CIRCUMNAVIGATE THE WHOLE THING?
THAT'S THE POINT! WHOEVER RACES AROUND THE ISLAND AND BACK TO DOCKSIDE FIRST, WINS.
WE WENT OVER THIS LIKE A BILLION TIMES!
YEAH, WELL, EVERYTHING LOOKS A LOT SMALLER ON THAT MAP.
MIGHT BE EASIER IF WE CUT THROUGH LAND. I'LL GPS US SOME SHORTCUTS.
SOUNDS BETTER THAN NAVIGATING THROUGH THE SOUND.
THAT'S IT! I'VE HAD IT WITH YOUR INCOMPETENCE!

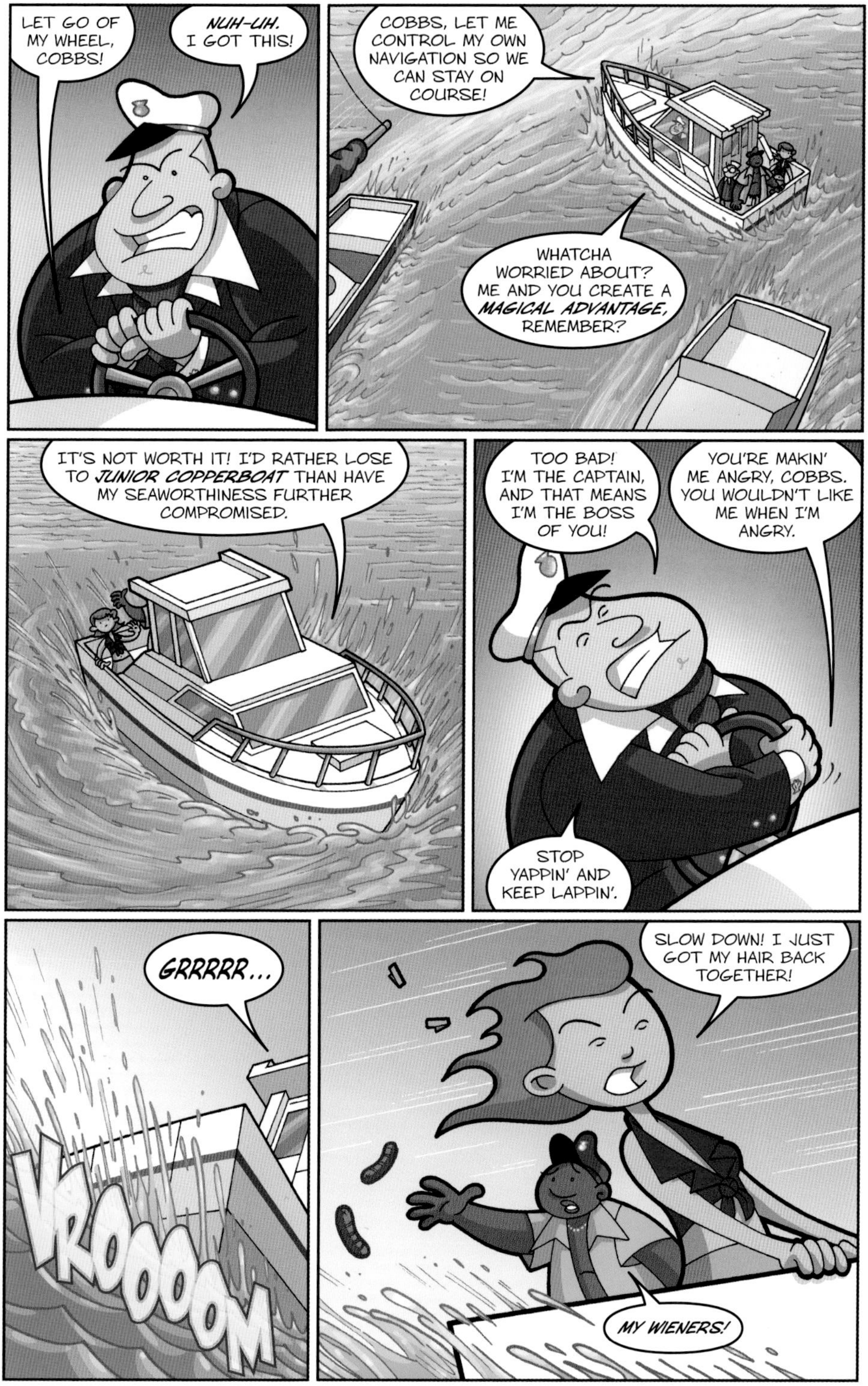
LET GO OF MY WHEEL, COBBS!
NUH-UH. I GOT THIS!
COBBS, LET ME CONTROL MY OWN NAVIGATION SO WE CAN STAY ON COURSE!
WHATCHA WORRIED ABOUT? ME AND YOU CREATE A MAGICAL ADVANTAGE, REMEMBER?
IT'S NOT WORTH IT! I'D RATHER LOSE TO JUNIOR COPPERBOAT THAN HAVE MY SEAWORTHINESS FURTHER COMPROMISED.
TOO BAD! I'M THE CAPTAIN, AND THAT MEANS I'M THE BOSS OF YOU!
YOU'RE MAKIN' ME ANGRY, COBBS. YOU WOULDN'T LIKE ME WHEN I'M ANGRY.
STOP YAPPIN' AND KEEP LAPPIN'.
GRRRRR...
VROOOOOM
SLOW DOWN! I JUST GOT MY HAIR BACK TOGETHER!
MY WIENERS!

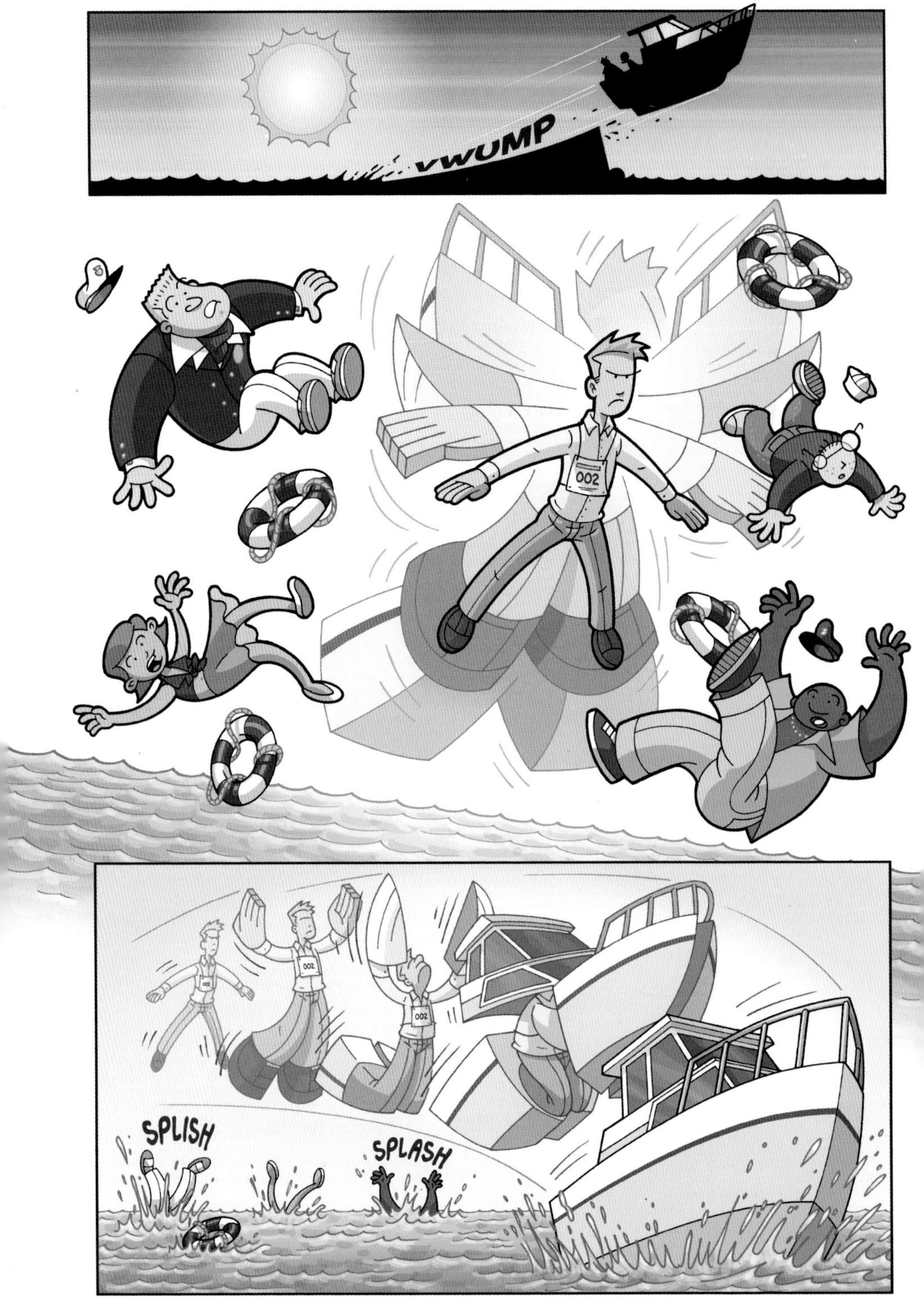
VWUMP
002
002
002
002
SPLISH
SPLASH

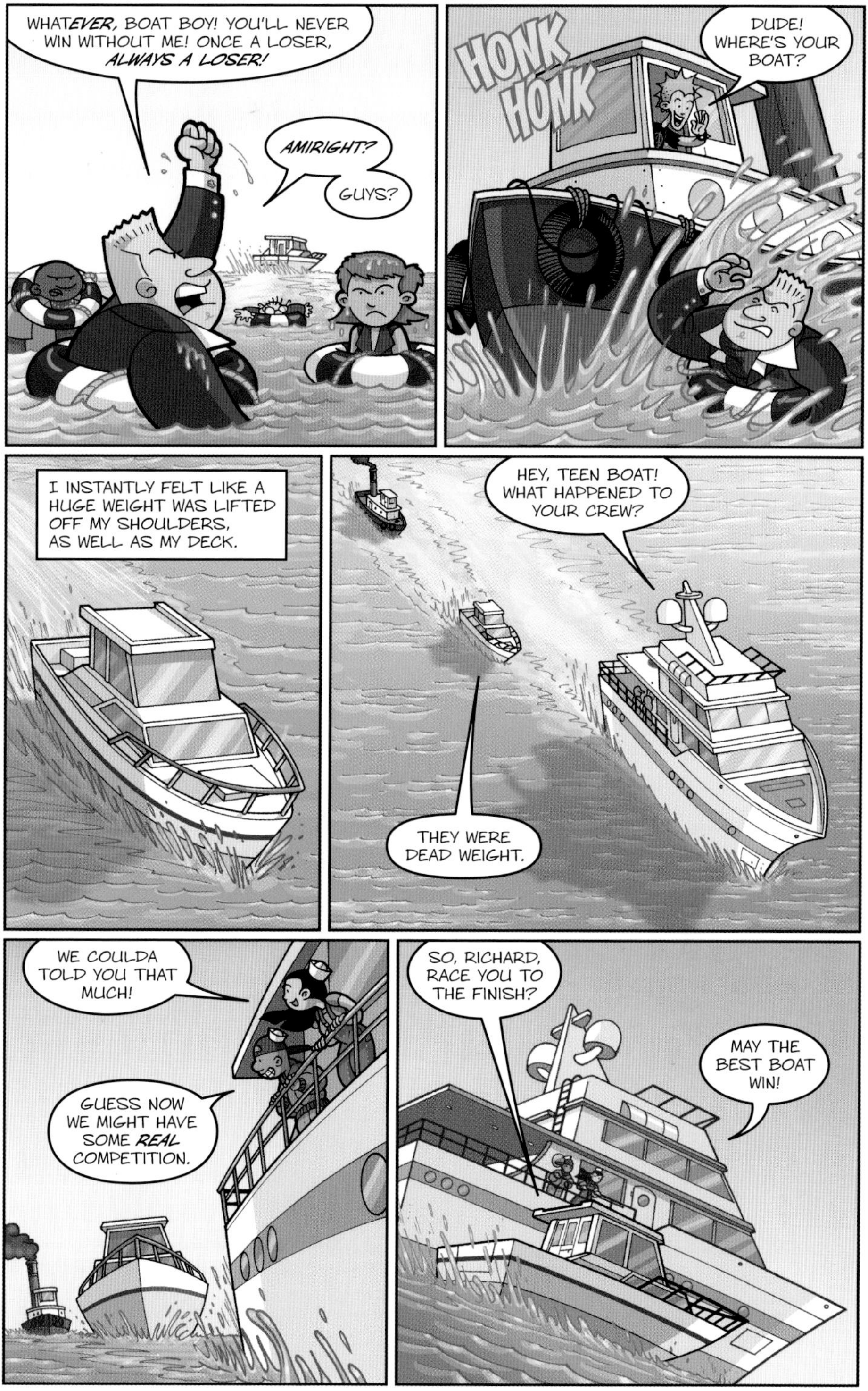
WHATEVER, BOAT BOY! YOU'LL NEVER WIN WITHOUT ME! ONCE A LOSER, ALWAYS A LOSER!
AMIRIGHT?
GUYS?
HONK HONK
DUDE! WHERE'S YOUR BOAT?
I INSTANTLY FELT LIKE A HUGE WEIGHT WAS LIFTED OFF MY SHOULDERS, AS WELL AS MY DECK.
HEY, TEEN BOAT! WHAT HAPPENED TO YOUR CREW?
THEY WERE DEAD WEIGHT.
WE COULDA TOLD YOU THAT MUCH!
GUESS NOW WE MIGHT HAVE SOME REAL COMPETITION.
SO, RICHARD, RACE YOU TO THE FINISH?
MAY THE BEST BOAT WIN!

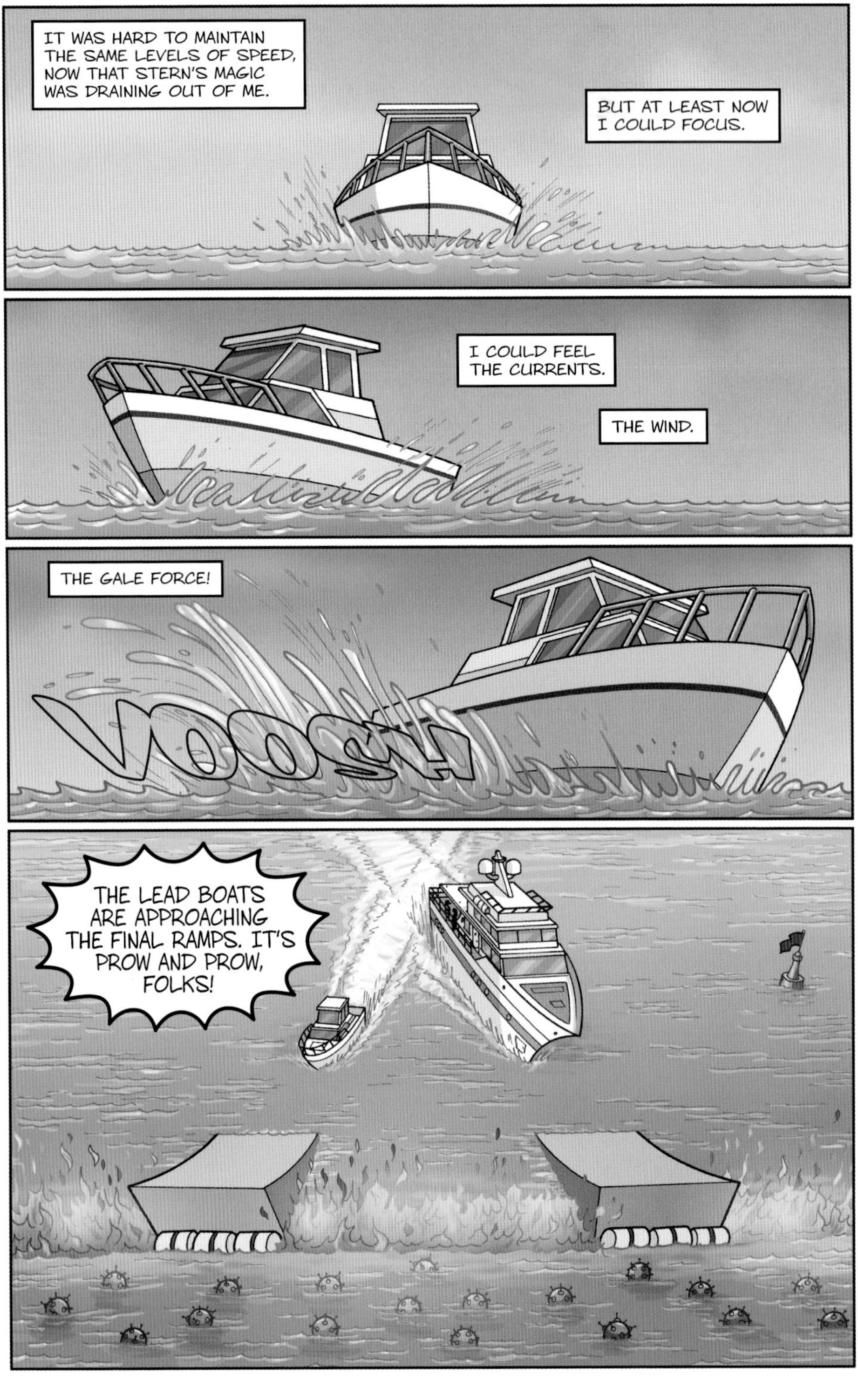
IT WAS HARD TO MAINTAIN THE SAME LEVELS OF SPEED, NOW THAT STERN'S MAGIC WAS DRAINING OUT OF ME.
BUT AT LEAST NOW I COULD FOCUS.
I COULD FEEL THE CURRENTS.
THE WIND.
THE GALE FORCE!
VOOSH
THE LEAD BOATS ARE APPROACHING THE FINAL RAMPS. IT'S PROW AND PROW, FOLKS!

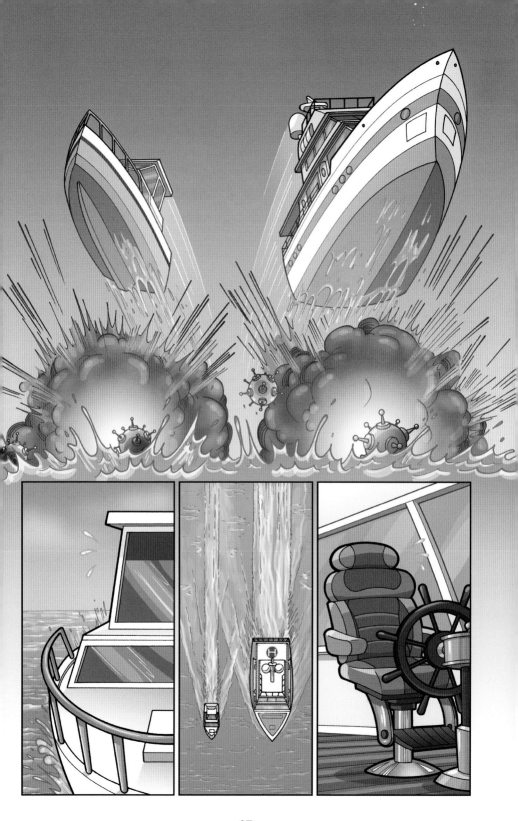

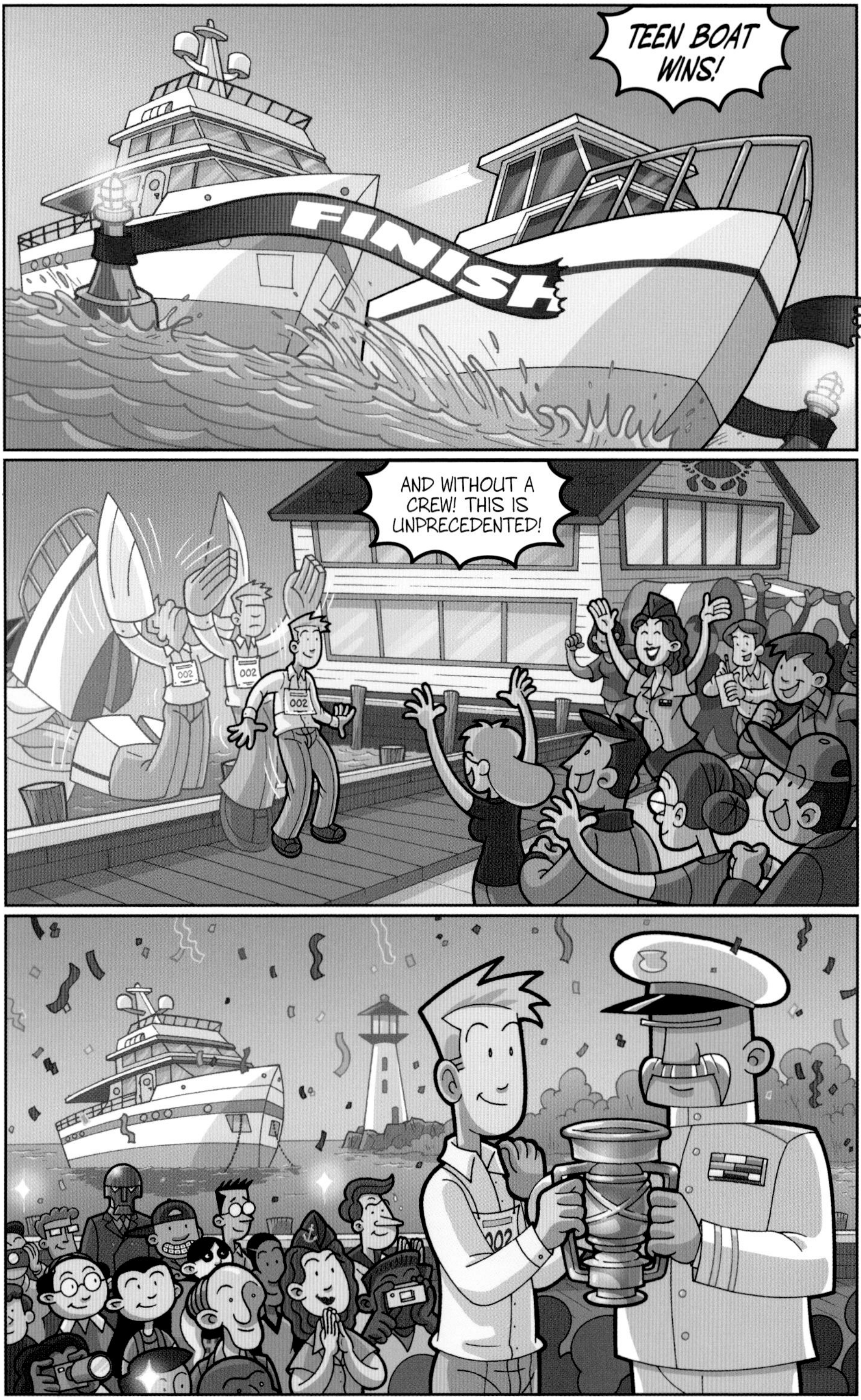
TEEN BOAT WINS!
FINISH
AND WITHOUT A CREW! THIS IS UNPRECEDENTED!

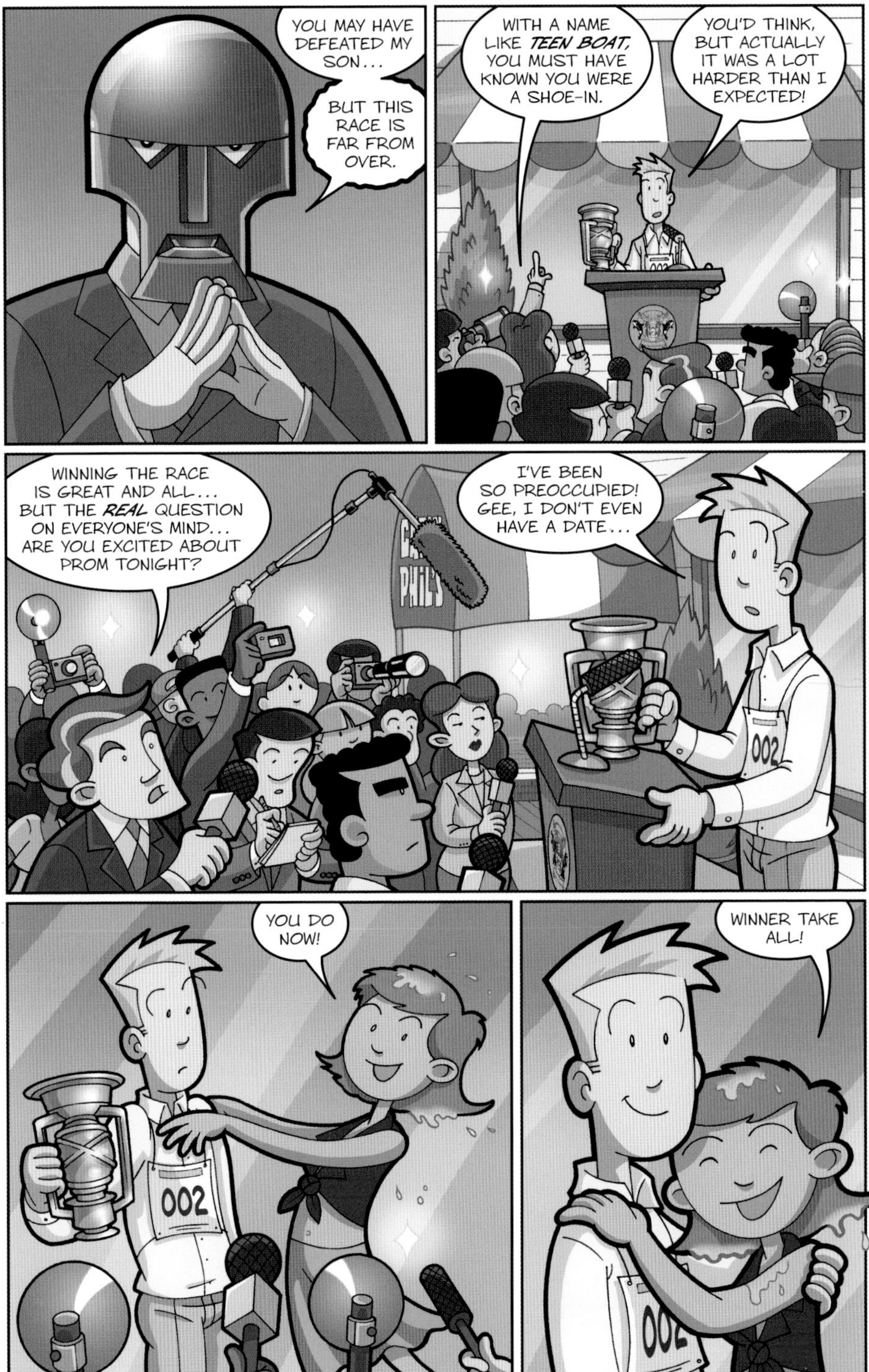
YOU MAY HAVE DEFEATED MY SON...
BUT THIS RACE IS FAR FROM OVER.
WITH A NAME LIKE *TEEN BOAT,* YOU MUST HAVE KNOWN YOU WERE A SHOE-IN.
YOU'D THINK, BUT ACTUALLY IT WAS A LOT HARDER THAN I EXPECTED!
WINNING THE RACE IS GREAT AND ALL... BUT THE *REAL* QUESTION ON EVERYONE'S MIND... ARE YOU EXCITED ABOUT PROM TONIGHT?
I'VE BEEN SO PREOCCUPIED! GEE, I DON'T EVEN HAVE A DATE...
YOU DO NOW!
WINNER TAKE ALL!

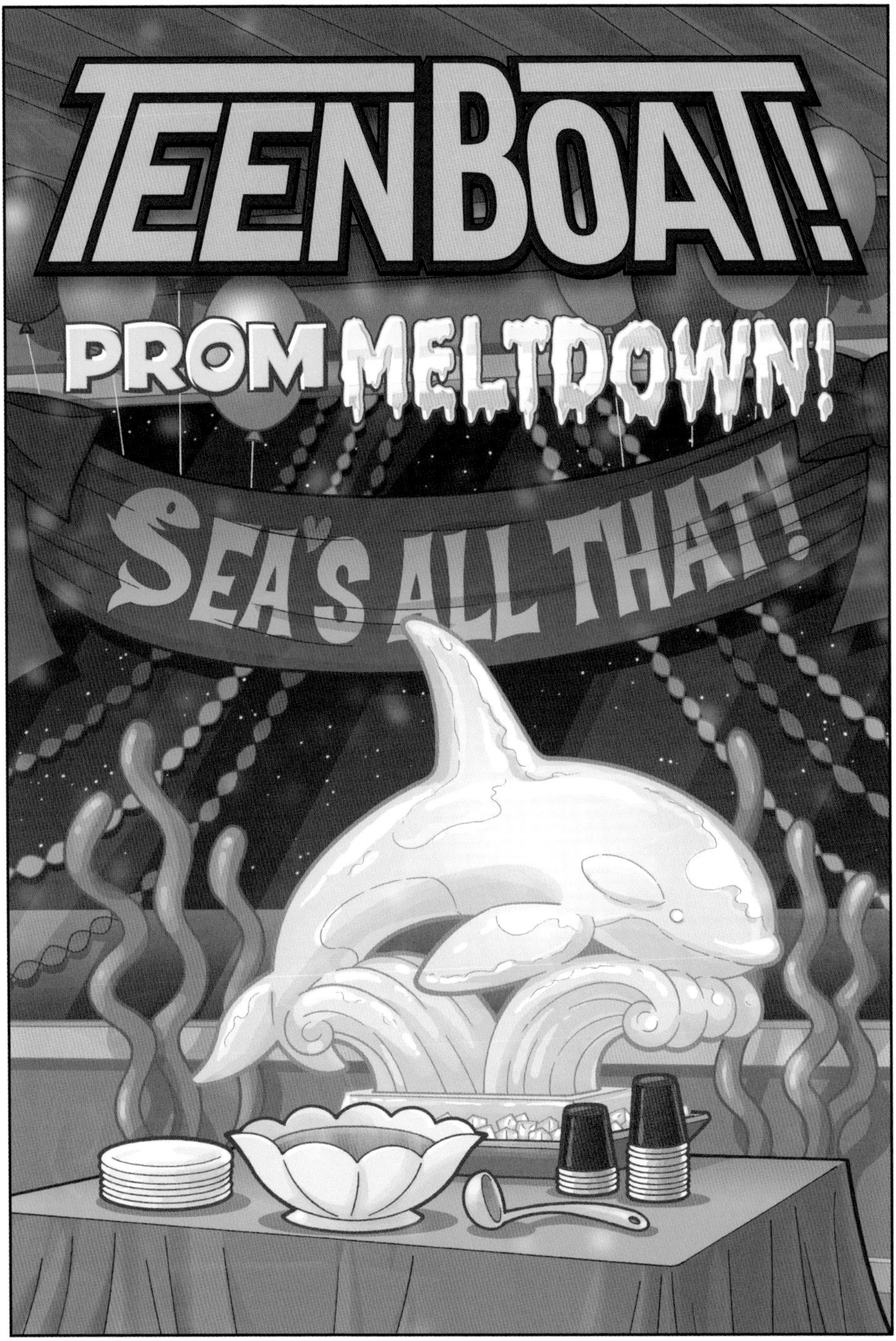
TEEN BOAT!
PROM MELTDOWN!
SEA'S ALL THAT!

The ***FUN*** of Parties—the ***ELEGANCE*** of Proper Attire!

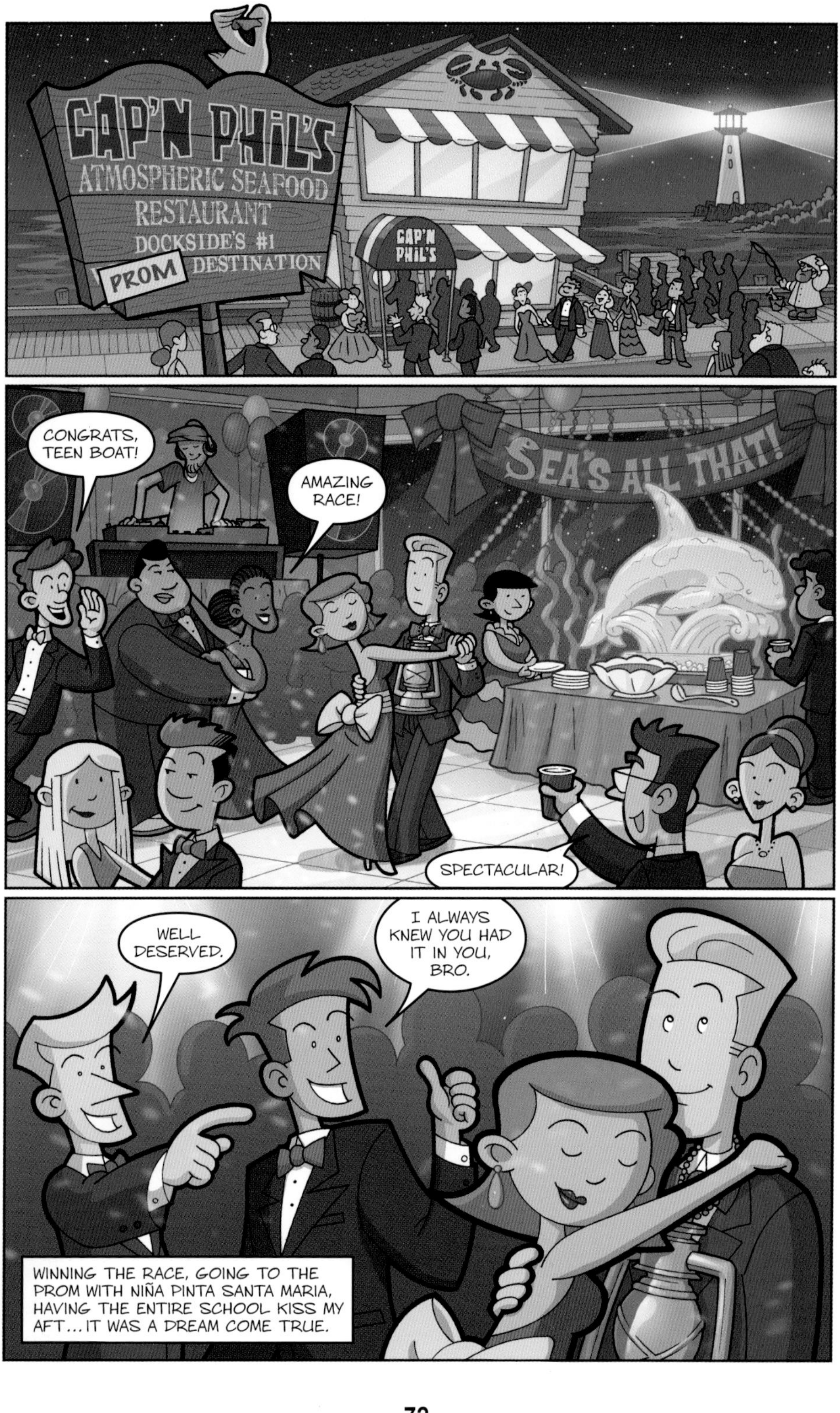
CAP'N PHIL'S
ATMOSPHERIC SEAFOOD
RESTAURANT
DOCKSIDE'S #1
PROM DESTINATION
CAP'N PHIL'S
CONGRATS, TEEN BOAT!
AMAZING RACE!
SEA'S ALL THAT!
SPECTACULAR!
WELL DESERVED.
I ALWAYS KNEW YOU HAD IT IN YOU, BRO.
WINNING THE RACE, GOING TO THE PROM WITH NIÑA PINTA SANTA MARIA, HAVING THE ENTIRE SCHOOL KISS MY AFT... IT WAS A DREAM COME TRUE.

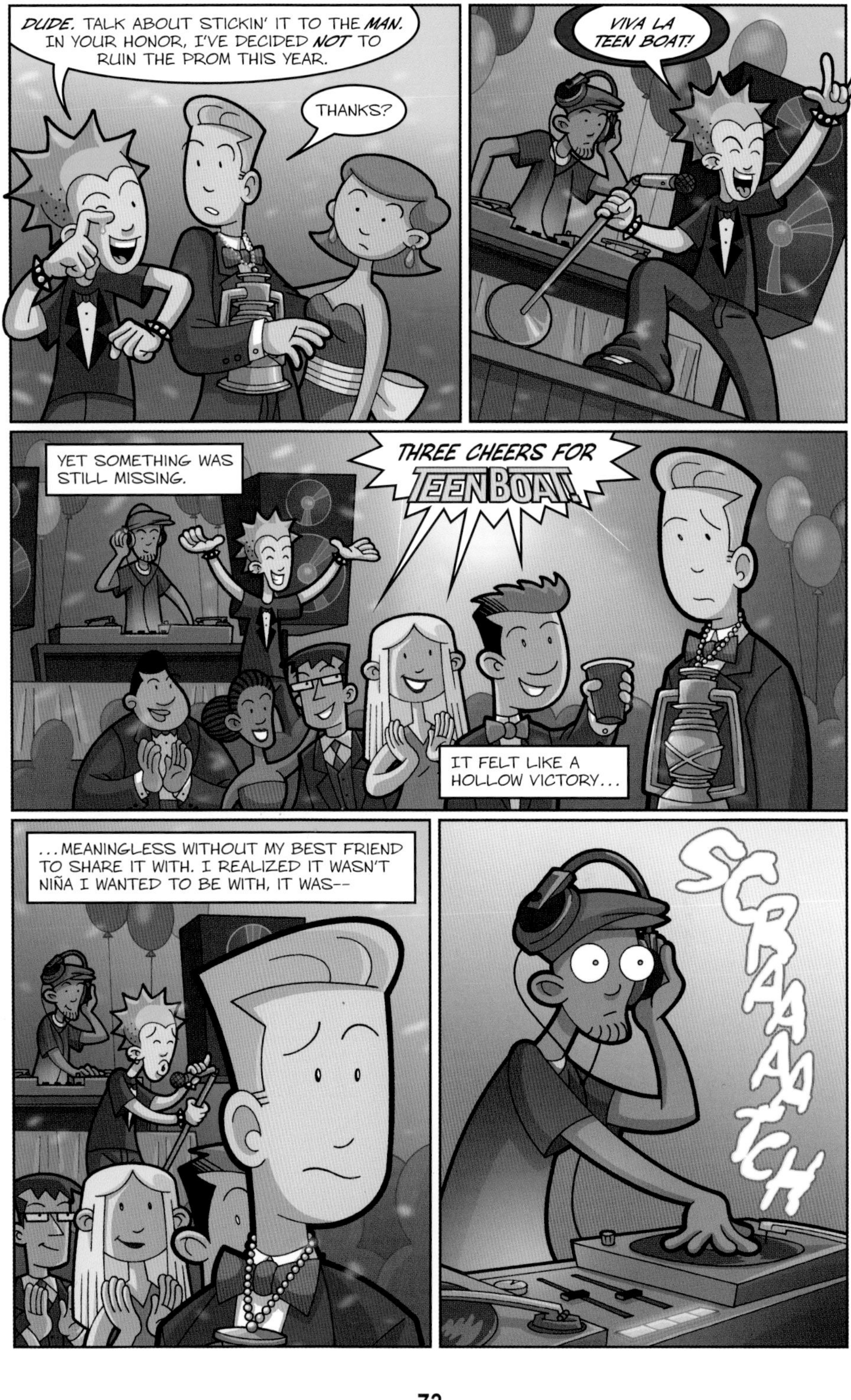
DUDE. TALK ABOUT STICKIN' IT TO THE MAN. IN YOUR HONOR, I'VE DECIDED NOT TO RUIN THE PROM THIS YEAR.
THANKS?
VIVA LA TEEN BOAT!
YET SOMETHING WAS STILL MISSING.
THREE CHEERS FOR TEEN BOAT!
IT FELT LIKE A HOLLOW VICTORY...
...MEANINGLESS WITHOUT MY BEST FRIEND TO SHARE IT WITH. I REALIZED IT WASN'T NIÑA I WANTED TO BE WITH, IT WAS--
SCRAAAATCH

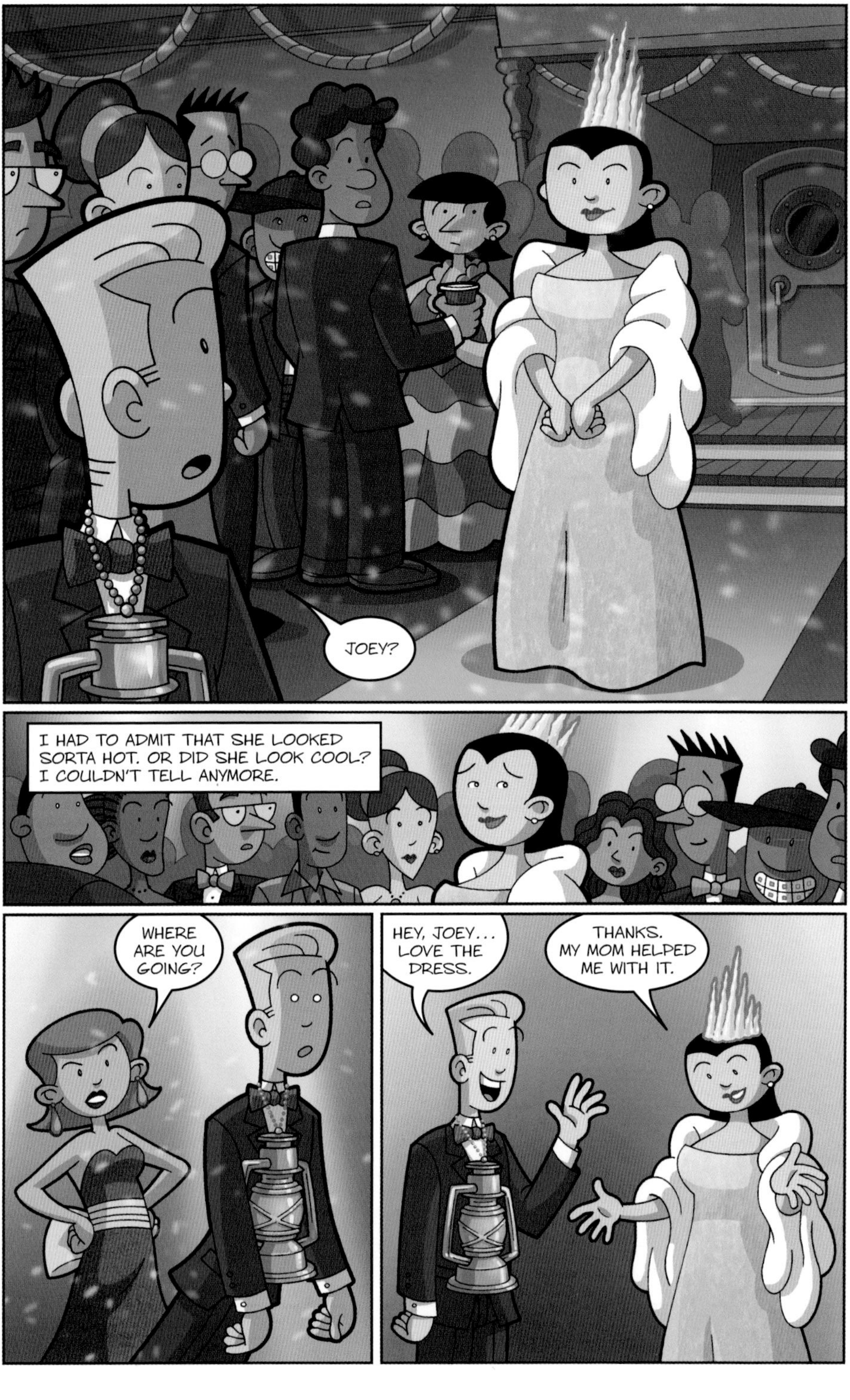
JOEY?
I HAD TO ADMIT THAT SHE LOOKED SORTA HOT. OR DID SHE LOOK COOL? I COULDN'T TELL ANYMORE.
WHERE ARE YOU GOING?
HEY, JOEY... LOVE THE DRESS.
THANKS. MY MOM HELPED ME WITH IT.

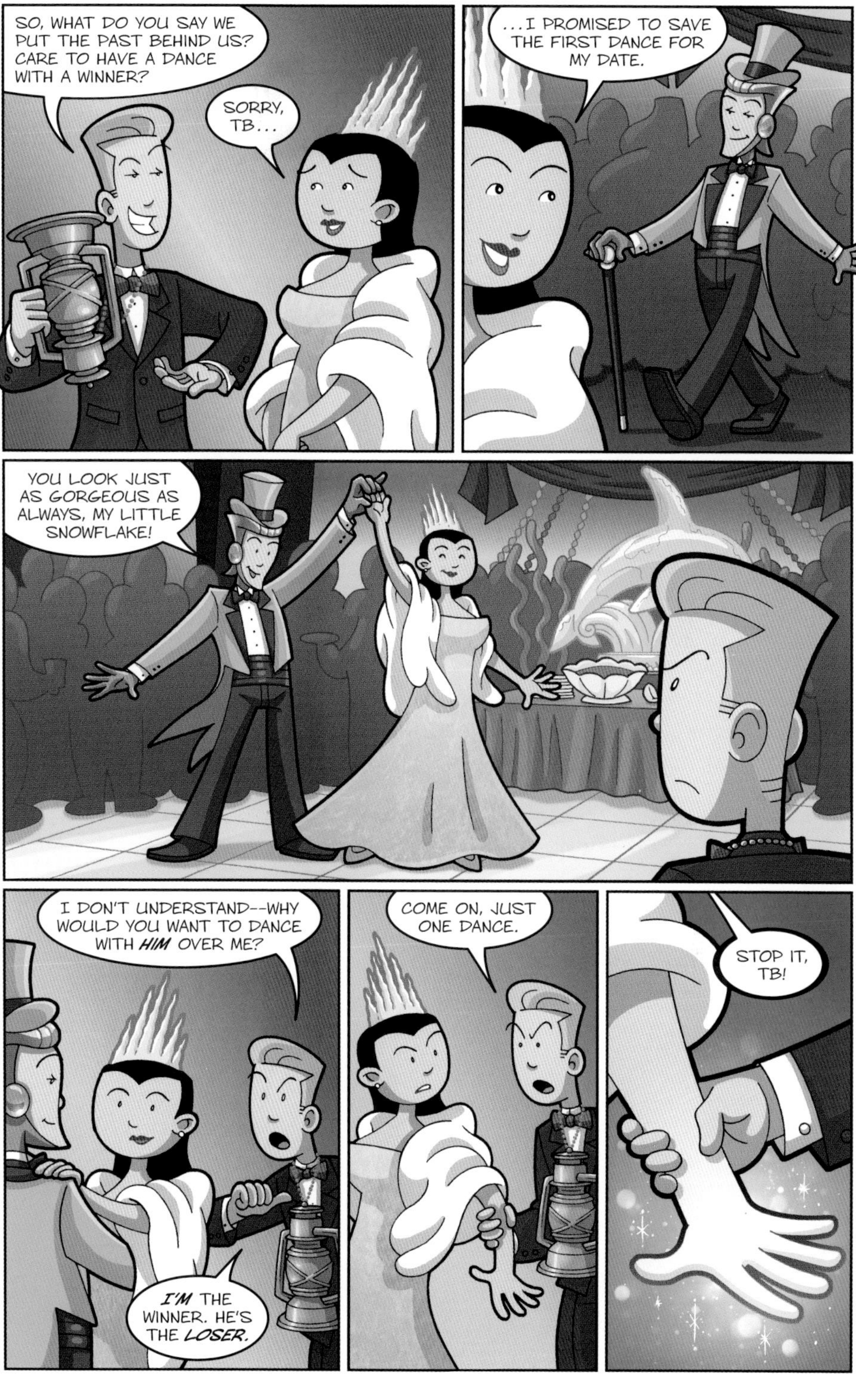
SO, WHAT DO YOU SAY WE PUT THE PAST BEHIND US? CARE TO HAVE A DANCE WITH A WINNER?
SORRY, TB...
...I PROMISED TO SAVE THE FIRST DANCE FOR MY DATE.
YOU LOOK JUST AS GORGEOUS AS ALWAYS, MY LITTLE SNOWFLAKE!
I DON'T UNDERSTAND--WHY WOULD YOU WANT TO DANCE WITH *HIM* OVER ME?
I'M THE WINNER. HE'S THE *LOSER.*
COME ON, JUST ONE DANCE.
STOP IT, TB!

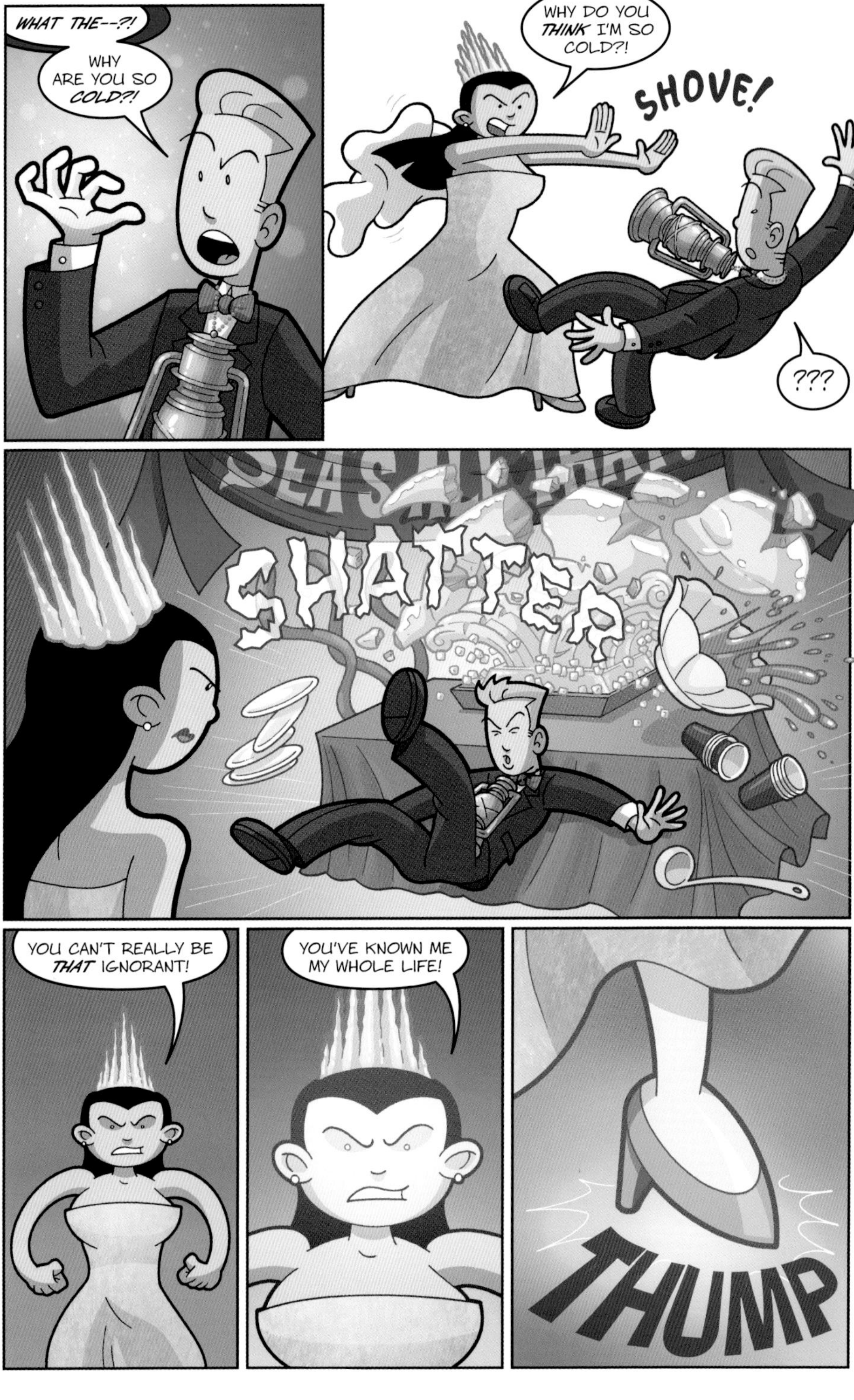
WHAT THE--?!
WHY ARE YOU SO COLD?!
WHY DO YOU THINK I'M SO COLD?!
SHOVE!
???
SHATTER
YOU CAN'T REALLY BE THAT IGNORANT!
YOU'VE KNOWN ME MY WHOLE LIFE!
THUMP

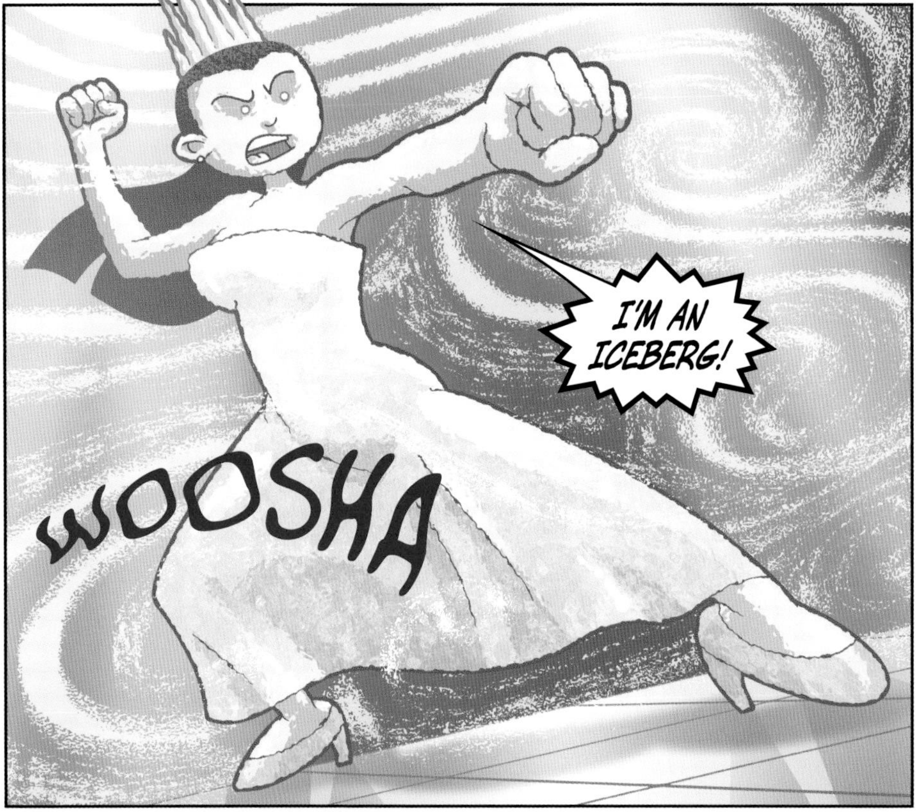
I'M AN ICEBERG!
WOOSHA

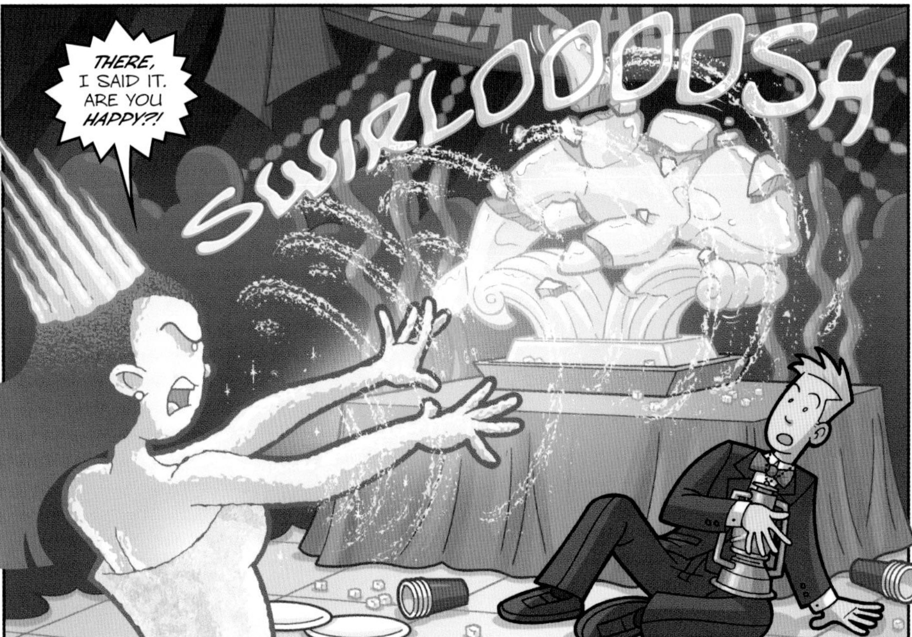
THERE, I SAID IT. ARE YOU HAPPY?!
SWIRLOOOOSH

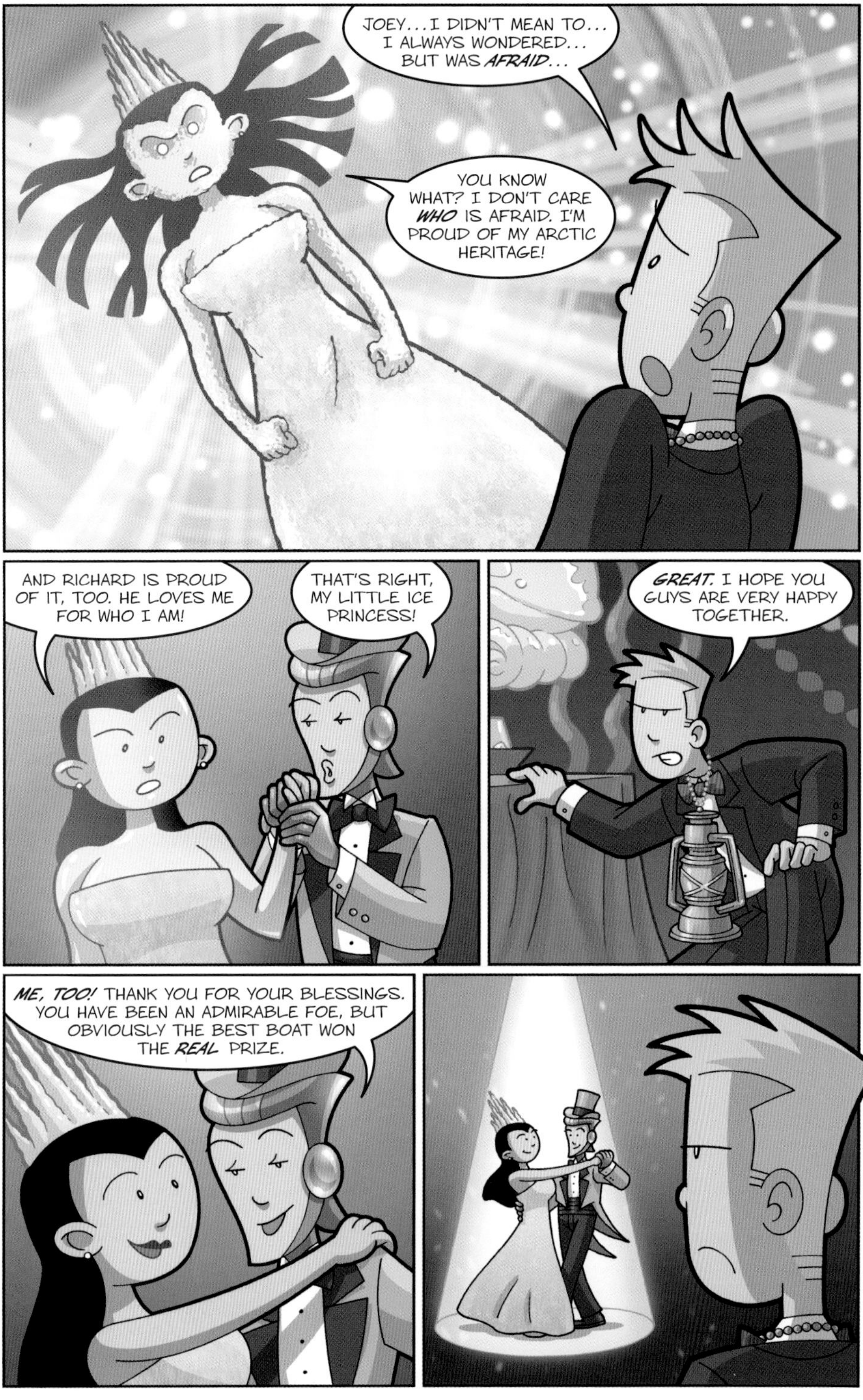
JOEY... I DIDN'T MEAN TO... I ALWAYS WONDERED... BUT WAS AFRAID...
YOU KNOW WHAT? I DON'T CARE WHO IS AFRAID. I'M PROUD OF MY ARCTIC HERITAGE!
AND RICHARD IS PROUD OF IT, TOO. HE LOVES ME FOR WHO I AM!
THAT'S RIGHT, MY LITTLE ICE PRINCESS!
GREAT. I HOPE YOU GUYS ARE VERY HAPPY TOGETHER.
ME, TOO! THANK YOU FOR YOUR BLESSINGS. YOU HAVE BEEN AN ADMIRABLE FOE, BUT OBVIOUSLY THE BEST BOAT WON THE REAL PRIZE.

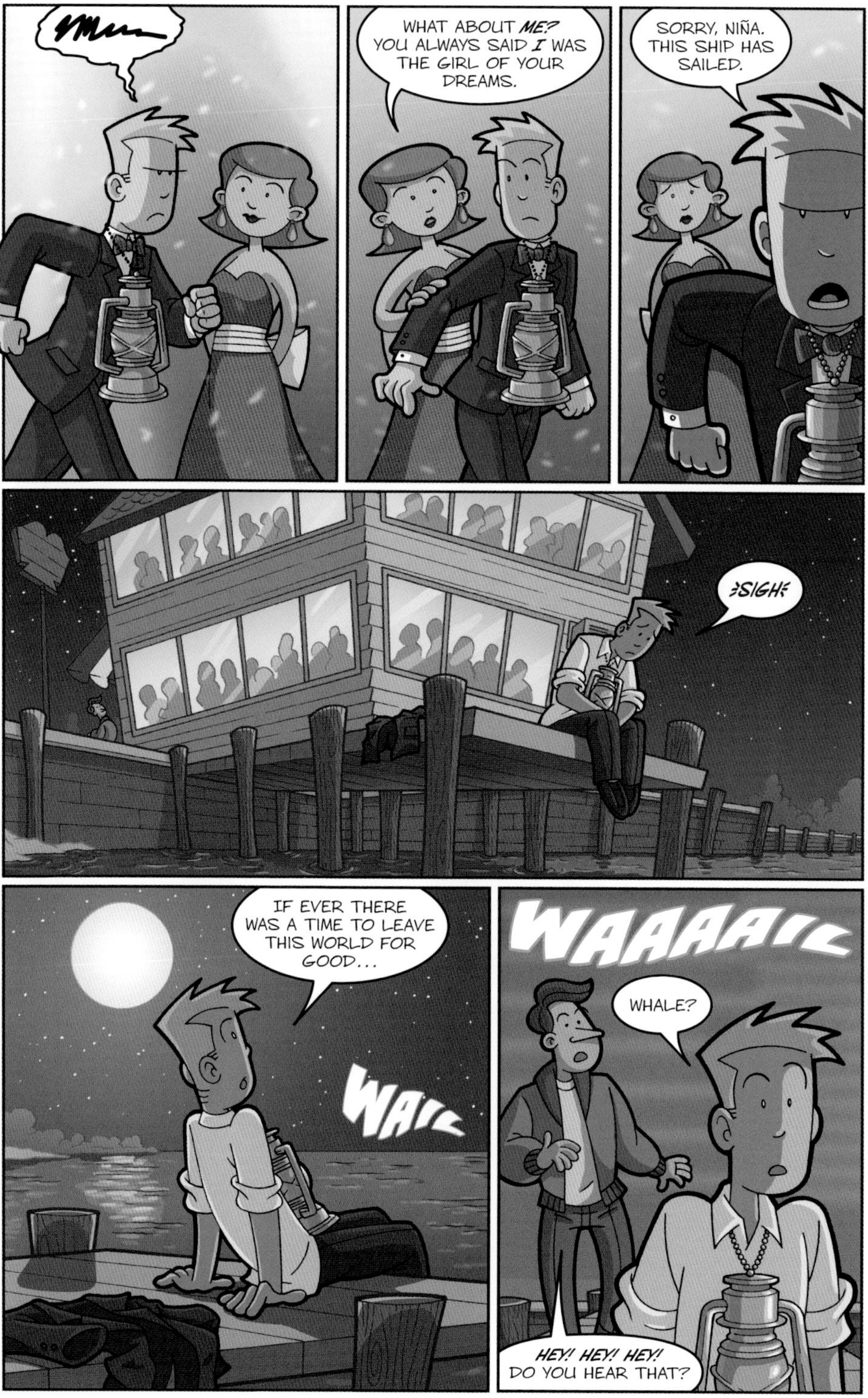
WHAT ABOUT ME? YOU ALWAYS SAID I WAS THE GIRL OF YOUR DREAMS.
SORRY, NIÑA. THIS SHIP HAS SAILED.
SIGH
IF EVER THERE WAS A TIME TO LEAVE THIS WORLD FOR GOOD...
WAIL
WAAAAIL
WHALE?
HEY! HEY! HEY! DO YOU HEAR THAT?

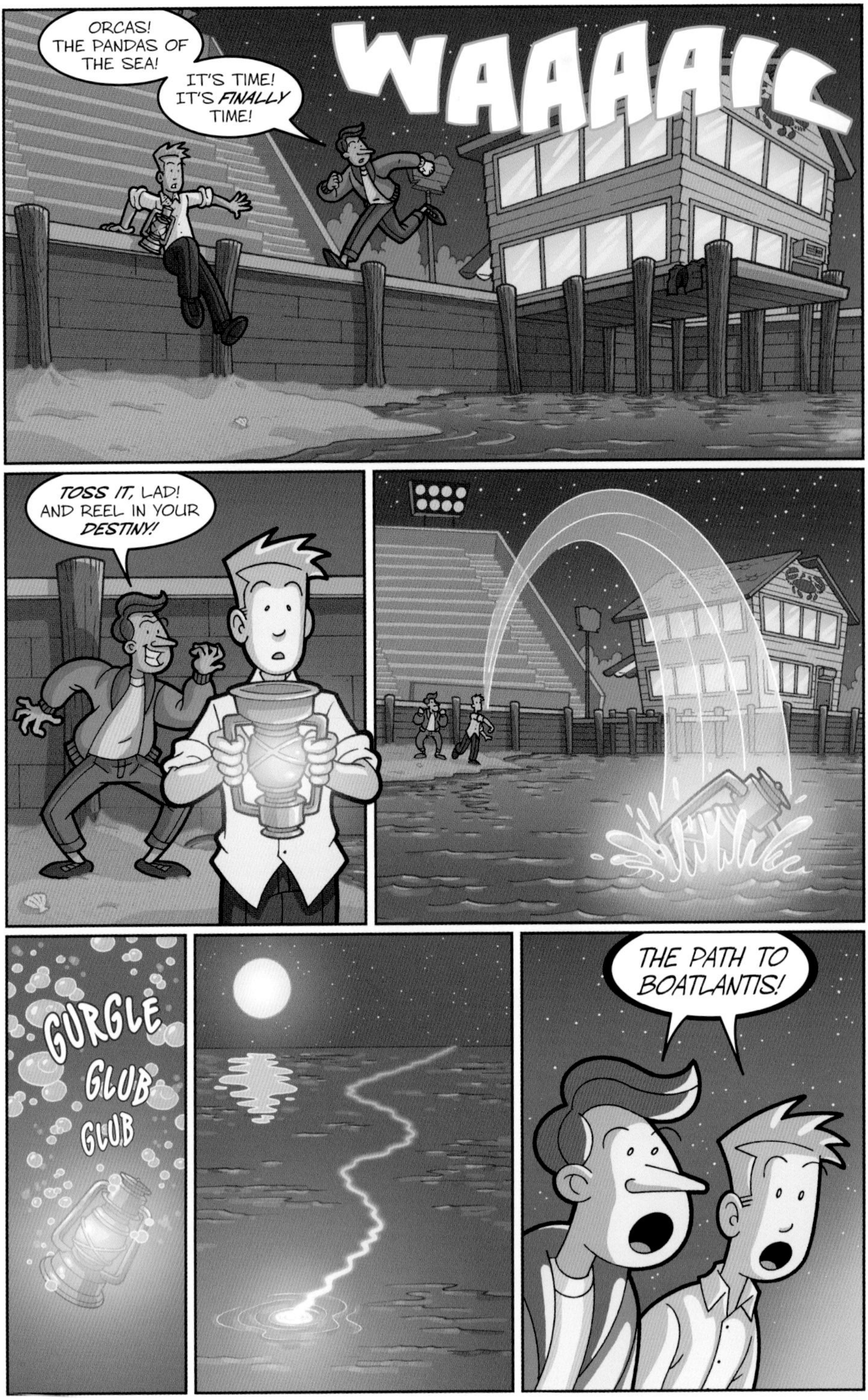
ORCAS! THE PANDAS OF THE SEA!
IT'S TIME! IT'S FINALLY TIME!
WAAAAIL
TOSS IT, LAD! AND REEL IN YOUR DESTINY!
GURGLE
GLUB
GLUB
THE PATH TO BOATLANTIS!

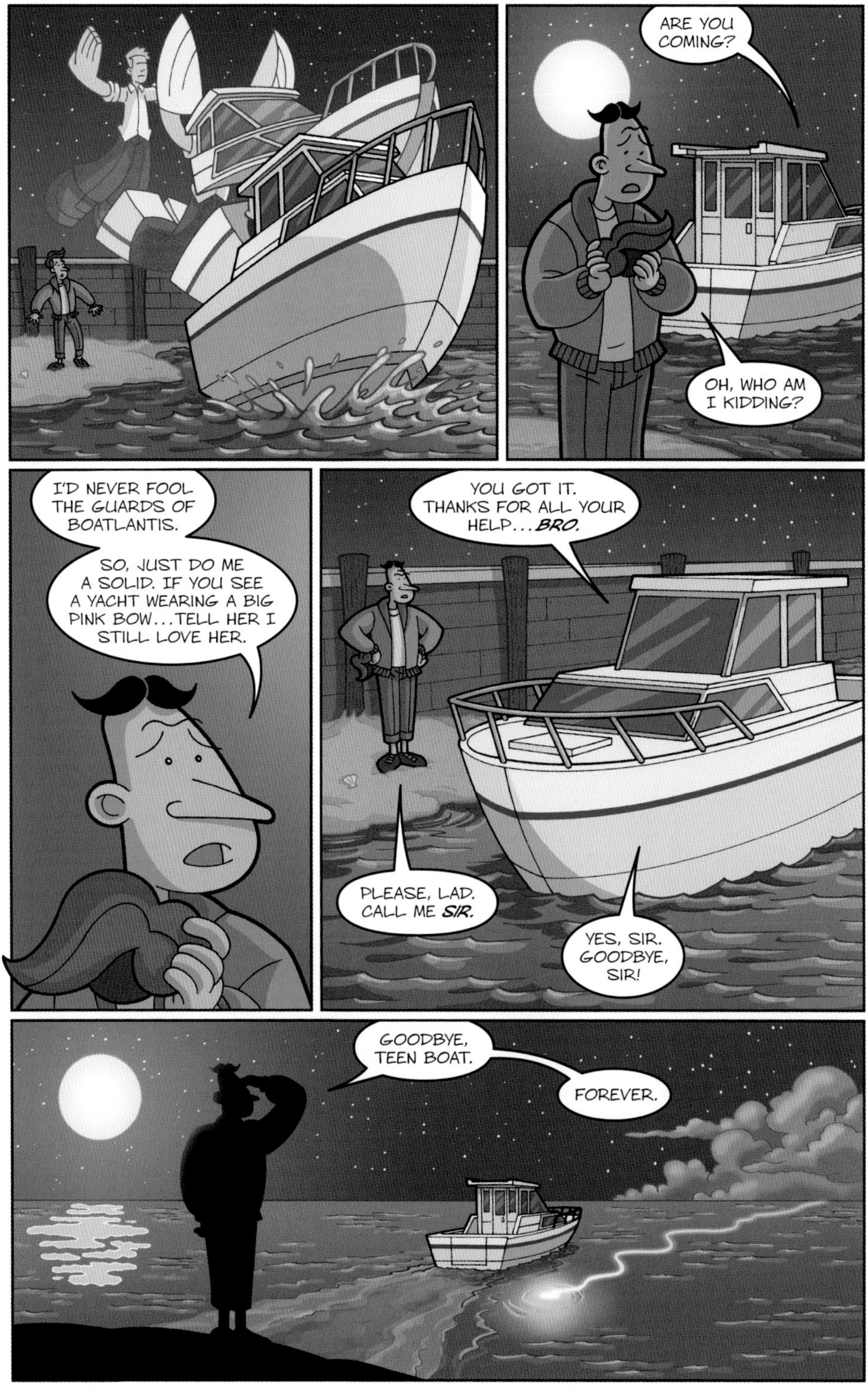
ARE YOU COMING?
OH, WHO AM I KIDDING?
I'D NEVER FOOL THE GUARDS OF BOATLANTIS.
SO, JUST DO ME A SOLID. IF YOU SEE A YACHT WEARING A BIG PINK BOW...TELL HER I STILL LOVE HER.
YOU GOT IT. THANKS FOR ALL YOUR HELP...*BRO.*
PLEASE, LAD. CALL ME *SIR.*
YES, SIR. GOODBYE, SIR!
GOODBYE, TEEN BOAT.
FOREVER.

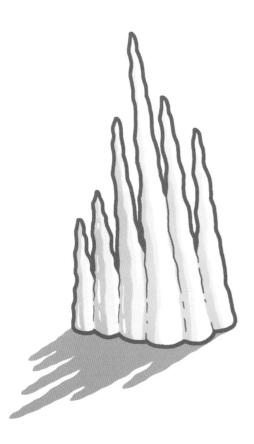

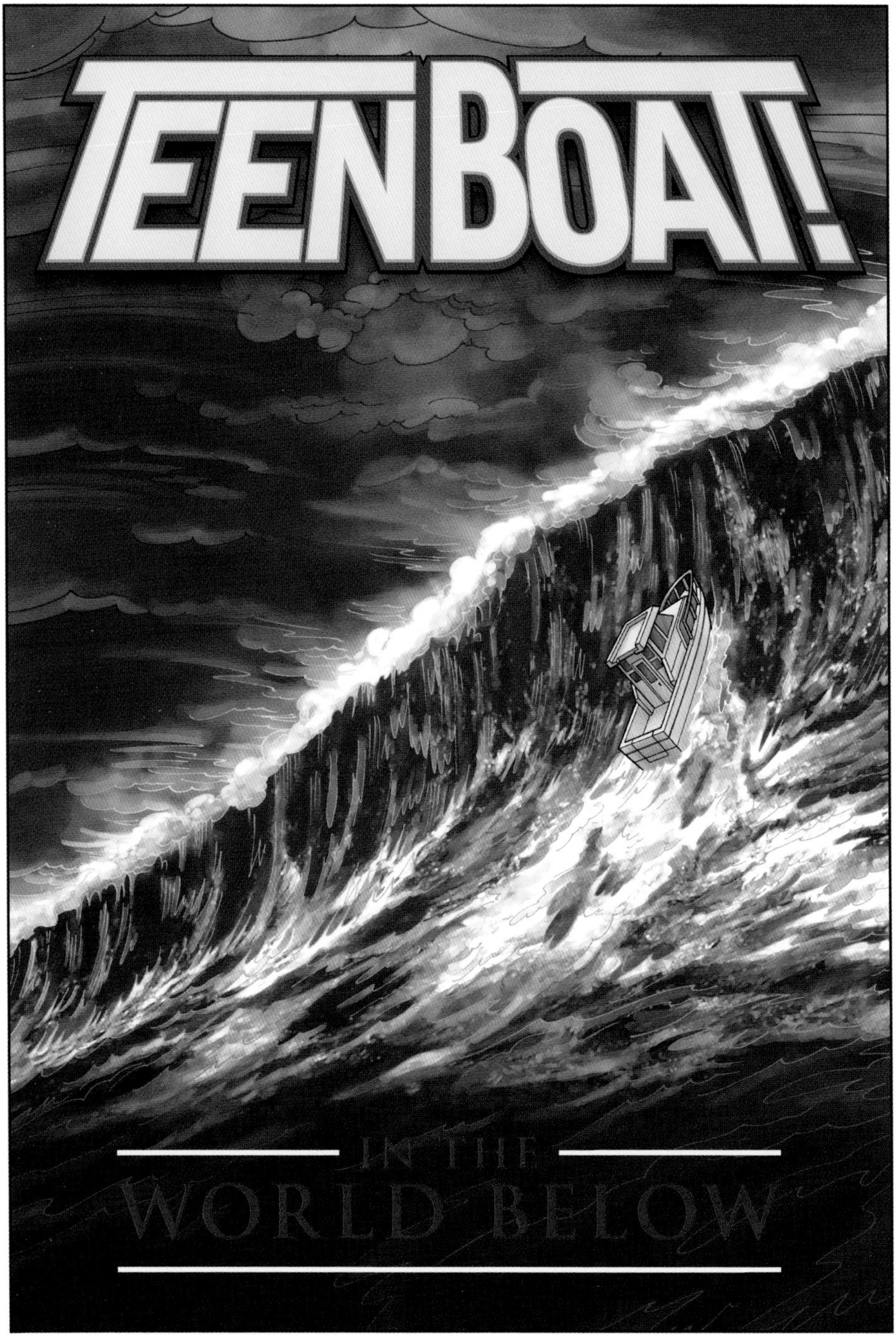
TEENBOAT!
IN THE
WORLD BELOW

The ***TINGE*** of Regret—the ***CALL*** of Destiny!

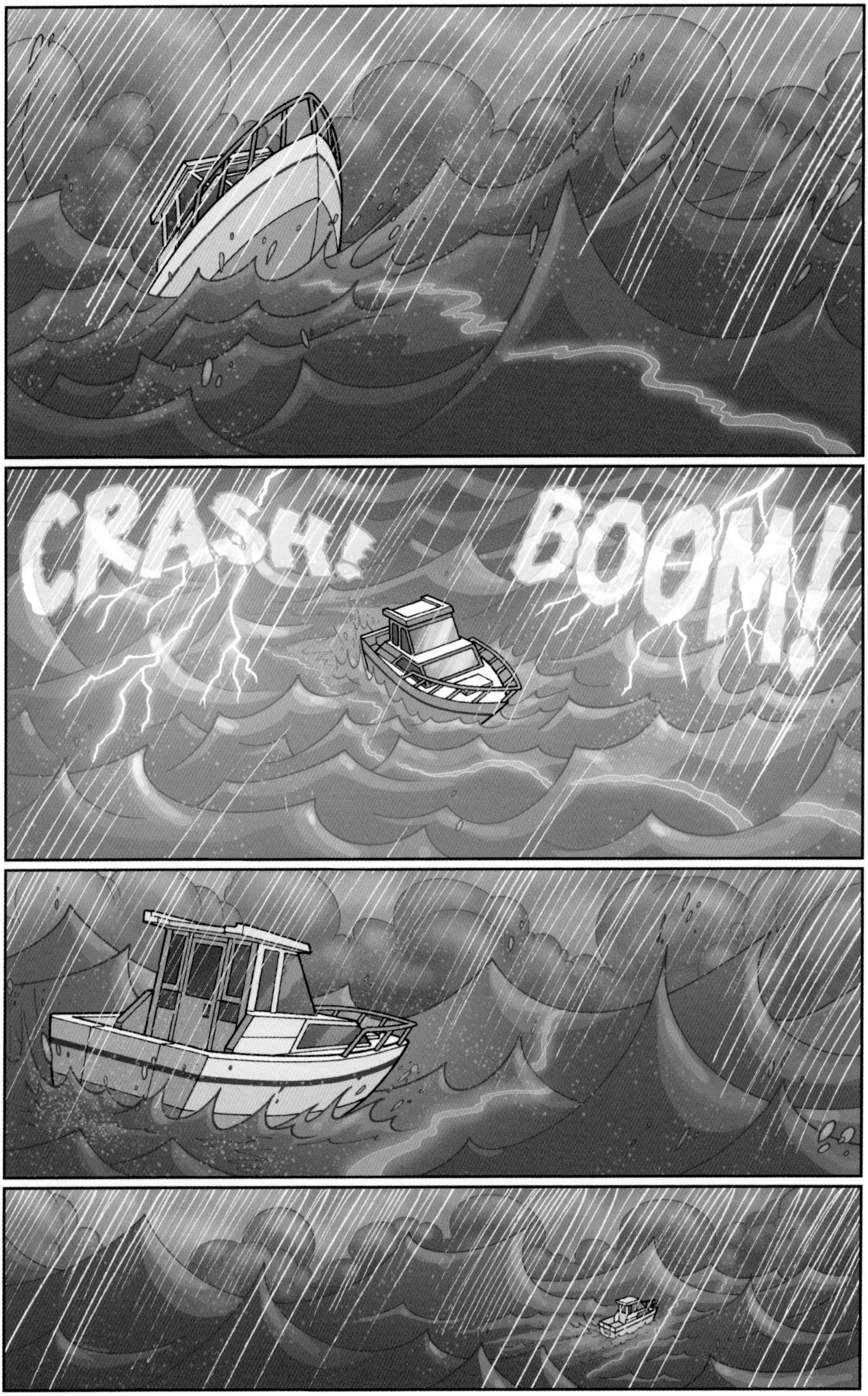
CRASH!
BOOM!

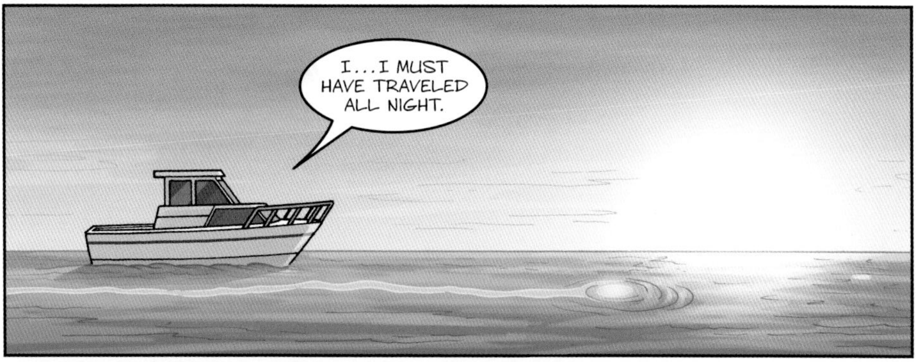
I...I MUST HAVE TRAVELED ALL NIGHT.

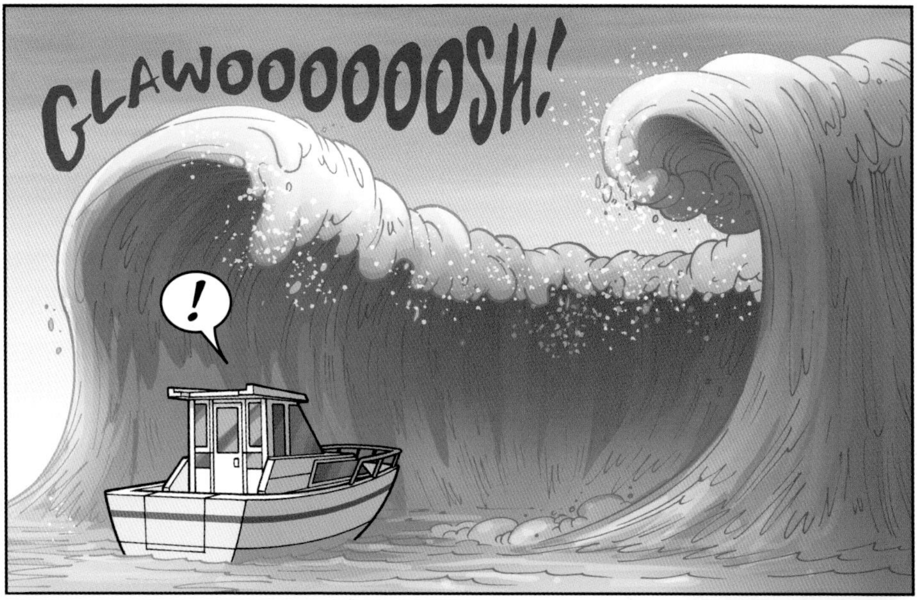
GLAWOOOOOOSH!
!

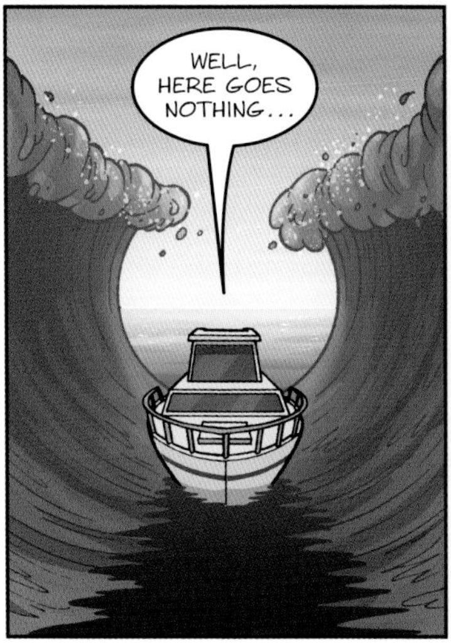
WELL, HERE GOES NOTHING...

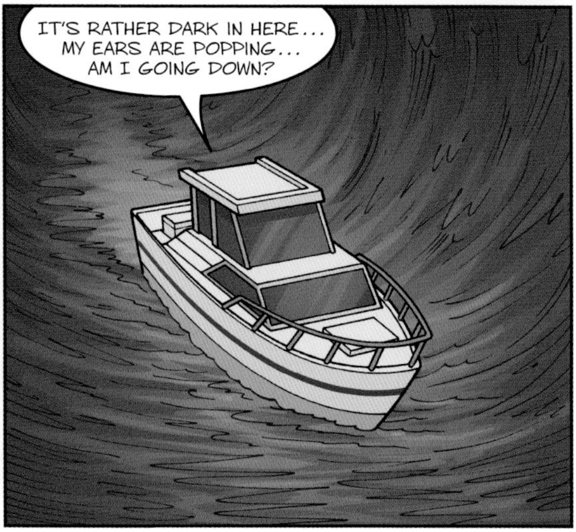
IT'S RATHER DARK IN HERE... MY EARS ARE POPPING... AM I GOING DOWN?

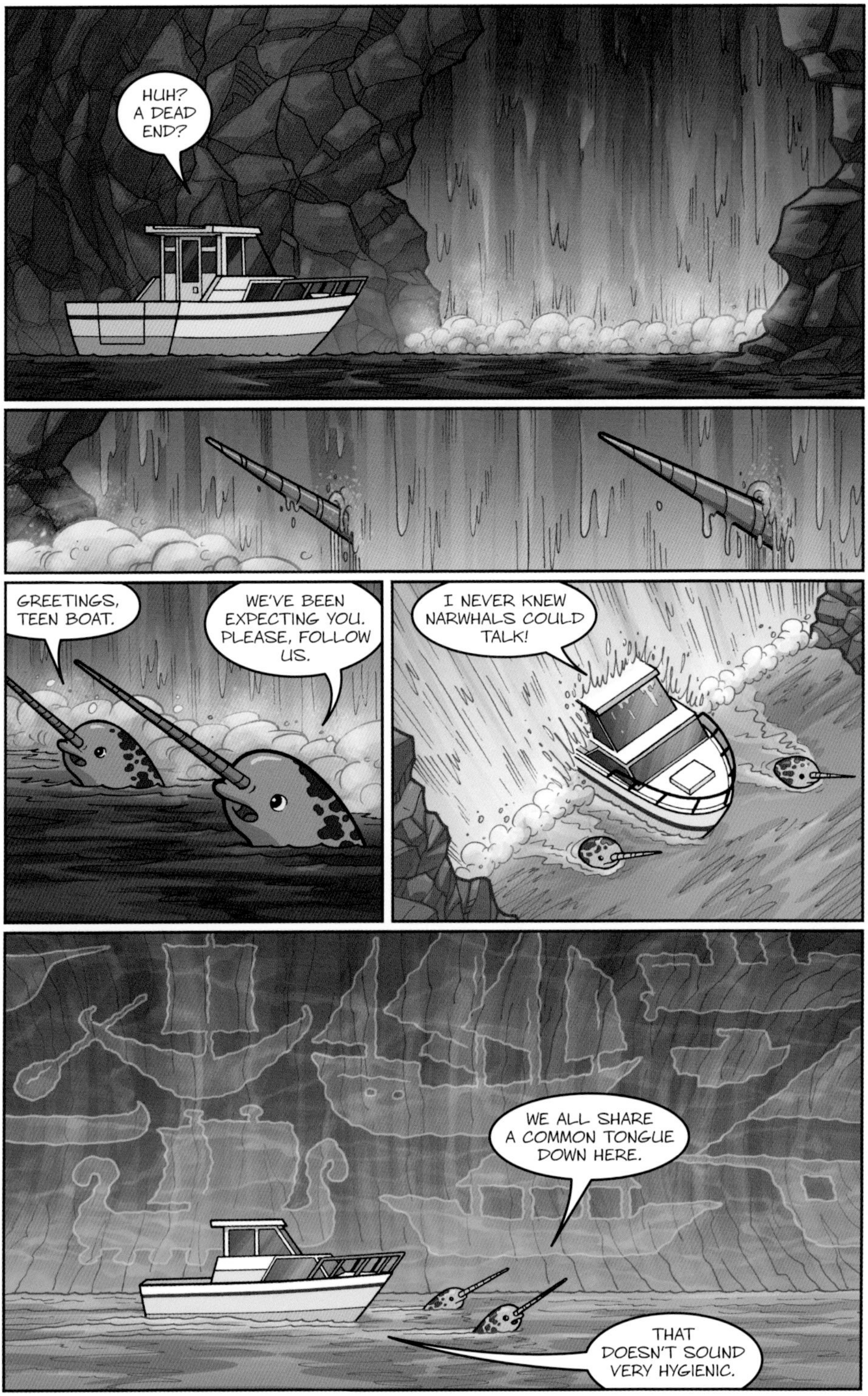
HUH? A DEAD END?
GREETINGS, TEEN BOAT.
WE'VE BEEN EXPECTING YOU. PLEASE, FOLLOW US.
I NEVER KNEW NARWHALS COULD TALK!
WE ALL SHARE A COMMON TONGUE DOWN HERE.
THAT DOESN'T SOUND VERY HYGIENIC.

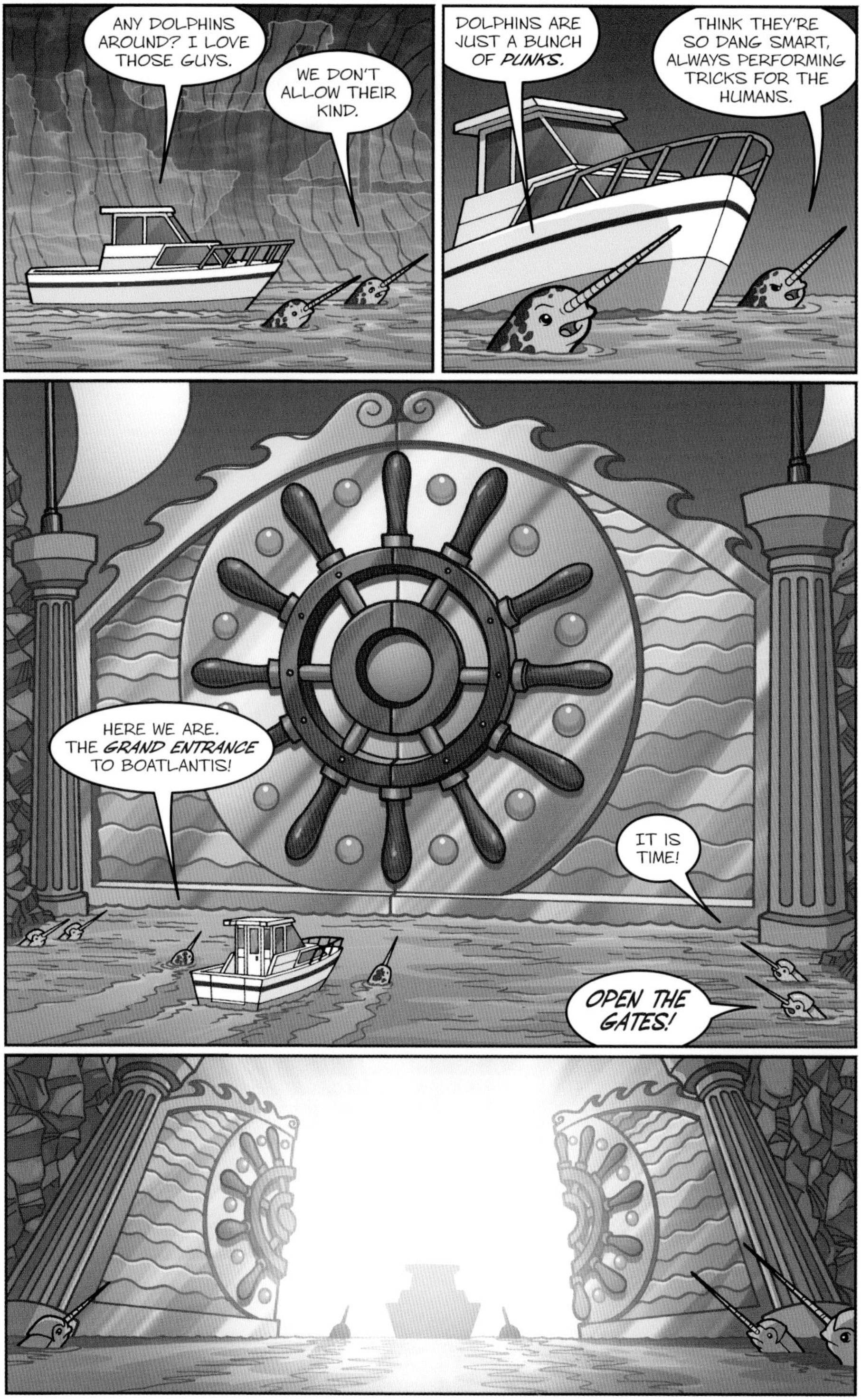
ANY DOLPHINS AROUND? I LOVE THOSE GUYS.
WE DON'T ALLOW THEIR KIND.
DOLPHINS ARE JUST A BUNCH OF PUNKS.
THINK THEY'RE SO DANG SMART, ALWAYS PERFORMING TRICKS FOR THE HUMANS.
HERE WE ARE. THE GRAND ENTRANCE TO BOATLANTIS!
IT IS TIME!
OPEN THE GATES!

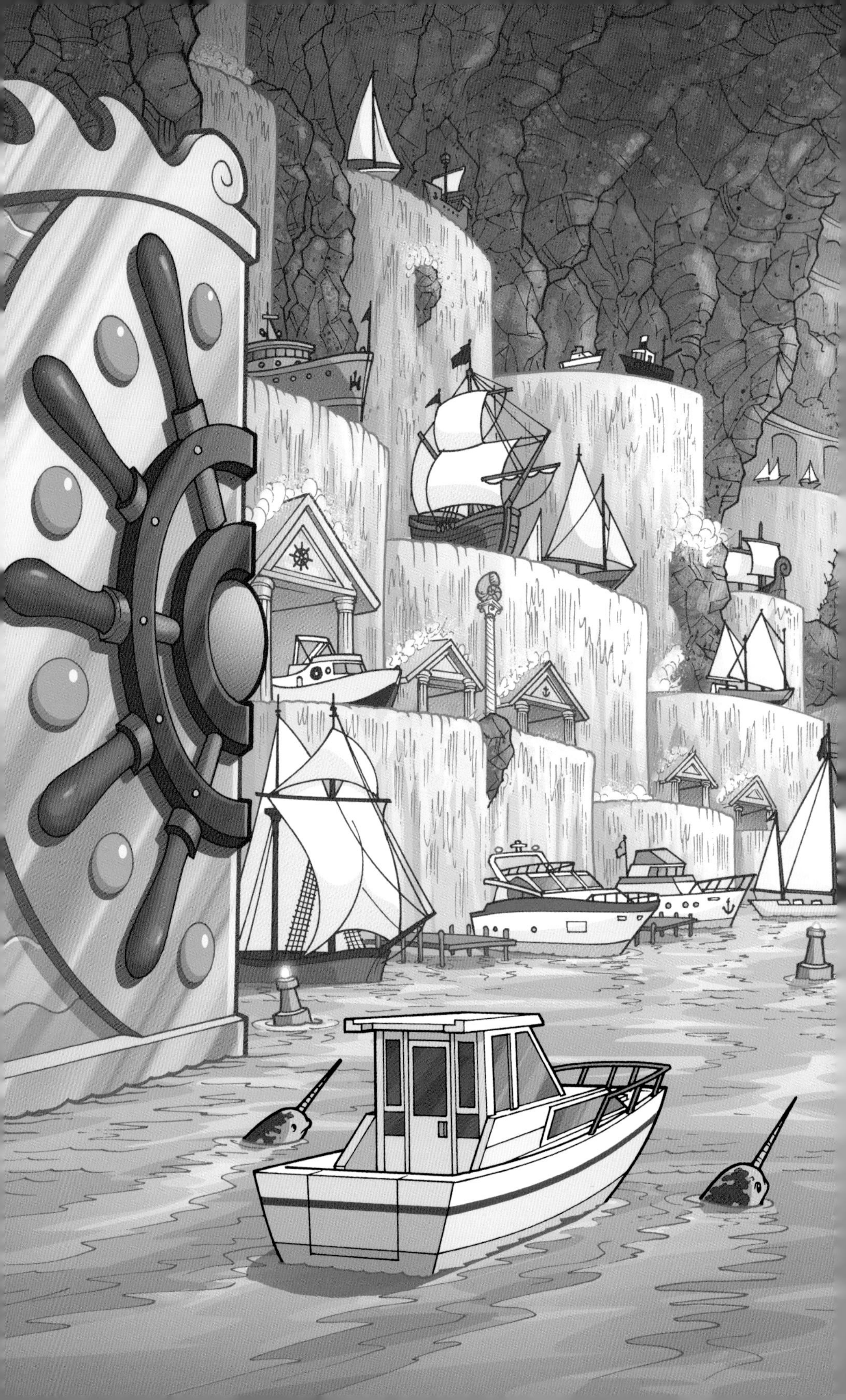

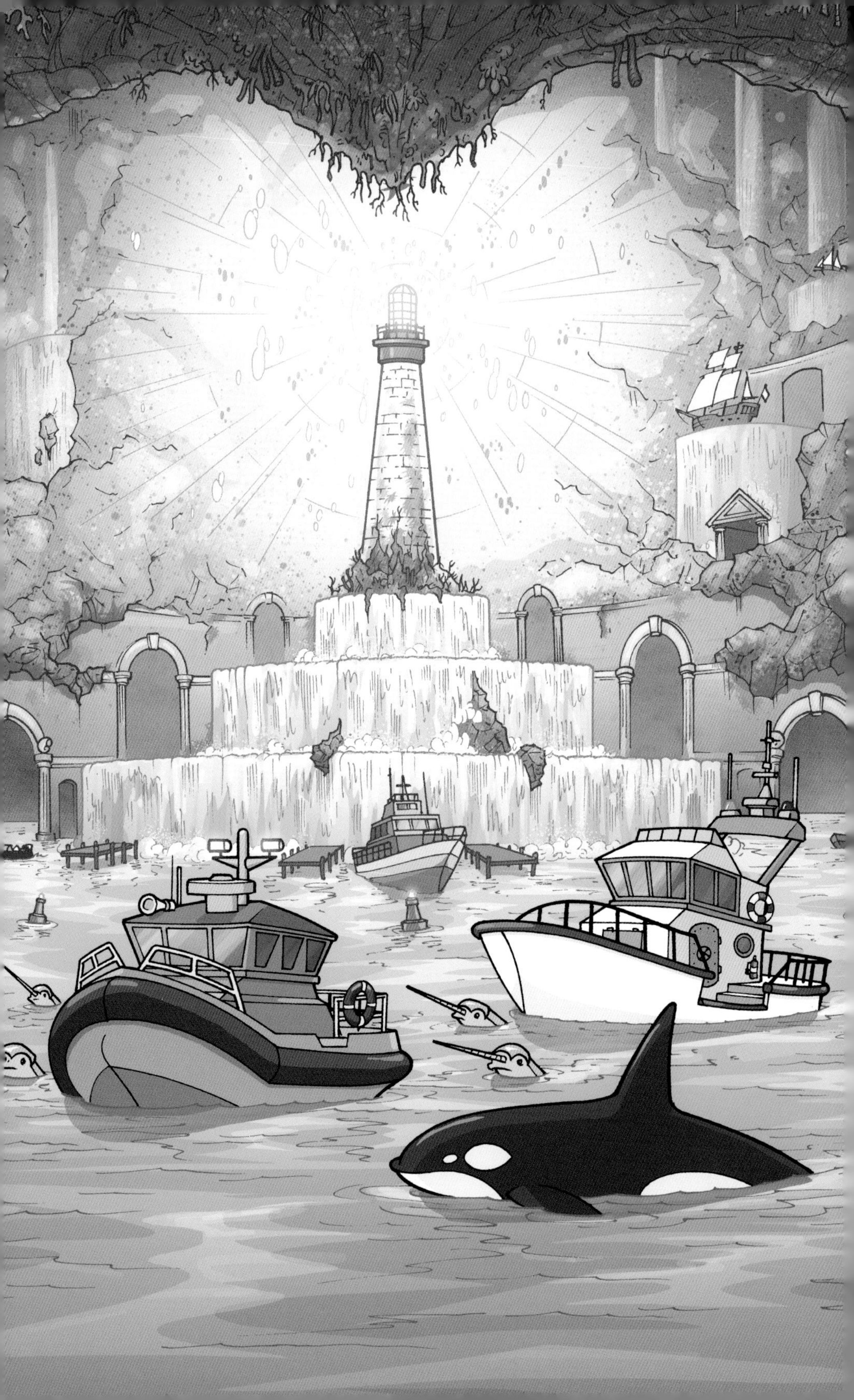

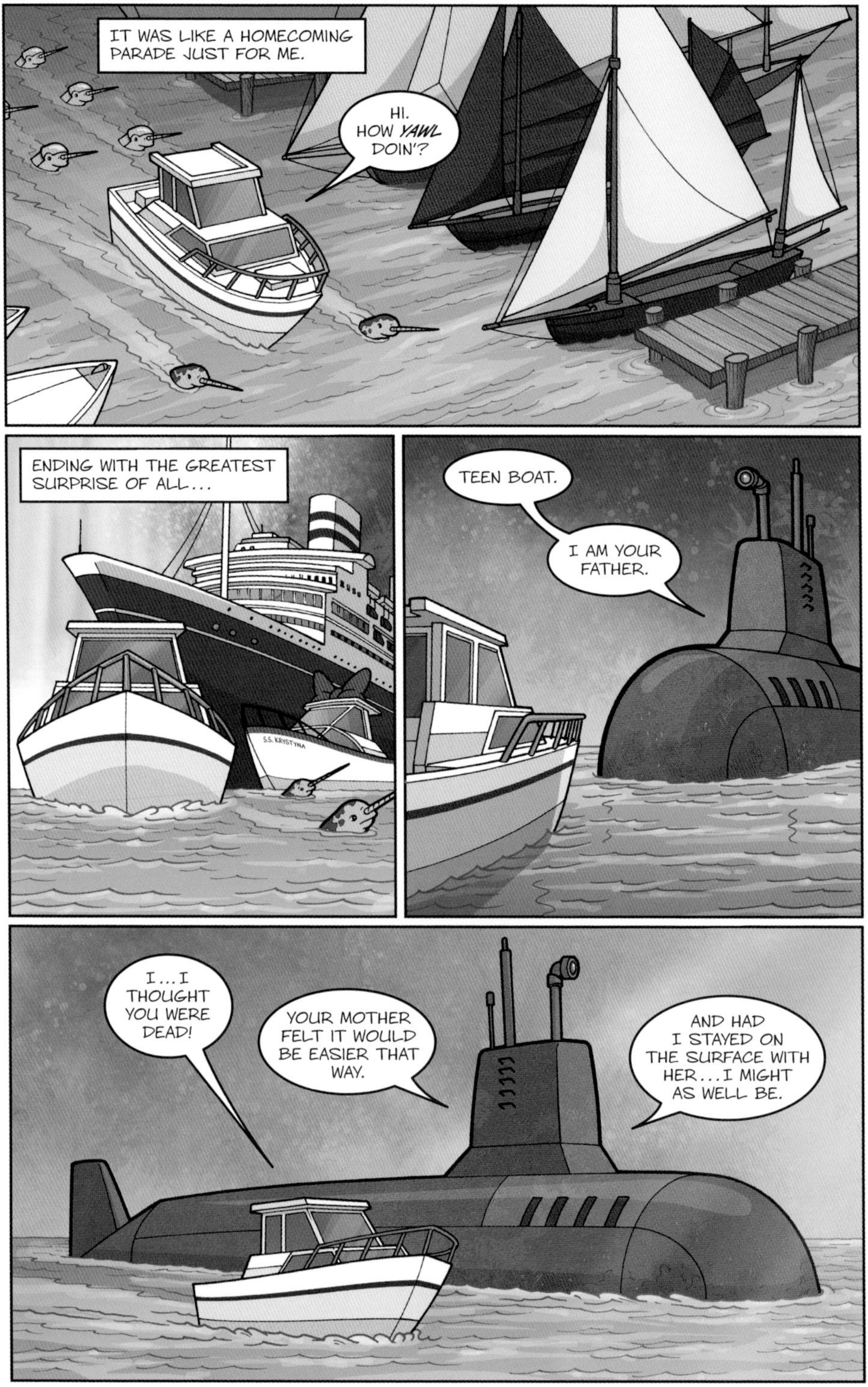
IT WAS LIKE A HOMECOMING PARADE JUST FOR ME.
HI. HOW YAWL DOIN'?
ENDING WITH THE GREATEST SURPRISE OF ALL...
S.S. KRYSTYNA
TEEN BOAT.
I AM YOUR FATHER.
I...I THOUGHT YOU WERE DEAD!
YOUR MOTHER FELT IT WOULD BE EASIER THAT WAY.
AND HAD I STAYED ON THE SURFACE WITH HER...I MIGHT AS WELL BE.

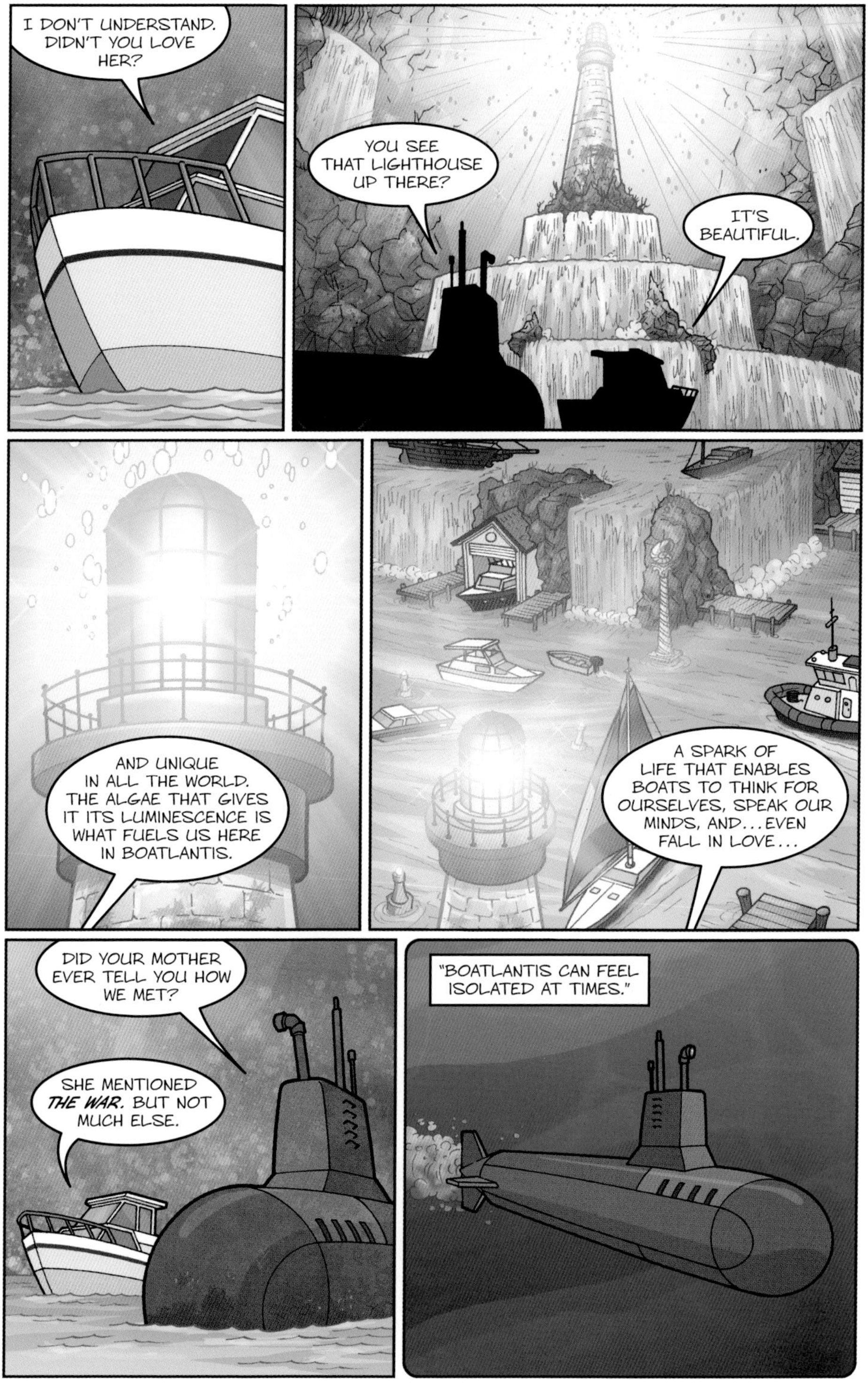

I DON'T UNDERSTAND. DIDN'T YOU LOVE HER?
YOU SEE THAT LIGHTHOUSE UP THERE?
IT'S BEAUTIFUL.
AND UNIQUE IN ALL THE WORLD. THE ALGAE THAT GIVES IT ITS LUMINESCENCE IS WHAT FUELS US HERE IN BOATLANTIS.
A SPARK OF LIFE THAT ENABLES BOATS TO THINK FOR OURSELVES, SPEAK OUR MINDS, AND...EVEN FALL IN LOVE...
DID YOUR MOTHER EVER TELL YOU HOW WE MET?
SHE MENTIONED *THE WAR.* BUT NOT MUCH ELSE.
"BOATLANTIS CAN FEEL ISOLATED AT TIMES."

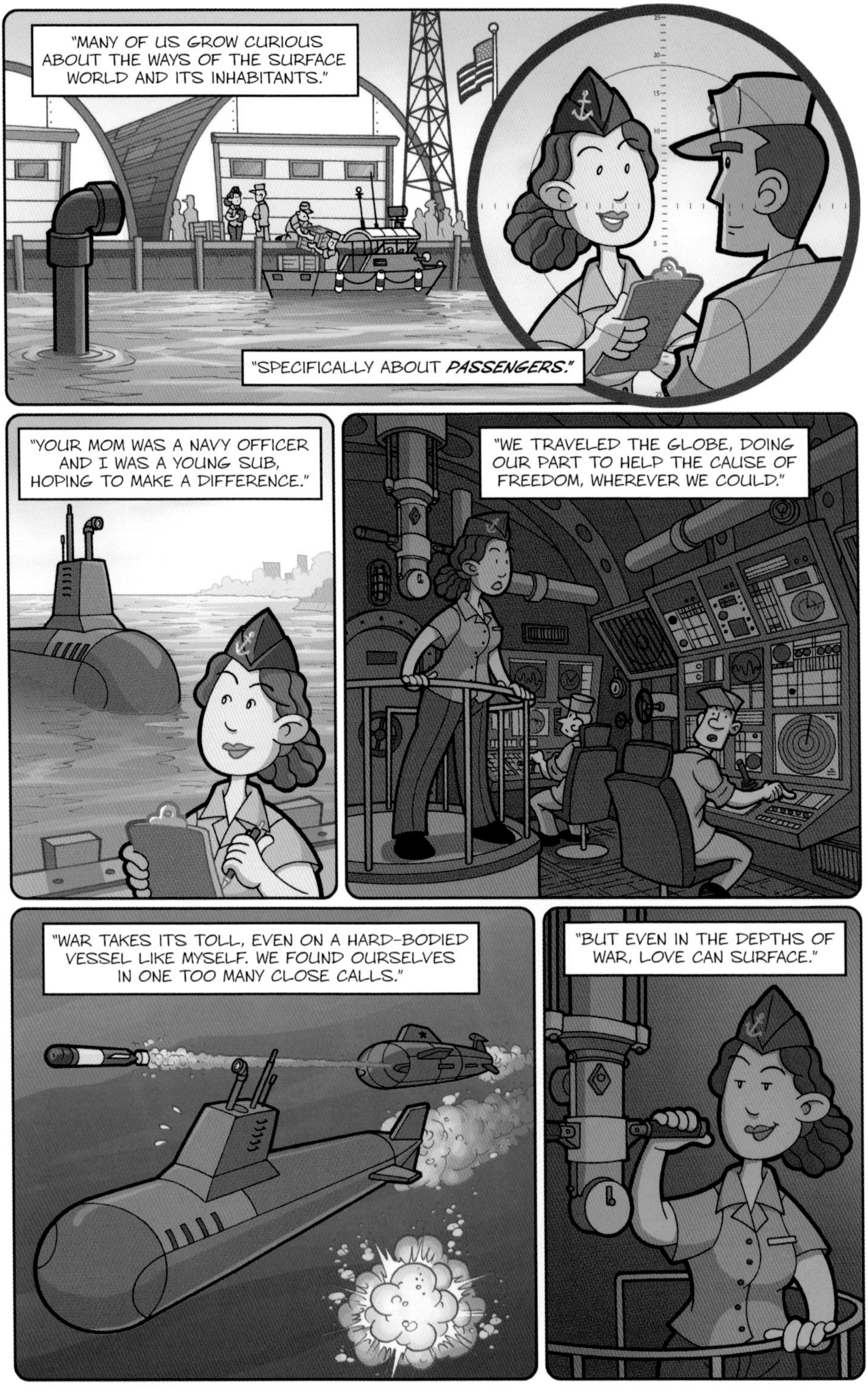
"MANY OF US GROW CURIOUS ABOUT THE WAYS OF THE SURFACE WORLD AND ITS INHABITANTS."
"SPECIFICALLY ABOUT *PASSENGERS.*"
"YOUR MOM WAS A NAVY OFFICER AND I WAS A YOUNG SUB, HOPING TO MAKE A DIFFERENCE."
"WE TRAVELED THE GLOBE, DOING OUR PART TO HELP THE CAUSE OF FREEDOM, WHEREVER WE COULD."
"WAR TAKES ITS TOLL, EVEN ON A HARD-BODIED VESSEL LIKE MYSELF. WE FOUND OURSELVES IN ONE TOO MANY CLOSE CALLS."
"BUT EVEN IN THE DEPTHS OF WAR, LOVE CAN SURFACE."

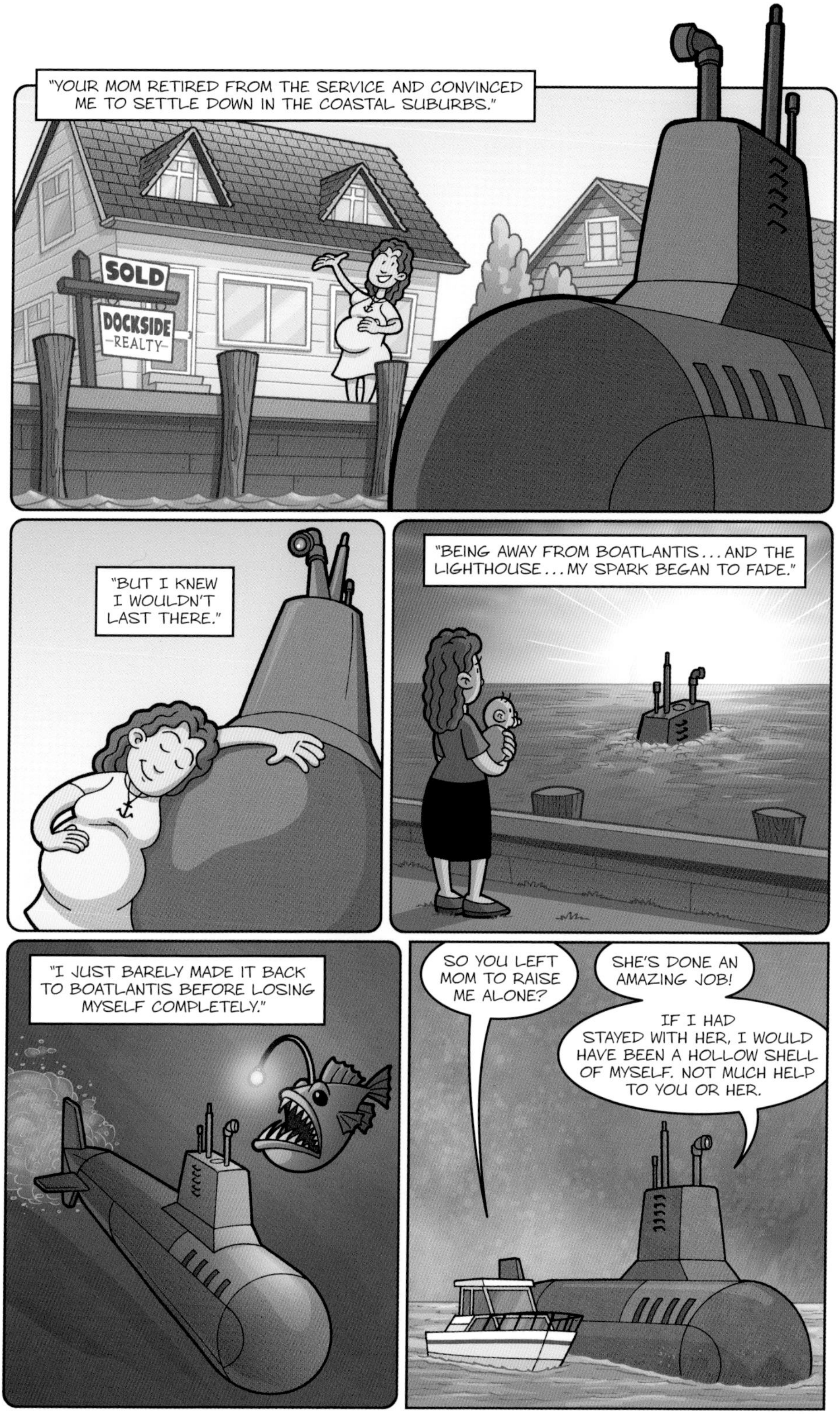
"YOUR MOM RETIRED FROM THE SERVICE AND CONVINCED ME TO SETTLE DOWN IN THE COASTAL SUBURBS."
SOLD
DOCKSIDE REALTY
"BUT I KNEW I WOULDN'T LAST THERE."
"BEING AWAY FROM BOATLANTIS... AND THE LIGHTHOUSE... MY SPARK BEGAN TO FADE."
"I JUST BARELY MADE IT BACK TO BOATLANTIS BEFORE LOSING MYSELF COMPLETELY."
SO YOU LEFT MOM TO RAISE ME ALONE?
SHE'S DONE AN AMAZING JOB!
IF I HAD STAYED WITH HER, I WOULD HAVE BEEN A HOLLOW SHELL OF MYSELF. NOT MUCH HELP TO YOU OR HER.

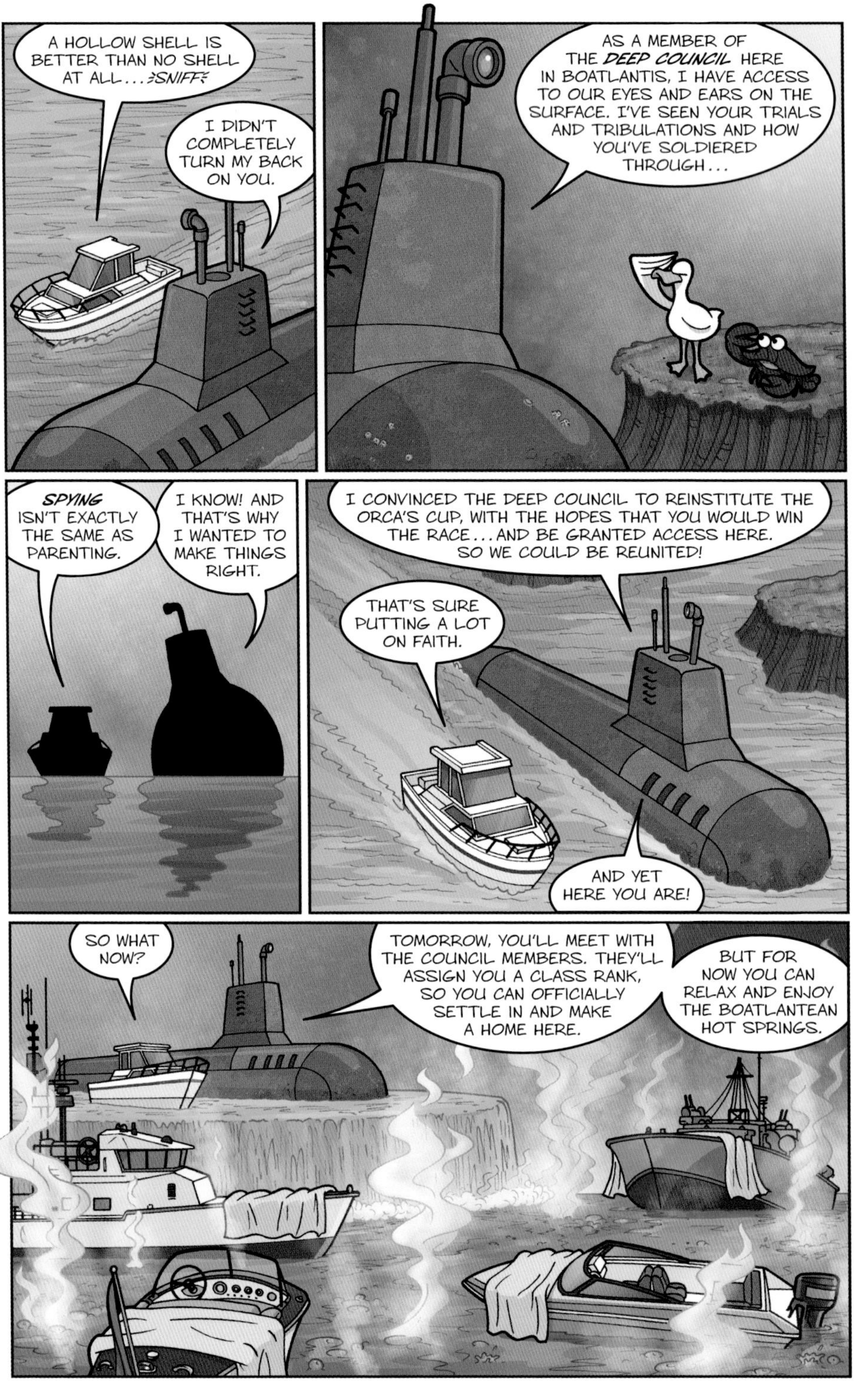
A HOLLOW SHELL IS BETTER THAN NO SHELL AT ALL... SNIFF
I DIDN'T COMPLETELY TURN MY BACK ON YOU.
AS A MEMBER OF THE DEEP COUNCIL HERE IN BOATLANTIS, I HAVE ACCESS TO OUR EYES AND EARS ON THE SURFACE. I'VE SEEN YOUR TRIALS AND TRIBULATIONS AND HOW YOU'VE SOLDIERED THROUGH...
SPYING ISN'T EXACTLY THE SAME AS PARENTING.
I KNOW! AND THAT'S WHY I WANTED TO MAKE THINGS RIGHT.
I CONVINCED THE DEEP COUNCIL TO REINSTITUTE THE ORCA'S CUP, WITH THE HOPES THAT YOU WOULD WIN THE RACE... AND BE GRANTED ACCESS HERE. SO WE COULD BE REUNITED!
THAT'S SURE PUTTING A LOT ON FAITH.
AND YET HERE YOU ARE!
SO WHAT NOW?
TOMORROW, YOU'LL MEET WITH THE COUNCIL MEMBERS. THEY'LL ASSIGN YOU A CLASS RANK, SO YOU CAN OFFICIALLY SETTLE IN AND MAKE A HOME HERE.
BUT FOR NOW YOU CAN RELAX AND ENJOY THE BOATLANTEAN HOT SPRINGS.

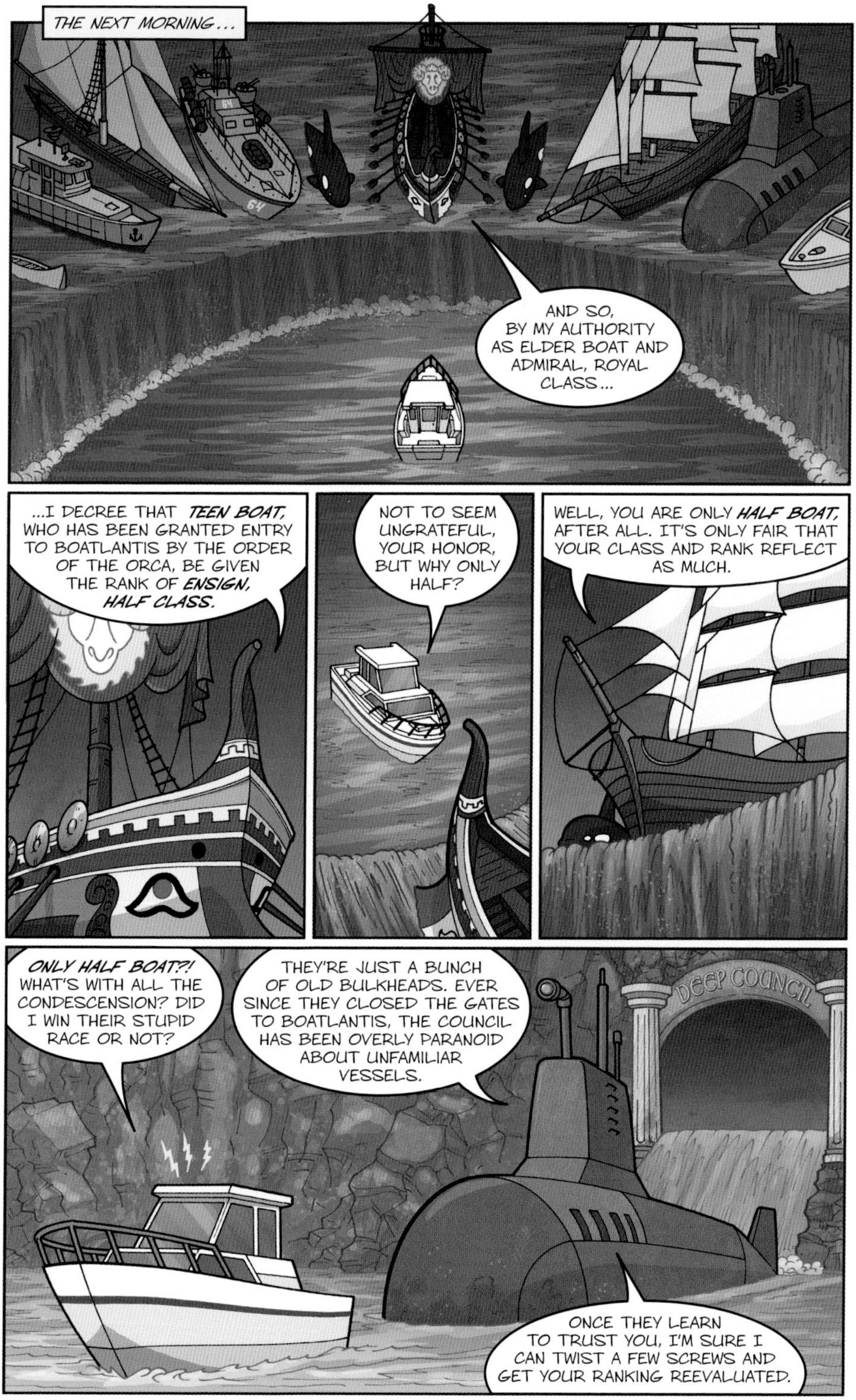
THE NEXT MORNING...
AND SO, BY MY AUTHORITY AS ELDER BOAT AND ADMIRAL, ROYAL CLASS...
...I DECREE THAT *TEEN BOAT,* WHO HAS BEEN GRANTED ENTRY TO BOATLANTIS BY THE ORDER OF THE ORCA, BE GIVEN THE RANK OF *ENSIGN, HALF CLASS.*
NOT TO SEEM UNGRATEFUL, YOUR HONOR, BUT WHY ONLY HALF?
WELL, YOU ARE ONLY *HALF BOAT,* AFTER ALL. IT'S ONLY FAIR THAT YOUR CLASS AND RANK REFLECT AS MUCH.
ONLY HALF BOAT?! WHAT'S WITH ALL THE CONDESCENSION? DID I WIN THEIR STUPID RACE OR NOT?
THEY'RE JUST A BUNCH OF OLD BULKHEADS. EVER SINCE THEY CLOSED THE GATES TO BOATLANTIS, THE COUNCIL HAS BEEN OVERLY PARANOID ABOUT UNFAMILIAR VESSELS.
DEEP COUNCIL
ONCE THEY LEARN TO TRUST YOU, I'M SURE I CAN TWIST A FEW SCREWS AND GET YOUR RANKING REEVALUATED.

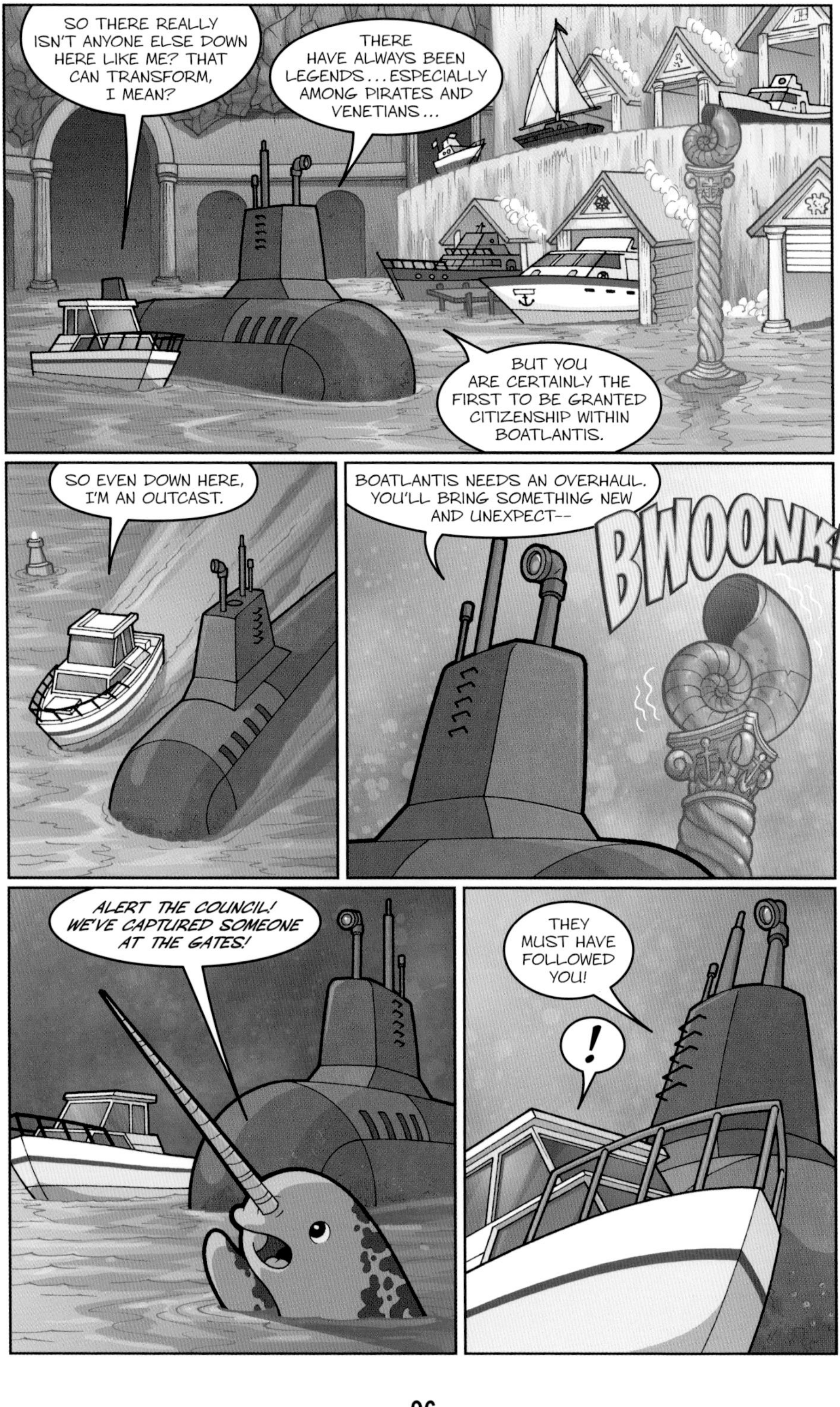
SO THERE REALLY ISN'T ANYONE ELSE DOWN HERE LIKE ME? THAT CAN TRANSFORM, I MEAN?
THERE HAVE ALWAYS BEEN LEGENDS... ESPECIALLY AMONG PIRATES AND VENETIANS...
BUT YOU ARE CERTAINLY THE FIRST TO BE GRANTED CITIZENSHIP WITHIN BOATLANTIS.
SO EVEN DOWN HERE, I'M AN OUTCAST.
BOATLANTIS NEEDS AN OVERHAUL. YOU'LL BRING SOMETHING NEW AND UNEXPECT--
BWOONK!
ALERT THE COUNCIL! WE'VE CAPTURED SOMEONE AT THE GATES!
THEY MUST HAVE FOLLOWED YOU!
!

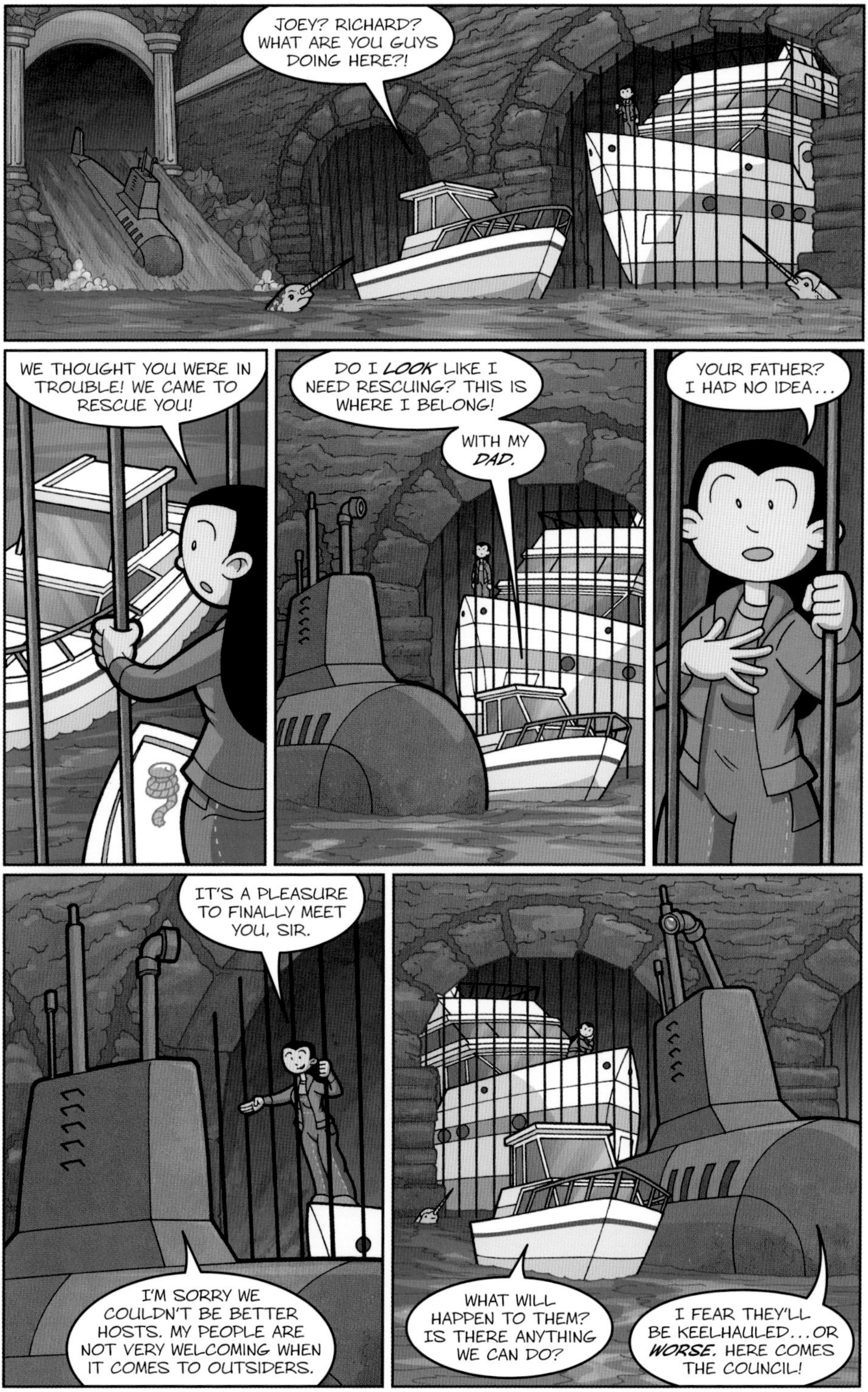
JOEY? RICHARD? WHAT ARE YOU GUYS DOING HERE?!
WE THOUGHT YOU WERE IN TROUBLE! WE CAME TO RESCUE YOU!
DO I *LOOK* LIKE I NEED RESCUING? THIS IS WHERE I BELONG!
WITH MY *DAD.*
YOUR FATHER? I HAD NO IDEA...
IT'S A PLEASURE TO FINALLY MEET YOU, SIR.
I'M SORRY WE COULDN'T BE BETTER HOSTS. MY PEOPLE ARE NOT VERY WELCOMING WHEN IT COMES TO OUTSIDERS.
WHAT WILL HAPPEN TO THEM? IS THERE ANYTHING WE CAN DO?
I FEAR THEY'LL BE KEELHAULED...OR *WORSE.* HERE COMES THE COUNCIL!

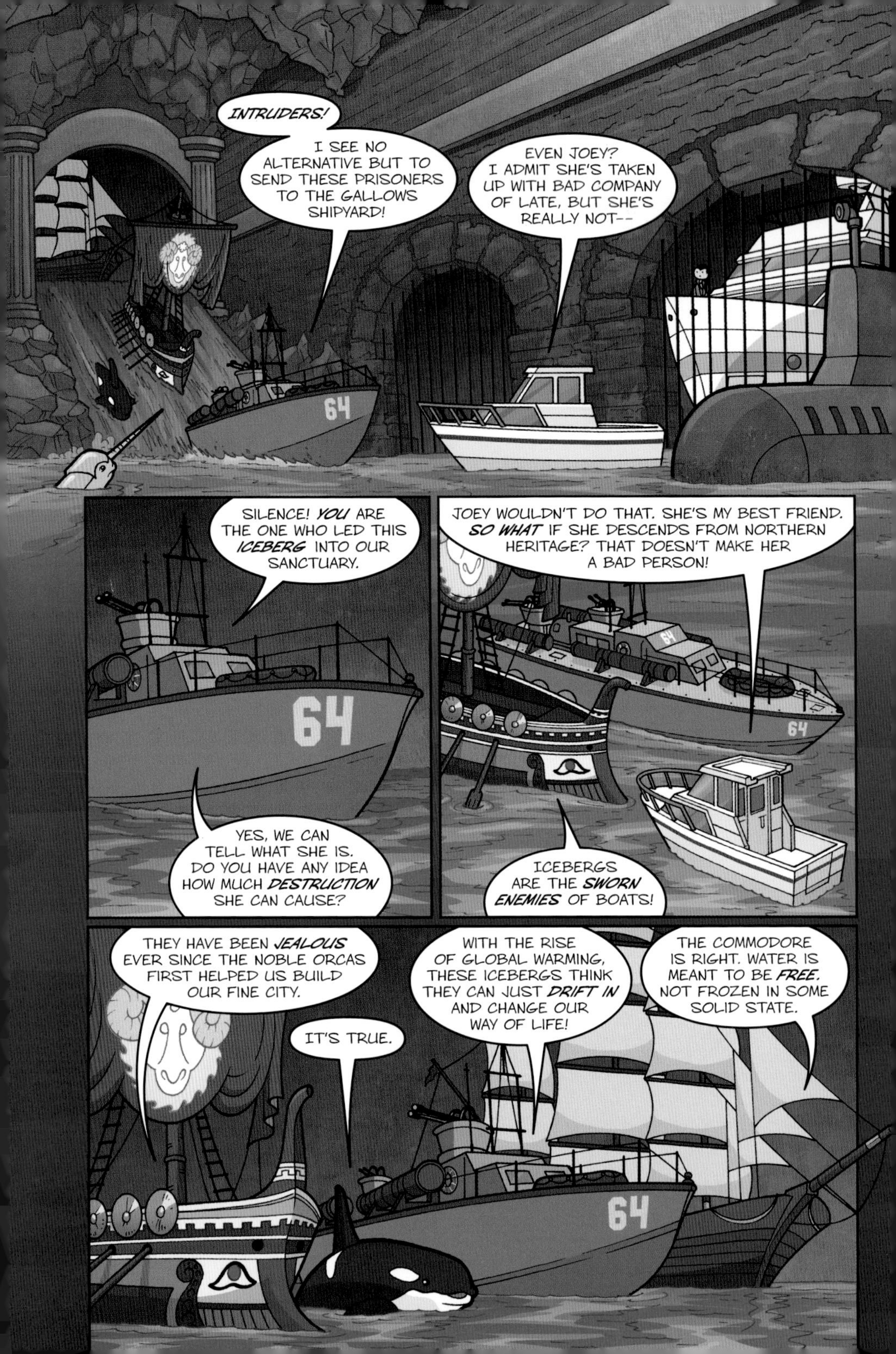
INTRUDERS!
I SEE NO ALTERNATIVE BUT TO SEND THESE PRISONERS TO THE GALLOWS SHIPYARD!
EVEN JOEY? I ADMIT SHE'S TAKEN UP WITH BAD COMPANY OF LATE, BUT SHE'S REALLY NOT--
64
SILENCE! YOU ARE THE ONE WHO LED THIS ICEBERG INTO OUR SANCTUARY.
64
YES, WE CAN TELL WHAT SHE IS. DO YOU HAVE ANY IDEA HOW MUCH DESTRUCTION SHE CAN CAUSE?
JOEY WOULDN'T DO THAT. SHE'S MY BEST FRIEND. SO WHAT IF SHE DESCENDS FROM NORTHERN HERITAGE? THAT DOESN'T MAKE HER A BAD PERSON!
64
ICEBERGS ARE THE SWORN ENEMIES OF BOATS!
THEY HAVE BEEN JEALOUS EVER SINCE THE NOBLE ORCAS FIRST HELPED US BUILD OUR FINE CITY.
IT'S TRUE.
WITH THE RISE OF GLOBAL WARMING, THESE ICEBERGS THINK THEY CAN JUST DRIFT IN AND CHANGE OUR WAY OF LIFE!
THE COMMODORE IS RIGHT. WATER IS MEANT TO BE FREE, NOT FROZEN IN SOME SOLID STATE.
64

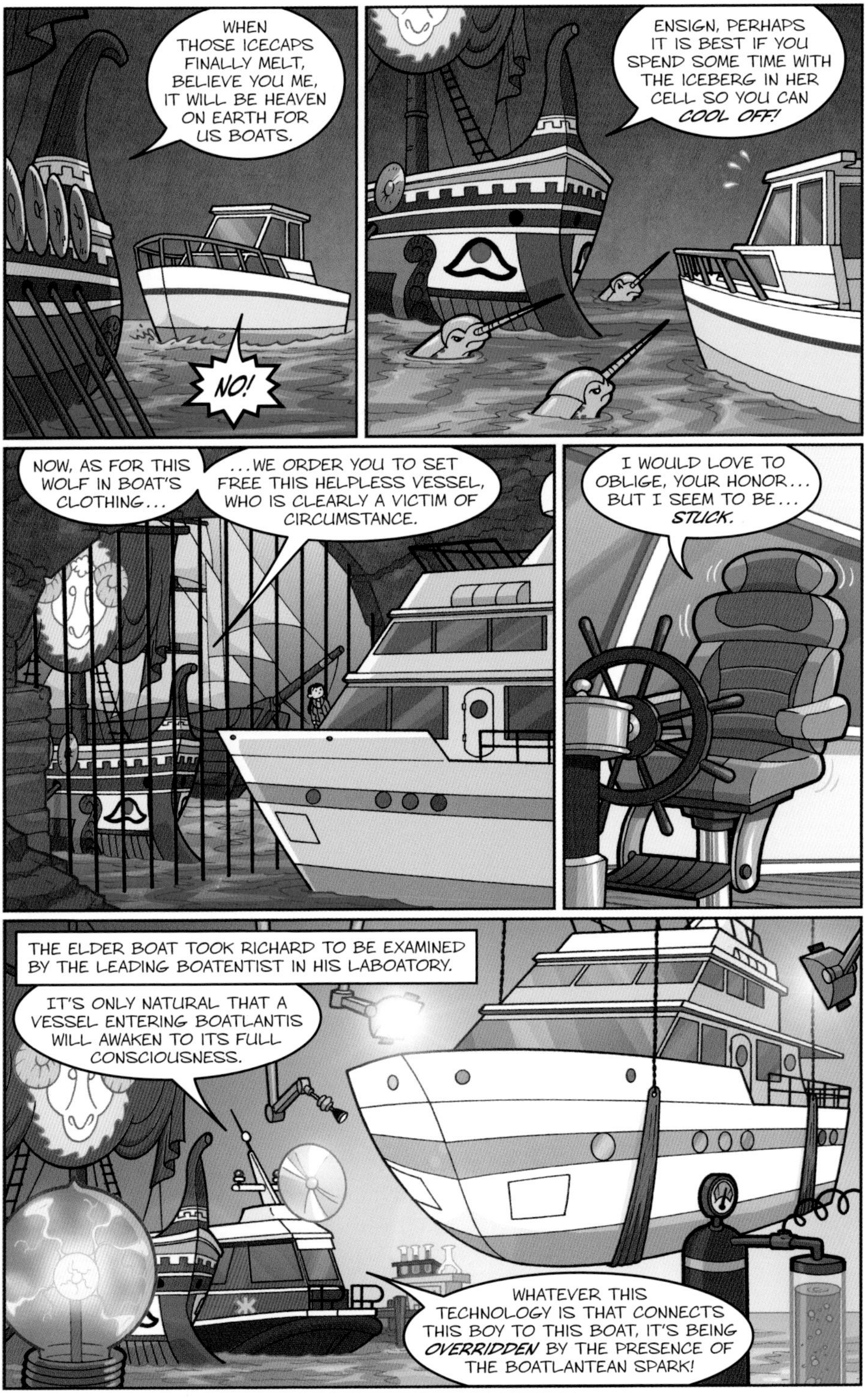
WHEN THOSE ICECAPS FINALLY MELT, BELIEVE YOU ME, IT WILL BE HEAVEN ON EARTH FOR US BOATS.
NO!
ENSIGN, PERHAPS IT IS BEST IF YOU SPEND SOME TIME WITH THE ICEBERG IN HER CELL SO YOU CAN *COOL OFF!*
NOW, AS FOR THIS WOLF IN BOAT'S CLOTHING...
...WE ORDER YOU TO SET FREE THIS HELPLESS VESSEL, WHO IS CLEARLY A VICTIM OF CIRCUMSTANCE.
I WOULD LOVE TO OBLIGE, YOUR HONOR... BUT I SEEM TO BE... *STUCK.*
THE ELDER BOAT TOOK RICHARD TO BE EXAMINED BY THE LEADING BOATENTIST IN HIS LABOATORY.
IT'S ONLY NATURAL THAT A VESSEL ENTERING BOATLANTIS WILL AWAKEN TO ITS FULL CONSCIOUSNESS.
WHATEVER THIS TECHNOLOGY IS THAT CONNECTS THIS BOY TO THIS BOAT, IT'S BEING *OVERRIDDEN* BY THE PRESENCE OF THE BOATLANTEAN SPARK!

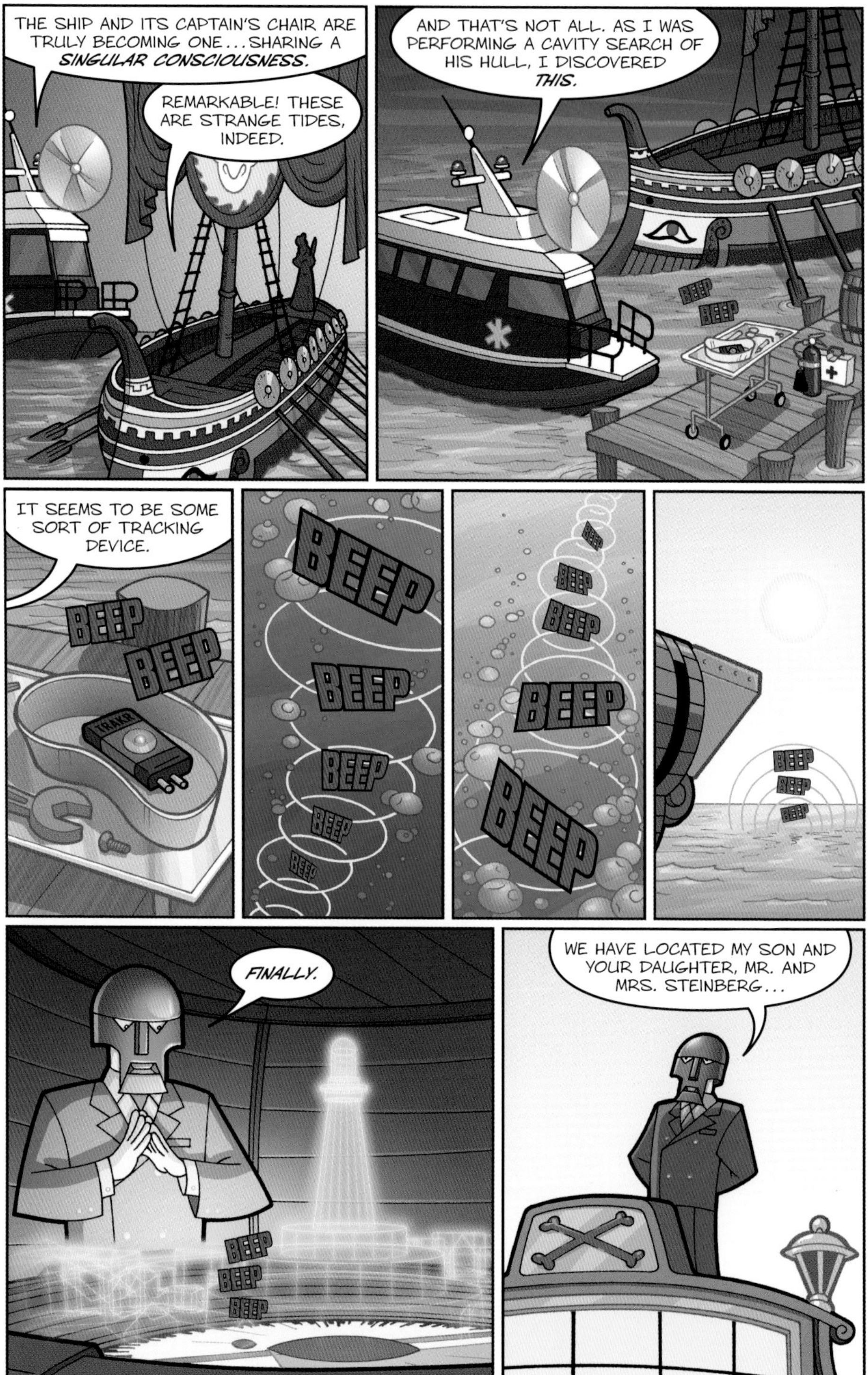
THE SHIP AND ITS CAPTAIN'S CHAIR ARE TRULY BECOMING ONE . . . SHARING A *SINGULAR CONSCIOUSNESS.*
REMARKABLE! THESE ARE STRANGE TIDES, INDEED.
AND THAT'S NOT ALL. AS I WAS PERFORMING A CAVITY SEARCH OF HIS HULL, I DISCOVERED *THIS.*
BEEP
BEEP
IT SEEMS TO BE SOME SORT OF TRACKING DEVICE.
BEEP
BEEP
TRAKR
BEEP
BEEP
BEEP
BEEP
BEEP
BEEP
BEEP
BEEP
BEEP
BEEP
BEEP
BEEP
BEEP
FINALLY.
BEEP
BEEP
BEEP
WE HAVE LOCATED MY SON AND YOUR DAUGHTER, MR. AND MRS. STEINBERG . . .

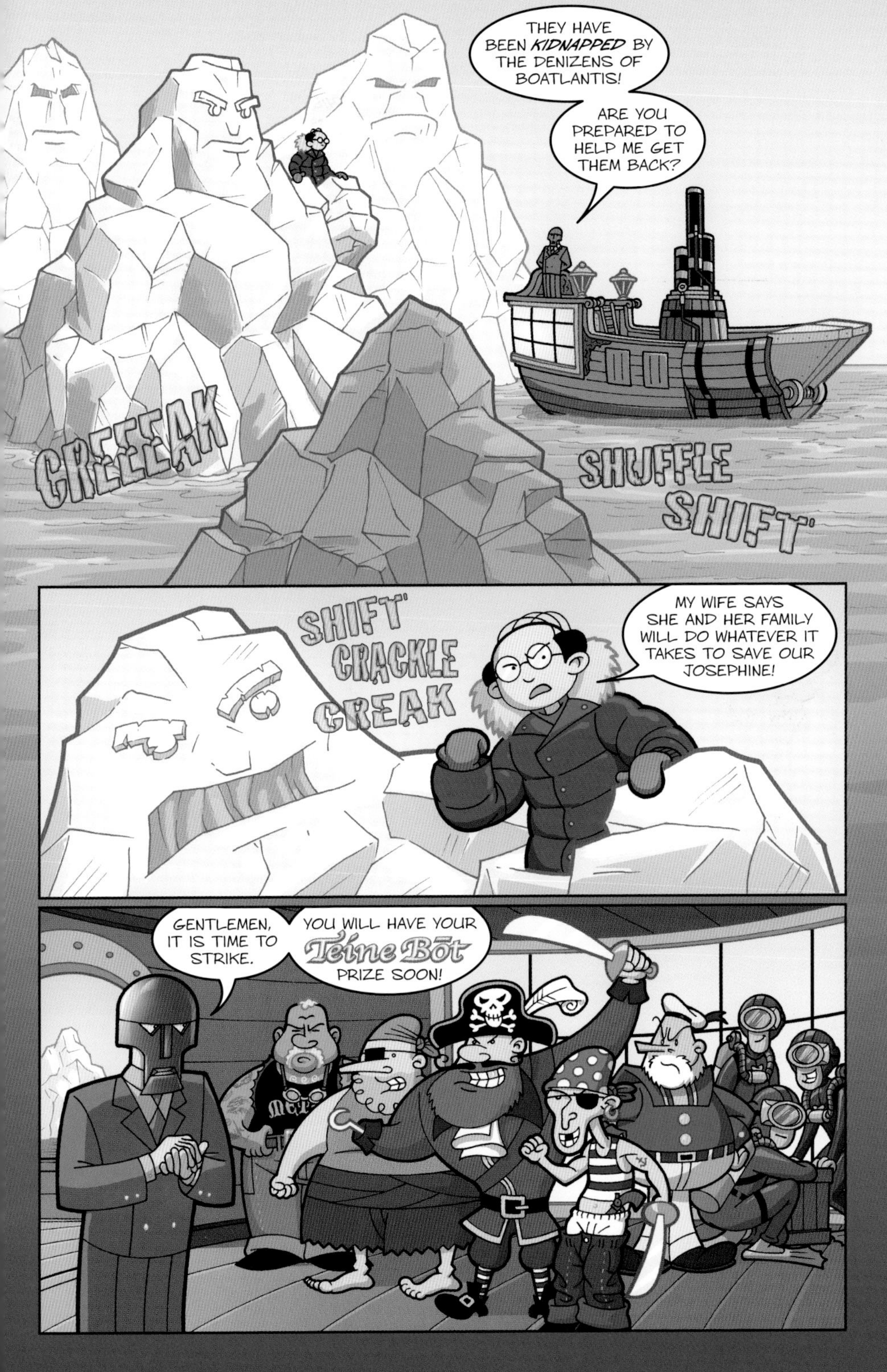
THEY HAVE BEEN KIDNAPPED BY THE DENIZENS OF BOATLANTIS!
ARE YOU PREPARED TO HELP ME GET THEM BACK?
CREEEAK
SHUFFLE
SHIFT
SHIFT
CRACKLE
CREAK
MY WIFE SAYS SHE AND HER FAMILY WILL DO WHATEVER IT TAKES TO SAVE OUR JOSEPHINE!
GENTLEMEN, IT IS TIME TO STRIKE.
YOU WILL HAVE YOUR Teine Bōt PRIZE SOON!

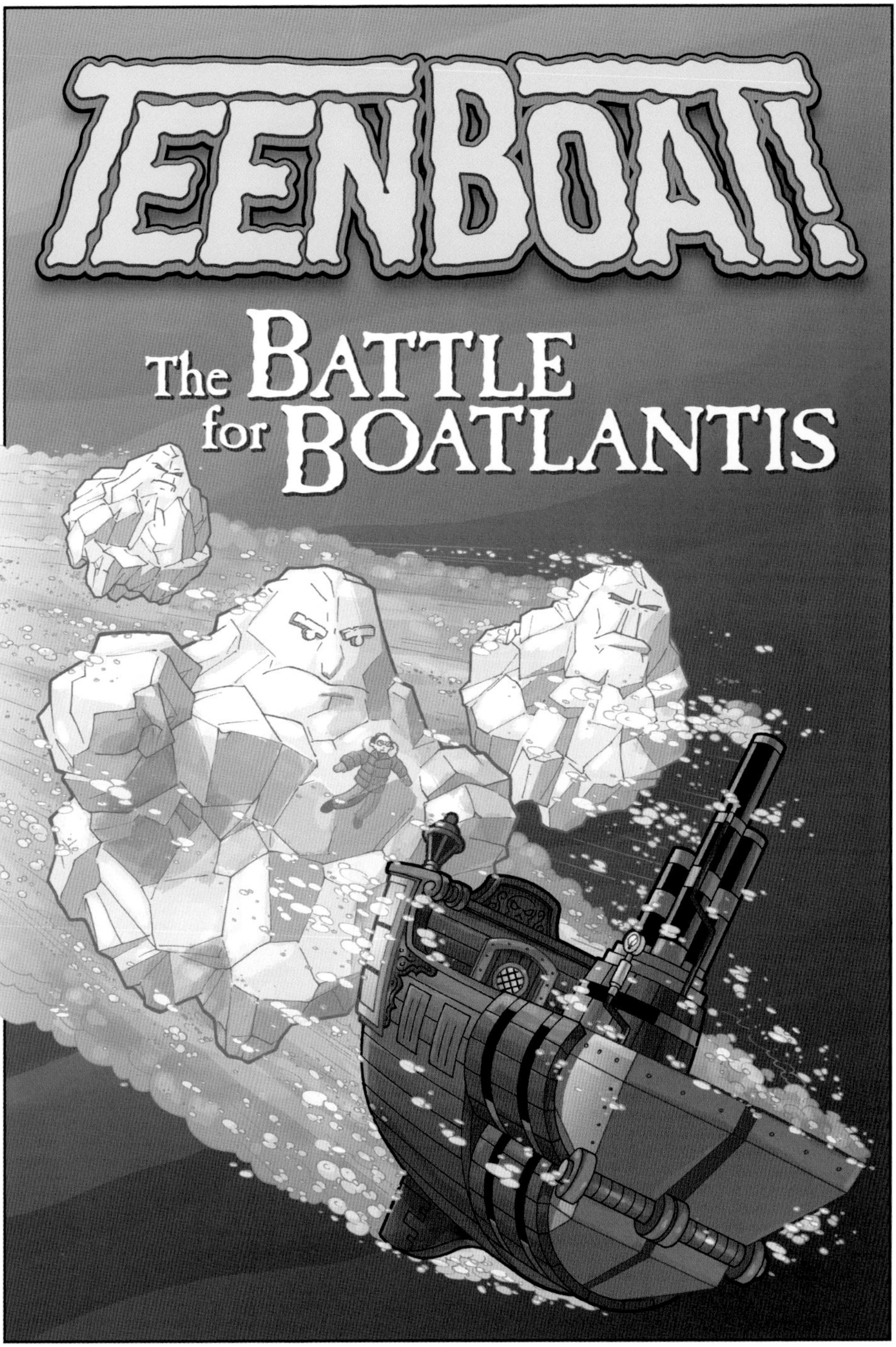
TEENBOAT!
The BATTLE for BOATLANTIS
The ***HERITAGE*** of being a Boat—the ***BATTLE*** for Survival!

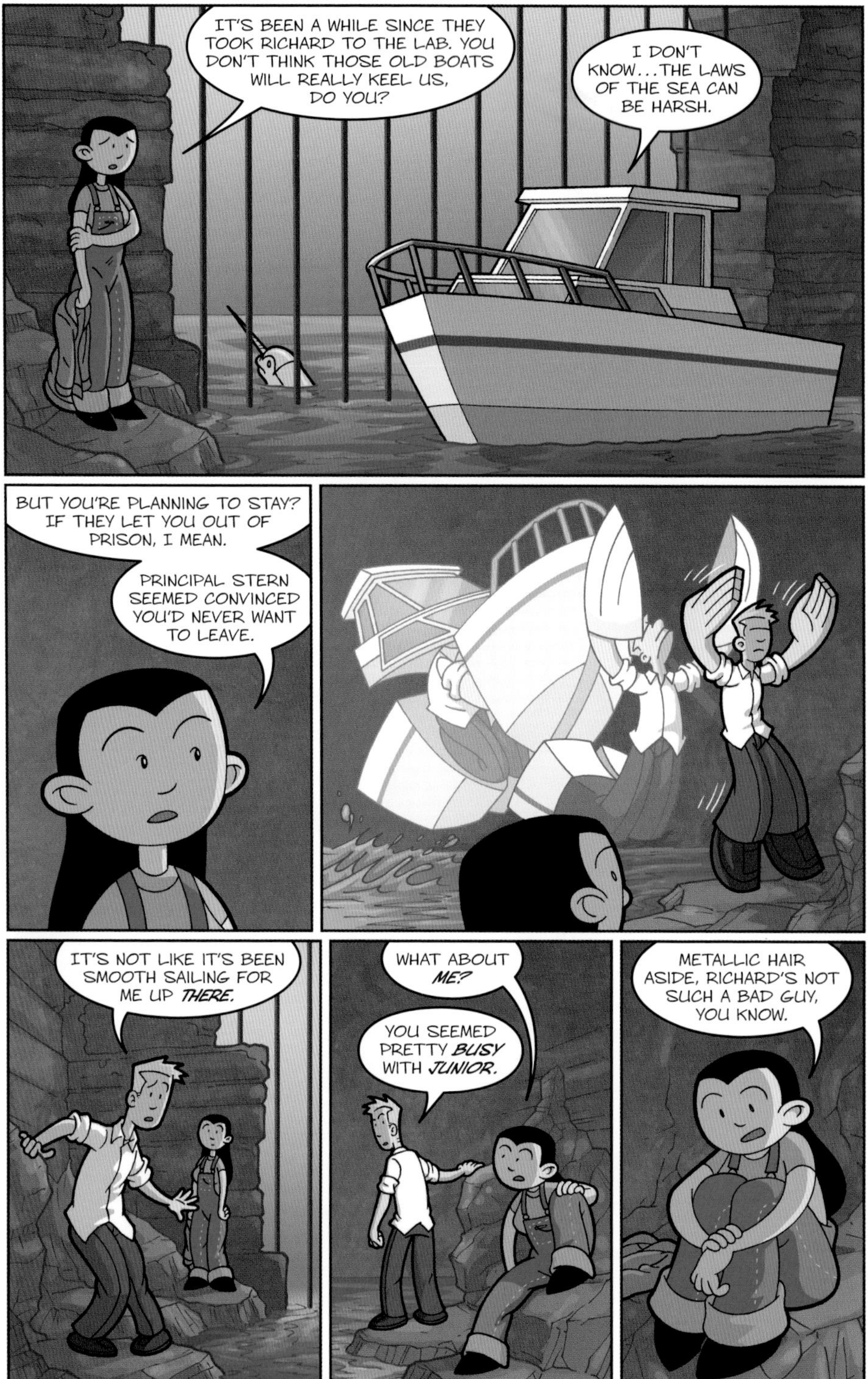
IT'S BEEN A WHILE SINCE THEY TOOK RICHARD TO THE LAB. YOU DON'T THINK THOSE OLD BOATS WILL REALLY KEEL US, DO YOU?
I DON'T KNOW...THE LAWS OF THE SEA CAN BE HARSH.
BUT YOU'RE PLANNING TO STAY? IF THEY LET YOU OUT OF PRISON, I MEAN.
PRINCIPAL STERN SEEMED CONVINCED YOU'D NEVER WANT TO LEAVE.
IT'S NOT LIKE IT'S BEEN SMOOTH SAILING FOR ME UP *THERE.*
WHAT ABOUT *ME?*
YOU SEEMED PRETTY *BUSY* WITH *JUNIOR.*
METALLIC HAIR ASIDE, RICHARD'S NOT SUCH A BAD GUY, YOU KNOW.

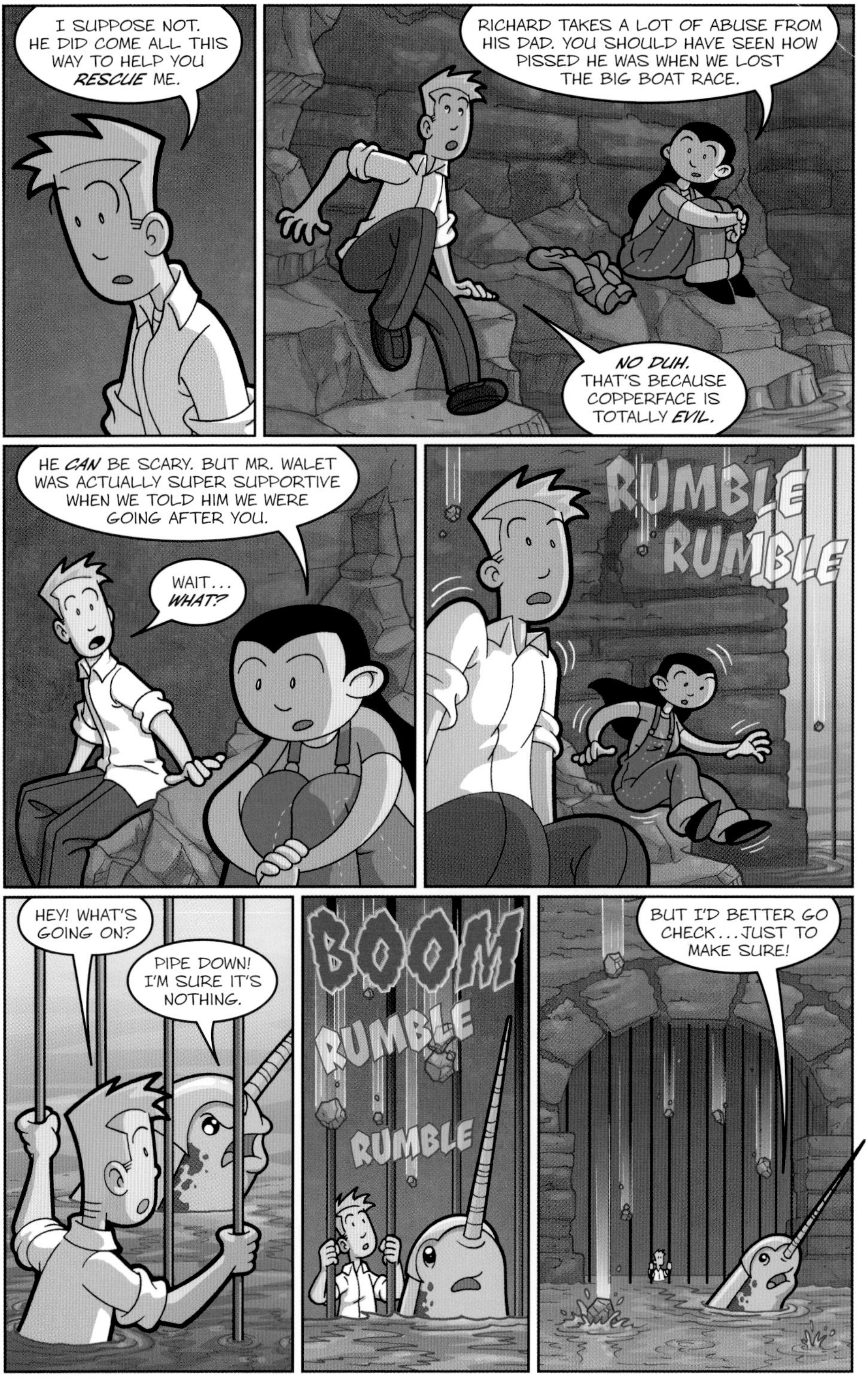
I SUPPOSE NOT. HE DID COME ALL THIS WAY TO HELP YOU *RESCUE* ME.
RICHARD TAKES A LOT OF ABUSE FROM HIS DAD. YOU SHOULD HAVE SEEN HOW PISSED HE WAS WHEN WE LOST THE BIG BOAT RACE.
NO DUH. THAT'S BECAUSE COPPERFACE IS TOTALLY *EVIL.*
HE *CAN* BE SCARY. BUT MR. WALET WAS ACTUALLY SUPER SUPPORTIVE WHEN WE TOLD HIM WE WERE GOING AFTER YOU.
WAIT... *WHAT?*
RUMBLE
RUMBLE
HEY! WHAT'S GOING ON?
PIPE DOWN! I'M SURE IT'S NOTHING.
BOOM
RUMBLE
RUMBLE
BUT I'D BETTER GO CHECK... JUST TO MAKE SURE!

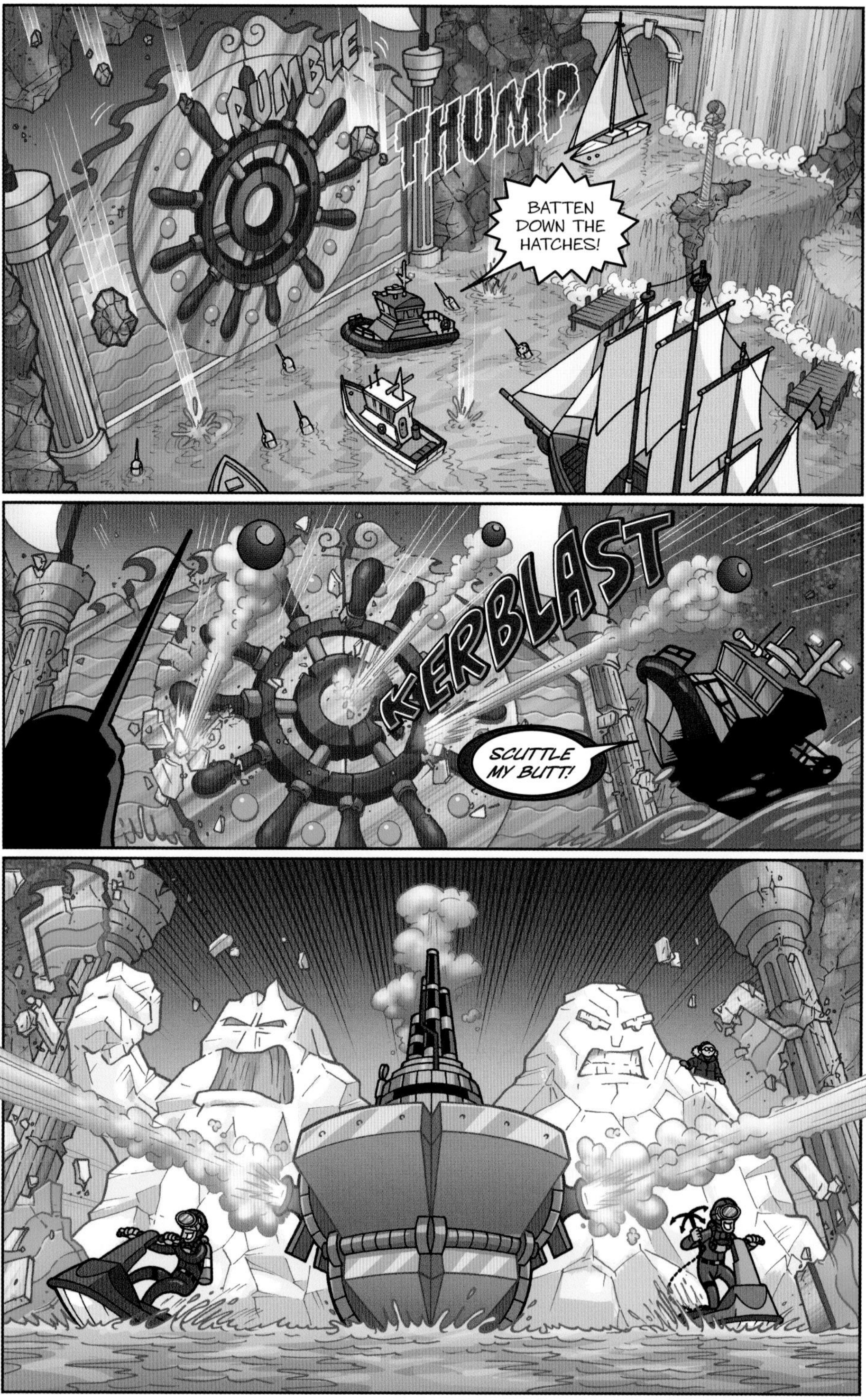
RUMBLE
THUMP
BATTEN DOWN THE HATCHES!
KERBLAST
SCUTTLE MY BUTT!

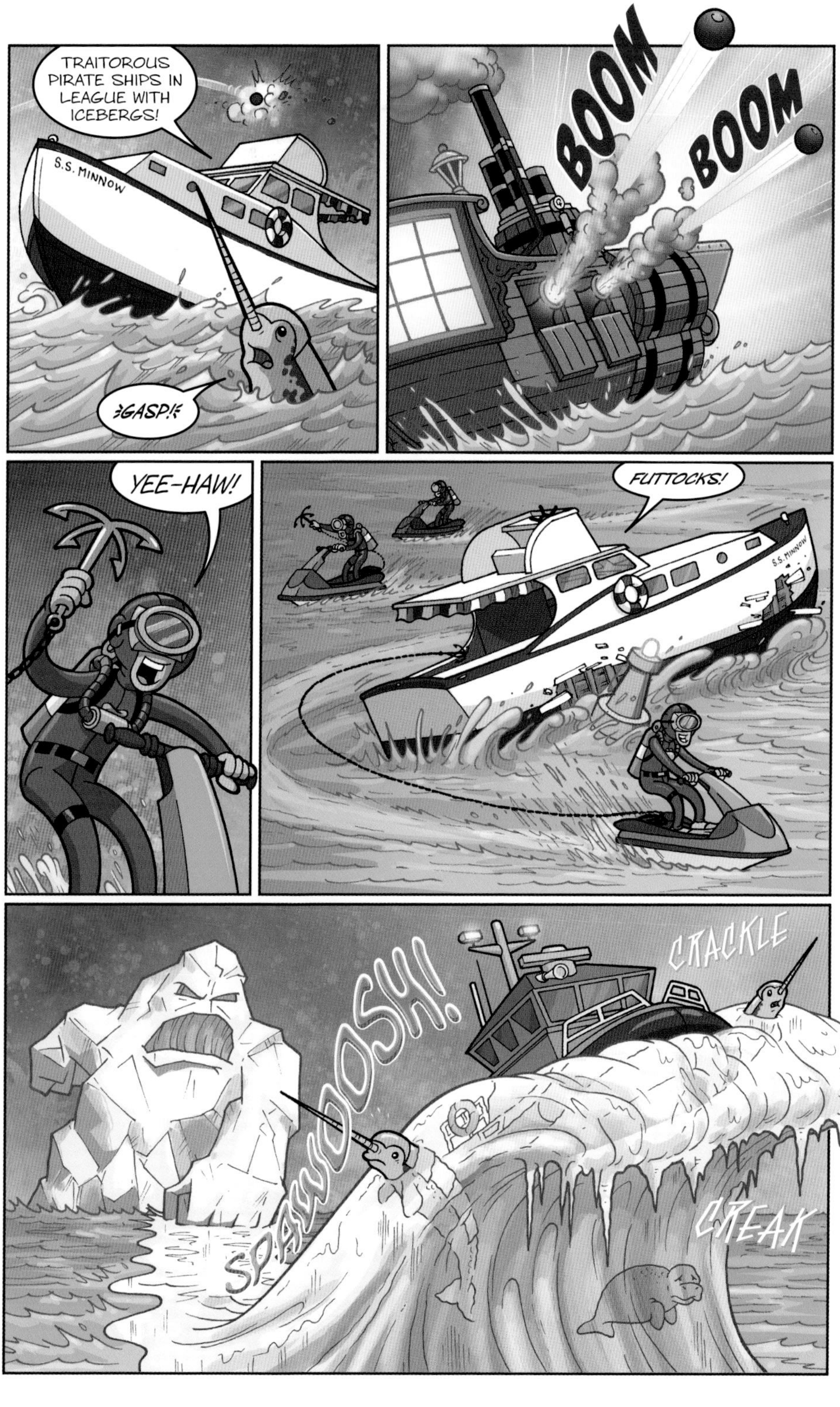

TRAITOROUS PIRATE SHIPS IN LEAGUE WITH ICEBERGS!
S.S. MINNOW
GASP!
BOOM
BOOM
YEE-HAW!
FUTTOCKS!
S.S. MINNOW
SPAWOOSH!
CRACKLE
CREAK

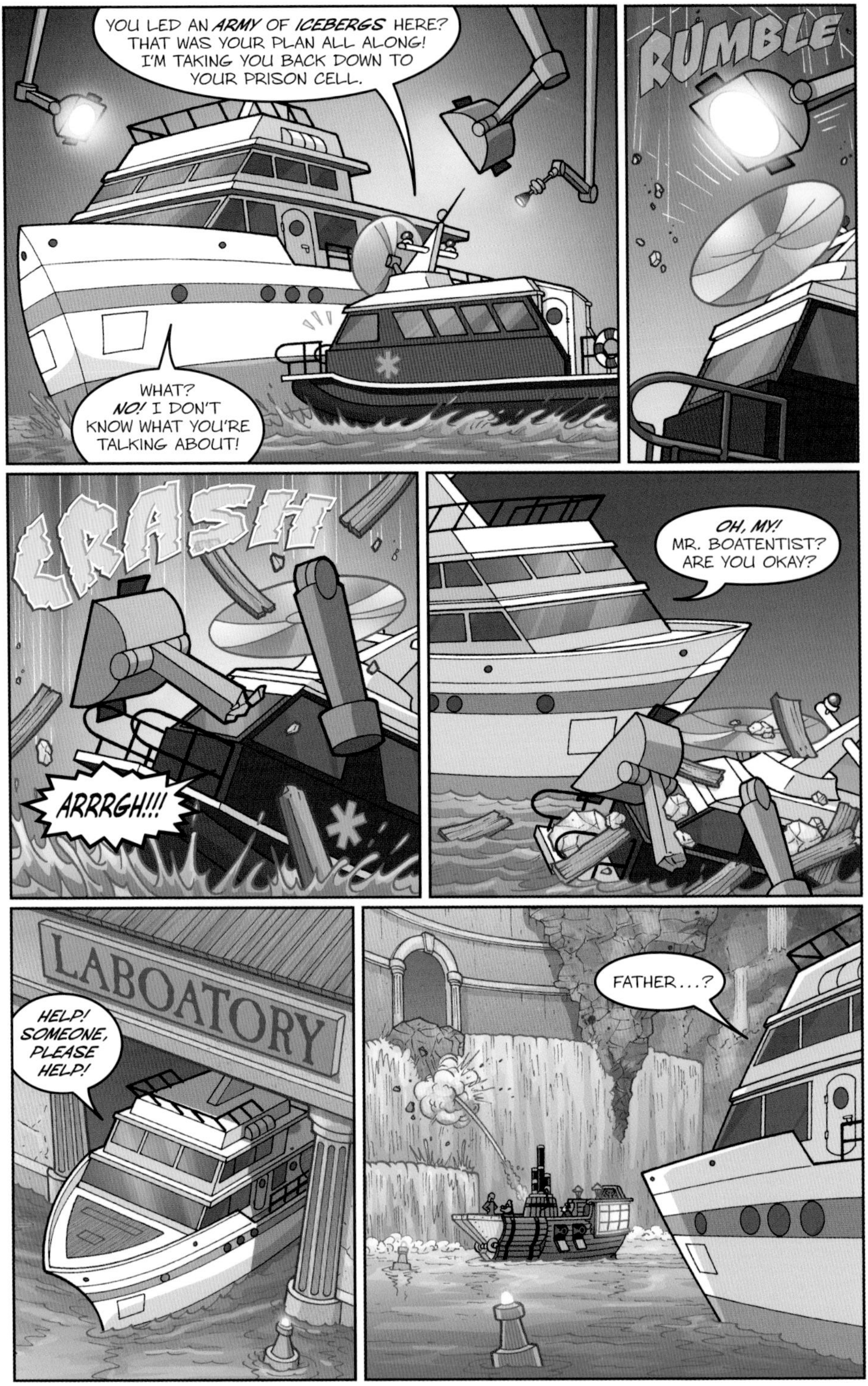
YOU LED AN ARMY OF ICEBERGS HERE? THAT WAS YOUR PLAN ALL ALONG! I'M TAKING YOU BACK DOWN TO YOUR PRISON CELL.
WHAT? NO! I DON'T KNOW WHAT YOU'RE TALKING ABOUT!
RUMBLE
CRASH
ARRRGH!!!
OH, MY! MR. BOATENTIST? ARE YOU OKAY?
LABOATORY
HELP! SOMEONE, PLEASE HELP!
FATHER . . . ?

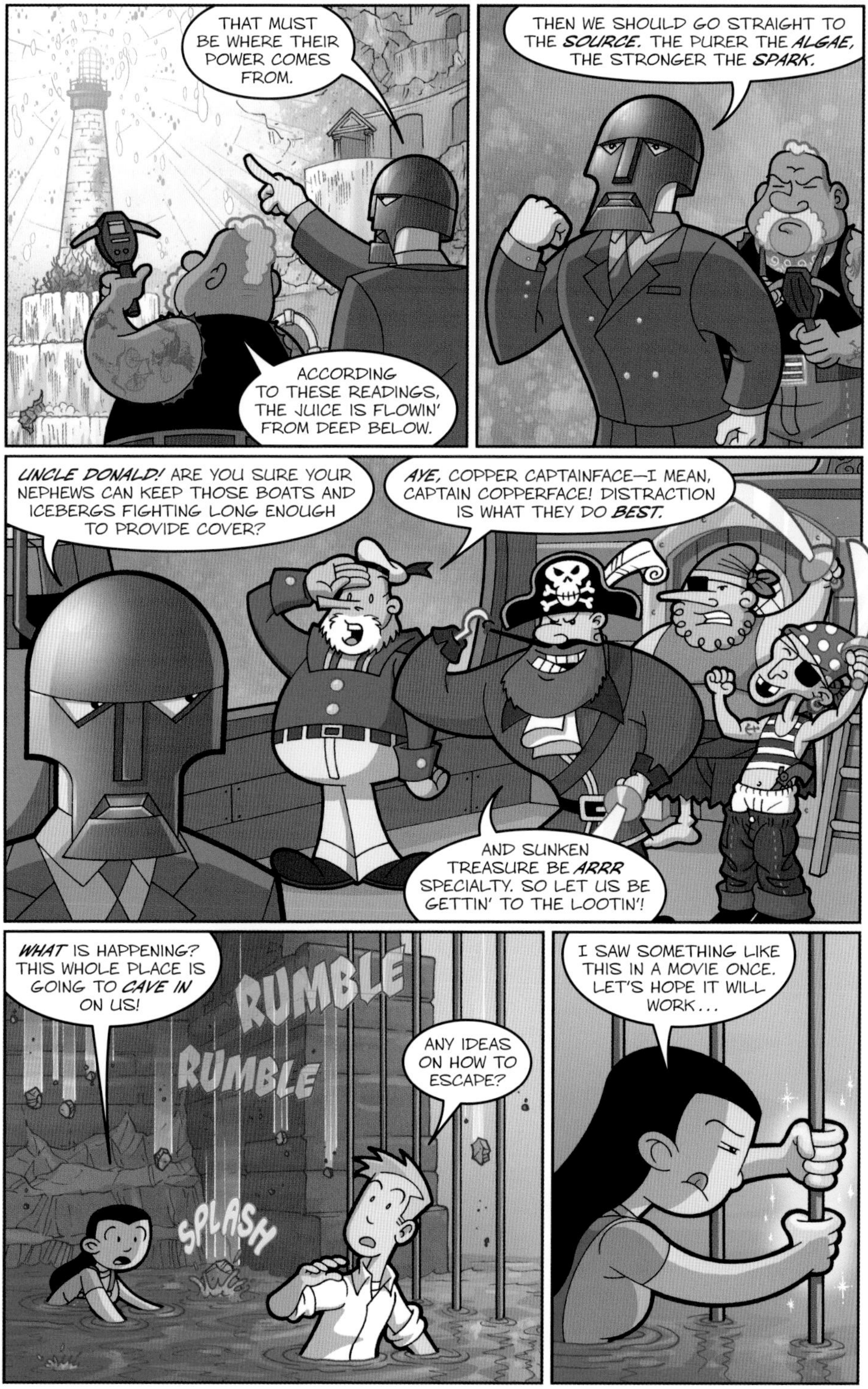
THAT MUST BE WHERE THEIR POWER COMES FROM.
ACCORDING TO THESE READINGS, THE JUICE IS FLOWIN' FROM DEEP BELOW.
THEN WE SHOULD GO STRAIGHT TO THE SOURCE. THE PURER THE ALGAE, THE STRONGER THE SPARK.
UNCLE DONALD! ARE YOU SURE YOUR NEPHEWS CAN KEEP THOSE BOATS AND ICEBERGS FIGHTING LONG ENOUGH TO PROVIDE COVER?
AYE, COPPER CAPTAINFACE—I MEAN, CAPTAIN COPPERFACE! DISTRACTION IS WHAT THEY DO BEST.
AND SUNKEN TREASURE BE ARRR SPECIALTY. SO LET US BE GETTIN' TO THE LOOTIN'!
WHAT IS HAPPENING? THIS WHOLE PLACE IS GOING TO CAVE IN ON US!
RUMBLE
RUMBLE
SPLASH
ANY IDEAS ON HOW TO ESCAPE?
I SAW SOMETHING LIKE THIS IN A MOVIE ONCE. LET'S HOPE IT WILL WORK...

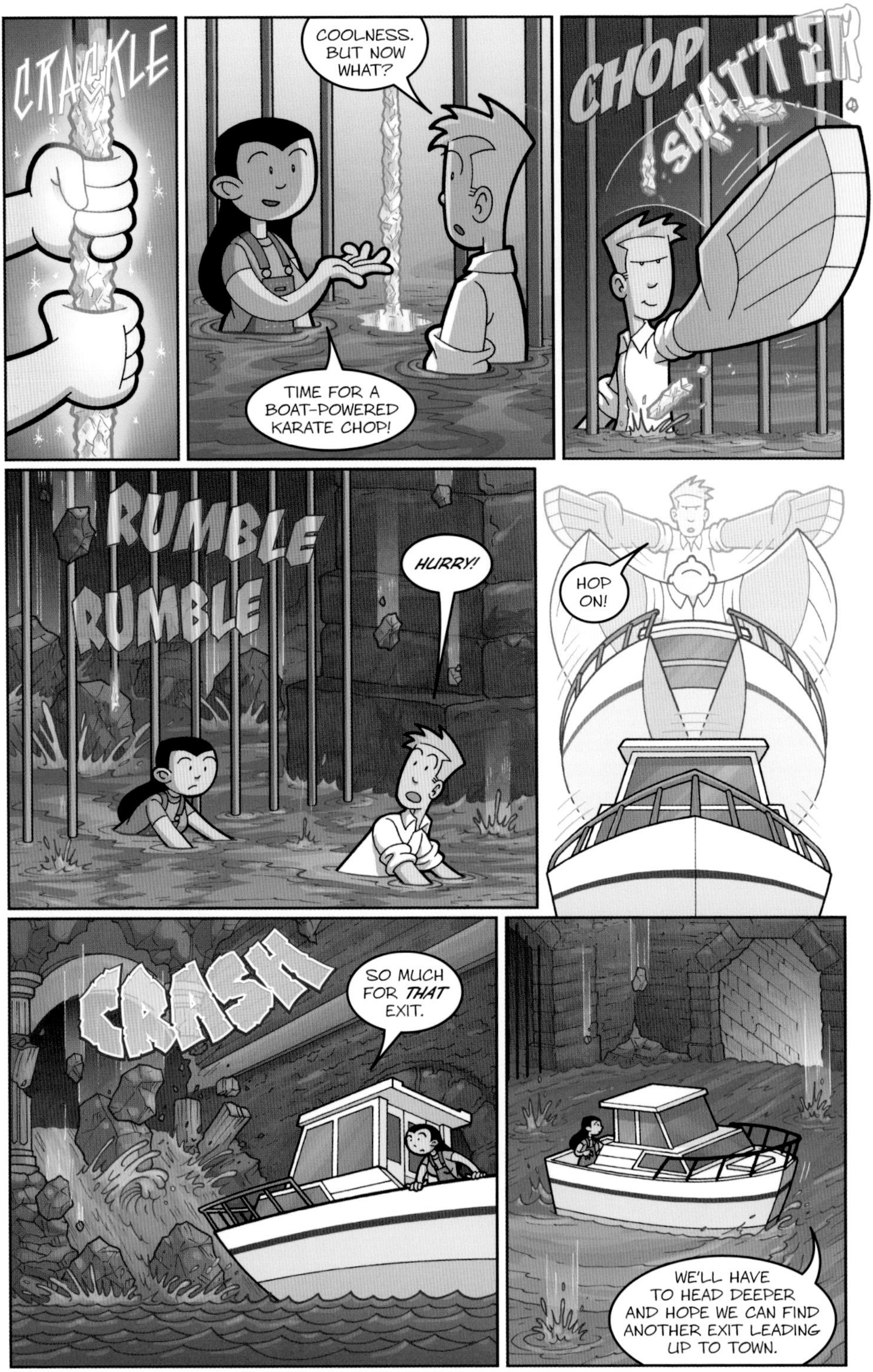
CRACKLE
COOLNESS. BUT NOW WHAT?
TIME FOR A BOAT-POWERED KARATE CHOP!
CHOP
SHATTER
RUMBLE
RUMBLE
HURRY!
HOP ON!
CRASH
SO MUCH FOR THAT EXIT.
WE'LL HAVE TO HEAD DEEPER AND HOPE WE CAN FIND ANOTHER EXIT LEADING UP TO TOWN.

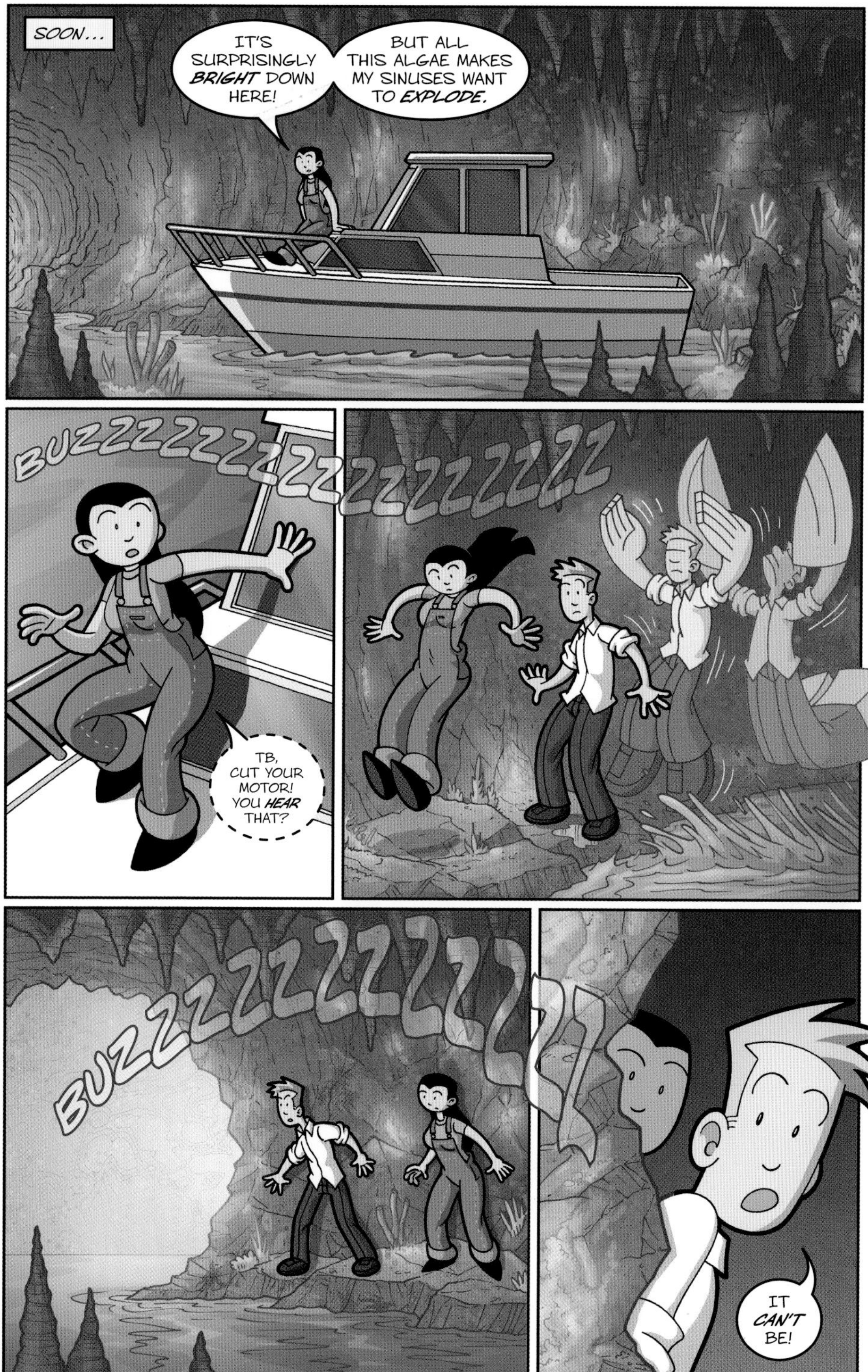
SOON...
IT'S SURPRISINGLY BRIGHT DOWN HERE!
BUT ALL THIS ALGAE MAKES MY SINUSES WANT TO EXPLODE.
BUZZZZZZZZZZZZZZZZZZ
TB, CUT YOUR MOTOR! YOU HEAR THAT?
BUZZZZZZZZZZZZZZ
IT CAN'T BE!

BUZZZZZZZZZZZZZZ

COPPERFACE!
THE MECHANIC!
UNCLE DONALD!
Totally PIRATES!

ALL WORKING TOGETHER!

WHAT'S WITH THEIR NEWFOUND INTEREST IN BOTANY?

WE MUST BE BELOW TOWN SQUARE...

THAT'S THE SAME ALGAE THAT POWERS THE LIGHTHOUSE AND FUELS THE CITY!

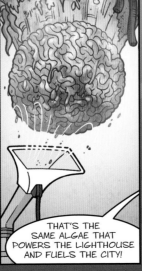

WHAT DO YOU THINK THEY PLAN TO DO WITH IT?

CAN'T BE GOOD. WE'D BETTER WARN MY DAD AND THE DEEP COUNCIL.

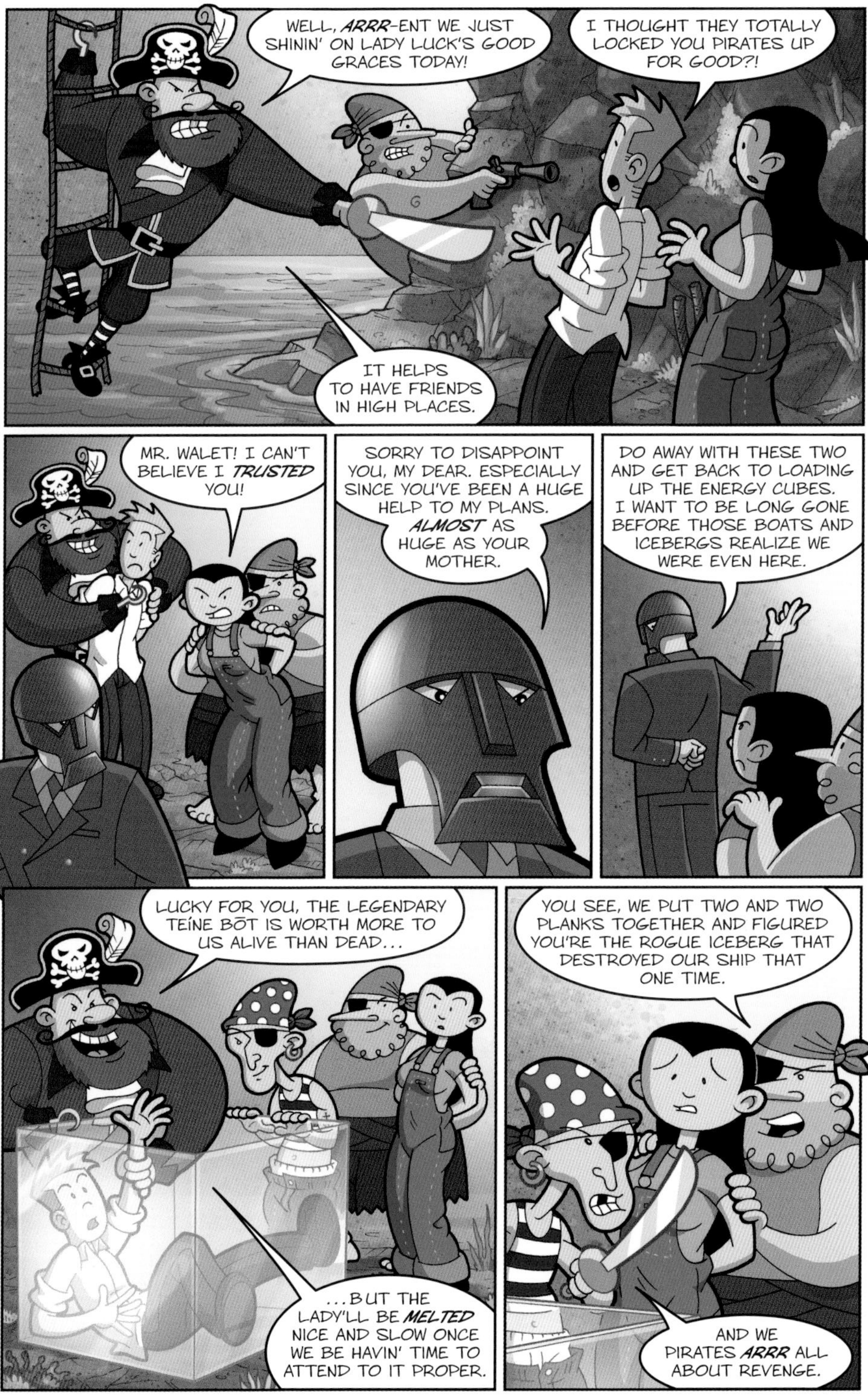
WELL, ARRR-ENT WE JUST SHININ' ON LADY LUCK'S GOOD GRACES TODAY!
I THOUGHT THEY TOTALLY LOCKED YOU PIRATES UP FOR GOOD?!
IT HELPS TO HAVE FRIENDS IN HIGH PLACES.
MR. WALET! I CAN'T BELIEVE I TRUSTED YOU!
SORRY TO DISAPPOINT YOU, MY DEAR. ESPECIALLY SINCE YOU'VE BEEN A HUGE HELP TO MY PLANS. ALMOST AS HUGE AS YOUR MOTHER.
DO AWAY WITH THESE TWO AND GET BACK TO LOADING UP THE ENERGY CUBES. I WANT TO BE LONG GONE BEFORE THOSE BOATS AND ICEBERGS REALIZE WE WERE EVEN HERE.
LUCKY FOR YOU, THE LEGENDARY TEíNE BŌT IS WORTH MORE TO US ALIVE THAN DEAD...
...BUT THE LADY'LL BE MELTED NICE AND SLOW ONCE WE BE HAVIN' TIME TO ATTEND TO IT PROPER.
YOU SEE, WE PUT TWO AND TWO PLANKS TOGETHER AND FIGURED YOU'RE THE ROGUE ICEBERG THAT DESTROYED OUR SHIP THAT ONE TIME.
AND WE PIRATES ARRR ALL ABOUT REVENGE.

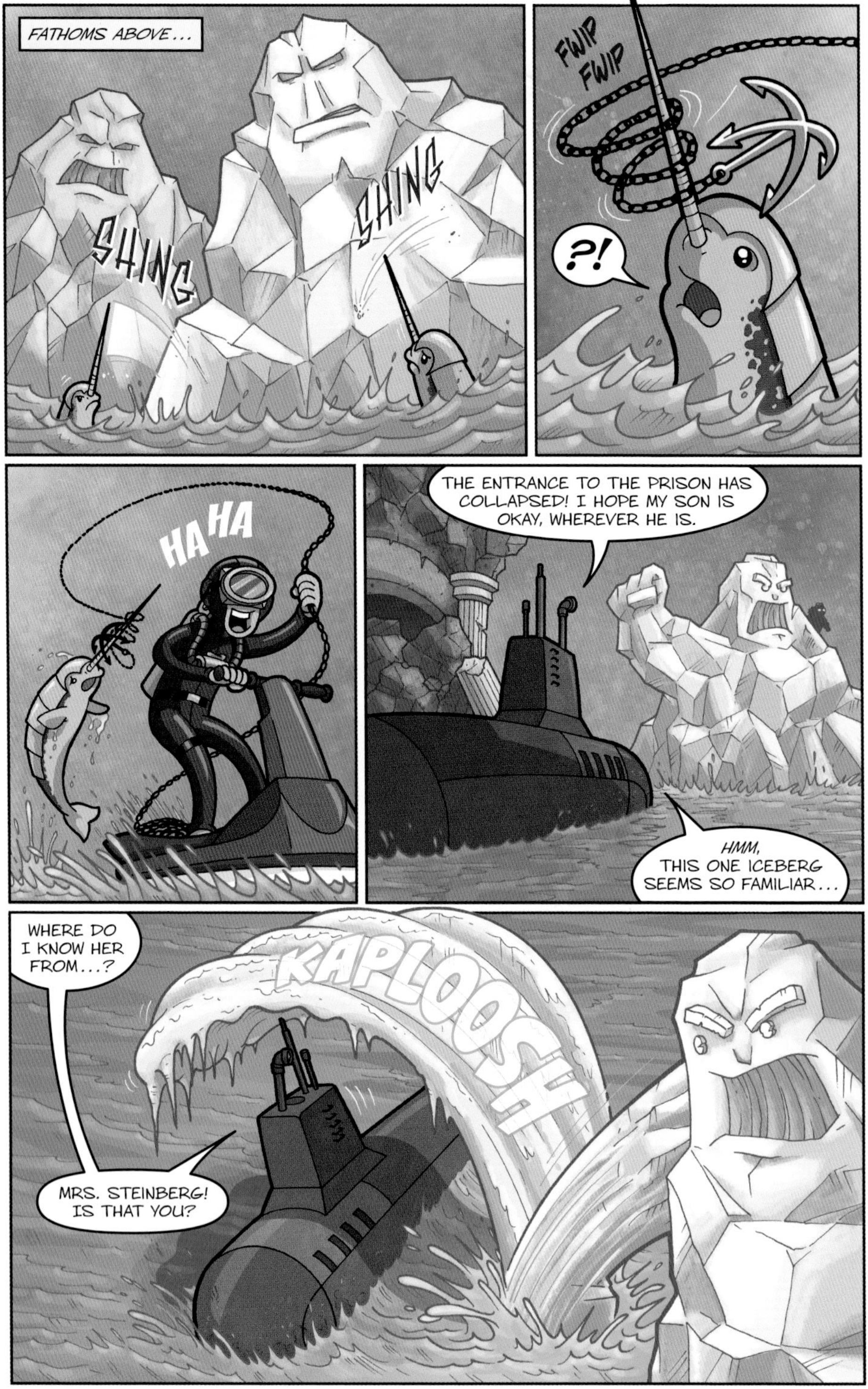
FATHOMS ABOVE...
SHING
SHING
FWIP
FWIP
?!
HAHA
THE ENTRANCE TO THE PRISON HAS COLLAPSED! I HOPE MY SON IS OKAY, WHEREVER HE IS.
HMM, THIS ONE ICEBERG SEEMS SO FAMILIAR...
WHERE DO I KNOW HER FROM...?
KAPLOOSH
MRS. STEINBERG! IS THAT YOU?

WAIT! MR. AND MRS. STEINBERG! PLEASE! I MEAN YOU NO HARM!
YOU KNOW US?
Crackle?
YOU'RE JOEY'S PARENTS! I USED TO LIVE BEHIND THE HOUSE NEXT TO YOURS... IN THE CANAL!
I'M TEEN BOAT'S FATHER.
OH, MY! WELL, IT HAS BEEN SOME TIME, HASN'T IT?
I'M SURE WE'RE ALL WORRIED ABOUT BOTH OUR MISSING KIDS...
...AND I THINK I MAY BE ABLE TO TRACK THEM DOWN.

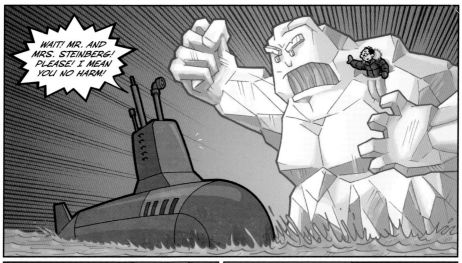

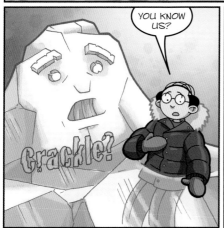

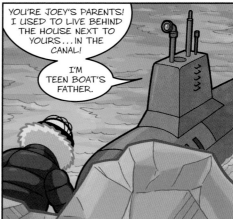

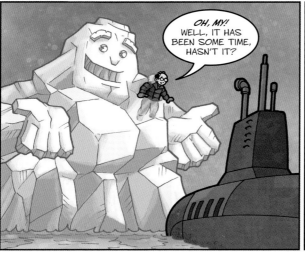

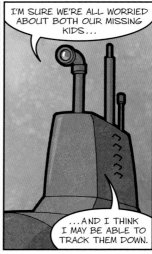

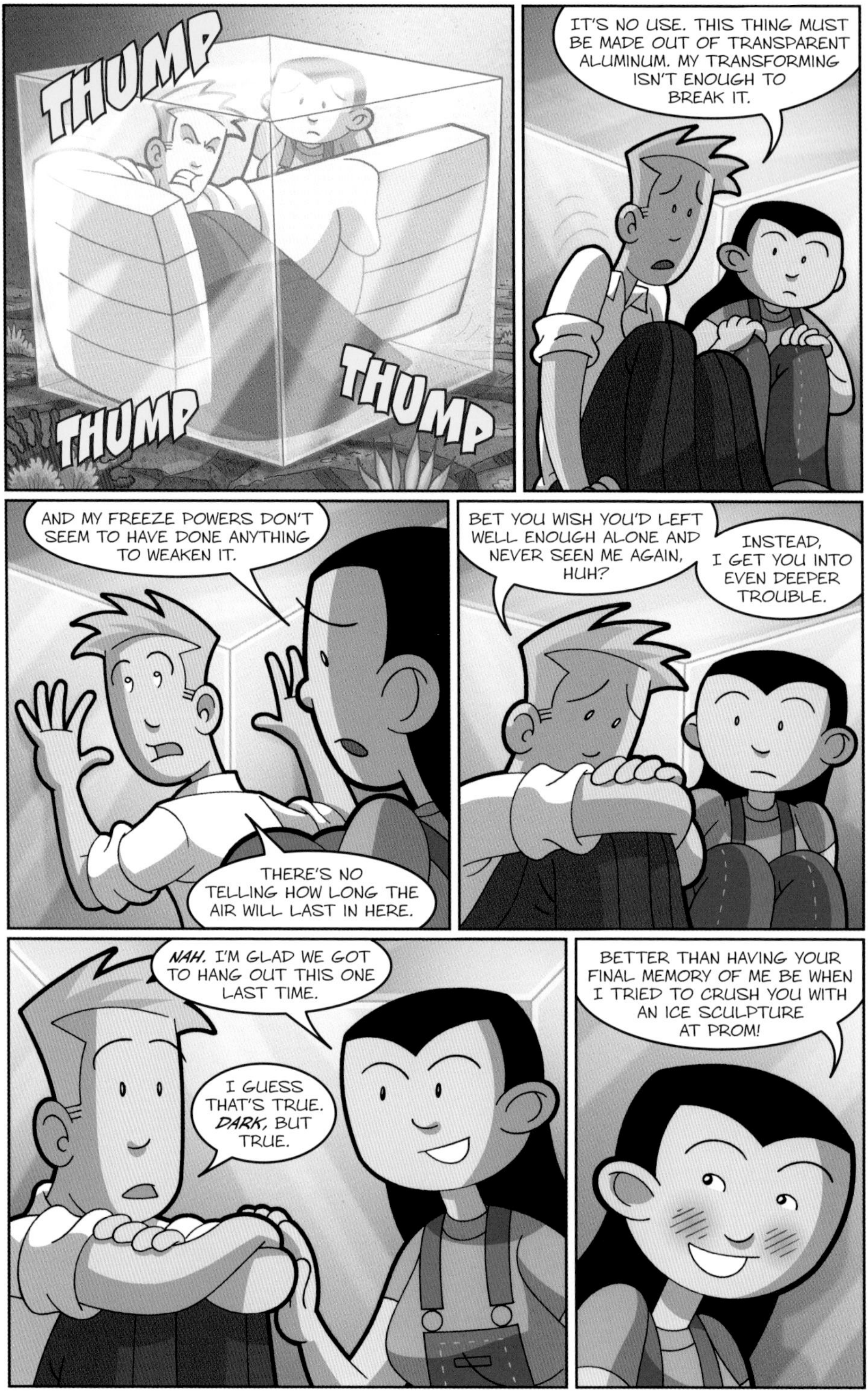
THUMP
THUMP
THUMP
IT'S NO USE. THIS THING MUST BE MADE OUT OF TRANSPARENT ALUMINUM. MY TRANSFORMING ISN'T ENOUGH TO BREAK IT.
AND MY FREEZE POWERS DON'T SEEM TO HAVE DONE ANYTHING TO WEAKEN IT.
THERE'S NO TELLING HOW LONG THE AIR WILL LAST IN HERE.
BET YOU WISH YOU'D LEFT WELL ENOUGH ALONE AND NEVER SEEN ME AGAIN, HUH?
INSTEAD, I GET YOU INTO EVEN DEEPER TROUBLE.
NAH. I'M GLAD WE GOT TO HANG OUT THIS ONE LAST TIME.
I GUESS THAT'S TRUE. DARK, BUT TRUE.
BETTER THAN HAVING YOUR FINAL MEMORY OF ME BE WHEN I TRIED TO CRUSH YOU WITH AN ICE SCULPTURE AT PROM!

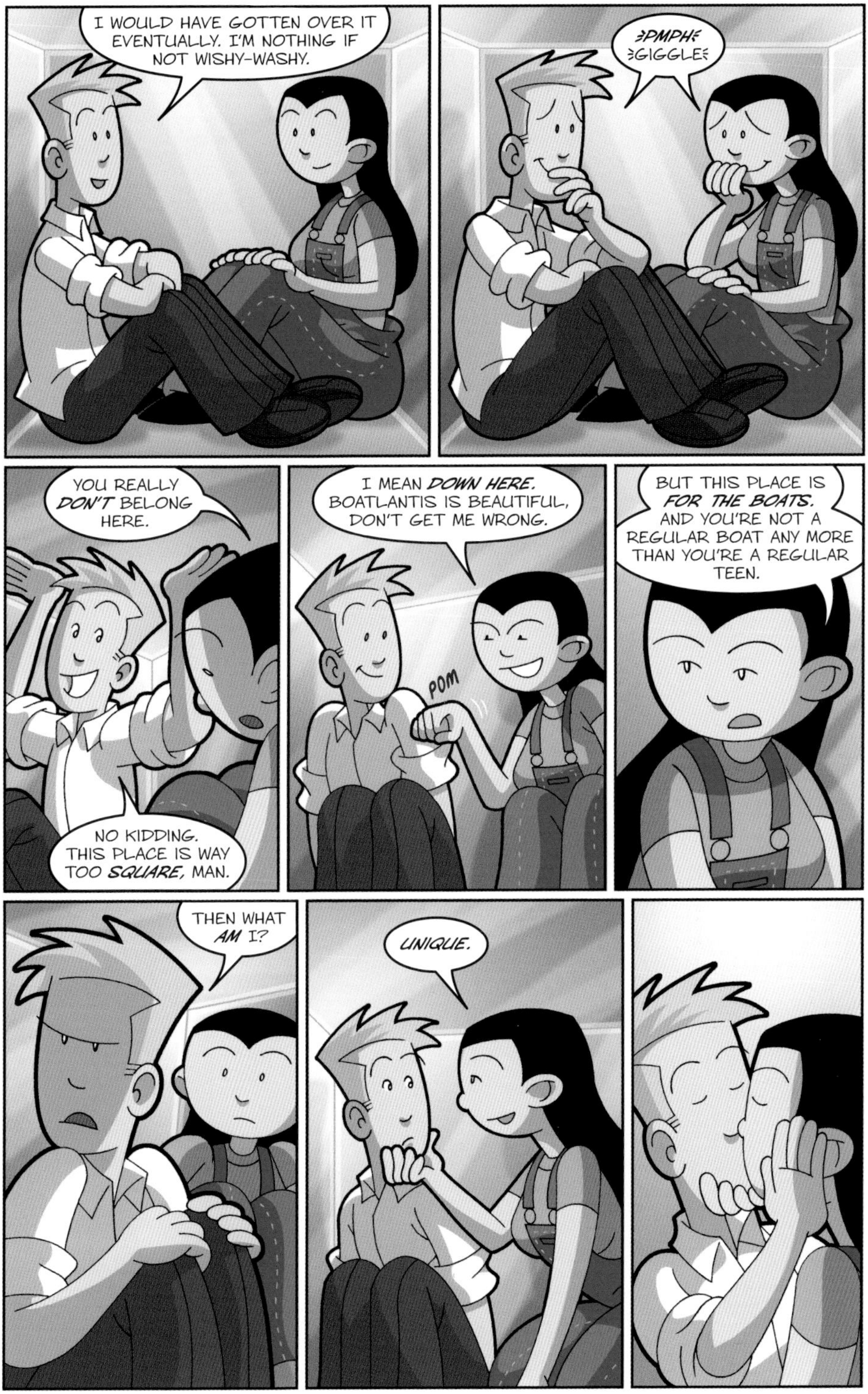
I WOULD HAVE GOTTEN OVER IT EVENTUALLY. I'M NOTHING IF NOT WISHY-WASHY.
PMPH
GIGGLE
YOU REALLY DON'T BELONG HERE.
NO KIDDING. THIS PLACE IS WAY TOO SQUARE, MAN.
I MEAN DOWN HERE. BOATLANTIS IS BEAUTIFUL, DON'T GET ME WRONG.
POM
BUT THIS PLACE IS FOR THE BOATS. AND YOU'RE NOT A REGULAR BOAT ANY MORE THAN YOU'RE A REGULAR TEEN.
THEN WHAT AM I?
UNIQUE.

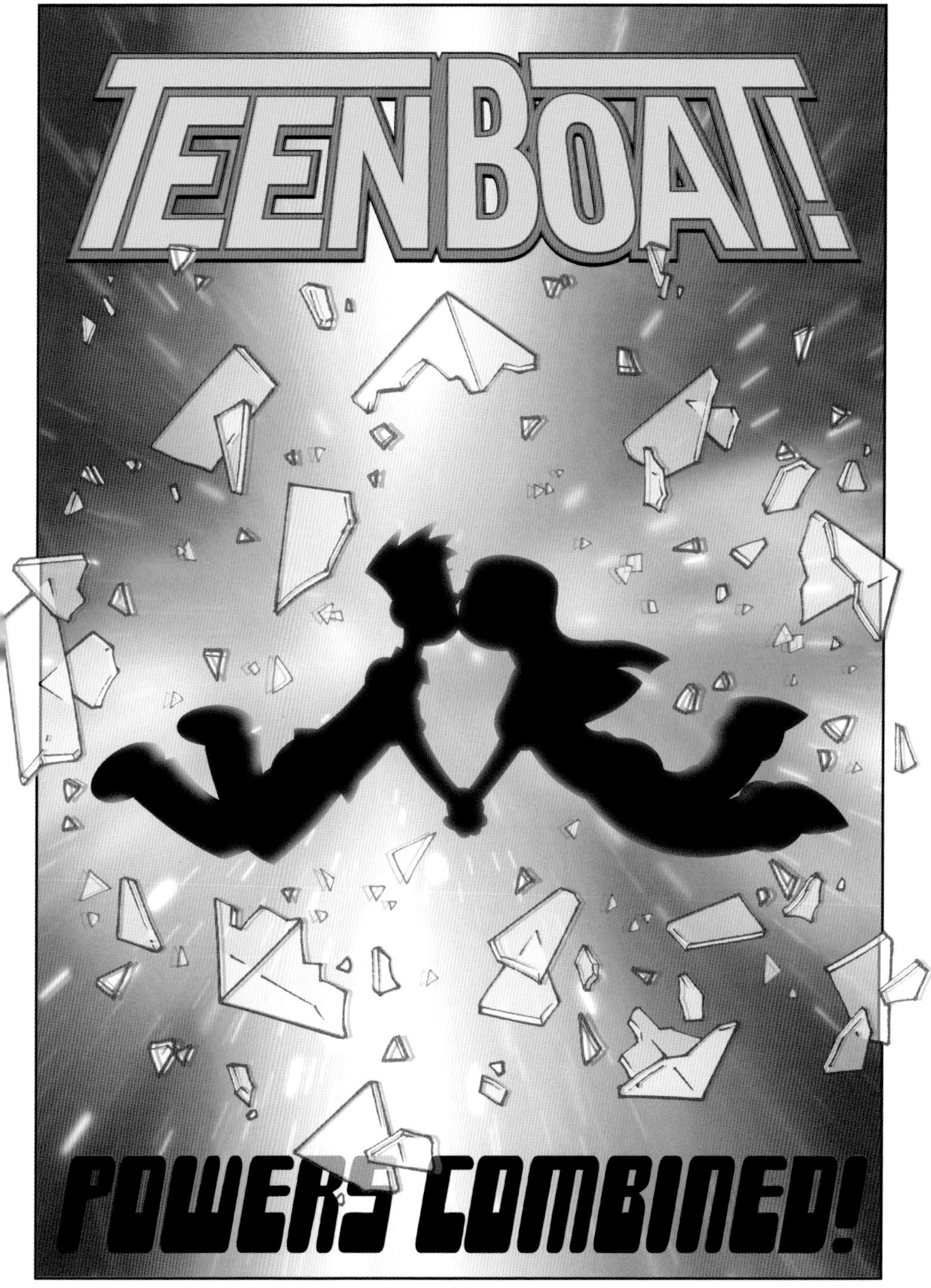
TEEN BOAT!
POWERS COMBINED!
The *THRILL* of being a Boat—the *CHILL* of being an Iceberg!

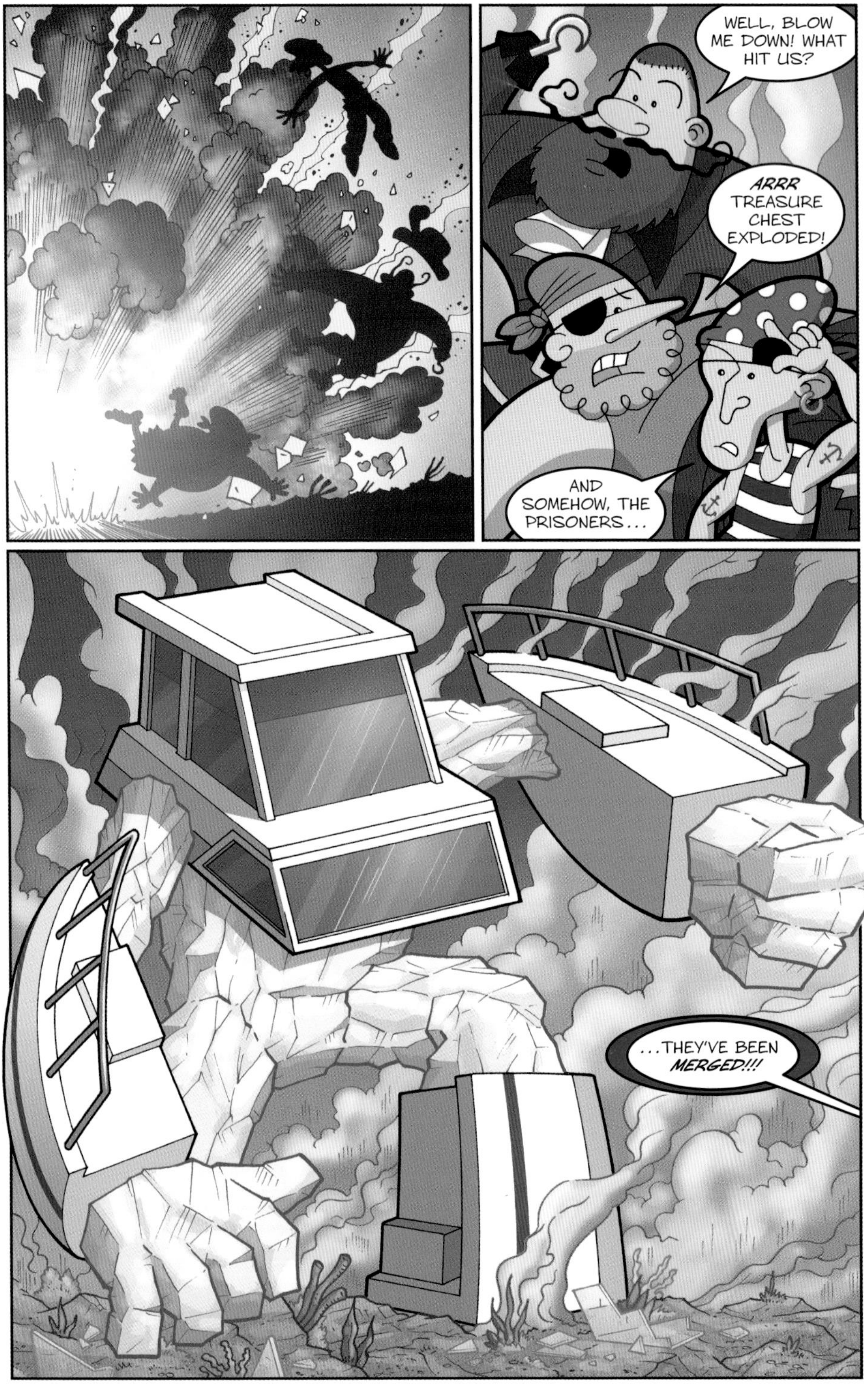
WELL, BLOW ME DOWN! WHAT HIT US?
ARRR TREASURE CHEST EXPLODED!
AND SOMEHOW, THE PRISONERS...
...THEY'VE BEEN MERGED!!!

I KNEW THE ENERGY OF BOATLANTIS HAD GREAT POTENTIAL, BUT THIS IS BEYOND EVEN MY GRANDEST VISION!

NOW DON'T BE HASTY... THAT EQUIPMENT IS VERY EXPENSIVE!

SMASH

STOP THEM, YOU FOOLS! I DIDN'T INVEST ALL THIS TIME AND RESOURCES TO HAVE MY PLANS SQUASHED!

PHSSH

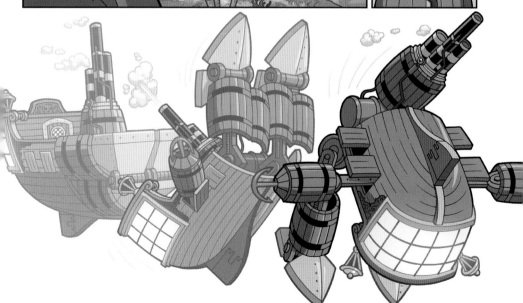

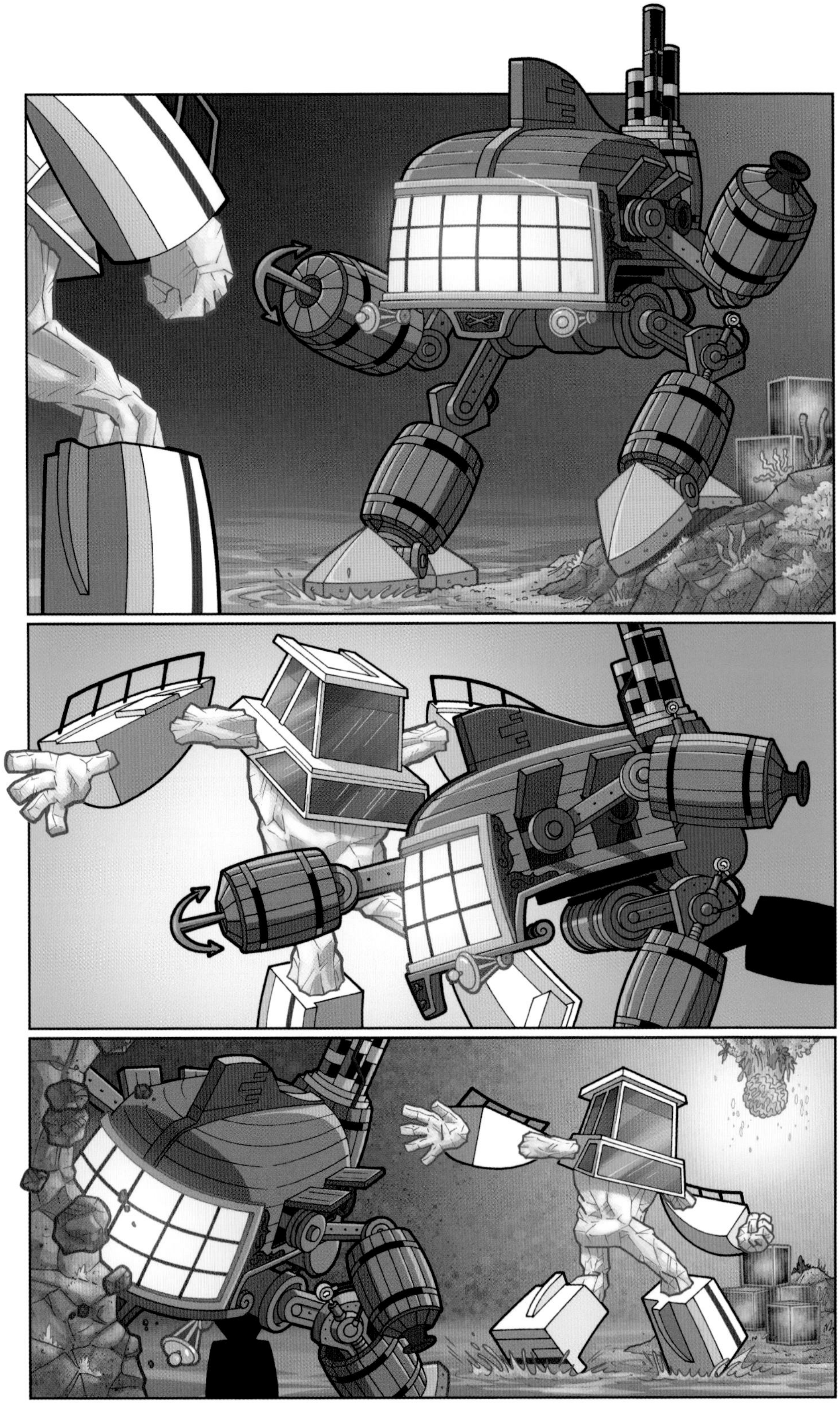

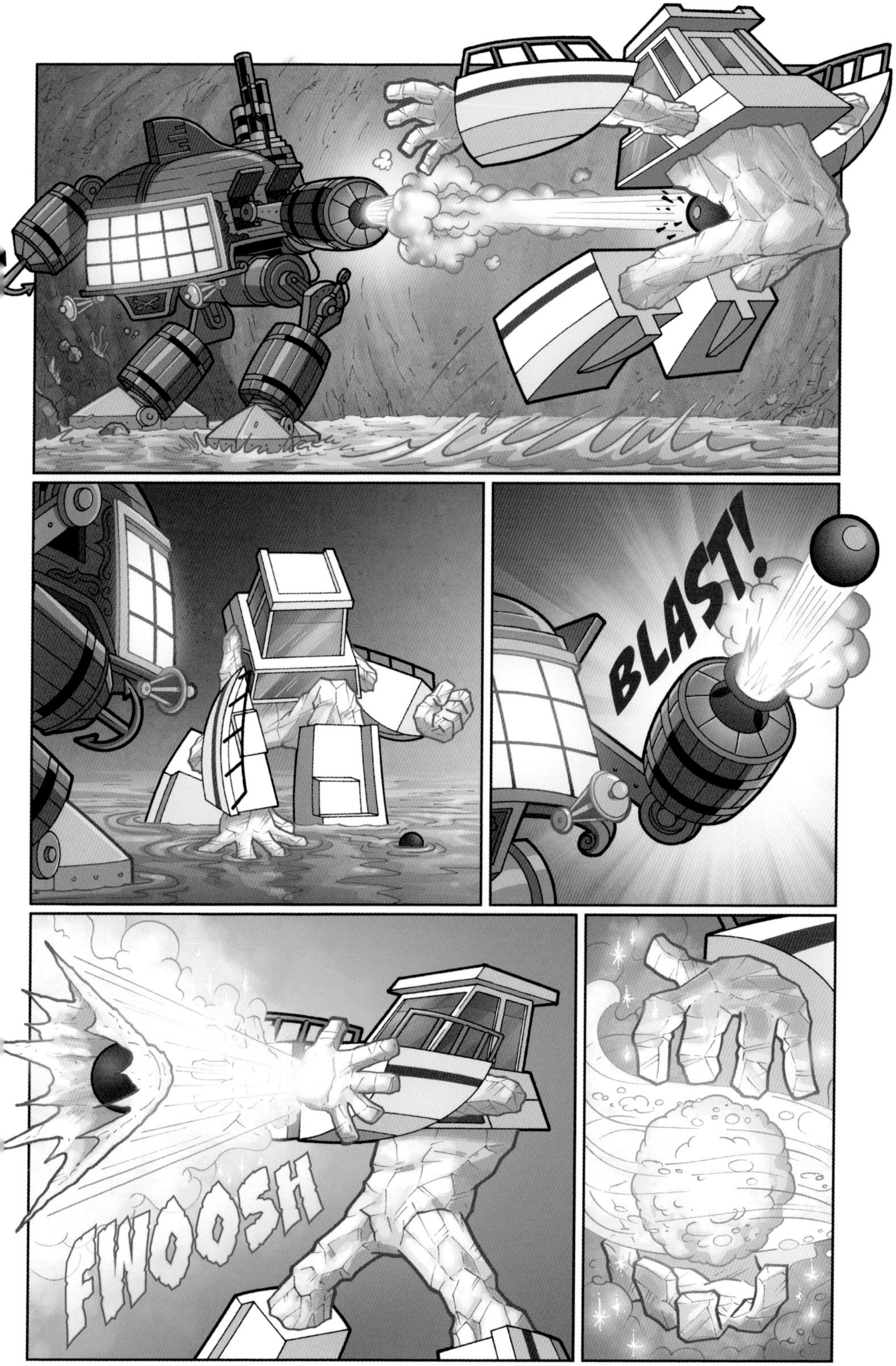
BLAST!
FWOOSH

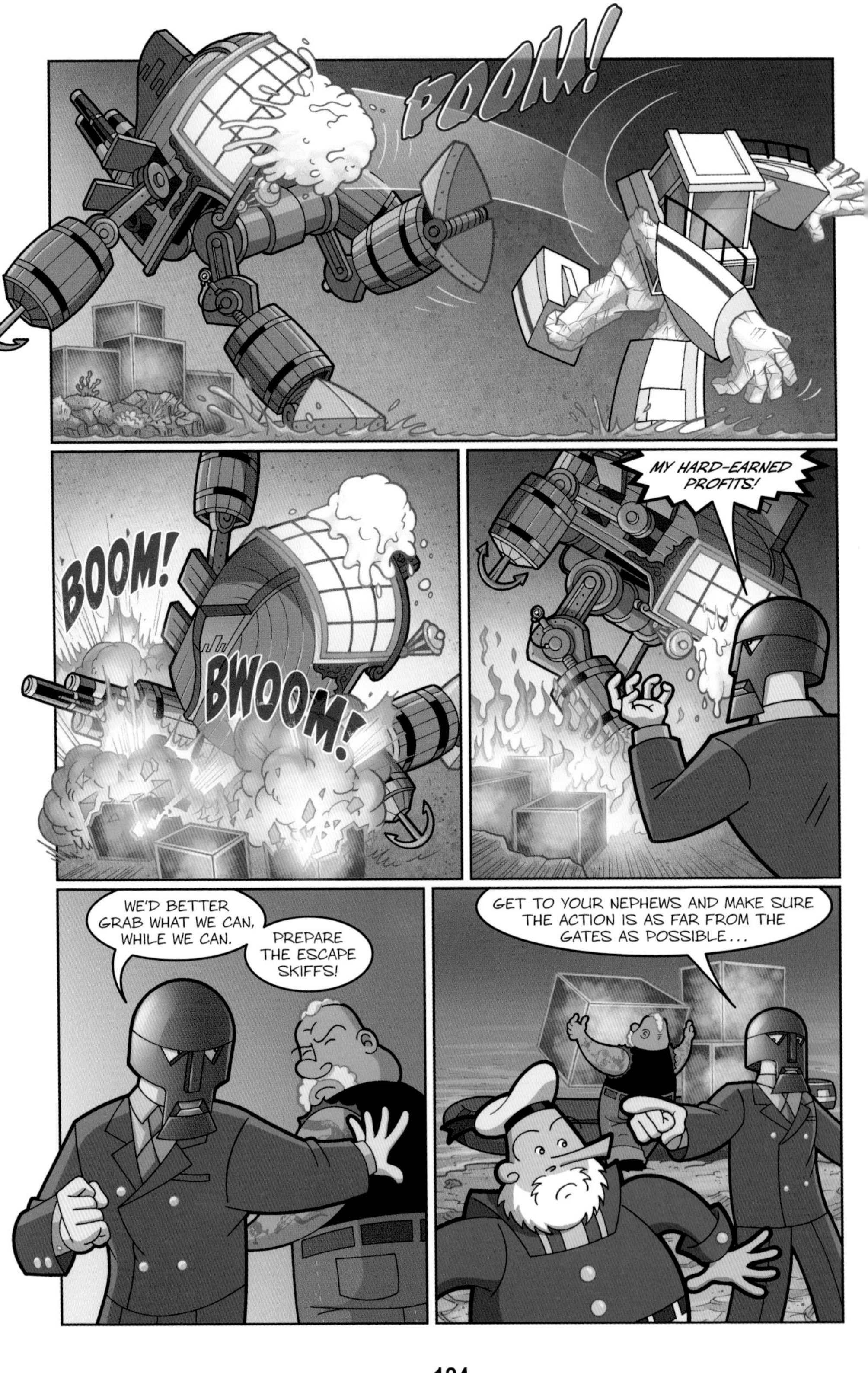
POOM!
BOOM!
BWOOM!
MY HARD-EARNED PROFITS!
WE'D BETTER GRAB WHAT WE CAN, WHILE WE CAN.
PREPARE THE ESCAPE SKIFFS!
GET TO YOUR NEPHEWS AND MAKE SURE THE ACTION IS AS FAR FROM THE GATES AS POSSIBLE . . .

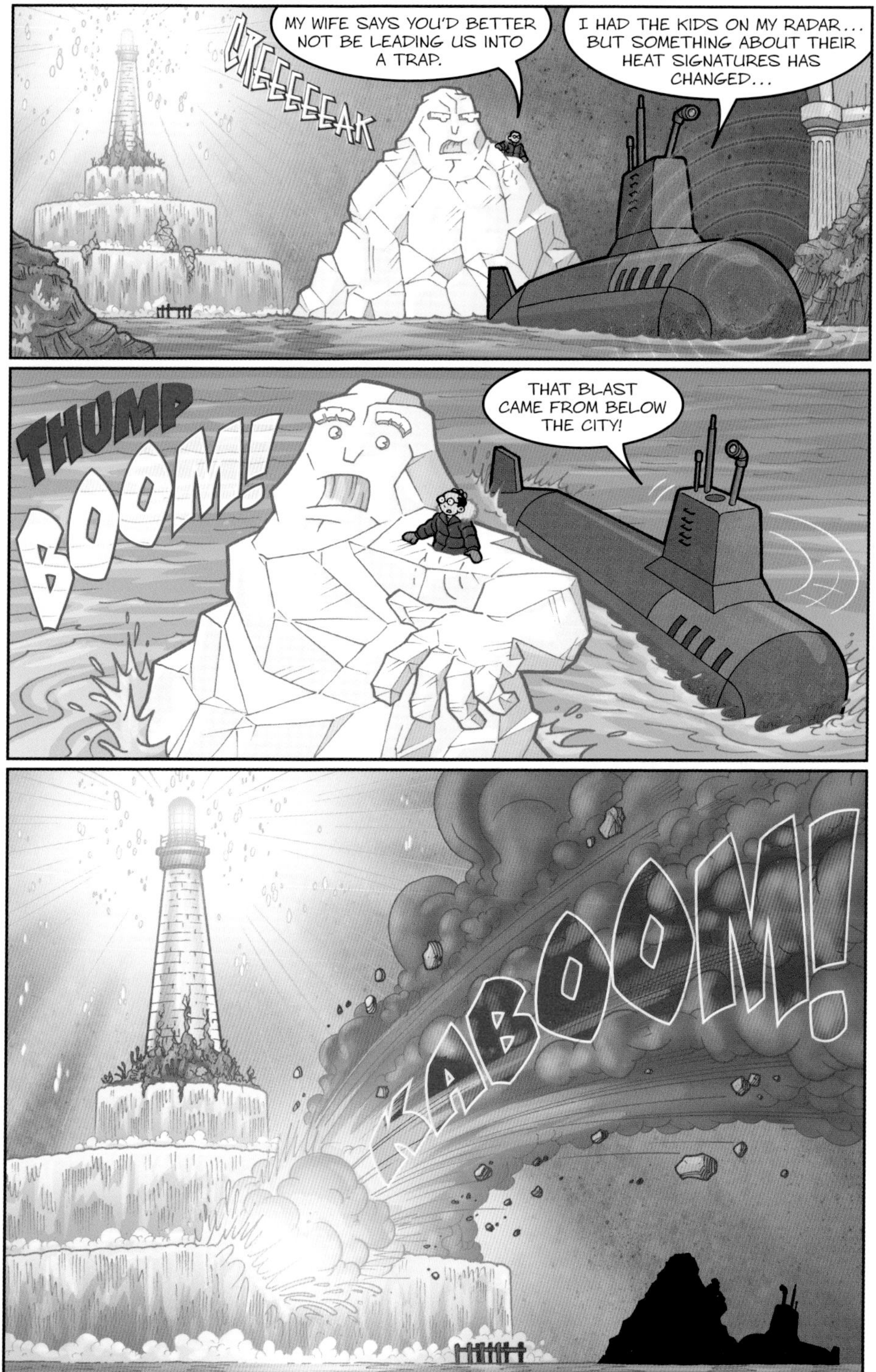
CREEEEEAK
MY WIFE SAYS YOU'D BETTER NOT BE LEADING US INTO A TRAP.
I HAD THE KIDS ON MY RADAR... BUT SOMETHING ABOUT THEIR HEAT SIGNATURES HAS CHANGED...
THUMP
BOOM!
THAT BLAST CAME FROM BELOW THE CITY!
KABOOM!

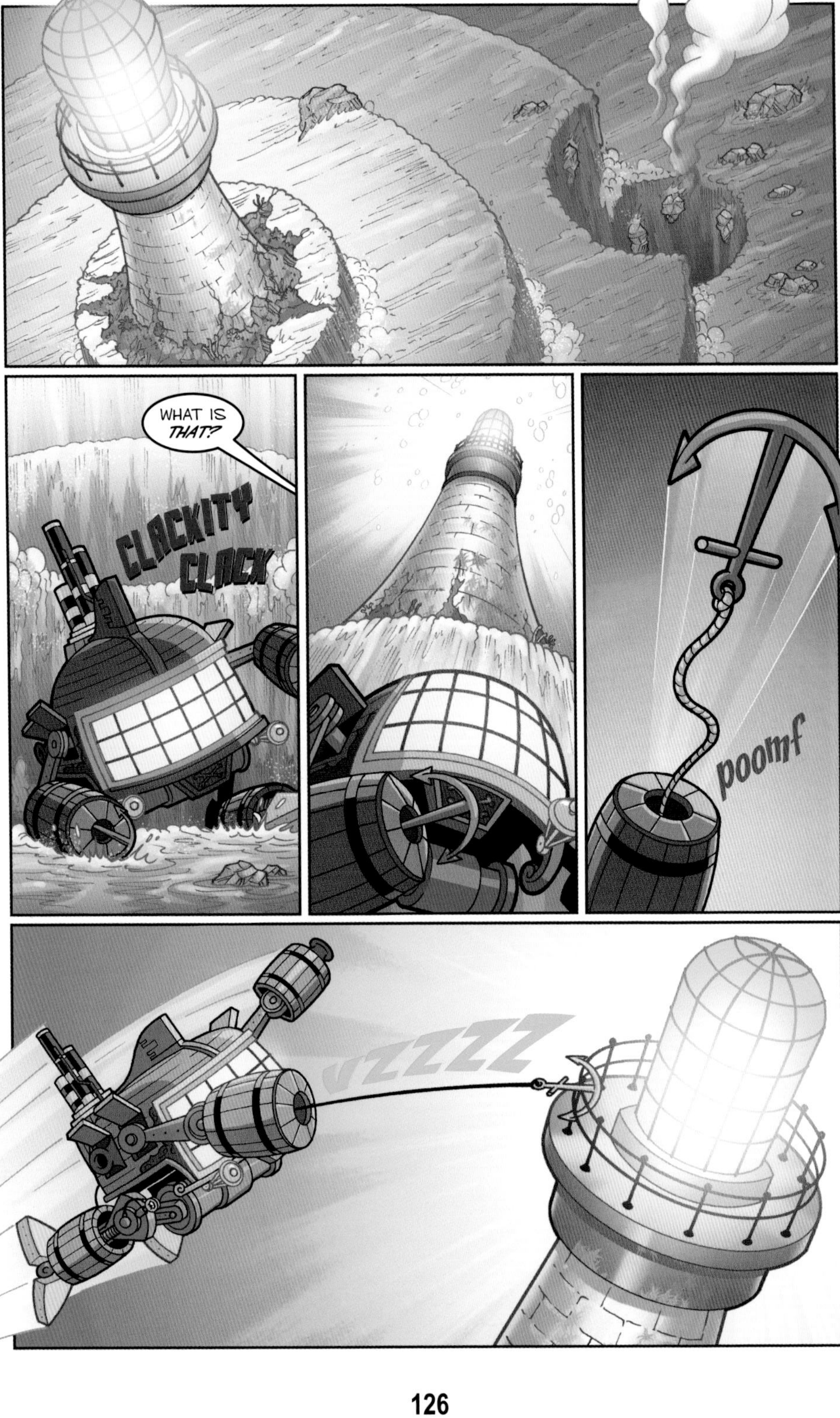
WHAT IS
THAT?
CLACKITY
CLACK
poomf
ZZZZZ

THUMP
THUMP

THAT'S... MY *SON!*

AND *OUR DAUGHTER!*

WELL, SINK MY BATTLESHIP!

THEY GROW UP SO FAST!

LEAP

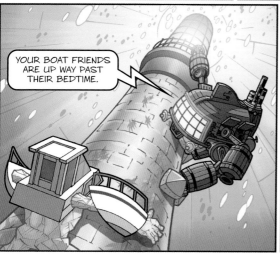

YOUR BOAT FRIENDS ARE UP WAY PAST THEIR BEDTIME.

TIME TO EXTINGUISH THEIR NIGHTLIGHT!

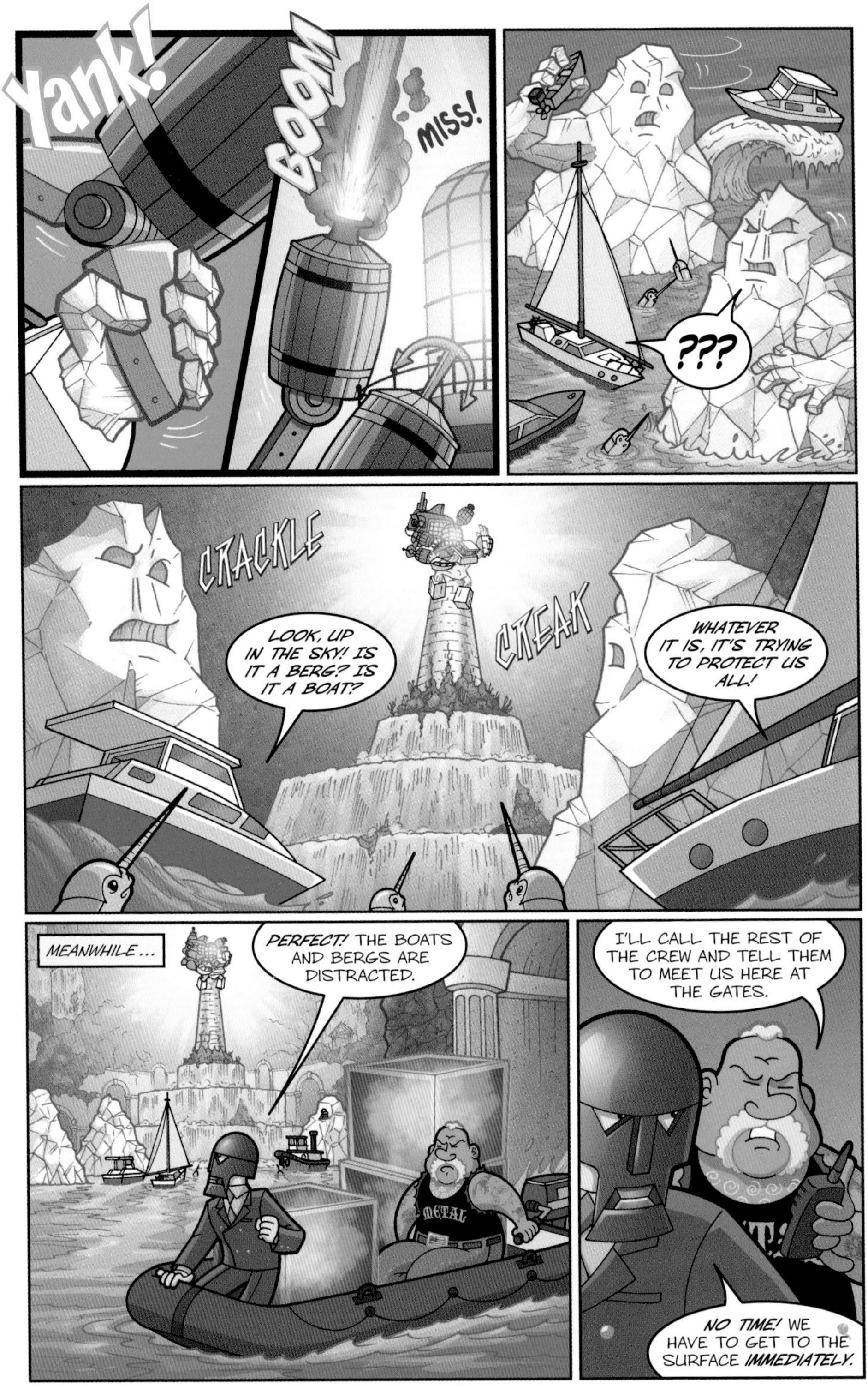
YANK!
BOOM!
MISS!
???
CRACKLE
CREAK
LOOK, UP IN THE SKY! IS IT A BERG? IS IT A BOAT?
WHATEVER IT IS, IT'S TRYING TO PROTECT US ALL!
MEANWHILE...
PERFECT! THE BOATS AND BERGS ARE DISTRACTED.
METAL
I'LL CALL THE REST OF THE CREW AND TELL THEM TO MEET US HERE AT THE GATES.
NO TIME! WE HAVE TO GET TO THE SURFACE IMMEDIATELY.

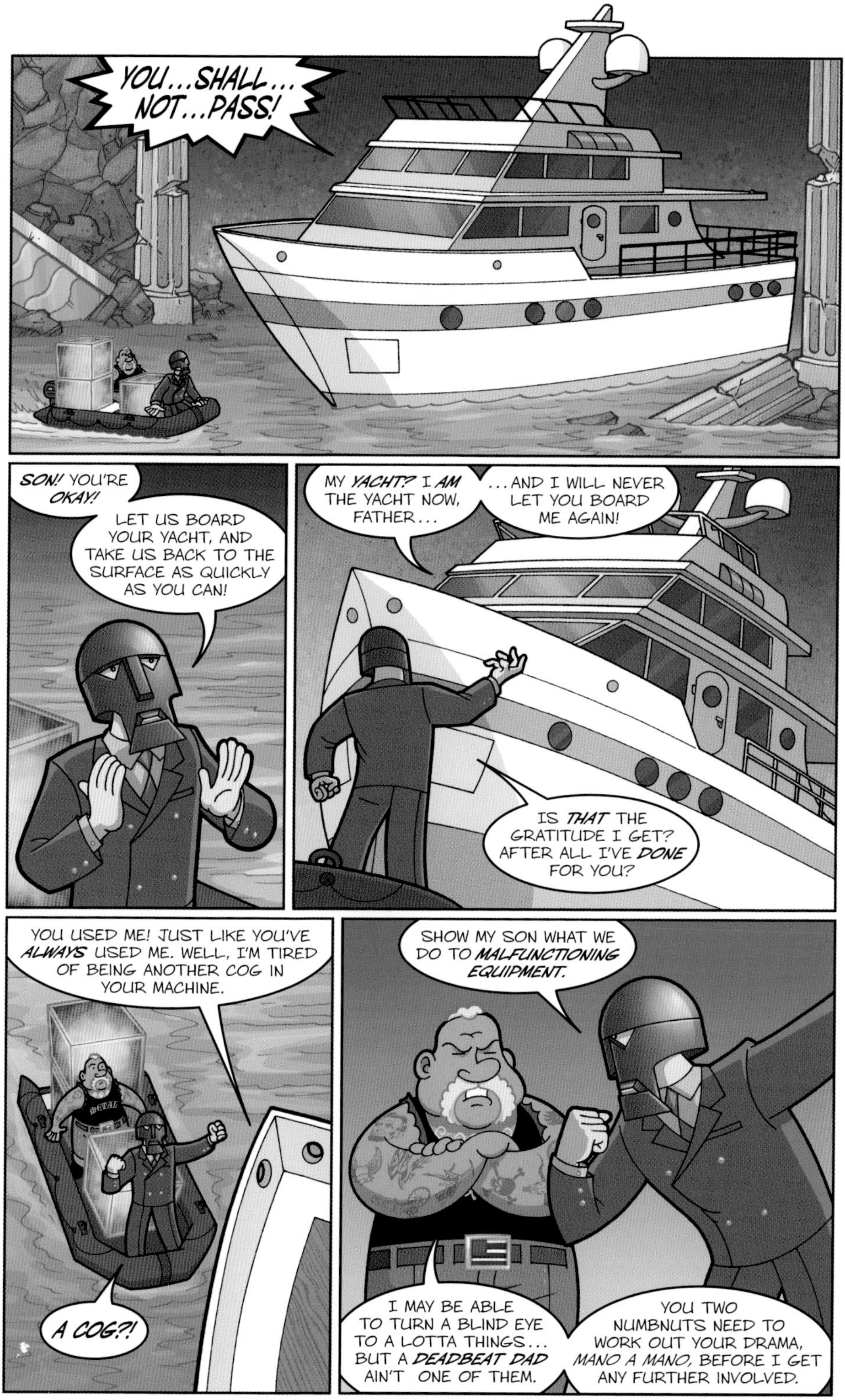
YOU...SHALL... NOT...PASS!
SON! YOU'RE OKAY!
LET US BOARD YOUR YACHT, AND TAKE US BACK TO THE SURFACE AS QUICKLY AS YOU CAN!
MY YACHT? I AM THE YACHT NOW, FATHER...
...AND I WILL NEVER LET YOU BOARD ME AGAIN!
IS THAT THE GRATITUDE I GET? AFTER ALL I'VE DONE FOR YOU?
YOU USED ME! JUST LIKE YOU'VE ALWAYS USED ME. WELL, I'M TIRED OF BEING ANOTHER COG IN YOUR MACHINE.
A COG?!
SHOW MY SON WHAT WE DO TO MALFUNCTIONING EQUIPMENT.
I MAY BE ABLE TO TURN A BLIND EYE TO A LOTTA THINGS... BUT A DEADBEAT DAD AIN'T ONE OF THEM.
YOU TWO NUMBNUTS NEED TO WORK OUT YOUR DRAMA, MANO A MANO, BEFORE I GET ANY FURTHER INVOLVED.

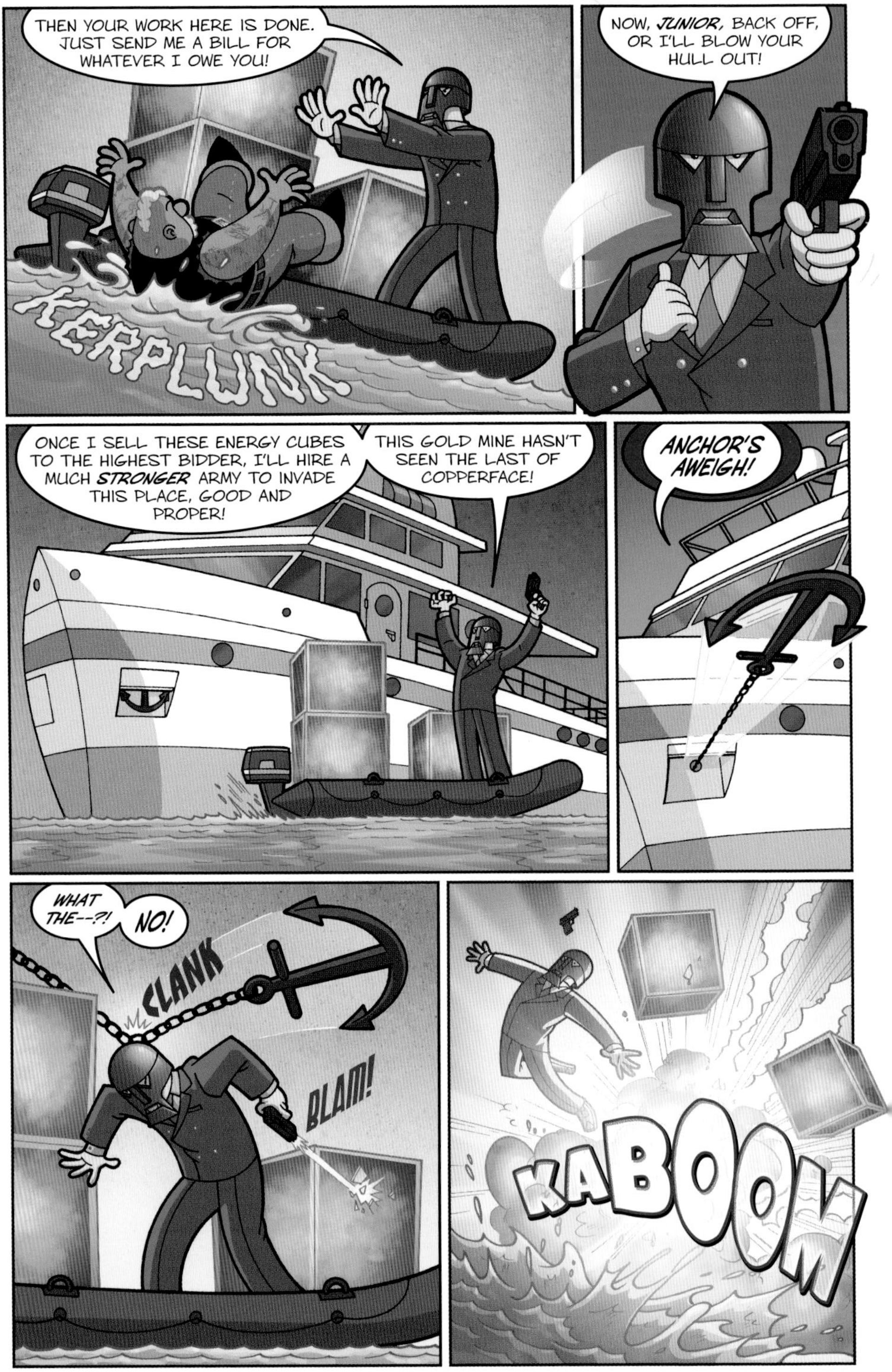
THEN YOUR WORK HERE IS DONE. JUST SEND ME A BILL FOR WHATEVER I OWE YOU!
KERPLUNK
NOW, JUNIOR, BACK OFF, OR I'LL BLOW YOUR HULL OUT!
ONCE I SELL THESE ENERGY CUBES TO THE HIGHEST BIDDER, I'LL HIRE A MUCH STRONGER ARMY TO INVADE THIS PLACE, GOOD AND PROPER!
THIS GOLD MINE HASN'T SEEN THE LAST OF COPPERFACE!
ANCHOR'S AWEIGH!
WHAT THE--?!
NO!
CLANK
BLAM!
KABOOM

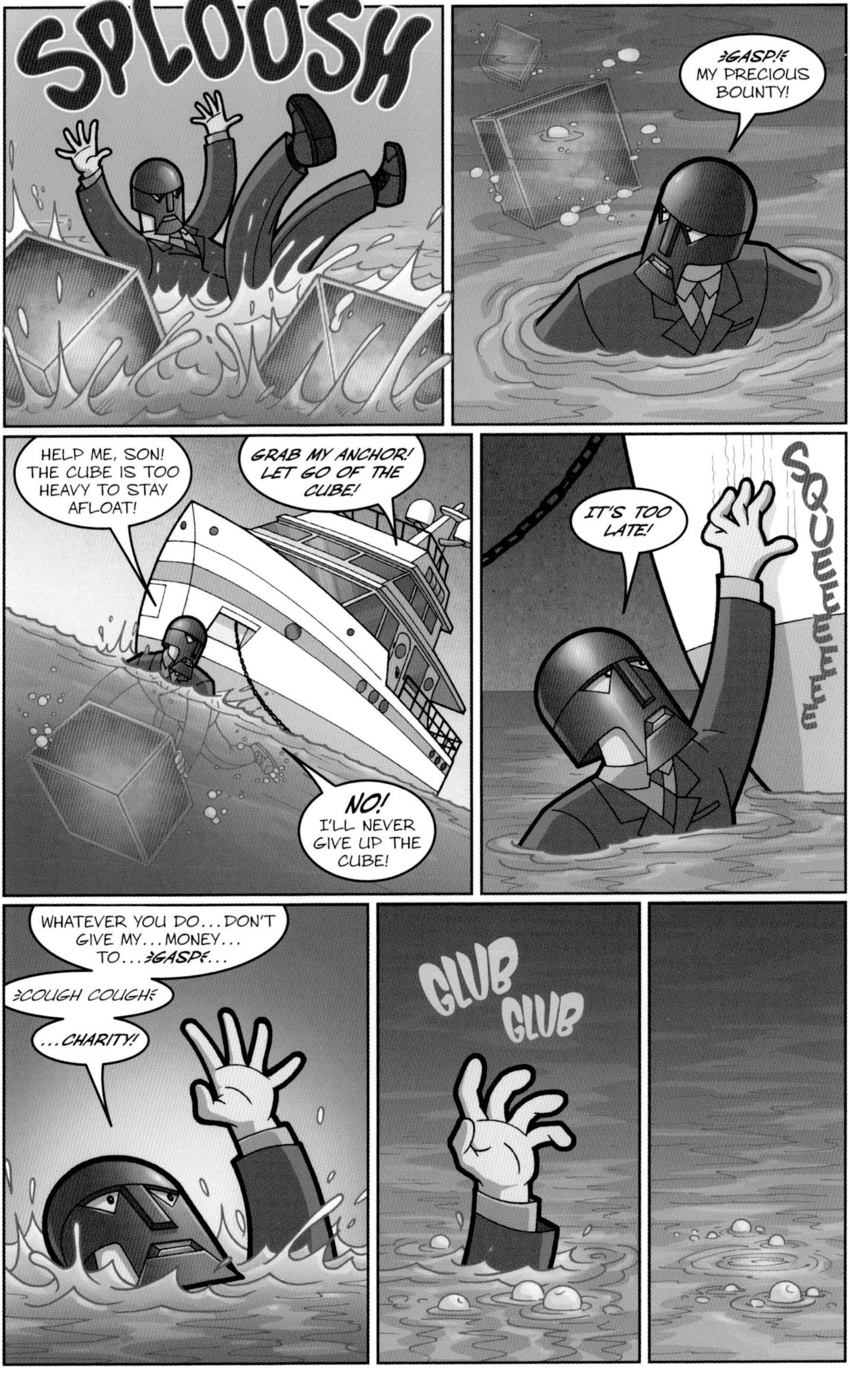
SPLOOSH
GASP! MY PRECIOUS BOUNTY!
HELP ME, SON! THE CUBE IS TOO HEAVY TO STAY AFLOAT!
GRAB MY ANCHOR! LET GO OF THE CUBE!
NO! I'LL NEVER GIVE UP THE CUBE!
IT'S TOO LATE!
SQUEEEEEEE
WHATEVER YOU DO... DON'T GIVE MY... MONEY... TO... GASP...
COUGH COUGH
...CHARITY!
GLUB GLUB

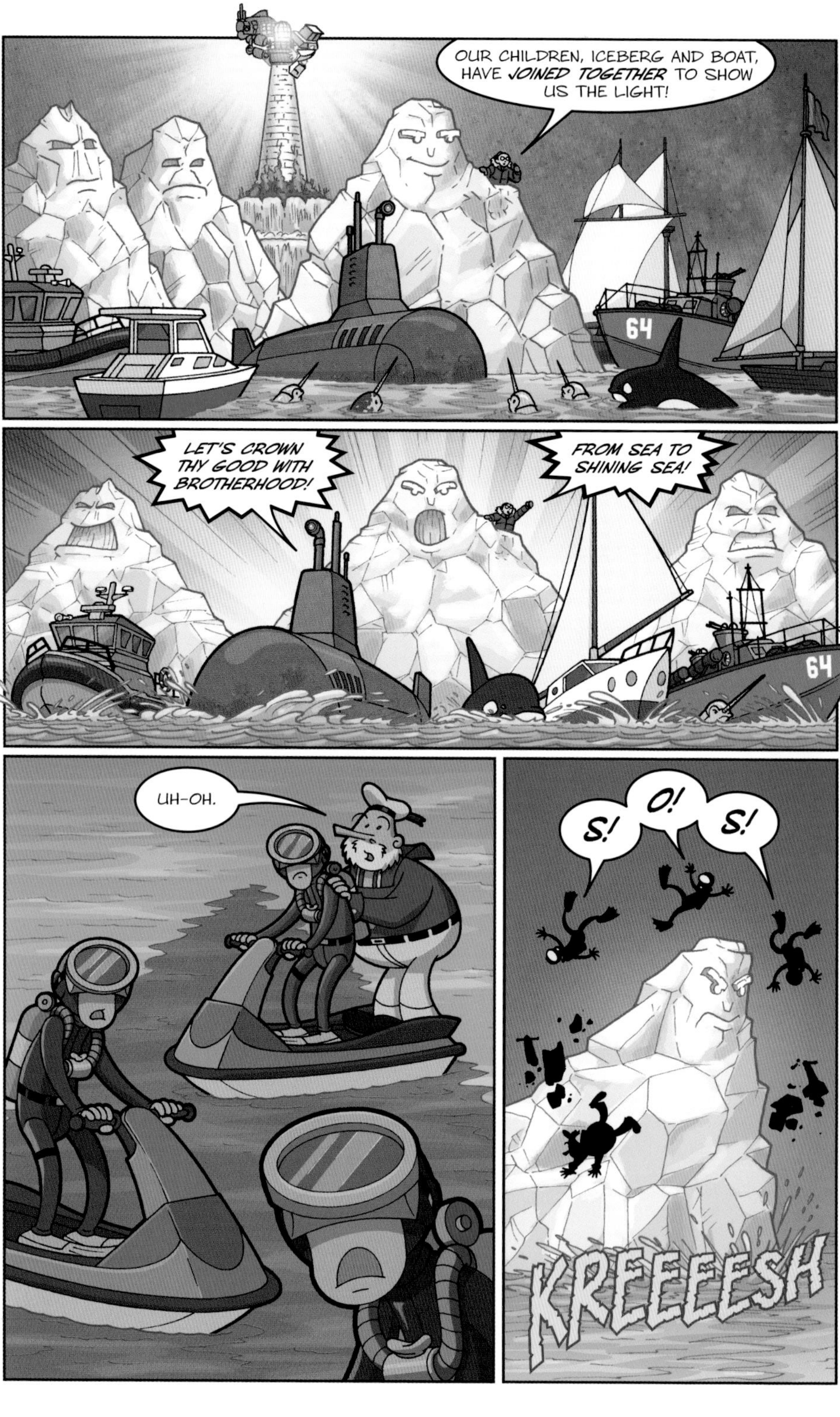
OUR CHILDREN, ICEBERG AND BOAT, HAVE *JOINED TOGETHER* TO SHOW US THE LIGHT!
64
LET'S CROWN THY GOOD WITH BROTHERHOOD!
FROM SEA TO SHINING SEA!
64
UH-OH.
S!
O!
S!
KREEEESH

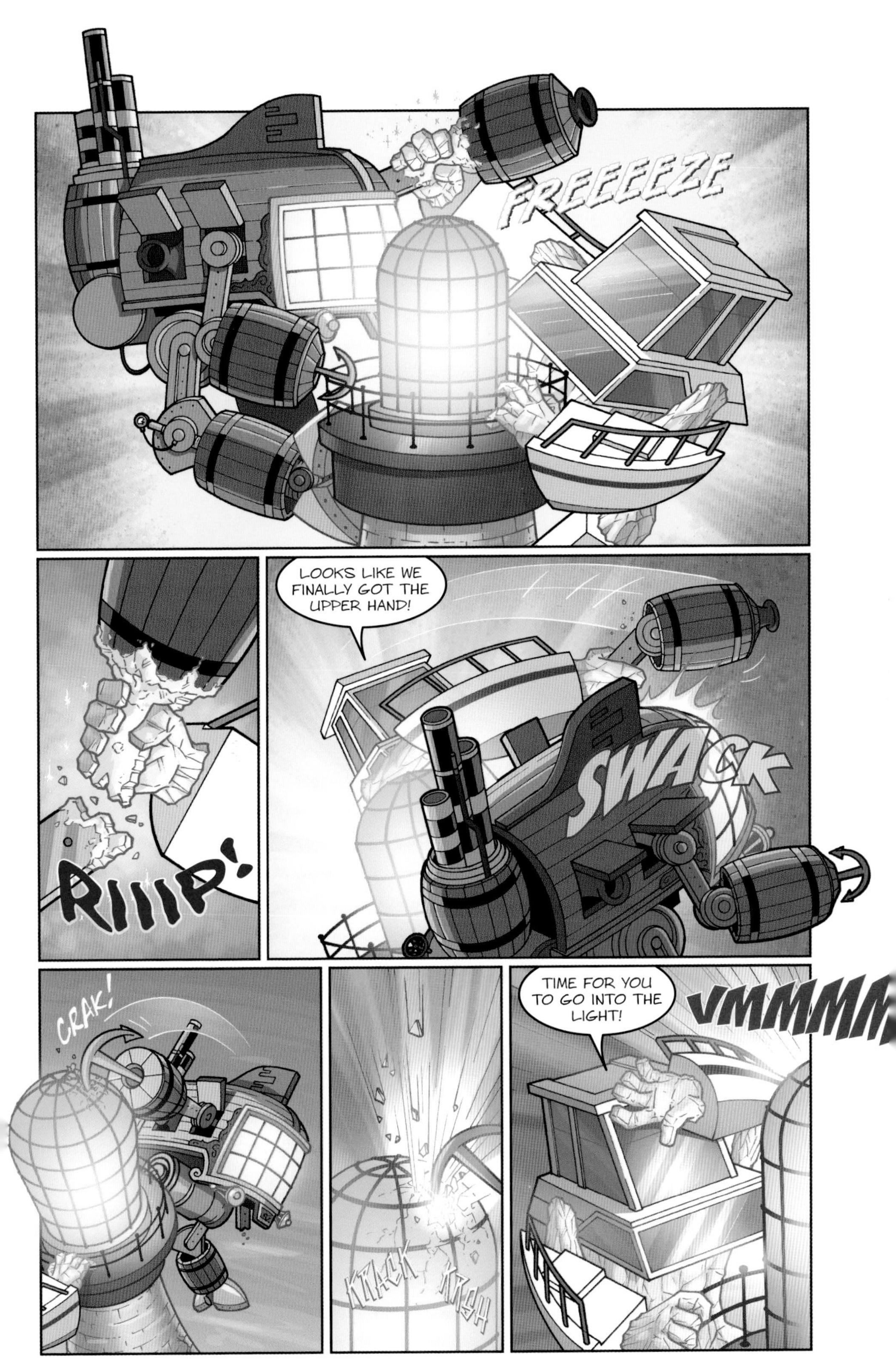
FREEEEZE
RIIIP!
LOOKS LIKE WE FINALLY GOT THE UPPER HAND!
SWACK
CRAK!
KRACK
KRSH
TIME FOR YOU TO GO INTO THE LIGHT!
VMMMM

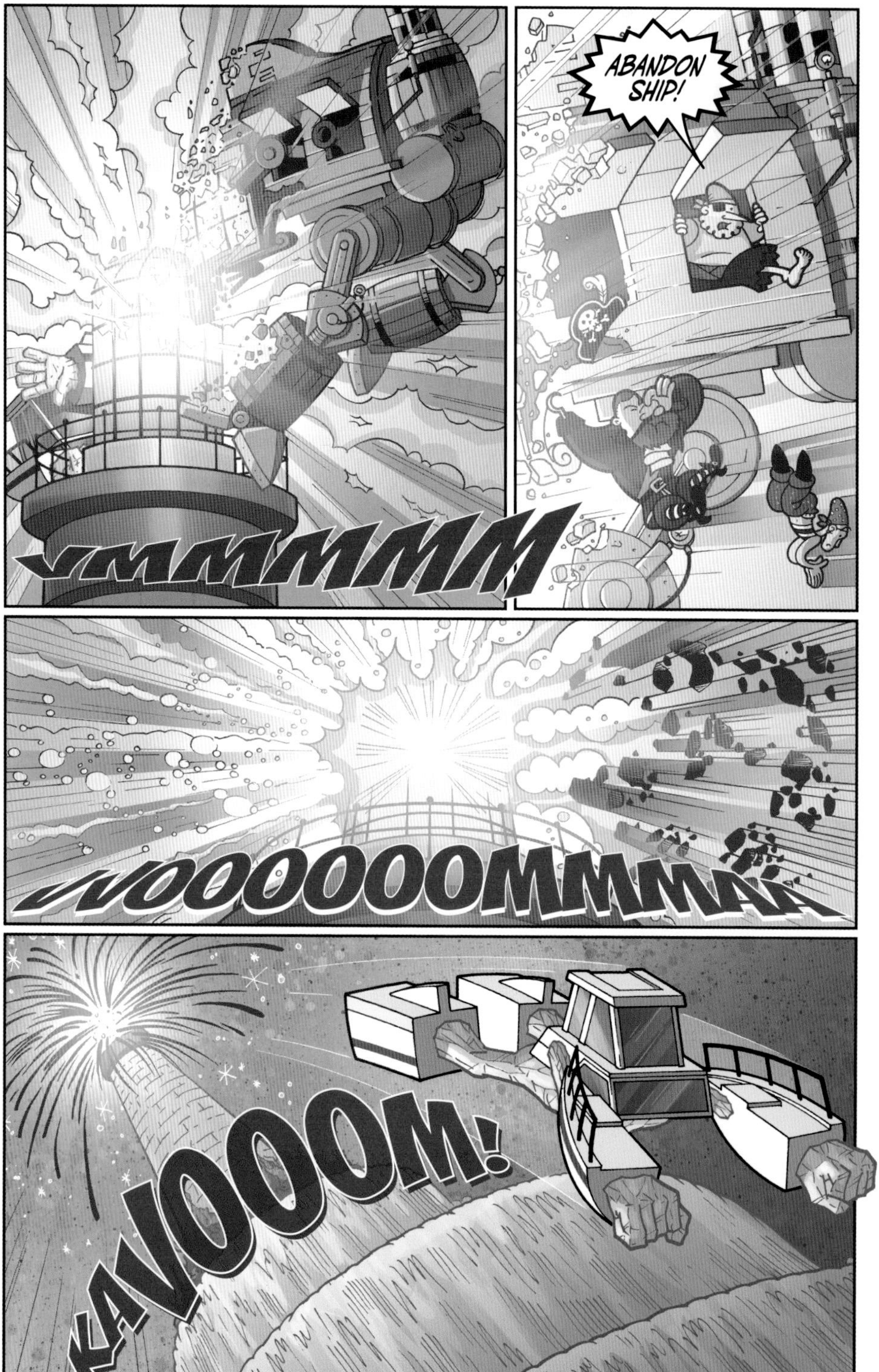
VMMMMMM
ABANDON SHIP!
VVOOOOOOMMMMAA
KAVOOOOM!

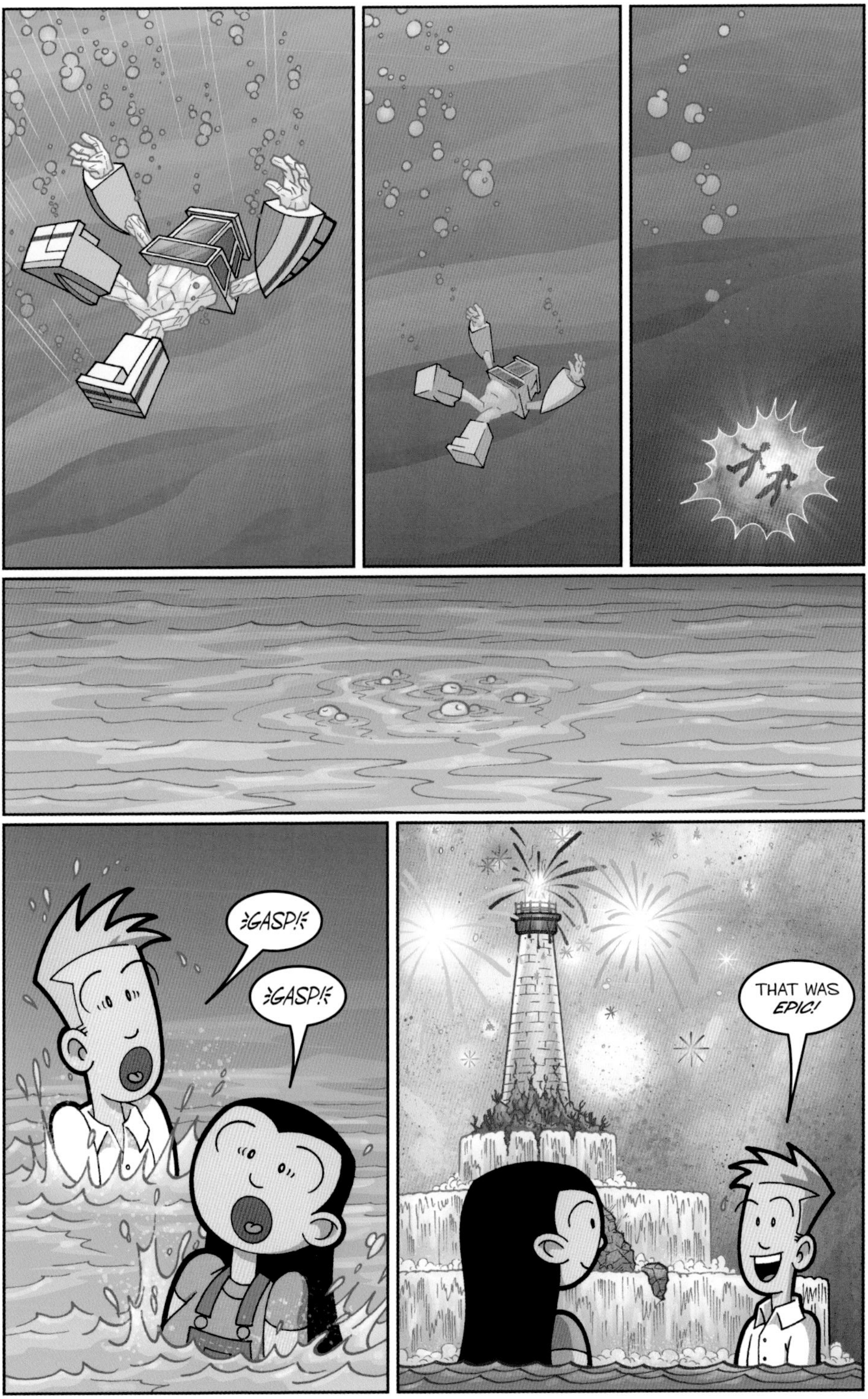
GASP!
GASP!
THAT WAS EPIC!

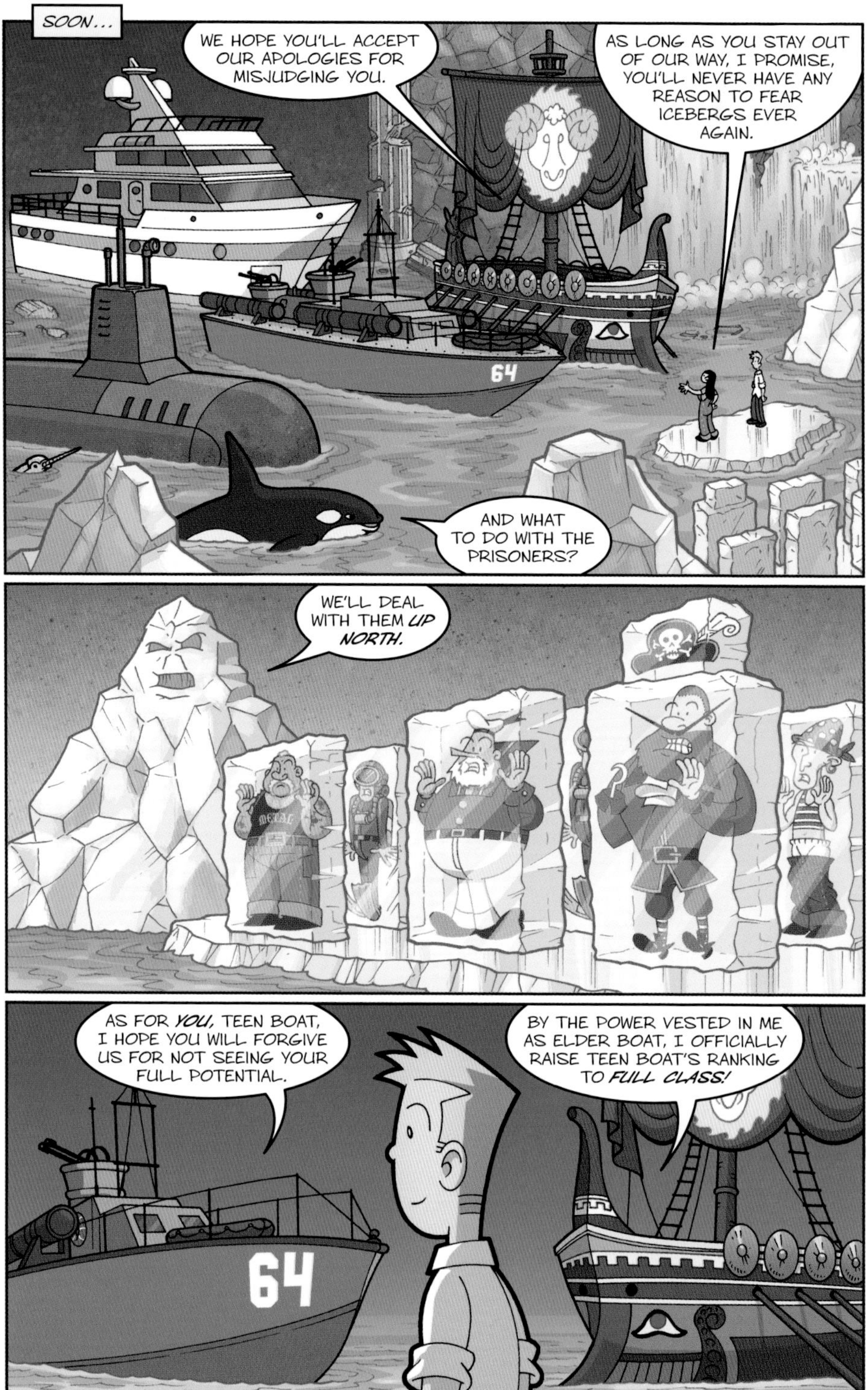
SOON...
WE HOPE YOU'LL ACCEPT OUR APOLOGIES FOR MISJUDGING YOU.
AS LONG AS YOU STAY OUT OF OUR WAY, I PROMISE, YOU'LL NEVER HAVE ANY REASON TO FEAR ICEBERGS EVER AGAIN.
64
AND WHAT TO DO WITH THE PRISONERS?
WE'LL DEAL WITH THEM *UP NORTH.*
AS FOR *YOU,* TEEN BOAT, I HOPE YOU WILL FORGIVE US FOR NOT SEEING YOUR FULL POTENTIAL.
BY THE POWER VESTED IN ME AS ELDER BOAT, I OFFICIALLY RAISE TEEN BOAT'S RANKING TO *FULL CLASS!*
64

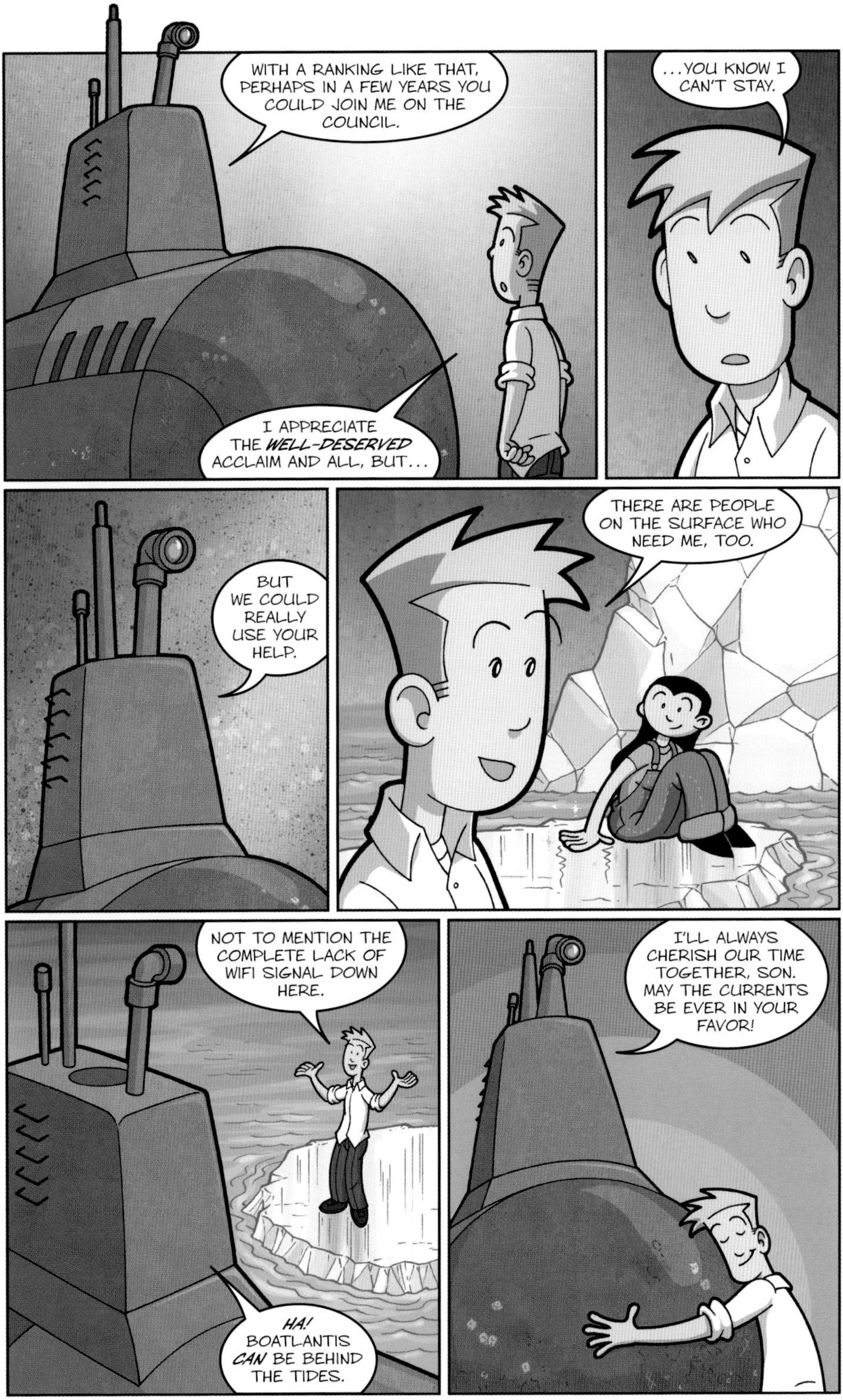
WITH A RANKING LIKE THAT, PERHAPS IN A FEW YEARS YOU COULD JOIN ME ON THE COUNCIL.
I APPRECIATE THE WELL-DESERVED ACCLAIM AND ALL, BUT...
...YOU KNOW I CAN'T STAY.
BUT WE COULD REALLY USE YOUR HELP.
THERE ARE PEOPLE ON THE SURFACE WHO NEED ME, TOO.
NOT TO MENTION THE COMPLETE LACK OF WIFI SIGNAL DOWN HERE.
HA! BOATLANTIS CAN BE BEHIND THE TIDES.
I'LL ALWAYS CHERISH OUR TIME TOGETHER, SON. MAY THE CURRENTS BE EVER IN YOUR FAVOR!

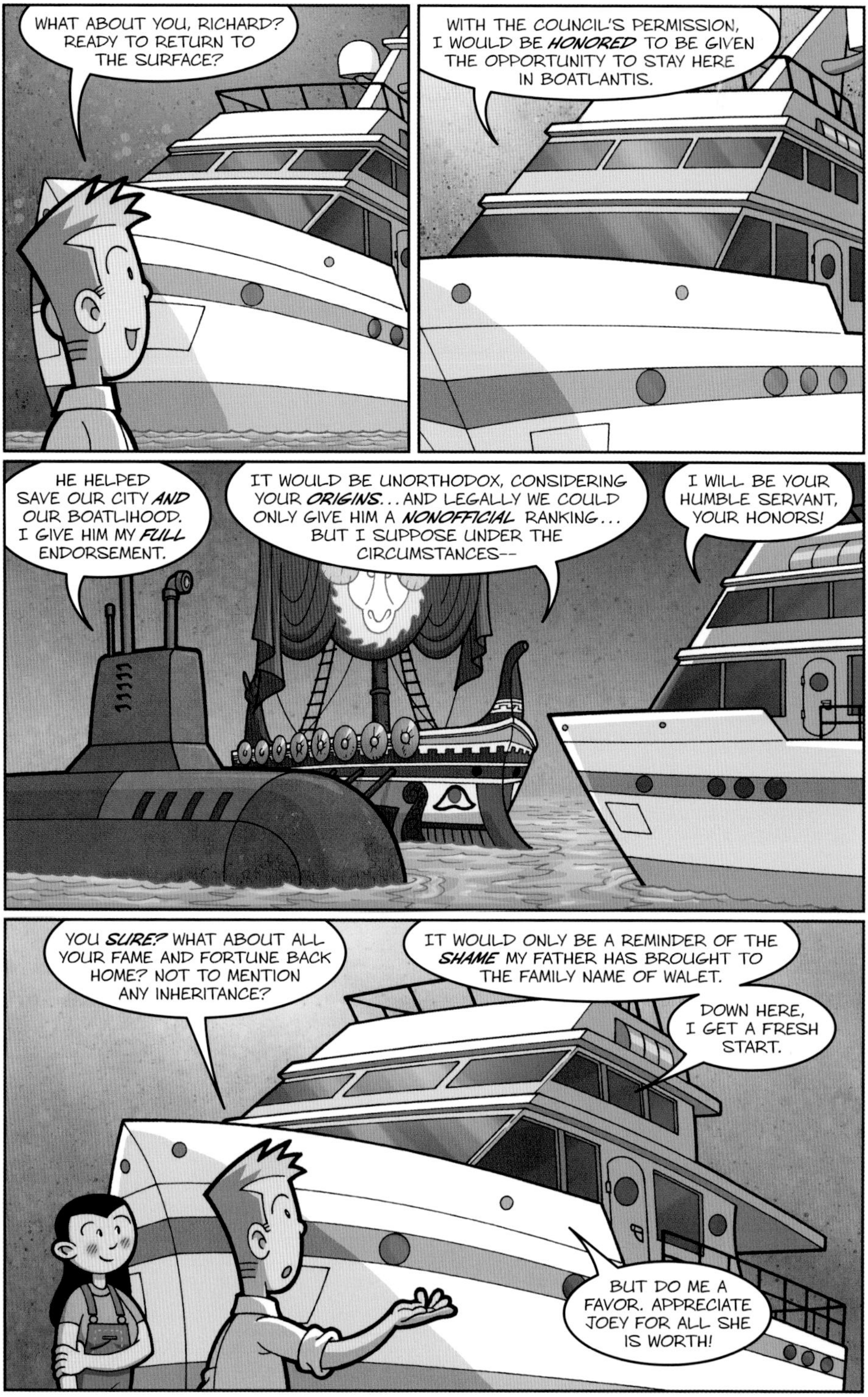
WHAT ABOUT YOU, RICHARD? READY TO RETURN TO THE SURFACE?
WITH THE COUNCIL'S PERMISSION, I WOULD BE *HONORED* TO BE GIVEN THE OPPORTUNITY TO STAY HERE IN BOATLANTIS.
HE HELPED SAVE OUR CITY *AND* OUR BOATLIHOOD. I GIVE HIM MY *FULL* ENDORSEMENT.
IT WOULD BE UNORTHODOX, CONSIDERING YOUR *ORIGINS*. . . AND LEGALLY WE COULD ONLY GIVE HIM A *NONOFFICIAL* RANKING . . . BUT I SUPPOSE UNDER THE CIRCUMSTANCES--
I WILL BE YOUR HUMBLE SERVANT, YOUR HONORS!
YOU *SURE?* WHAT ABOUT ALL YOUR FAME AND FORTUNE BACK HOME? NOT TO MENTION ANY INHERITANCE?
IT WOULD ONLY BE A REMINDER OF THE *SHAME* MY FATHER HAS BROUGHT TO THE FAMILY NAME OF WALET.
DOWN HERE, I GET A FRESH START.
BUT DO ME A FAVOR. APPRECIATE JOEY FOR ALL SHE IS WORTH!

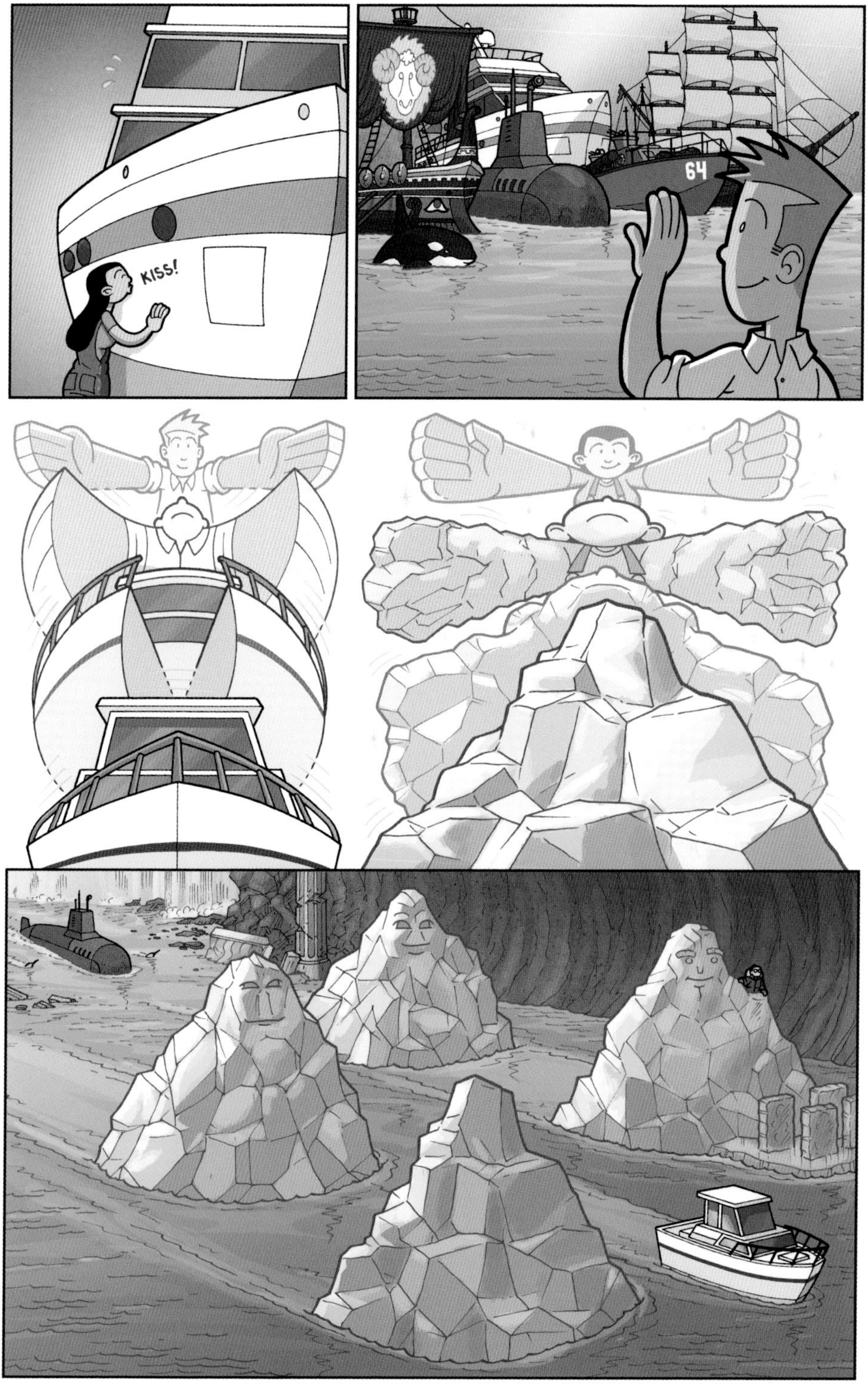
KISS!
64

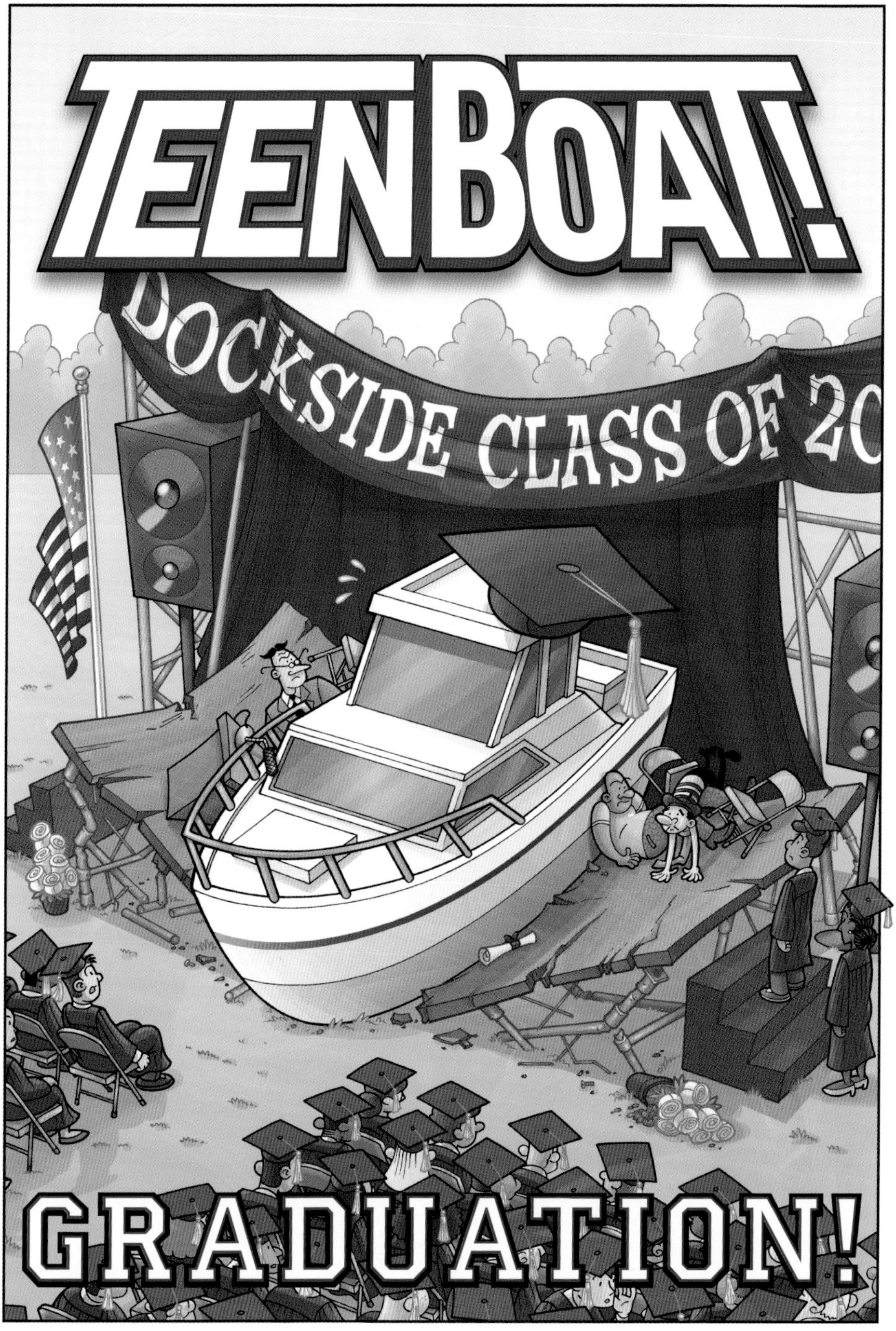
TEEN BOAT!
DOCKSIDE CLASS OF 20
GRADUATION!

The ***AFTERMATH*** of Adventure—the ***RESOLUTION*** of Story!

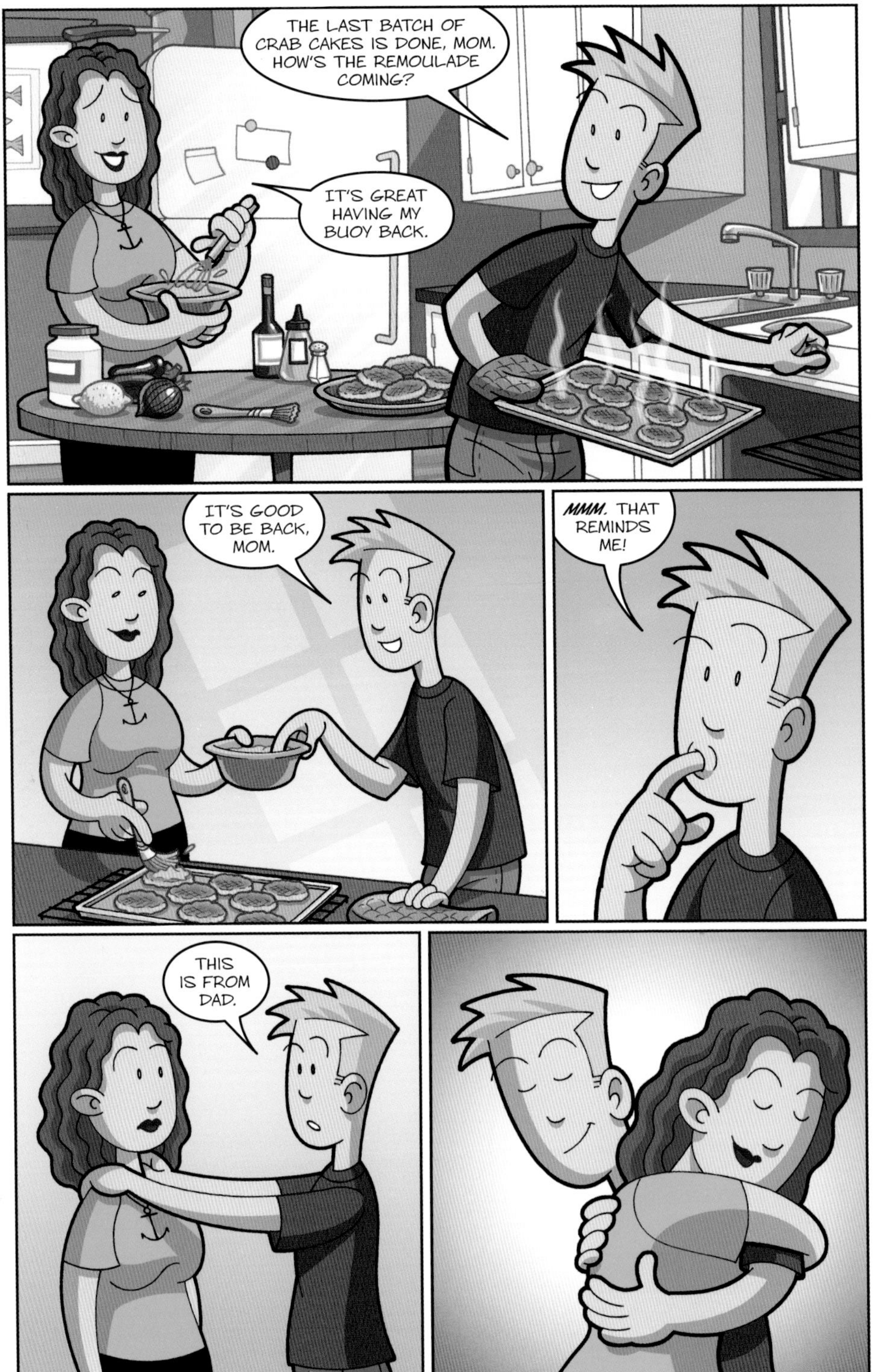
THE LAST BATCH OF CRAB CAKES IS DONE, MOM. HOW'S THE REMOULADE COMING?
IT'S GREAT HAVING MY BUOY BACK.
IT'S GOOD TO BE BACK, MOM.
MMM. THAT REMINDS ME!
THIS IS FROM DAD.

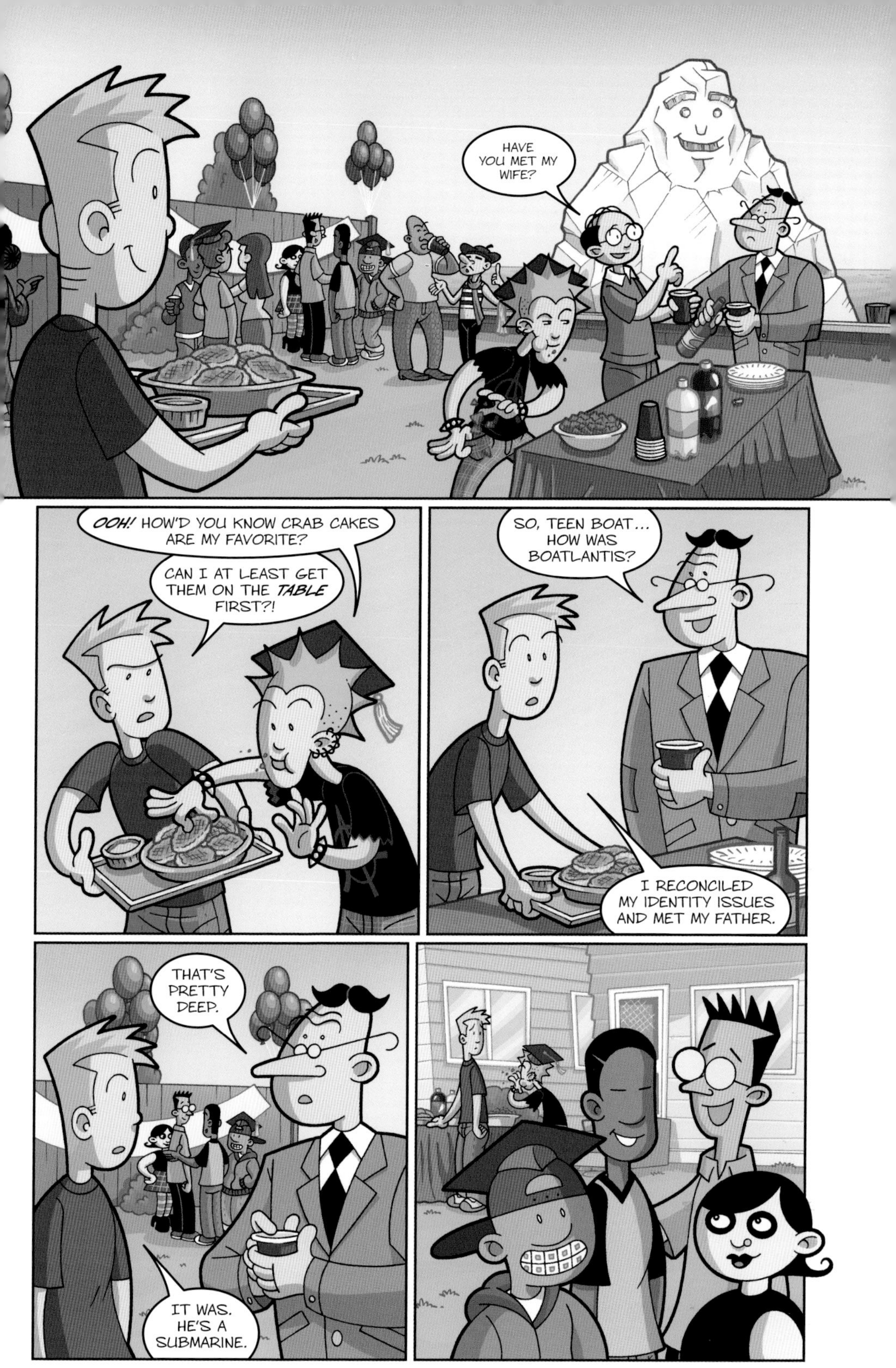
HAVE YOU MET MY WIFE?
OOH! HOW'D YOU KNOW CRAB CAKES ARE MY FAVORITE?
CAN I AT LEAST GET THEM ON THE TABLE FIRST?!
SO, TEEN BOAT... HOW WAS BOATLANTIS?
I RECONCILED MY IDENTITY ISSUES AND MET MY FATHER.
THAT'S PRETTY DEEP.
IT WAS. HE'S A SUBMARINE.

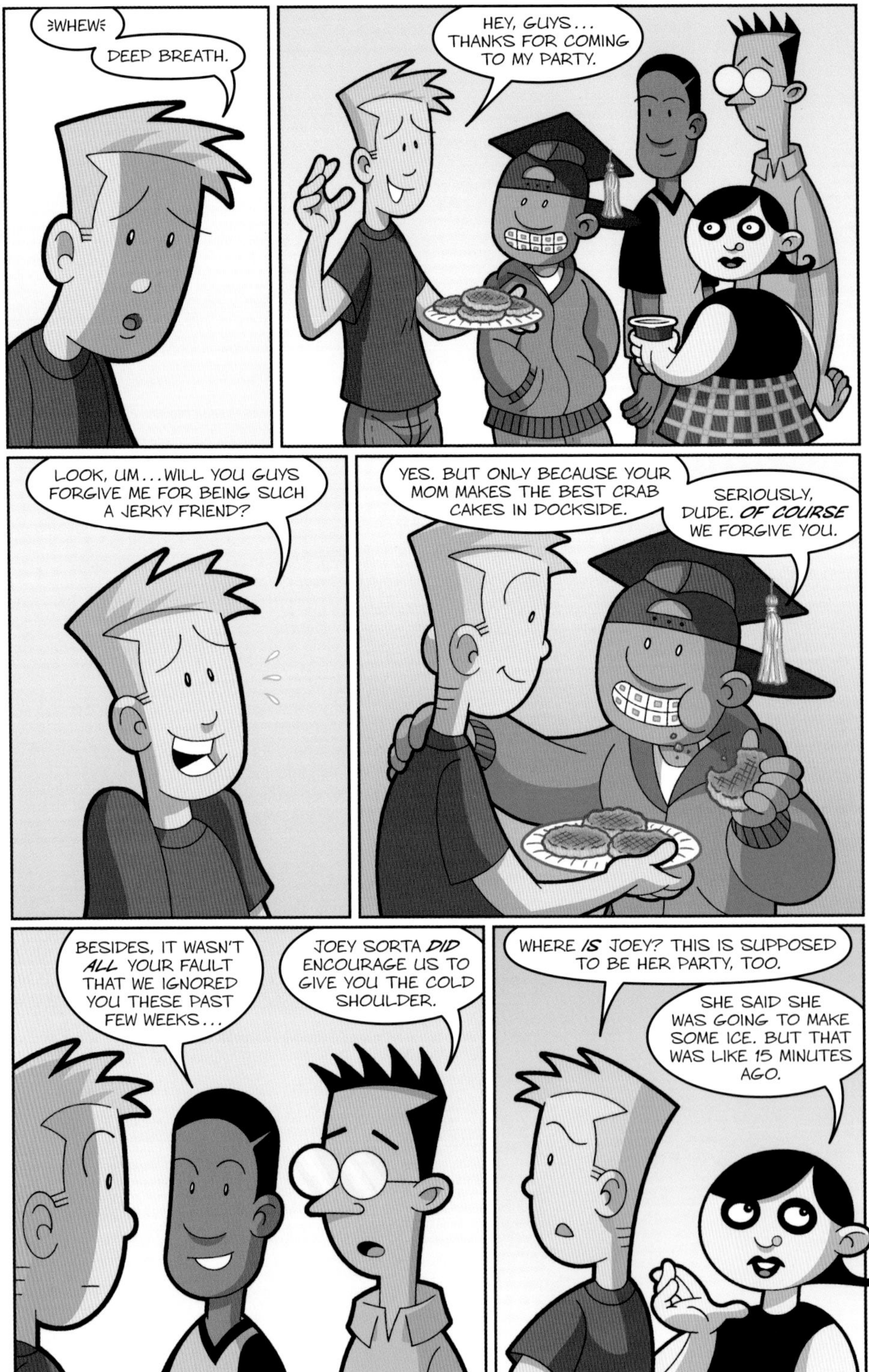

WHEW
DEEP BREATH.
HEY, GUYS... THANKS FOR COMING TO MY PARTY.
LOOK, UM... WILL YOU GUYS FORGIVE ME FOR BEING SUCH A JERKY FRIEND?
YES. BUT ONLY BECAUSE YOUR MOM MAKES THE BEST CRAB CAKES IN DOCKSIDE.
SERIOUSLY, DUDE. *OF COURSE* WE FORGIVE YOU.
BESIDES, IT WASN'T *ALL* YOUR FAULT THAT WE IGNORED YOU THESE PAST FEW WEEKS...
JOEY SORTA *DID* ENCOURAGE US TO GIVE YOU THE COLD SHOULDER.
WHERE *IS* JOEY? THIS IS SUPPOSED TO BE HER PARTY, TOO.
SHE SAID SHE WAS GOING TO MAKE SOME ICE. BUT THAT WAS LIKE 15 MINUTES AGO.

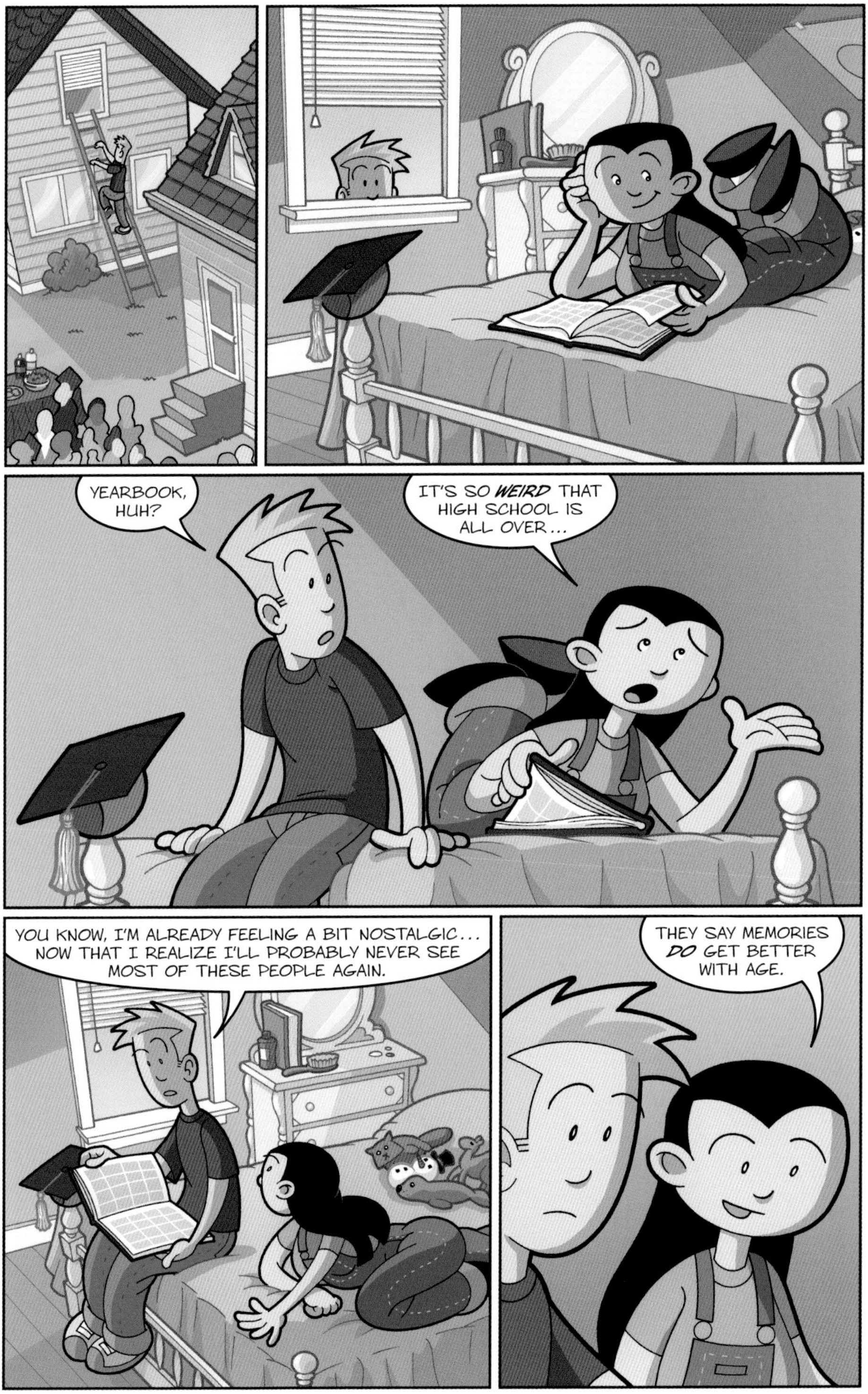
YEARBOOK, HUH?
IT'S SO WEIRD THAT HIGH SCHOOL IS ALL OVER...
YOU KNOW, I'M ALREADY FEELING A BIT NOSTALGIC... NOW THAT I REALIZE I'LL PROBABLY NEVER SEE MOST OF THESE PEOPLE AGAIN.
THEY SAY MEMORIES DO GET BETTER WITH AGE.

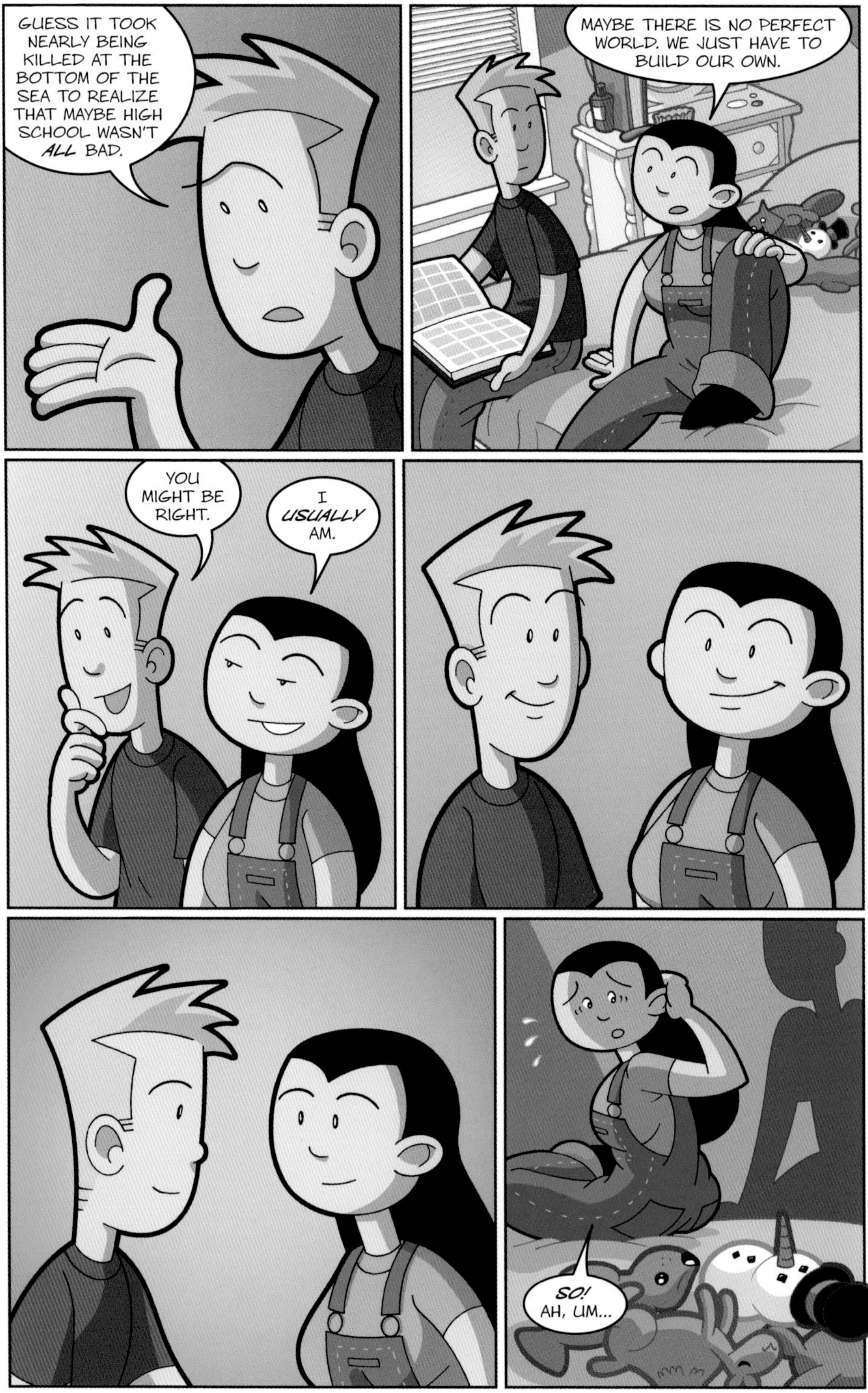
GUESS IT TOOK NEARLY BEING KILLED AT THE BOTTOM OF THE SEA TO REALIZE THAT MAYBE HIGH SCHOOL WASN'T ALL BAD.
MAYBE THERE IS NO PERFECT WORLD. WE JUST HAVE TO BUILD OUR OWN.
YOU MIGHT BE RIGHT.
I USUALLY AM.
SO! AH, UM...

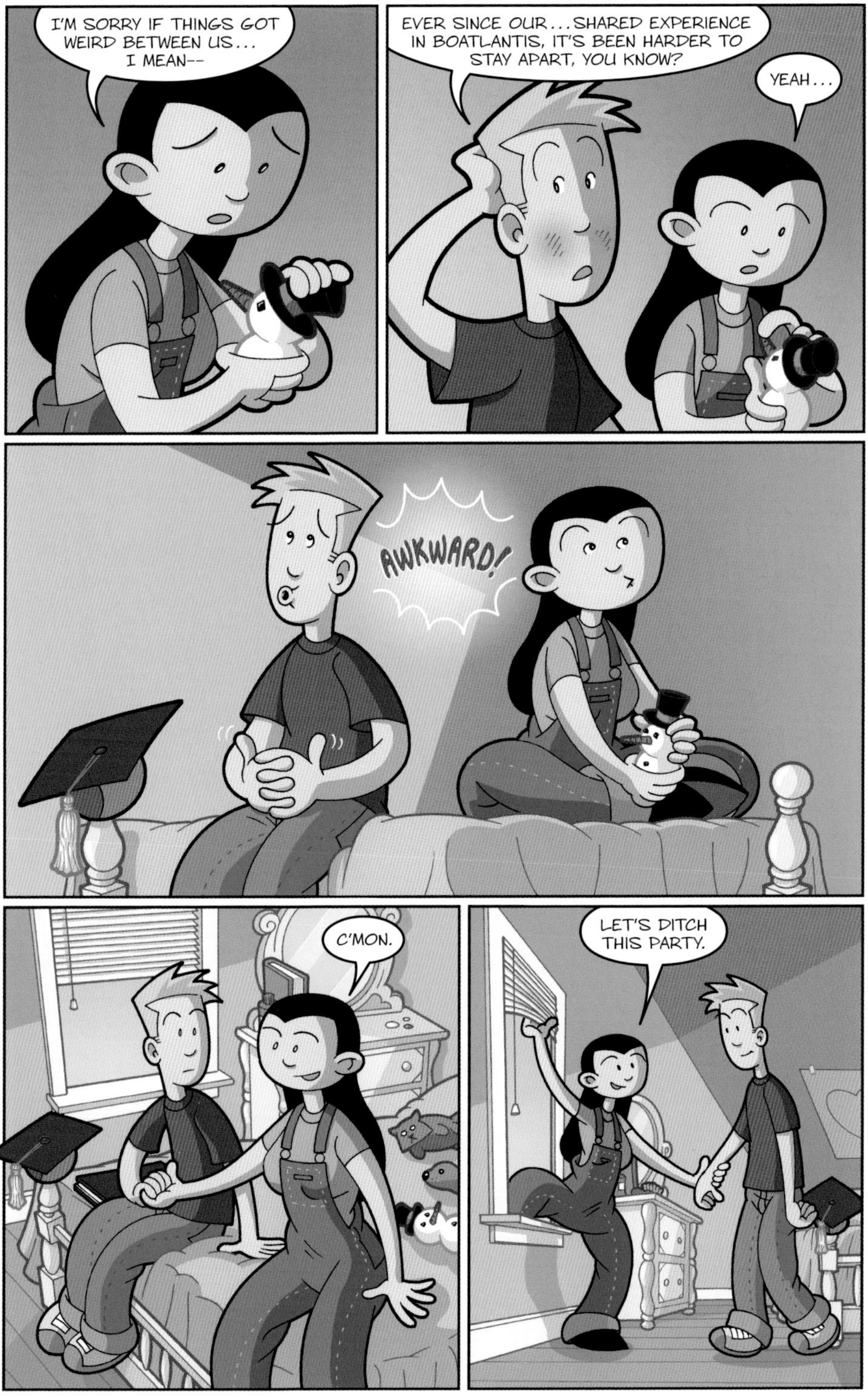
I'M SORRY IF THINGS GOT WEIRD BETWEEN US... I MEAN--
EVER SINCE OUR...SHARED EXPERIENCE IN BOATLANTIS, IT'S BEEN HARDER TO STAY APART, YOU KNOW?
YEAH...
AWKWARD!
C'MON.
LET'S DITCH THIS PARTY.

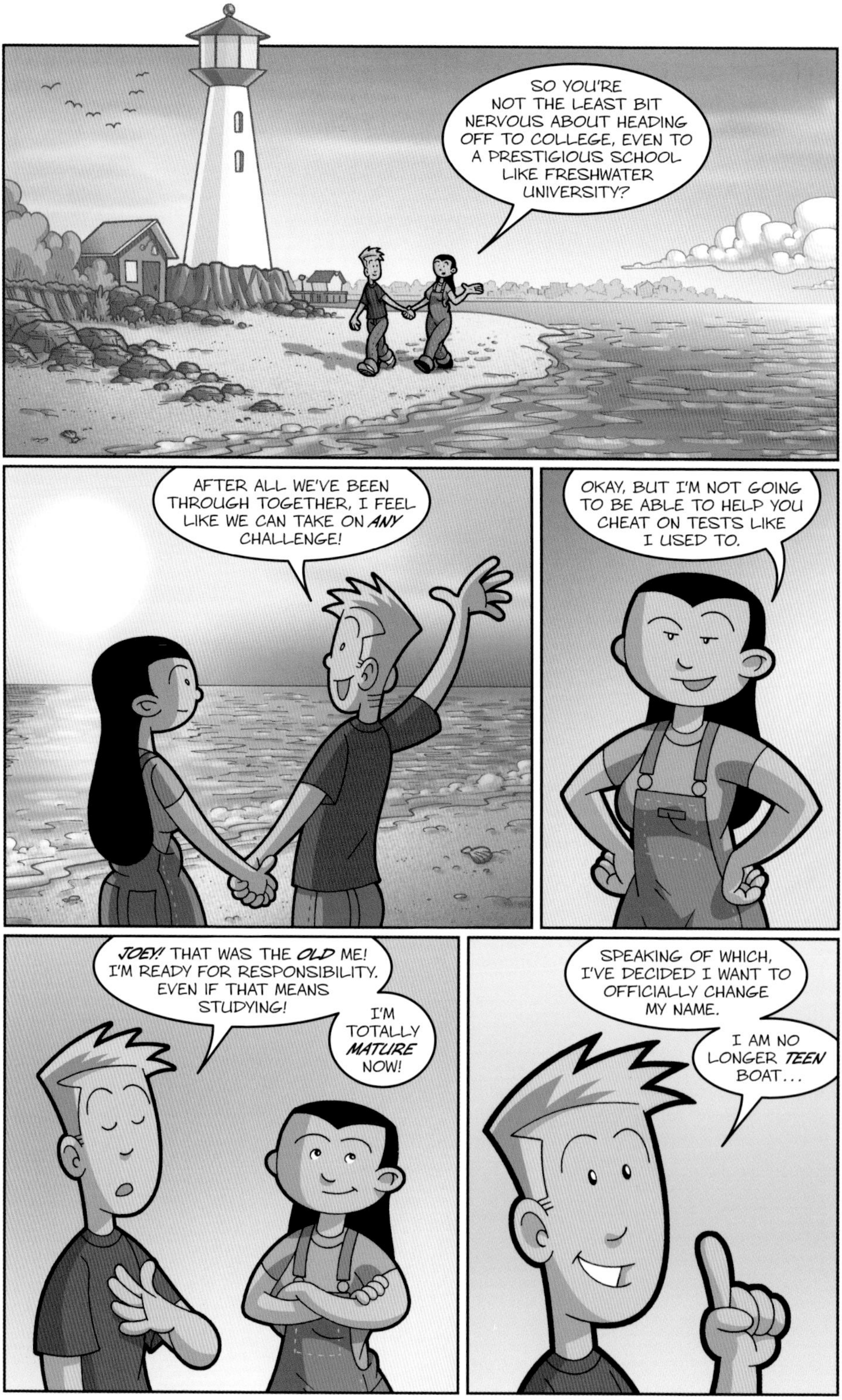
SO YOU'RE NOT THE LEAST BIT NERVOUS ABOUT HEADING OFF TO COLLEGE, EVEN TO A PRESTIGIOUS SCHOOL LIKE FRESHWATER UNIVERSITY?
AFTER ALL WE'VE BEEN THROUGH TOGETHER, I FEEL LIKE WE CAN TAKE ON *ANY* CHALLENGE!
OKAY, BUT I'M NOT GOING TO BE ABLE TO HELP YOU CHEAT ON TESTS LIKE I USED TO.
JOEY! THAT WAS THE *OLD* ME! I'M READY FOR RESPONSIBILITY. EVEN IF THAT MEANS STUDYING!
I'M TOTALLY *MATURE* NOW!
SPEAKING OF WHICH, I'VE DECIDED I WANT TO OFFICIALLY CHANGE MY NAME.
I AM NO LONGER *TEEN* BOAT...

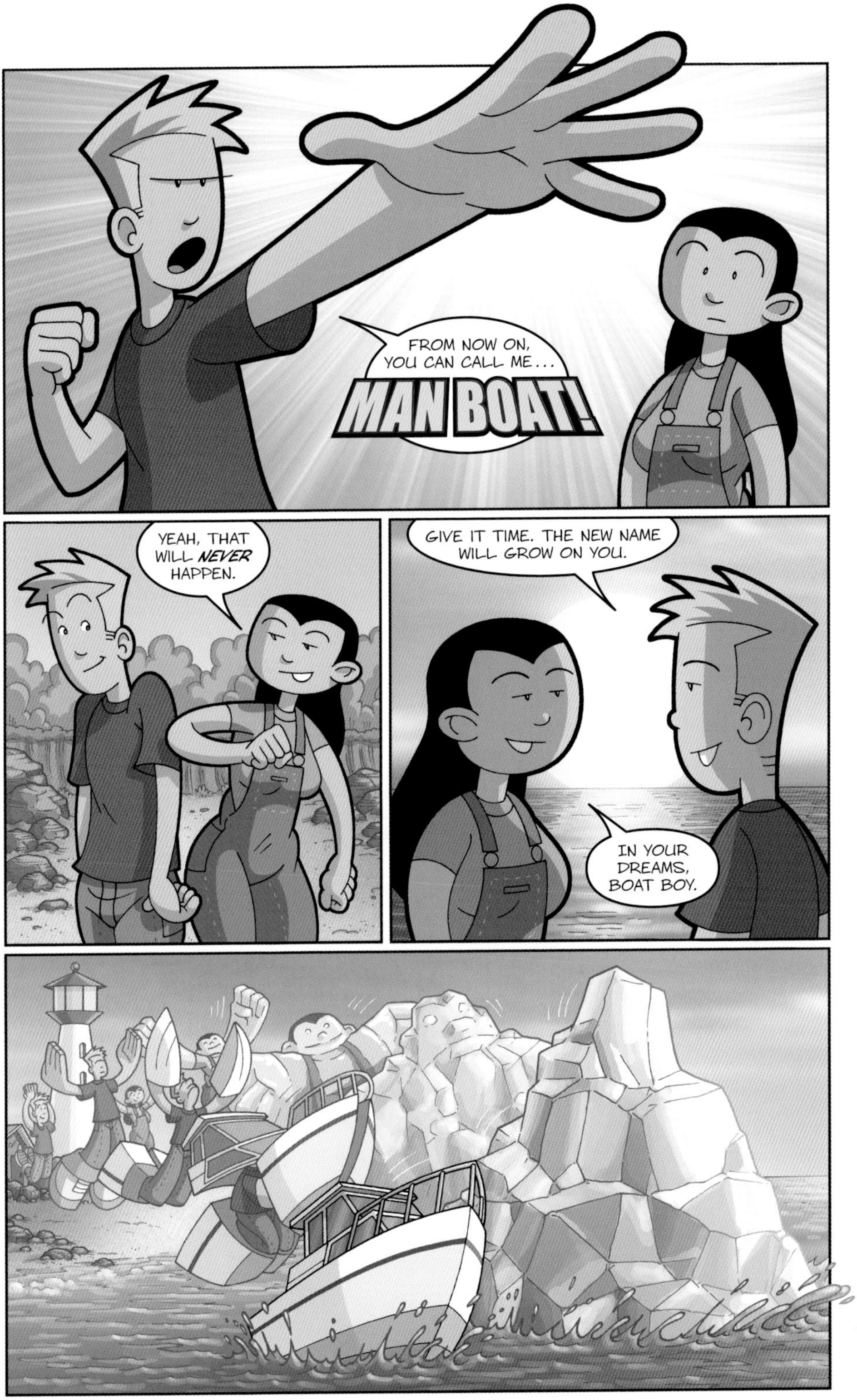
FROM NOW ON, YOU CAN CALL ME...
MAN BOAT!
YEAH, THAT WILL *NEVER* HAPPEN.
GIVE IT TIME. THE NEW NAME WILL GROW ON YOU.
IN YOUR DREAMS, BOAT BOY.

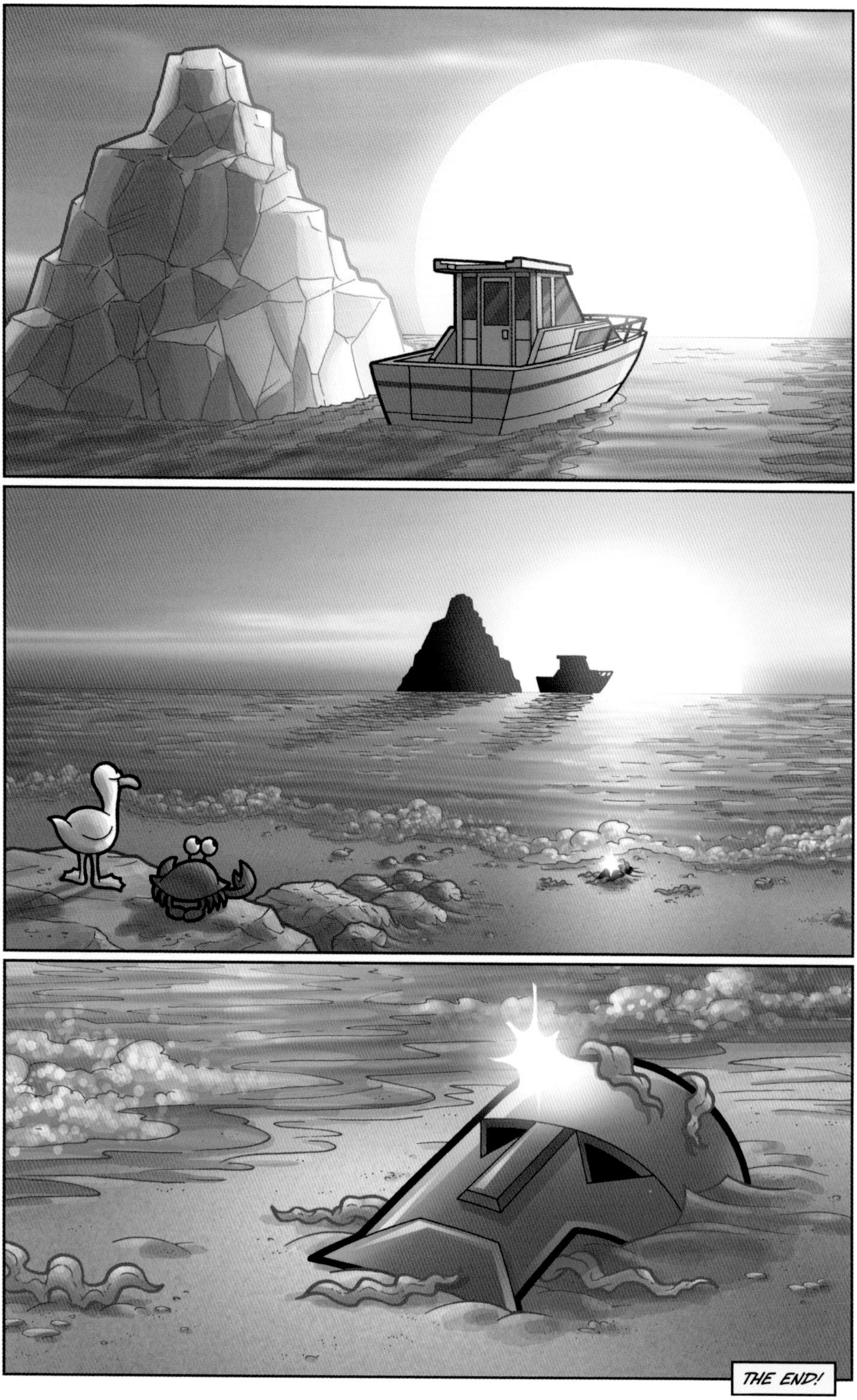
THE END!

THANKS TO

Savage Steve Holland, Robert Zemeckis, Richard Donner, Sunbow Productions, Stan Bush, Sebastian, King Triton, Jason, The Argonauts, Herman the Manatee, James Spader, Carl Barks, the cast and crew of Waterworld: A Live Sea War Spectacular at Universal Studios, David Sharps at the Waterfront Museum & Showboat Barge, the other John Green, Raina Telgemeier, Gina Gagliano, Judith Hansen, Lynne Polvino, Jim Secula, Daniel Nayeri, Dodie Ownes, Jerzy Drozd, Jarett Krosoczka, Jason Viola, Gene Luen Yang, Kazu Kibuishi, Faith Erin Hicks, Hal Johnson, Brian Wyzlic, Becca Grace, Laura Given, Kelly Mueller, the Nerdy Book Club, everyone who has ever bought a mini-comic from a cartoonist, and all the kind people who have supported our books over the years and said nice things about them on the internet.

*No boats were harmed in the making of this book.

dave & John

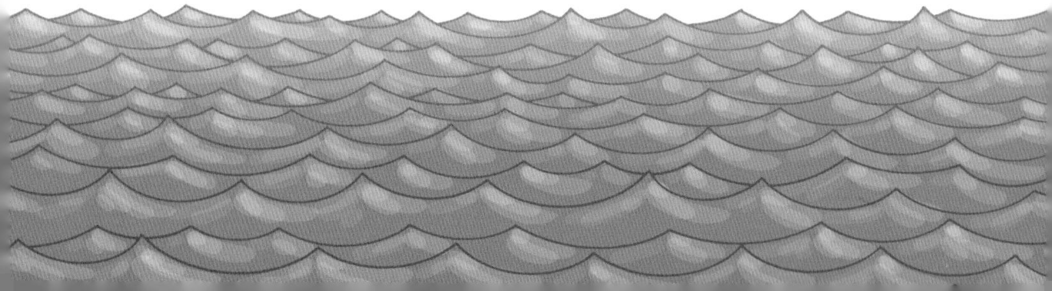

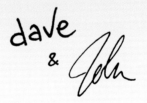

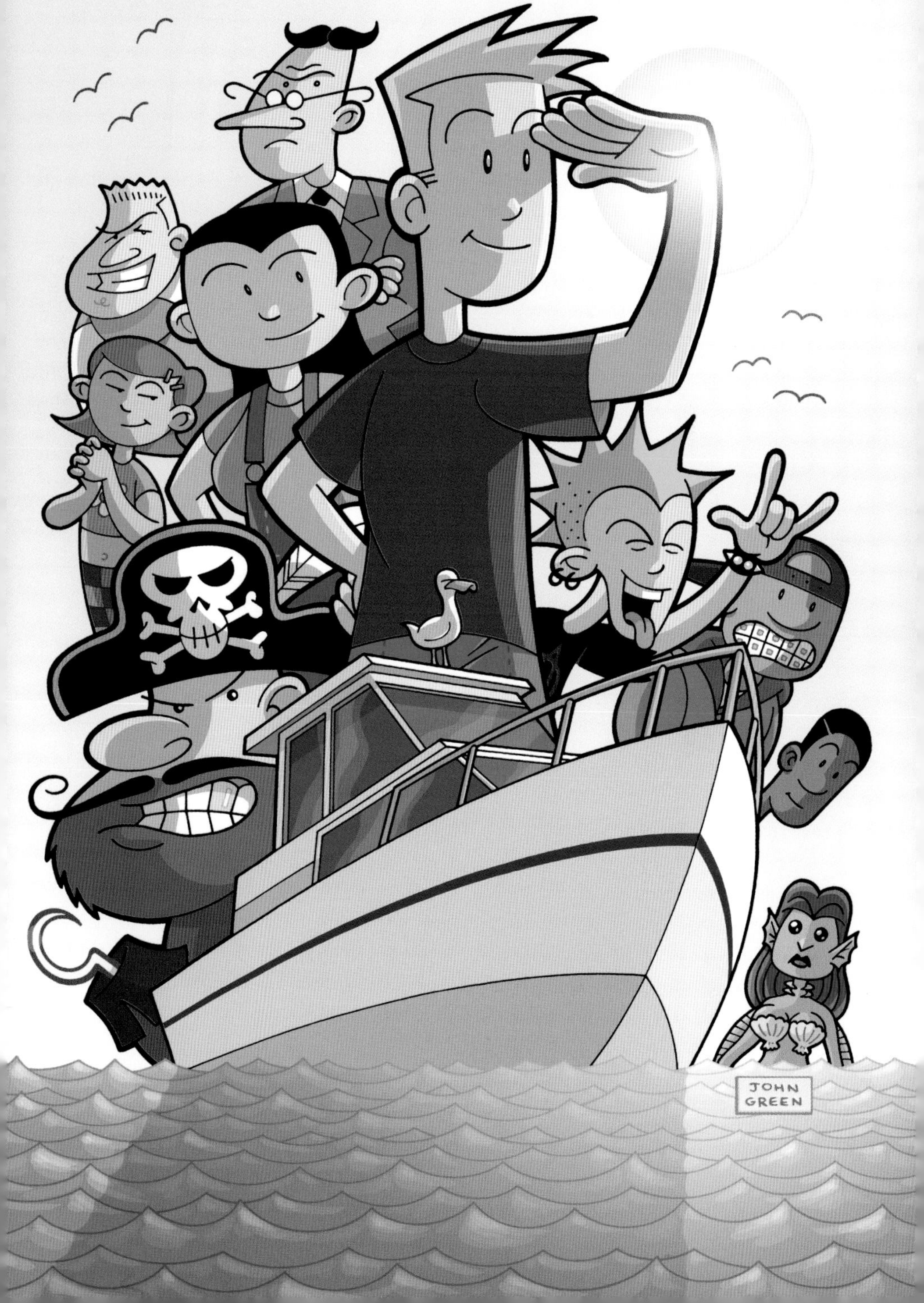
JOHN GREEN

DAVE ROMAN is the creator of the graphic novel series *Astronaut Academy* and *Agnes Quill: An Anthology of Mystery*. He has contributed stories to *Comic Squad: Recess!*, *Explorer: The Lost Islands,* and is the co-author of two *New York Times* best-selling graphic novels, *X-Men: Misfits* and *The Last Airbender: Zuko's Story*. He is also the writer of *Jax Epoch and the Quicken Forbidden,* which he co-created with John Green when they were students at the School of Visual Arts. Dave worked as an editor for the groundbreaking *Nickelodeon* magazine and lives in New York City with his wife and fellow cartoonist, Raina Telgemeier. See more of Dave's work at **www.yaytime.com**.

JOHN GREEN grew up on Long Island and has worked in New York City since graduating from the School of Visual Arts with a degree in graphic design. He was the comics consultant for *Disney Adventures* magazine and has also worked on comics for Nickelodeon, DreamWorks, Scholastic, DC Comics, and First Second Books. His latest project is *Hippopotamister,* his first graphic novel as writer and artist. John lives in Brooklyn with zero cats and way too many LEGOs. See more of John's work at **www.johngreenart.com**.

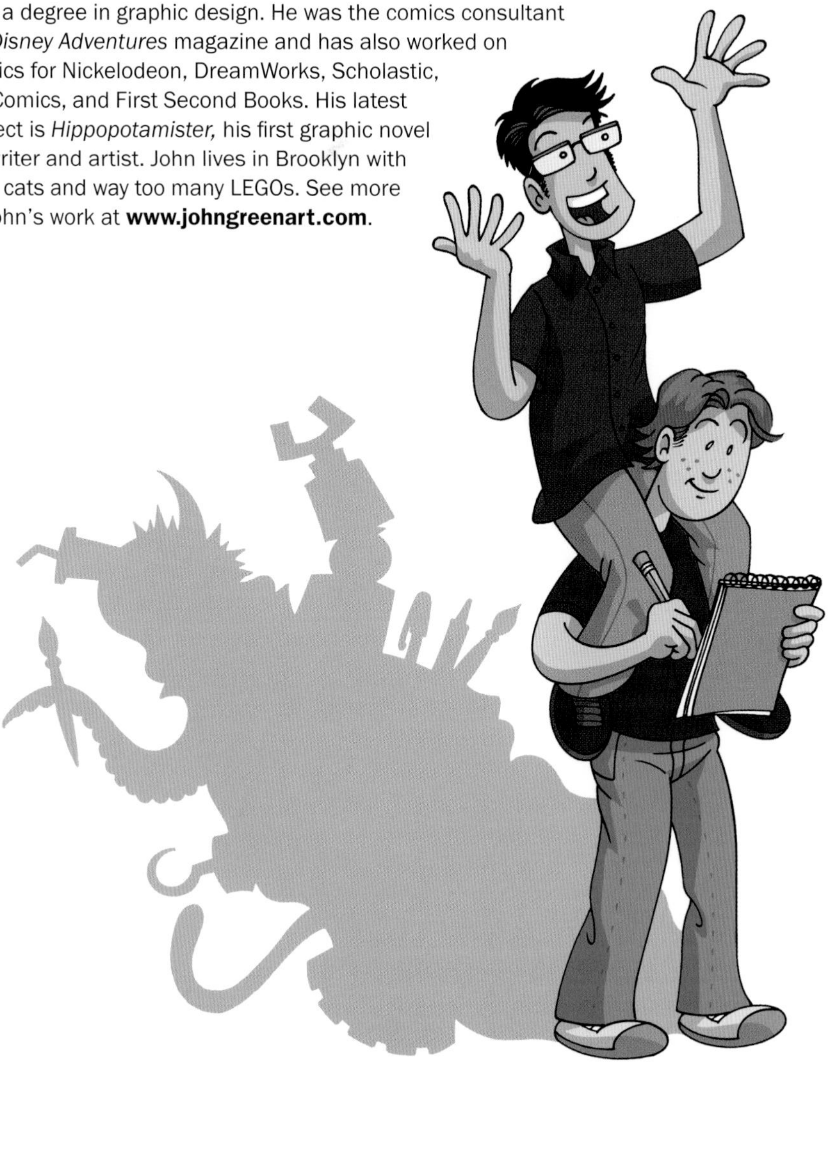